I am the youngest of four, born under the star sign of Taurus and am older than I want to be but escaping to Spain two years ago, I found a rejuvenated spirit to enjoy life once again. Putting careers of casino and marketing behind me some sixteen years ago, I began writing, but it took a time of apprenticeship to be confident readers might want to see what I have written. My time in gaming allowed me to travel the world to appreciate different cultures, but more satisfying, people paid me to do it. My transition into marketing proved effortless, if you can convince a goat herder to put his life savings on a roulette table, then persuading a company to invest fortunes on advertising campaigns to sell a pot of jam came easy.

Married life disappeared as fast as it began and with a few failed relationships behind me, I'm probably not the ideal person to share a life with. I'm single again and thankfully (for them) have no offspring to brag about.

My education came to an abrupt stop when expelled from private school in Brighton without an 'A' level to my name, but this fortunately didn't seem to matter back then. At that age, money and how to get it seemed to be the target, not too dissimilar to today's youngster's aspirations. But I was fortunate to have had parents who permitted me to tread my own 'Yellow Brick Road', possibly the journey educated me far more than any university could muster.

Some call me lucky, but I disagree. There is no such thing as luck. Like to the lead character in this novel, Mathew Hobbs, you have to take your chances in the game of life to succeed.

I would like to thank all those at Austin Macauley for their faith in my ability to write this novel, especially Magan, Grace and Rajaj for their sterling work in making this novel legible, but there are too many more to single out. I thank you all. I also would like to thank a nameless person (you know who you are) who left me no other option but to leave Brighton and save me the heartache of seeing you with another. It gave me the impetus to begin writing again.

Thank you.

David Spear

THE MAJOR
AND MINER

AUSTIN MACAULEY
PUBLISHERS LTD.

A CIP catalogue record for this title is available from the British Library.

ISBN 9781786294531 (Paperback)
ISBN 9781786294548 (Hardback)
ISBN 9781786294555 (E-Book)
www.austinmacauley.com

First Published (2016)
Austin Macauley Publishers Ltd.
25 Canada Square
Canary Wharf
London
E14 5LQ

CHAPTER 1

Concealing its ferocious intentions, a mischievous dawning sun eagerly anticipates the Planets daily rotation before fully materialising into a transparent azure sky from below the horizon. Rising unchallenged, its power progressively strengthening, the orb erupts from behind a tranquil disguise to unleash explosive forces of overwhelming heat upon the population of planet Earth below on the fourth day of August, in the year 1914. Unbeknown to millions of innocents throughout the world regardless of wealth, race or creed, the morning heralds the ignition of a ticking time bomb. Its malicious countdown determining in the next four years, the precise day on which so many would meet their premature death.

Pre-empting Greenwich Mean Time's authority propelling two hands at a snail's pace on the face of *Big Ben,* Lord Edward Grey loathingly anticipates the eventual chimes which would announce the hour of eleven o'clock. The Liberal Foreign Secretary stands uneasily, waiting under the shade of western democracy for the swelled attendance of the members of parliament to be seated, squeezed together in a rapidly overheating House of Commons. Attired in his customary black worsted tailcoat, tailored to ward off chill winds blowing through the corridors of Westminster, a white fidgeting handkerchief attempts to staunch droplets of sweat dribbling down an ageing face before they dampen a starched, white winged-collar. Concealed by his uniform of office, every pore contained within his skin uncontrollably leaks. Conscious of the enormity of the occasion, Lord Grey stoically stands fast, ignoring an overwhelming desire to collapse. Nothing shall deter him from timing his speech to coincide with the first chime of the giant clock. Randomly scanning the privileged, elected all male membership within the second highest echelon of British politics, he notices cronies he'd long thought to have passed away seated amongst unfamiliar faces, such was the pulling power of the perceived contents of his announcement. Deep within the assembly, ears crane in anticipation to catch every word, words Lord Grey would dread declaring, but was adamant the gathering understood the dire consequences of every spoken syllable. The first of eleven chimes resounds.

"Due to reasons of intolerable provocation."

He began, but paused, guaranteeing silence as the entire House focused their attention on the lone speaker. Needlessly scanning a sheet of paper hurriedly thrust into his hand by a faceless civil servant confirms his first memorised reading of the declaration, but on this occasion there is no need for prompts.

"Triggered by a massing aggressive force threatening friendly frontiers, the Government of the United Kingdom has no other option but to side with its endangered allies and regrettably declare war against the aggressor Germany and its subordinate allies."

By the time afforded to complete its cycle of chimes, eloquently delivered rhetoric resigns the people of the United Kingdom and its colonies to a grave, uncertain future. Standing, head bowed, before a silent packed House, Lord Grey's final poignant words aren't scripted but come from a loathing conscious, echoing the thoughts of the silent majority.

"The lamps are going out all over Europe; we shall not see them lit again in our lifetime."

In eerie silence, a number of heads similarly bow, not in sympathy for heralding the obvious forthcoming loss of life both sides would undoubtedly suffer, but a visual act of digesting the impending financial disaster to any investment unconnected to supplementing the forthcoming war effort. Whilst a scattering of jingoists broke ranks applauding this retaliatory decision, the majority remain seated, bemused as to why an insurgence of this magnitude was allowed to gather so much momentum. Amongst varying differences of opinion, a smattering of the faithful couldn't comprehend why direct descendants to the British crown could sanction such a threat. Illuminated by 'midnight oil', arguments from both sides of the House continued into the early hours. Voiced opinions from the most subdued members are heard for the first time in decades, but regardless of the ravenous splits and despite lengthy intense discussions, the elders of the chamber disregard the hard facts of Germanic intention, heartened instead by the banal view that this skirmish is only that and would be squashed by Christmas. Conscious of the assured backing from the Commonwealth and the combined strength of its own armed forces, surely no country would be foolish enough to continue such an aggressive insurgence.

***

Whilst the gravity of Lord Grey's unambiguous words stunned the general literate public, His Lordship's grim analogy for the future of the British Isles went unheard outside the circulation of those able to read a daily newspaper. With radio broadcasts yet to be invented, a state of war was announced to only a fraction of the population who understood the ramifications such a proclamation meant to the common man.

Politically ignorant of what was being decided on their behalf in Westminster, the illiterate working class relied solely on 'word-of-mouth' as access to current political affairs, but the further the message travelled north to the heartland of British industry, especially into rural domains, the more diluted the statement became. During a time when wealthy gentry wallowed in the industrial revolution that had swept across Great Britain for the past half century, only those involved in manufacturing armaments and ammunitions accepted the situation with relish. The more pragmatic investors foresaw hard times, knowing labourers responsible for accumulating their fortunes in the past would be the first to be asked to lay down their hammer, scythe or shovel and replace them with a helmet, rifle and bayonet.

**

Disregarding diplomatic sympathy from the British Government, the assassination of Archduke Franz Ferdinand on the sleepy streets of Sarajevo ignited immediate retribution from the Austro-Germanic royal alliance. This killing by a sole member of a students' revolt in a city lying deep within Serbia, more famous for freezing winters than a hotbed of political turmoil, was precisely the excuse needed by Kaiser Wilhelm to pursue an irrational dream of becoming Europe's largest 'landlord', regardless of the dire consequences. To nullify the United Kingdom's navy; the largest in the world and double that of any other world power, the Kaiser covertly supplemented his submarine fleet but surreptitiously prioritised his planned main attack overland. The Kaiser's rapidly developing armed land force raised eyebrows across neighbouring foreign borders for a number of years, but none believed Wilhelm's irrational political behaviour aligned with national revenge could encompass the entire continent of

Europe into a full blooded war. Contrary to how the British politicians interpreted this action, in the Germanic mind-set, royal bloodline bore no relevance to the argument. Should there be opposition against their uninvited tyrannical march across borders onto foreign sovereign soil, then so be it.

And so on this unbearably hot, August day, Lord Grey admitted the severity of the situation. Endorsing his words, he acknowledged to a loyal group of equally worried allies a fact they already knew. It would be the backbone of the country's industrial work force who would shoulder arms to bolster resistance against an enemy never witnessed before in past conflicts. Naively believing his message would be instantly heard by the entire nation, it failed to reach the ears of those he had in mind until weeks after the declaration of hostilities and in some isolated outcrops, months later.

Initially, an expeditionary force of regular army fronted the brunt of the first assaults mustered by a large but inexperienced enemy, but the opposition's intent and growing expertise on the battlefield soon became clear. Previous numbers thought to be adequate to quell this uprising required immediate revision as it became very obvious, if there was to be a victory before Christmas, enforcements would be drastically needed. Predictions by the military hierarchy and those within the press melted into oblivion as a new year heralded stronger resistance. Initially unthinkable by those who ridiculed Lord Grey's assessment, even with the addition of the Commonwealth's assistance, the day for national conscription of 'The Tommy' grew ever closer.

***

Similar to many isolated hamlets situated in deprived, forgotten outer city rural wastelands, Twickton, an impoverished mining community hidden under the camouflage of the Yorkshire Dales, contained all the ingredients where the fortunes of the wealthy originated and where the fighting reserve would be earmarked to be harvested. Previously ignored, the people of Twickton could barely afford the cost of candles, let alone the luxury of possessing the oil generated illumination so metaphorically described by His Lordship. Bereft of education, the folk wished for nothing more than to continue living their mundane lives, thankful for an employer putting a roof over their family's heads and providing food to fill empty bellies in return for hard, physical labour.

To an outsider's eye, treeless Twickton would be difficult to describe as it neither bore a resemblance to a town nor a village. The visual effect of drab, crudely grafted grey slates adorning chunky York stone dwellings paid little respect to the art of planning, architecture or construction, and with just one road capable of supporting anything more than four hooves, the sight was one of dire poverty and decay. Away from this one cobble-stoned thoroughfare, dirt tracks fronted most dwellings. In dry conditions they adapted positively, but in this region of Yorkshire, regardless of season, torrential downpours are constantly expected. Within the hour of clouds turning hostile, torrents unable to soak into already sodden landscape cascaded off discarded slag-heaps searching for the easiest route to escape. Churned into an untreated cocktail of coal dust and mud, the black infected liquid quagmire instinctively chose the same direction to disperse. Unfortunately for the folk living below, gravity decided the sliding mass headed straight for Twickton.

Newspapers, an imperative source of information within the metropolises, offered nothing more to the ignorant than a luxury alternative within the toilet. Accommodating overwhelming numbers of illiterates in a plethora of similar townships only confirmed publisher's decisions not to waste precious paper-stock in these educational wastelands. It was no wonder the future fighting force knew nothing about their country being at war, especially when employers thought it financially prudent not to inform them. Unbeknown to these folk, the journalistic word proclaimed a swift victory, but on pages buried amongst advertising trivia and cricket scoreboards, spiralling numbers of deaths portrayed a graver picture. Crucially, on orders from the moguls of Fleet Street, positive headlines were essential, not so much to ease the worried investors when choosing which journal best to advertise, but to retain a high degree of moral from its readers. Responding discreetly to prompting by Downing Street, reports from the front line required tinkering before going to press so as not to hinder enlistment - a definite possibility if graphic descriptions of the horror happening on the opposite side of the English Channel were allowed to go to press.

**

For the people of Twickton with a modicum of home-taught education, the choice between a newspaper and a jug of ale never entered the equation. The liquid nectar proved a powerful victor every time. Apart from this liquid nullifier relieving the trauma of living under such extreme diabolical conditions, availability of a luxury item was rare on a miner's pay. That is to say, all except for the one affordable extravagance - a tin bath, essential to every mining household. Using water drawn from an outside well heated over a constantly burning coal stove, the eldest male, usually the father, benefited from the first use followed by the eldest of the children, that is, if it was a Sunday. Situated alongside the stove - the only communal space large enough within the dwelling to accommodate

15

these public ablutions - it was possible to count the number of previous bathers before the youngest took its turn in decreasing tepid frothy grey water, by counting the staggered descending black lines encircling the infant.

These hovels, constructed at minimal cost by the mine owners, offered the barest of essentials. Managerial thoughts concerning the welfare of the worker's family in the guise of education, health or nutrition, never came before the board of directors for consideration. A nationwide labour force far outnumbering demand decided a worker's standard of living. Long before unions could champion a workers cause, a complaint initiated instant dismissal. In Twickton's case, only the relief of the chapel roof, towering slag heaps and the mine's lifting wheel interrupted the bleak skyline viewed from these humble dwellings.

Accepting illness and death as acceptable causes to disrupt a honed, beholding allegiance, intelligent individuals soon became apparent and dissuaded, by one way or another, from further employment.

To the community's mothers bearing a son - another wage packet bolstering the household coffers - was a godsend, as long as the sibling survived past his tenth birthday, but once into their teens, inquisitive young virile males earning adult mining rates naturally followed in their father's footsteps and sourced amusement in one or both of the alternatives the township offered. The choice was simple, warm ale or the warmth between a girl's thighs.

Daughters on the other hand were considered a burden, that is to say, until they reached the age of puberty. Whilst incest was never condoned, fraternisation within the family circle regularly occurred. When a girl became pregnant, even if the boy-father was related, they married before the birth and took up residence in one of the already crowded squats of a relation. No one complained because no one listened.

***

It was late November, over three months after the outbreak of war, when word trickled through the township concerning hostilities building up on mainland Europe. Though most of the population understood the gravity of the hostile situation, Twickton's mine owners deemed it unnecessary to disrupt their worker's monotonous but profitable daily routine by informing them of what was happening in the world outside their community. It would take more than a skirmish oversees to disorganise the strict regime laid down by the Noble dynasty concerning mining procedure and the quantity of coal retrieved daily from the bowls of the earth. The daily grind would have remained unaffected had it not been for overheard whispers circulating the manager's office.

Against his wife's advice fearing managerial reprisals, Jack Fowler, a burly thirty-six year old shift foreman, confronted the most approachable superior person within head-office to ratify or dismiss the gossip. On November 26th Fowler unwisely, but bravely, requested answers to his questions from Robert Noble, the mine manager and eldest son and heir to the formidable founder of the business, Sir Richard Noble.

Expecting dire repercussions, Fowler's sweated anticipation about the outcome of this meeting paled into insignificance compared to that of Robert Noble's relief. To finally unburden the truth which, up until this day had been deliberately kept from the workers, for no other reason but profit, unshackled him from his father's style of management. Having no choice when taking over the helm from his father a few years before, Sir Richard's etched in stone draconian directives required smashing and replacing with a new code of practice, clearly re-engraved, so that every worker understood their rites. Family arguments undoubtedly would follow, but on this day, against his father's wishes, Robert rewrote the rulebook by instructing his foreman to spread the word of truth amongst his fellow workers as soon as physically possible. At the likely cost of his livelihood, extracting this news was a chance Fowler was prepared to take. Unexpectedly, but relieved by Robert's response, Fowler wasted little time calling a meeting of the entire community. Nobody, he ordered, was allowed to be absent.

***

Allowing one of his father's old directives to remain in Robert's new block of stone, the family's fervent belief in the bible allowed a few hours of rest on the Sabbath. This would be the perfect time when the population of Twickton, all six hundred and seventy-two, were free to attend the meeting without fear of managerial reprisals.

As luck would have it for this time of year, Sunday arrived without a cloud in the sky, albeit with a low weak sun in the heavens radiating insufficient heat to melt the first frost of winter covering the landscape, but Fowler chose well for his venue to hold this impromptu meeting. Twickton's lack of a building large enough to hold the expected turnout directed Fowler's thoughts to a plot of land featuring a raised knoll, half a mile outside the commune's perimeter. An ideal setting to act as his forum. At the stroke of ten, allowing for those of the parish who wished to first attend chapel, Fowler waited, perched above the crowd for the last of the stragglers to arrive.

Dressed in the only clothes unaffected by coal dust, the imposing figure spread his arms skywards, demanding silence. Nobody could remember a meeting of this magnitude before, each sensing they were about to witness something special. Though Fowler was a hard man in every respect, he uncannily possessed a second sense for the theatrical. Waiting fully half a minute to ensure the throng's attention was focused solely on him; even the youngest in the gathering took note and ceased their grizzling. Looking down at his boots, he thought it a strange time to decide he needed a new pair. They'd seen too many years of work, but further disappointment crossed his brow when noticing they refused to accept a shine despite all his laborious attempts to polish them that morning.

"Good folk of Twickton," a local Yorkshire brogue bellowed across the clearing.

His wife Gladys stood at his side, slightly to the rear but sufficiently in view to show off a relatively new frock to the envious wives gathered below. Unwilling to cover the garment with an ageing overcoat, though the temperature suggested it might be wiser, she smiled radiantly whilst ensuring her siblings, clothed no better than ragamuffins, huddled together. Pulling her shoulders back to a point of pain, her ample bosom emphasised her pride in her man.

"I have some very grave news for you all." Fowler purposely paused, guaranteeing attention. "I, like you, have heard the tittle-tattle going round the patch. So, as shift foreman, I took it upon myself to confront Master Robert. I asked him if it was true what I've been hearing and I'm afraid, my good people of Twickton, it ain't gossip any longer. It's all true. Our great nation is at war with Germany."

A stunned silence swept across the gathering for a few seconds, sufficient time for the ramifications of what was said to fully sink in. Taking a lead from the first mutterings, a low bee-like drone grumbled from the gathering confronting Fowler and his family.

***

19

In the distance, across open fields half a mile away, the manor house stood dominating the landscape. Built on majestic, opulent lines, Robert Noble openly spied on the spectacle through a drawing room window. Focusing his binoculars on Fowler, Robert's enthusiastic running commentary of the proceedings wasn't greeted with the same fervour by his family, ordered to assemble by his father.

"Good man, that Fowler. It appears he's got everything under control," Robert mockingly announced, ignoring a schooner of sherry offered by Thomas the butler. Sensing his father privately seething at Fowler's audacity and power over a workforce he'd never personally met, prompted Robert to keep the lenses firmly attached to his eyes, fearful his father might detect amusement emanating from behind the binoculars. An awkward silence descended within the grandly decorated and sumptuous residence, testament to thirty years of a profitably run business. Whilst Robert enjoyed Fowler's performance, His mother and three younger brothers sat uneasily on an assortment of expensive Louis XIV settees circling a huge ornate, marble fireplace where Sir Richard, seriously affected by the proceedings and appearing ashen grey, stood straight as his military background had taught, legs slightly bent at the knee, rocking from toe to heal and back again. Noble senior scowled at his eldest son's refusal to acknowledge his anger. Pompously obnoxious, Sir Richard ignored the offered sherry, preferring to swirl a large cut-glass brandy goblet in his right hand, whilst his left fidgeted with the elongated whiskers of a waxed moustache.

"I hope this chap Fowler has got everything under control." Endeavouring to appear in command of the situation, Sir Richard questioned Robert, but knew better than to expect an answer. "Though the word coming from London endorses *The Times'* assessment about all this being over by Christmas, I'm not at all convinced. By next week we'll be in December and I can't see this ending in four weeks. Could play havoc with the mine. A miner going to war means one less to dig out coal and you know what that means? Less profits."

***

Fowler allowed nervous chattering amongst the gathering before retaking control.

"I came back from fighting the Boers some fourteen years ago. I fought for Queen and Country back then and lived to tell the tale. If my country needs my services again, I'll willingly oblige. We beat the Dutch in their own back yard, thousands of miles away, so we can bloody-well beat the Germans next door across the Channel. All they have to do is ask. This is my land and God forbid anyone who tries to take it away from me. If the Almighty wants me that bad, I'll die before I'll allow some German bastard take away what isn't his."

Punching the air with a raised fist, Fowler waited. The spellbound, silent crowd suddenly transformed into a rumbling, shivering mass. Quickly growing vocal support reached a high pitch of fervent approval. Where there was once subdued obedience, hysteria took control of the leaping masses; all imitating Fowler's clenched fist salute.

Deeply encompassed by frenzied bodies, the Hobbs family reacted no differently to those around them, that is to say, all except young Mathew, the last born of three sons to George and Dorothy. Standing open mouthed, the amazed fifteen-year old youth stared at Fowler through flailing bodies, marvelling at how one man could influence so many. He gazed at faces he knew well, all laughing and appearing overwhelmed with joy. He'd never witnessed such happiness in his parents even though Fowler's announcement meant their country was at war. Unable to imitate their reactions despite the surrounding euphoria,

Mathew felt scared. He would remember this day for as long as he lived. Nothing could be the same again.

***

"What on earth is happening out there? What's that fearful noise I can hear?"

Visibly shaken, Sir Richard outstretched a trembling hand, a silent instruction for Thomas to refill his glass. Seemingly ignored when in family attendance, Thomas knew his position and was thankful of his status within the household. Clean clothes, bed sheets and the right to dine below stairs at Cook's kitchen table confirmed a butler's standard of living far exceeded that of a miner.

"You won't believe this father. They're all jumping up and down and cheering their heads off. It appears they've all gone quite berserk. What, I wonder, has Fowler just said to them?" Grinning broadly, Robert turned to face his father. "I hope he hasn't taken it upon himself to offer a pay rise."

Robert laughs alone. The family see the reaction of his summary on the face of Sir Richard and decide it wiser to remain stiff lipped.

"Get down there, man, and see what all this fuss is about," the head of the household orders, his anger festering.

"Oh, you have to be joking, father. We'll find out all in good time without me putting my life on the line."

Being the only son who dared answer back to his father, Robert managed it always with a smile. Sir Richard saw beyond this façade, knowing full well, under his light hearted exterior his eldest was serious and spoke with calculated authority. Camouflaged pride didn't cloud his knowledge when deciding the time was right for Robert to inherit the right to run the business, Sir Richard knew he would make the ideal replacement. The company would be safe in his hands as the miners appeared to respect his decisions far better than they respected his own. Robert fitted in behind his father's desk with consummate ease. Success was never in doubt but required new methods born of the twentieth century to remain healthy. Unsympathetic to his father's past iron fisted directives, Robert chose to suggest changes to workers and note the reaction, rather than dictate. Loathe to admit the mine required alterations, Sir Richard admitted the new formula worked, as production figures proved, but having only a past military experience for comparisons he harboured reservations about how long it might last. During a career as an army colonel, there was no reasoning to a given order. A trooper's disobedience on the field of battle resulted in the firing squad or a lengthy spell in the glass-house. On occasions, when Robert was a boy, Sir Richard reminisced about occasions when he oversaw field court marshals, hoping his son might learn the meaning of respect and obedience, but typically with traits carried into adulthood, Robert argued that respect could only be earned reciprocally.

***

"Come on, Mathew. Time to go home. You've had enough excitement for one day." George Hobbs put a fatherly arm around his youngest son's shoulders. "You saw a good man up there talking today. You'll remember it for a long time."

George Hobbs only confirmed what Mathew knew already.

CHAPTER 2

By Monday - the following morning - life returned to relative normality, though conversation between the early shifts contained a different topic. There also appeared to be less absenteeism after a Sunday night's debauchery, care of the township's solitary drinking hole.

Arriving some three hours later, Robert Noble's attention was also drawn by a subtle difference only a trained eye might notice amongst the usual activity of a coal mine's daily workings. Entering the main, wrought-iron gates, surface workers doffed their caps, a courtesy never bestowed even to his father. Bypassing the reception, he chose a different route and ascended the exterior iron staircase leading to his office. Reaching the top step, he turned to take in an elevated view of the yard spread out below. Three youths armed with stiff brooms swept the area with somewhat military precision. Again it was a first. He pondered if this was of Fowler's doing.

Inheriting his father's office, a domain in total contrast to the drab decorative state to the rest of the building, a theme of wanton opulence challenged any who entered. Enclosed in chunky, gilt frames, fine artworks depicting various subjects obscured reams of rich, ruby wallpaper. Hidden under thick Oriental rugs shouldering an assortment of antique settees, a highly polished wooden floor occasionally found out rare visitor's inability to ice-skate. Situated directly opposite a carved interior oak door, a huge desk sprawled under a disgruntled looking portrait of the founder, a deliberate subtle placing to deter over-confidence from those who entered. Times were rapidly changing and this wasn't the impression Robert wanted an impoverished worker to view his style of management, but further impending father to son disagreements concerning the décor would have to wait.

***

Taking his private secretary by surprise, Robert poked his head round the door leading to her small but adequate office.

"Mrs Booth, before you bring in my tea, could you get someone to find Fowler for me and bring him to my office. He's the large chap who spoke at yesterday's meeting. I believe he's working this shift."

Thankful for the distraction from mundane paperwork some twenty minutes after his directive, a handful of knuckles rapped the oak panelling on Robert's door opposite.

"Come in."

Gradually the barrier opened sufficiently to display Fowler standing sheepishly, the opposite characteristic to how he appeared the day before, perched confidently on the knoll in front of the entire community. Now dressed in shapeless, coal encrusted trousers held aloft by braces draped over a collarless, what was once a white shirt with its sleeves rolled to the elbow; he clutched his cap to his chest with both hands.

"Come in man, don't just stand there."

It was the first time in the worker's memory when a pit face miner had been given the accolade to enter this inner sanctum. It would be a day when there would be quite a few firsts.

"Pull up one of those chairs and sit yourself down."

Fowler scanned the suggested area for a seat he wouldn't embarrassingly foul with black coal dust.

"You're probably wondering why I've called you here to see me. But before we have our chat, would you care for a cup of tea?"

Before his foreman could answer, Mathew poured a cup, deliberately stifling a smile at Fowler's attempt to pick up the fine china with filthy, stubby fingers.

"I observed you yesterday speaking to the workforce. Not being in the vicinity to hear what you had to say, my father and I were amazed to witness their reaction from afar. Tell me, what exactly did you say to them?"

Robert watched Fowler awkwardly juggle the cup back onto the saucer whilst still clutching his cap to his chest with his other hand. Robert guessed he was illiterate, but judging the way he conducted the crowd, he knew this person, squatting so uncomfortably before his desk, possessed great integrity, loyalty and strength of character.

"I just told them what you told me, that we are at war with Germany. I also told them I fought in the last one we had in South Africa and if need be, would do it all over again."

Avoiding eye contact, his uncertainty confirmed why Robert needed to alter his workers' opinion of management. Judging by the size of Fowler, Robert saw an immense strength hidden under a humble exterior. He was impressive. Gradually nurtured, Robert knew he possessed the trusted raw material to act as his go-between when voicing ideas for improved conditions. Breaking this interesting, silent interlude, an erratic knock from Mrs Booth side of the door refocused Robert's attention.

His secretary appeared flustered.

"An army vehicle has just pulled up in the yard, Sir. There are two uniformed gentlemen coming this way."

"Haven't you anything better to do Mrs Booth than to look out of the window?"

Robert's intended mockery backfired. A shocked intake of breath and a complexion turning ever redder prompted a swift apology.

"Oh Mrs Booth, I'm only jesting. Make a note; we must make it a rule to have more humour in this workplace."

Having been his father's private secretary for over twenty years, she smiled uncertainly at his brand new formula of management.

"Okay, Mrs Booth. When they arrive send them in."

Robert's attention returned to Fowler.

"If I'm right in my assumption, I believe this could be the end of our closeted, peaceful existence here in Twickton. Thank you for coming to see me, I've enjoyed our little chat. So I understand from my office staff, they consider you very brave to approach me the other day. I must admit, Fowler, I didn't realise there was such an unbreachable gap between my office and the workers. Believe me that will change. There is no doubt we shall get together again, probably sooner than you think. Congratulate your shift on my behalf for their loyalty. They are good, honest workers. You should be very proud of them."

For the first time since they met, Fowler's eyes made contact with Robert's.

"Oh, Master Robert. You can be sure I am."

Inadvertently, seeds for a new beginning had been sown with a shake of the big man's hand.

Obligingly pressing his back to the narrow corridor wall, Fowler's unwashed torso allowed two pristine uniformed officers to pass.

"It's alright, Mrs Booth. I'll take it from here."

Ushering his visitors into his office, Robert firmly secured the barrier between himself and the outside world. As much as he trusted his staff, he didn't want more gossip filtering through to the coal face.

"Good morning gentlemen. May I introduce myself? I'm Robert Noble, the Managing Director. What can I do for you?"

The question was short and to the point, affording the officers to be in no doubt of Robert's intent. Pointing to two easy chairs, Robert beckoned them to be seated and waited for what he already knew was the inevitable reason for their visit.

The higher ranking officer spoke.

"It's good of you to see us so promptly, Mr Noble. I am Major Frobisher and this is my adjutant, Lieutenant Myers. As you no doubt have read in *The Times,* things are starting to heat up across the Channel. At the moment the regular army are doing a sterling job, but we require a reserve force to be on hand should it be needed. This is, of course, by no means compulsory, not yet anyway, but we would appreciate your assistance in this matter. By what we have witnessed already, you have a tight, hardworking community which we could well use."

"Tea, gentlemen?"

Dissecting the major's well-rehearsed speech before he could rattle off more predictable words written by a faceless civil servant back at the War Office, Robert pondered on how many other small communities had heard the same words before his arrival at Twickton.

"Er, yes. Thank you. One sugar for me, please."

Pausing as he stood to pour the refreshments to their required taste, the officers wrongly felt they could relax.

"Please, feel free to interrupt if you believe I'm getting hold of the wrong end of the stick."

Whilst at Baliol College, Cambridge, Robert achieved an honours degree in history, but it was his uncanny ability to verbally manipulate himself out of sticky situations that caught the eye of his astute professor. Watching him progress through university, he witnessed a polished orator blossom, the ideal candidate to enter politics. His confrontational capabilities weren't wasted however - when he chose to join the family business, Robert's father became the member for the opposition.

"I am not ignorant to the reason why you are here. I know precisely. Reading between the lines of the published journalistic word, your war in Europe isn't going the way your boys in Whitehall planned. It appears we are getting our arse smacked. So to cover your ineptness when forecasting a victory before Christmas, you want to take away my boys to fight on foreign soil to hurry things up. Maybe you don't require them just yet, but I'm sure one day in the not too distant future you'll need them to put their lives on the line. Inform me if I've made a mistake in my assumption."

The major turned to his adjutant for words that weren't forthcoming from his own mouth.

"Come now, Major. You require my workforce without a thought about what they have already given to the nation. Obviously, you have no idea how long it took my father to establish this mine. Without these men bringing up coal from the bowls of the earth, your army wouldn't be going anywhere, let alone the continent. Who do you think supplies all the raw material to supply your guns? It's men down the pit and many others doing the same, dangerous backbreaking work. Tell me, Major, have you ever been down a pit?"

Glaring down at the seated duo from his standing position, Robert restrained his rage. Always take the high ground before attacking; his father's words rang out clearly. The men from the military left their teacups untouched.

"Sir, all we ask of you is to form a company of men between the ages of seventeen and thirty. Of course, we would prefer volunteers so as not to hinder production. Where would we be without coal? We can train them here so as to keep disruption down to a minimum. To begin with, it would only take up three afternoons a week under the watchful eye of a drill sergeant to learn the rudiments of basic army life. I cannot deny it, Sir. One day we might require their assistance. I must remind you, we are at war against a very powerful enemy."

Turning his back on the officers, Robert walked across to the adjacent window reluctantly accepting the reality of the major's reasoning. The view overlooked his father's empire, built on farmland bequeathed from his late father. Understanding only army life from a young man, Sir Richard assumed greater ambitions than to succeed in farming, where his father had failed. Having never milked a cow, he gambled on an alternative use for the land as surrounding areas started to reap benefits from exploratory mining. The day before bailiffs arrived to possess their last worthwhile belongings, Sir Richard's theory of coal deposits beneath his land proved positive. Within four years of striking black gold, profits and employment flourished where once a man struggled to afford a loaf of bread.

Whilst at university, Robert studied transcripts describing the Boer conflict against the Dutch, South African farmers. Though the uprising was quelled, some reports even mentioned the word victorious, the loss of life was enormous. However on this occasion, replacing ageing weaponry, the enemy had at its disposal the wealth of a powerful nation to provide far deadlier equipment in the hands of a vast trained army, not to mention a sizeable navy and a flying corps capable of dropping bombs. The opposition was more powerful than had been seen before in any previous conflicts. Knowing the consequences to expect on the front line, if he asked his workers to put their life on the line, his honour dictated he do the same.

"I have a proposition to put to you, Major." Robert finely turned to face the officers. "I agree to your suggestions. We shall form a company made up solely from my workforce, but on one condition. As I know and trust my men, I require a high rank to lead them and the authority to choose my own NCOs from within my workforce. If this is agreeable, then we have a deal to all the training you wish to put us through, in which I shall participate. Also, should my men become a company within your regiment; they shall need to look the part. So no bloodstained, bullet holed uniforms taken from dead soldiers. Do I make myself clear?"

Clearly taken back by the veracity of the delivery, Frobisher listened and readily agreed.

"I must say, Sir." Lieutenant Myers unwisely stood and spoke for the first time, a sardonic smile creasing his lips to accompany a cold, calculating efficiency. "We really don't require you to be part of the exercises. Your place is here managing the mine. It's just numbers of men we need, the good old foot soldier, don't you know."

Engulfed with rage, Robert confronted Myers at close quarters, an unexpected action causing the lieutenant to sprawl backwards into his vacated chair, his smirk just a memory.

"How dare you. No, I don't bloody-well know, you condescending bastard. To you they might be considered just gun fodder, but to me they are the life blood of this community. Where they go, I go. Do you understand me?"

CHAPTER 3

Six weeks passed since Frobisher's visit when uncensored news reports outlined the seriousness of the conflict being contested on foreign soil. Daily, the review worsened, confirming Robert's worse fears that it would be only a matter of time before Twickton Company would be called upon to go into action. All the talk of a swift victory was long forgotten with numbers of spiralling deaths published, not tucked away on previously hidden pages, but highlighted in large printed headlines. Where there was once perceived excitement, induced by glamorised writing, hard-nosed journalists now wrote it how they saw it, leaving nothing to the imagination for those dreading to be called forward to fill the gaps vacated by the dead

Awarded the rank of captain, Robert became privy to whispers circulated by home based officers, mostly all from privileged, wealthy stock and fresh out of university. This criterion to automatically become an officer worried Robert. Adding family connections to the list of fundamental qualities essential in the eyes of regimental hierarchy to qualify for an officer's rank only endorsed his apprehension. Once Robert was acquainted and trusted by his fellow officers, these misgivings were finally endorsed, as most demanded expensive, bespoke tailored uniforms to glorify their masculine indulgence by portraying gladiatorial qualities, not to men under their command, but to attract the opposite sex when attending nightly social gatherings. A trusted officer friend of Robert described this charade as 'continuous daily remakes of New Year's Eve fancy dress parties'. A low ranking batman was also imperative for the battle field, as was a trunk containing a dinner suit, fine wines and sufficient space for a golf bag. He sympathised with the men these imposters commanded, whose plight would be secondary to the comfort of these officers who viewed conflict much the same as a gentleman's game of cricket. This bravado would soon be put to the test. Few would return with their same sense of humour.

Should he be directed to the front line, Robert took every opportunity, listening not to the brigadiers who fought a good battle over a bottle of expensive brandy, but to words of wisdom on how to stay alive from the sergeant majors and corporals who chose an army life as a career.

***

Twickton Company became a reality. Under the auspices of a drill sergeant major, a soldier from a bye gone age considered beyond the acceptable age to fight but frighteningly vocally adequate to scare the pants off raw recruits, Twickton Company surfaced to resemble a worthwhile addition to the regiment. Training sessions initially made little impact to mining quotas, but as fighting abroad approached a critical stage, Robert and his men spent a further two days away from home 'practising' how to become serious soldiers. Inevitably, production waned, coinciding with families suffering financially due to volunteers unquestionably following their commander.

Spending less time behind his desk and more on the simulated killing fields of The Yorkshire Dales, Robert juggled his dual responsibilities but was resigned to accept his father's reintroduction to the post he retired from a few years before. If his war effort meant the mine returned to draconian ways, then Robert needed to rethink where he and the future lay. Either commit all his energy to Twickton

Company and allow the mine to drift into an uncertain future or take Myers advice and concentrate on the war effort from behind a desk. The long delayed confrontation with his father couldn't be postponed any longer, as blind obedience from his workers couldn't be rewarded by allowing their families to suffer financially.

Expecting an angry reaction, Sir Richard's suggestion for an uncomplicated scheme of compensation surprised Robert. Standing below his portrait, Robert saw no resemblance from the stony faced man in the painting compared to the man standing before him. Something significantly had changed.

"We all are living in difficult times, Robert. Who would have dared to think that over the last couple of months I would admit money is not the most important commodity in life? As a family, we have sufficient collateral to last a multitude of lifetimes. I'm so very proud of what you have achieved. I believe the same men who are prepared to follow you to war should not be penalised but instead be rewarded with a share of the profits."

Placing a fatherly hand on Robert's uniformed shoulder, his voice lowered emotionally.

"By the way things are escalating; your three brothers shall probably follow your example. I admire your initiative and only wish I was younger so it was I who wore the uniform. Whatever happens, my boy, take care of yourself and your men. I know they'll follow you with pride."

Standing half hidden by the manager's open office door, Mrs Booth wiped away developing tears with a handkerchief usually tucked up the sleeve of a hand-knitted cardigan.

"You saw your own share of action, Father. Now it's my turn. Don't worry; I have good men by my side and Fowler's been a bloody marvel. He makes other sergeants look ordinary and Twickton Company knows it. I know you understand, what with all this looming over the horizon, fate determined the path I needed to tread. Thank you on behalf of the workers and me for everything you've done."

They embraced.

***

Consisting of two hundred men, Twickton Company formed part of the East Riding Regiment. Across Yorkshire, similar companies formed, all undertaking similar basic training and field exercises, but Robert knew his company would have a head start when it came to fitness. It takes a man in excellent physical condition to labour down a mine.

***

Apprehension grew on an overcast afternoon in May when Robert saw a military motorbike outrider arrive at the main building. No good news was ever delivered in such a manner, he thought, but it cheered up the community as most of the elderly had never witnessed such a vehicle before. A small gathering engulfed the gates to peer at this strange, noisy contraption trailing a plume of white smoke in its wake. Squeezing his way through the inquisitive crowd, Fowler traced the rider into the compound, meeting Robert descending the iron staircase. Confronting a superior officer, the rider dismounted and saluted.

"Message from HQ, Sir. I'm to wait for a reply."

"Thank you, Corporal."

Returning the salute, Robert tore open the brown envelope. A hundred pair of eyes, mostly women and children's, watched in silence as Robert extracted a typed official memorandum. Under an array of coloured insignia and scrolled printing, he read the order loud enough for those in close proximity to hear.

"'To;- Captain Robert Noble. Twickton Company. 2nd
Rifle Battalion. East Riding Regiment.

You are advised to report to Battalion Headquarters with Twickton Company of two hundred (200) recruits no later than 1500 hours, Monday, 6th May, 1915. All personnel to be attired in full battle fatigues and prepared for embarkation by locomotive to London. Times and transfers from London to Folkestone for embarkation to a French port to be arranged on arrival at London. Full supplies and armaments to be issued at HQ quartermasters.

Signed. General .B. Sparrow.'"

Staring silently down at the order sheet, Robert knew word would quickly spread, causing grief to engulf the families of Twickton. It was likely he was announcing their death warrant. It also might be possibly his own.

"Thank you, Corporal. Please confirm to General Sparrow, that Twickton Company shall be honoured to attend the party." Salutes exchanged. Seconds later, Robert watched the rider disappear through the growing crowd.

Fowler, the only personnel within Twickton Company to have experienced the trauma of battle, witnessed the same departure wondering if his luck could hold for a second time. Some will face the enemy with aggression, but most will not have the stomach to plunge a bayonet into a body probably belonging to another fledgling soldier.

"Well, Sergeant Fowler. The time we've all been expecting has come. Inform all the Company. Get them mustered here in the yard in full battledress by 1000 hours on Monday. I've decided we're not going to use our filthy rolling stock to get to Isley, instead, we'll march in formation. I'll have an engine and coaches standing by to take us to Catterick from there. We might be miners at heart but we'll arrive at HQ in style looking like soldiers."

Robert winked at Fowler, allowing an elongated smile to crease his lips.

"As I'm an official captain in the eyes of the military, I can commandeer any bloody thing I want. We're at war, don't you know."

Though dressed in clothes more suitable for subterranean labour, Fowler disregarded protocol by standing to attention and saluted his commanding officer in one well-rehearsed movement.

"You're correct, Sir. If it's anything like my past recollections of the army, captains can do anything they bloody like."

And yet there was still adequate time for another first to be registered on this day. Robert witnessing Fowler smile.

***

The day began sombrely in the Noble household. Sir Richard, walking ahead, led his family, showing his solidarity with the other families of volunteers ordered to assemble at the colliery, leaving Robert to say his lone farewells to domestic household servants he'd known since he was a boy. Fortunately for the male staff, their age eliminated them from any involvement.

For the community, it was a rare sight to witness the Nobles as a family unit, but marching purposely, Sir Richard led the way closely followed by and trying to stay in touch, his wife Lady Mary. Bringing up the rear, Robert's brothers followed, the eldest in front. Approaching the colliery gates, villagers from surrounding parishes swelled the crowd, joining those living in the community. Hearing a ripple of applause rising above mutterings, Sir Richard appeared bemused. No more than twenty paces from reaching the main gate, this sprinkling accolade grew stronger whereby people he'd never seen before lined the route. Putting their hands together, the mass created a noise more akin to an audience showing their satisfaction to a theatre performance. Quite bewildered, Sir Richard raised an uneasy, acknowledging hand.

Reaching down, Lady Mary grabbed the hem of her embroidered dress, freeing her legs from the encumbrance to allow quickened paces to draw alongside her husband. Elevating her panting mouth closer to her husband's ear, she endeavoured a ventriloquist-like attempt at not being overheard.

"They appear to like you, Richard...At last."

Dressed for battle before his family rose from their beds, Fowler recalled the previous night's emotion of saying farewell to his wife and young daughters. Deciding it best for all concerned, he banished negative thoughts and took to the countryside, walking three miles to where he knew he could borrow a dray and cart from an ageing farmer. Perched high on the four wheeled carriage, Fowler allowed the nag to proceed at its own pace, arriving at the mansion as Robert emerged from the front door, respectfully followed by Thomas and the entire household.

"Best I could find at short notice, Captain. Thought you might like a ride instead of walking."

From his lofty position, Fowler lowered a hand, a vice-like grip assisted his commanding officer on board. At the same speed as he approached, Fowler traced the route taken earlier by the Noble family, leaving behind a tearful, waving group of servants engrossed in their own private, black thoughts. Ahead, a mile away from the colliery, the outline of the familiar lifting wheel stood out, silhouetted against a grey sky manufacturing a light drizzle, falling on unperturbed, unfamiliar faces voicing their patriotic approval. Waving home-made union flags they obediently parted, creating a passage for the dray to slowly press forward seemingly oblivious to the growing noise echoing round his ears, but without warning, despite Fowler's sympathetic urging, planted itself to a spot surrounded by crowds outside the main gates. Every eye focused on Robert. Though there was a carnival-like atmosphere in the air for those viewing this solely as a pageant, it wasn't an occasion for Robert to emulate Fowler's stylish disembarkation from the cart. For the loved ones of those whose men were about to march off to war, the seriousness of the situation demanded a temper on adrenalin by cautiously slithering down the side ensuring his feet hit the ground before his posterior.

Simulating his father's approach, the crowd parted sufficiently for the duo to proceed unhindered but within reach to deliver spontaneous back slapping gestures. Catching occasional glimpses through flailing bodies, Robert saw his family huddled together alongside the picture of other family groups in the courtyard, separated from the massing crowd by the wrought iron main gates. The vision on his arrival of a column, fifty man long by four abreast, quickened Robert's heart-rate. Standing at ease, Twickton Company looked resplendent in new khaki uniforms, strapped webbing over shining boots and tilted forage caps. For many, it would be their first opportunity to wear clothes unaffected by coal dust, or those other than worn hand-me-downs. Timing his captain's approach to the second, Corporal Mallory's cry of, "Attention," instigated a crunch of two hundred pairs of boots simultaneously slamming down on the cobbled surface. Each stood bolt upright, unflinching in their allotted, measured space. Tears of pride freely flowed from the eyes of those families whose father, uncle, son or brother were about to go into battle. The Noble family were no exemption from this affliction. Robert witnessed his father weep for the first time.

Succeeding to be heard over the din of raucous cheering, Captain Robert Noble calmly gave his order to Sergeant Fowler, saluted, then marched to take his rightful place at the front of the line. Putting to the back of his mind all the emotional hugging and kissing from the previous night, Fowler glanced to his wife, lingered on eye contact with two small daughters before roaring the order back to the troops.

"Twickton Company. Wait for it Smithers. By-the-right. Quick march." In perfect harmony, the formation strode forward as one.

"Eyes left."

On command, every soldier's head turned to face the Noble family as they marched past, accompanied by Robert's lone salute.

Arriving early to guarantee a prime position with the other families, George Hobbs gathered his wife and youngest son between his arms, glowing with pride watching his two eldest sons march away. His wife, Dorothy, inconsolable, his son, Mathew, overawed.

"When can I go and join them?" Mathew pestered his mother.

"I've already told you. Not until you're old enough," she repeated, praying the war was over before the time arrived.

"When's that?" he persisted.

"God forbid. When you're eighteen and not a day before."

Accepting the answer, no more badgering was needed. Mathew achieved his objective of having a day and a target to aim for.

***

An alien sound of men marching in unison echoed across the fields, causing a handful of underfed cattle to scatter to far corners of their barren territory, but their following entourage continued their tirade of flag waving and cheering until the last man in the formation was fully a mile out from the colliery. Twickton Company's pace remained constant, arriving at Isley Station precisely on time with Robert's calculations and true to his promise with Fowler, the commandeered train waited on platform one, smoke lazily wafting from its stack on a line pointing in the direction of Catterick.

CHAPTER 4

Mathew Hobbs stared blankly out of his elevated bedroom window. Induced by overnight snow, a film of ice formed on the small panes, confirming the indoor temperature was below zero. Winter had arrived early this year.

Over two years had passed since word came back from the frontline describing Twickton Company's heroic advance leading to their decimation at Ypres. The question no one answered was, how only fourteen troopers out of the original company of two hundred could survive to fight another day. Sadly, for Mathew's family, both his elder brothers were not amongst the fortunate, though Fowler overcame the carnage, surviving unscathed and by what Mathew could glean from snippets of unsubstantiated reports, was recommended for a medal for outstanding bravery. Each family mourned in their own private way, but as a community, bereavement continued up until this day. A length of black cloth remained draped over the Noble's mansion's portico signifying the loss of their son, but the faded banner only served as a reminder to continue Twickton's mourning.

In his grief, Sir Richard demanded a large marble memorial to be erected at the colliery inscribed with all the names of those who perished, but Lady Mary wisely advised him to wait until the end of hostilities as it was likely more names might need to be added. When hearing the news of her two sons, Mathew's mother retreated into a dark chasm of remorse, regretting ever giving her youngest permission to follow in their footsteps. Shy of becoming eighteen years old by one day, Mathew vividly remembered the day when Twickton Company marched proudly to war and his persistence for a date when he could join his brothers. At a time when the sight of Twickton Company in their resplendent uniforms gave great joy to many, the reality of war was now all too prevalent. It seemed a long time in the distant past, but after the terrible massacre, Mathew stopped reminding his mother of her promise.

Adding to the accumulation covering the ground, snow began to fall again. Watching the flakes descend, Mathew dreaded reminding his mother of her promise, that on the morrow, the 15th of November, it would herald the morning of his eighteenth birthday. Fully aware of her continued suffering, he loathed repeating his intention. Grabbing his coat and cap, he slipped out of the house without attracting attention, heading for the open fields.

Freezing conditions percolated through inadequate outer layers of clothing as he squinted to the heavens, hoping the falling snowflakes freezing on his face could inspire divine help. Choosing a low stone wall partly sheltered by a lone leafless maple tree, the sole timber growth within miles offering an umbrella of overhanging snow laden branches, he sat, contemplating his dilemma. Extracting a tobacco tin from an inside pocket, protected against a stiff, snow filled breeze blowing against his back, frustrated, frozen fingers attempted to prise open the lid. Unable to fall back on brothers to teach him the practiced art of rolling a cigarette, his feeble attempt resulted in more tobacco falling to the snow around his feet than in the finished article. Protecting a flame from his eldest brother's bequeathed lighter feared no better until burying his face under the coat collar to light the skinny object between his lips. Amongst a crumpled photograph of his mother, two leather identity tags and a wooden comb, the lighter was only one of five articles retrieved from the bodies and returned to the Hobbs family.

Taking a deep pull on lit tobacco without releasing his breath, the effect sobered his thoughts before allowing lungs to liberate a cocktail of smoke mixed with warm vapour. From across the fields in the direction of the community, Mathew's picked out a huddled figure approaching. Wearing a similar coat to his with a collar wrapped tightly round a hidden face to ward off the cold, Mathew was baffled as to its identity. Its gait, so indigenous to pit face miners, offered a clue apart from one peculiarity, a slight limp. When the shape was no more than twenty paces away Mathew confirmed his earlier assumption that it was his father.

"Hallo, son. I saw you from back home sitting out here like some big, lonesome crow in need of a mate. So I thought I'd join you."

From under the peak of his well-worn cap pulled low over his eyes, Mathew welcomed his father's warm smile.

"I know there's only one reason why you're out here by yourself in this bloody, god awful weather. It's your birthday tomorrow."

Pausing to brush snow off the top of the wall, he sat close to his son. Mimicking his sole surviving heir, he removed his tobacco tin and rolled a perfect cigarette with educated fingers in a matter of seconds allowing nothing to drop to the floor.

"You're out here wondering how to tell your mother that you're off to war. I'm right, aren't I, son? She'll take it badly, you know. You're the only one she has left, so before you make your final decision, there's something you have to ponder on. War only happens when someone wearing a white, starched collar and a suit fucks up."

In his entire life, Mathew had never heard his father swear and hearing him do so for the first time, guaranteed he listened.

"You have to realise since the start of all this trouble, thousands, if not millions of innocent young blokes just like

44

your brothers have gone to their deaths and all for what? We hear the old farts who are supposed to be running this country down in London barking out orders. Your country needs you, so they keep saying, but none of the bleeders go anywhere near the sodding front line. I know you have your heart set upon going, but just ponder on what I have to say for a moment. If everyone under the rank of corporal refused to fight, what would happen next? There would be no wars 'cos there ain't enough prisons to hold the deserters and they couldn't stick 'em up against a brick wall and shoot 'em 'cos they know the guns would be turned on the fuckers ordering the execution. Believe me son, whilst all this is going on, there's plenty of bastards out there laughing all the way to the bank."

George Hobbs tempered his anger by taking a deep intake of breath. This was not the time to air his grievances about a policy written by centuries of megalomaniac warmongers. His son required an open mind to come to his own conclusions, not prejudiced by a father's ranting.

"Take your time to decide, I'll understand."

If this was the divine intervention Mathew asked for, it was a strange way of showing itself, but he took the advice and sat deep in thought until flicking the cigarette end into the deep snow.

"If I stay here, I'll never be able to look any of those people in the eye who have lost someone. I have to go, not because I want to fight, but it gives me a reason to leave here. Forgive me, Pa, but I can't work down the pit all my life like you. There must be more to life than existing in this place and I want to taste some of it. If I stay I'll definitely die someday, begrudging the time I had an opportunity to leave, but if I go to the front, I might just live a little. I know I won't regret it. What would you do, Pa, if you could turn back the clock and were in my shoes?"

George Hobbs turned, resting a hand on his son's shoulder.

"I'd do precisely what you're going to do."

"That's not an answer."

"I'm surprised you expect one. It's been a long time since your mother wiped your arse. You're a man not a child. You have to weigh up these awkward decisions without my help, god forbid, I made some right bloomers even after the advice my father gave to me. Just remember one small morsel of wisdom he gave me and it still works to this day, when you make a mistake and believe me you will, try and make it as small as possible. I've said enough for one day, so I'll let you be. Don't be too long, it's getting colder out here and I know your mother has something special in for tea."

His infectious smile squashed any lingering anger.

Watching his father retrace his footprints until his image merged into the white landscape, Mathew pondered if he was right to tell of his anxiety. To appear ungrateful to parents who struggled with so little to bring up a family would be the wrong message he tried to send. They supplied a modicum of home-learnt education, sufficient to be one of only a few of his age to be able to read and write, but love was always available in large quantities. He couldn't bring his brothers back, but he would make sure any success he carved out for himself, he would share. He swore to uphold this promise, even though he had no idea how to achieve it.

***

"You must be freezing you silly boy, here, give me your coat and get by the fire."

Fussing around her son, Dorothy Hobbs guided Mathew into his father's chair by the grate. Disguising a smile behind a gnarled knuckled hand, George winked knowingly at his son.

46

"Good time to tell her what you're going to do, Mathew. But, do me one last favour before you do, leave it until after she's cut your birthday cake. I haven't seen that smile on her face for such a long time. Let me see it for a little while longer."

***

By the light of a full moon shining through a frosted window, Mathew packed his meagre belongings into a battered hold-all before a final visit to collect uncollected wages from the colliery paymaster. Prepared for his mother to be waiting when he returned, he hadn't accounted for his father's misplaced wisdom of borrowing the same dray and cart that memorably transported Fowler and Captain Noble some two years earlier.

Barely able to look at his mother, the fleeting glances he dared only showed that the happiness she openly showed the day before was now just a memory for him to take on his travels. Dorothy Hobbs sore, half closed red eyes contrasted pitifully against her stone white complexion. Clinging at every opportunity to Mathew's arm, she only released her grip when Mathew gently eased her away.

"Time to go, Ma."

Through her agony she managed a false smile. Quietly she whispered, "I'll be thinking of you, Son. Take care."

"I'll write," Mathew promised approaching the cart.

"You'll always be my baby."

Mathew couldn't trust his emotions to turn and wave a final farewell.

***

Not a word passed between Mathew and his father for the duration of the journey to Isley Station. The only sound interrupting the stillness of winter came from the dray's crunching, dinner plate sized hooves compressing snow with each of its lumbering steps. Only when the train was about to pull away from the station did George break the self-imposed silence.

"Be lucky, son, and remember. You know where we live but your mother and I won't know where you are."

George grabbed his son with a last loving gesture, he levered Mathew's upper torso out of the carriage window with entwined arms in a bear-like embrace, only releasing when a shrill whistle came from the guard's van at the rear. Keeping pace as the train began its journey to Catterick, George walked alongside attached to the moving carriage with fingers wrapped tightly on the door-handle.

"Remember to write you little bugger."

Mathew laughed, encouraging his father to do likewise. He hadn't heard this fond reprimand since he was a small boy. Only when the speed of the locomotive increased to more than a walking pace did George finally release his grip. Imitating every school-boy's dream for employment, the footplate man elevated a lever to open floodgates of pent up steam-power roaring into action. Belching from the fiery furnace below, white smoke blasted from its funnel across the station platform obliterating the last sight of Mathew's waving, tearful father.

CHAPTER 5

On Mathew's arrival, Catterick resembled the opposite of the snowbound Christmas card image he'd left behind on the Yorkshire Dales. What he would describe back home as the perfect nature made children's playground for toboggans, here outside the station, ice churned up with dirty mush created deep dark puddles. A mass of strangers shuffling in different directions appeared none too friendly, transforming the area outside the station into a hazardous wasteland. Confined to a life of viewing monotonous Twickton, Mathew stood in awe at his first sight of large buildings. Even under this depressive sky, he never dreamt anything could be so grand. The spectacle of fine workmanship rekindled his mother's stories of big cities and her courting days with his father, but this wasn't a time or place to stop and daydream. Bustled by a crowd larger than Fowler's memorable gathering a few years earlier hampered Mathew's attempts to scan the horizon above bobbing heads for a clue of which direction to take out of this human labyrinth to find the barracks. Everyone, including those dressed in uniform, criss-crossed his path without a hint of where they were heading.

It would be too much of a gamble to follow an individual hoping the trail led to the barracks. Feeling vulnerable but also very conspicuous carrying a suitcase, his appearance would justify to anyone caring to notice, he'd just arrived from out of town. A cigarette might quell his anxiety but his hands twitched, not so much with cold, but with nervous anticipation. Not a suitable place for a novice to roll tobacco and not an image to relate in his first letter home. Breathing deeply, Mathew adjusted his collar to meet the rim of his cap and randomly chose a direction. Forcing his way through, faced with horse drawn carriages and a first sighting of automobiles, the opposite side of the road beckoned a safe haven outside the front door of a public house. Unlike most males working down a mine, Mathew's taste-buds never acclimatised to the taste of ale, but to get directions from someone inside the hostelry, he was prepared to suffer. Wedging his cash deep within an inside pocket, Mathew pushed the pub door open and entered.

Knowing only Twickton's sole drinking house to use as a comparison, Mathew's nostrils instantly reacted to the aroma of an unwashed and decaying interior camouflaging unsavoury clients. Every eye in the premises turned, witnessing his arrival. Though early morning, a brisk trade contributed to the heavy haze of stale air and tobacco smoke engulfing an atmosphere that was anything but friendly. Not daring to make eye contact, Mathew focused on a vacant plot by the bar and briskly sidestepped obstacles of tables and seated customers to reach his chosen spot. Feeling the discomfiture of stares on his back, it wasn't long before a scrawny barman took his order.

Digging deep inside a pocket to discern the shape of a penny without bringing a handful of cash into view for those watching his movements, Mathew waited for the barman's return, fully aware his suitcase depicted him as a traveller and travellers carried money. Silently he chastised his choice of where to find directions. Remembering on several occasions when his father advised his elder brothers to give similar places a wide berth, he never imagined the first place he would encounter would be on one of his father's 'don't do' list. Some of his last words rang alarm bells.

"If you're going to make a mistake, make sure it's a small one."

Clutching the tankard, his attempt to down the ale failed miserably, his strangled epiglottis, refusing to accept the foul liquid. Spluttering for breath, Mathew removed the pot from his lips.

"Who's a thirsty lad, then?"

A wizen, unshaven face appeared from behind carrying a similar earthenware jug filled with the same dregs. Shuffling aggressively closer for an answer, the eighteen year old picked up an obnoxious odour emanating from the stranger. Having lost his teeth many years before, the stranger's lips curled inwards resembling a stretched, facial naval.

"Sorry, Sir. Are you speaking to me?" Though garbled, Mathew understood the question only too well but stalled, weighing up the intended threats.

A surreptitious nod by the unwanted guest in the direction of an equally ugly accomplice standing not three yards away heightened Mathew's awareness to the danger of the situation.

"I said, who's a thirsty lad, then?" The naval shaped mouth opened, spewing drops of spittle on Mathew's coat as he menacingly stepped closer.

"Sorry, I don't know what you're talking about."

Confident of his ability, Mathew stood his ground. Working in a colliery since his twelfth birthday produced strength and quick growth and though only eighteen, his developed body might have dissuaded the more vigilant, but masked by an ageing overcoat, the pest only saw the teenager as a soft touch.

"You don't want to sup alone do you, not a lad like you. How about buying me and my friend a drink?"

"Buy your own fucking ale," Mathew snapped back.

The intention of the stranger was obvious by his pronounced nodding, an invitation for his collaborator to join and bolster the force of confrontation. Mathew's education might have been basic, but he didn't require a university degree to know it was time to leave. Grabbing his case, Mathew turned on his heels and sprinted for the exit, bludgeoning a path through tables, chairs and static customers. Quick thinking to put as much space between him and his pursuers proved successful as a glance over his shoulder confirmed he'd managed a five-yard advantage, a plenty big enough gap for what he planned. Remembering the doors opened opposite to each other when entering, Mathew's chosen barrier flew open and immediately swung back, masking his movements once outside. The urgency of his leaving the premises fooled his followers into thinking he would keep running and easy prey once outside, but instead of escaping, Mathew restricted his forward momentum by grabbing a lamppost and swinging back towards the pub, pushing his back tight against the wall. Using both hands, he brought the case up to chest level in anticipation of the inevitable onslaught.

Taken completely by surprise, the first body through the door received the swinging suitcase fully in the face, bringing the pursuer's head to an abrupt standstill whilst his torso and legs continued their forward journey. Having little chance of avoiding the sprawled body, his accomplice tumbled over the pavement leaving his unprotected trunk a prime target for a well-aimed kick in the stomach. The ferocity of Mathew's deliveries confirmed the assailants weren't about to get to their feet for quite a while.

Satisfied there was no need to continue the onslaught, Mathew mockingly smiled down at the writhing bodies. As though it was an everyday occurrence in these parts, those hurrying past to go to work or just to get somewhere warmer totally ignored the bloodied injured.

"I've left half-a-pint of that piss on the bar. If it was a drink you're after, you can finish mine. It'll match nicely with the stink coming out of your mouth."

Rejuvenated, Mathew rejoined the protection of the crowd with a new found spring in his step. Mathew's first letter home might after all interest his father.

"Hey, kiddo," Mathew called, trying to attract the attention of a youngster shouting out news headline from under a makeshift canvas protection covering his news-stand. "Where can I find the barracks?"

Unfazed by Mathew's interruption, the boy pointed down the street, diverting Mathew's eyes to follow the direction. Completely surrounded by eight foot railings, a parade ground capable of holding the entire garrison fronted the austere building.

***

"Trying to conjure up the guts to go in and join-up, are we son?"

Surprised by the sudden voice interrupting his thoughts of what lay ahead, Mathew turned towards the source. Standing to his side, a resplendent uniformed mountain-of-a-man advertising three stripes on each well pressed sleeve to complement the insignia of rank on encrusted epaulettes, stared down under the shiny black peak of a cap positioned flush against his forehead.

"No, Sir. I've got the guts. It's just I'm trying to figure out how to get in to join up."

"Don't call me sir, son. I'm Colour Sergeant Higgins. So, you want to earn the King's shilling do you? Well, do you see those gates down there? Tell the sentries what you want to do and they'll let you in. Then proceed until you'll see a great big sign giving directions."

Directing with gusto, Higgins expanded his chest, straining the resisting buttons on his red tunic whilst extravagantly placing a regimental baton tightly under his arm.

"That's if you can read of course... From the country, are we?"

A supercilious smile creased Higgins's face when noticing Mathew's tatty suitcase.

Mathew's first half-hour in the 'Big City' hadn't gone as planned. Twice, since he'd arrived, his intelligence had been brought into question, not by superior academics but by individuals possessing more brawn than brain. Increasingly becoming deaf to his father's advice, this character appeared no better than the two he'd left sprawling outside the pub, even though he wore the King's uniform and towered above his height.

"I've been educated and I can read and write, Colour Sergeant, but can I ask a question."

"Of course you can. Fire away, sonny."

"Just how tall are you?"

Higgins looked bemused, peering down at Mathew. Being one of the regiment's longest serving NCO's since joining when sixteen, his twenty-four years of service installed into him to never fudge a question and to answer even it meant lying, if it couldn't be ratified. Unmarried and unlikely ever to find a woman foolish or sober enough to take on the mantle as his wife, unbeknown to Higgins, his sole love, the regiment, was planning a divorce. Only the outbreak of war reconciled his relationship and reprieved him from being pensioned off.

Colour sergeants are not renowned for their tolerance or understanding, but Higgins, an infamous name within the regiment, took these qualities to greater depths of loathing. If circumstances had been different, papers demanding his demobilisation from duty were in the pipeline awaiting a signature from a commanding officer. The advent of fresh, young officers deployed directly from officer training school effectively ended the likes of Higgins. To confirm this ideology, when Higgins persisted voicing unwarranted opinions in an officer's ear, it only made him more of an outcast and a considered liability. The hierarchy believed there was no place in the modern army for a remnant of the last century regardless that most of the generals in command were also relics of bygone years when cavalry charges played a major part during strategic frontline manoeuvres.

"Six feet three, why do you ask, sonny?" Higgins answered.

Without delay, Mathew replied.

"I didn't think they could stack shit that high."

Mathew ducked a swinging fist and sprinted to the barrack gates before Higgins unravelled his sergeant's stick from under his arm. Knowing it wasn't the wisest thing to have said, Mathew heard Higgins's voice bellow out over the humdrum of the passing crowd.

"Piss off you little prick. I'll remember your face and when we get the chance to meet again, I'll have your fucking balls on the end of my bayonet. Do you hear me? That's a promise."

***

It wasn't as hard as Mathew thought to sign away his liberty. After signing a few innocuous forms and having a bare chest probed by a faceless character wearing a white coat brandishing a stethoscope, he joined the ranks of wary new recruits queuing for uniforms outside the quartermaster's store. Approaching the front of the line as each individual peeled off clutching a parcel, his heart that only minutes before entertained a fumbling doctor, quickened, pumping adrenalin to a brain questioning his decision, but The King had his name written on a dotted line. There would be no turning back.

"Boot size?" a stern, uninterested corporal questioned from the opposite side of a well-used, wooden counter.

Signed up to be a foot soldier, this article of clothing needed to fit. The rest of the uniform depended on the visual skills of the two-striper to decide which of the many bundles squashed on the shelves appeared to contain a similar sized uniform to the trooper's shape. Adhering to British army regulations, regardless of the size of the uniform, it was the trooper's responsibility whether it fitted or not. The onus later fell on Mathew to swap with another trooper if it didn't. Treated similarly to a line of cattle, once fitted out, the recruits stood in ram-shackle formation on the parade ground, each fledgling's bundle and suitcase by their sides waiting until sufficient numbers gathered to form a new company. And then, the process began all over again.

CHAPTER 6

By the close of the following day, Mathew's fitness became obvious to the training corporals and sergeants screaming threats of castration in the ears of the majority of the disillusioned new conscripts. Nine hours of continuous 'square-bashing' divided those who understood an order from those too exhausted to listen. Within these early hours of conscription, Mathew witnessed that the majority found it a struggle to keep up to the daily pressure the army demanded. His personal physical strength, though nurtured from a young boy, hadn't prepared him to be able to shoot, hit targets or plunge a bayonet into the fleshy midriff of a complete stranger.

On the second morning, before the sun broke the horizon, lines of recruits stood shivering with anticipation for another day of torture on the parade ground. From a distant mouth of a screaming drill sergeant, Mathew heard his name called along with six others, ordering to drop out and report for special firearms practice. Having never held a gun, let alone fired one, Mathew chose his moment to ask why he'd been given this privilege, as it meant certain promotion to corporal and relief from mundane daily square-bashing.

"Because your name on my list is the first one beginning with an H," answered an uninterested corporal.

Mathew couldn't decipher if the instructor was jesting or if this was the way all specialists were chosen. Nothing like it, Mathew thought, for keeping the moral of the men up to scratch.

During this period of barrack internment, Mathew made few friends, the situation not conducive to nurture a close relationship. On a daily basis when training was over for the day, most were too tired to do anything but clean their equipment and go to bed, knowing reveille would sound in a few hours to kick-start another bout of hell. Spared most of these mundane exercises by his specialized instructor, Mathew practiced with a new found friend, a specially adapted Lee Enfield sniper's rifle, alongside others whose surname also began with the letter 'H'. Mathew never asked, but maybe the corporal wasn't joking after all.

A natural phenomenon happens when a thousand individuals are squashed into barrack dormitories; gossip spreads like wildfire, so it wasn't surprising when word filtered through that when training was completed, Mathew's company of trainee, virgin soldiers would join their battalion already on the front line. Orders were given to the literate to write letters home and for those owning anything over the value of a five pounds, to fill out a last will and testament. Mathew knew it was only a matter of time before being sent to the place where his two brothers fell in combat. He wasn't nervous at the prospect but wondered if he was capable of killing. As training continued, this became one of the main topics of conversation. It soon became apparent, most kept reservations of their capabilities to themselves, despite being screamed at from dawn to dusk to plunge their bayonet in, twist and remove it with the aid of a boot firmly planted on the foe's chest. Simulating on straw filled dummies required no reasoning, but when the time came, Mathew wondered just how many would have the mental strength and willpower to actually kill.

A wispy sun heralded the morning every cadet loathed arriving. Emphasising the poignancy of the moment, low snow-laden clouds swept in from the north. Two years before, under similar climatic conditions, Mathew watched his two brothers march away, never to be seen again. Imitating the same scenario, Mathew scanned the fragmented gathering of onlookers for a wide-eyed youth soaking up the glamour and pageantry of uniformed men marching in unison to war. The sound of hob-nailed boots on cobbles accelerates the heartbeat and mesmerises even the most musically deaf, but to a teenager undecided about his future, this rhythm certainly bolsters a recruitment campaign.

Lining the route, crowds gave his company a similar, noisy farewell as that from the people of Twickton. Looking to the sky, Mathew whispered a prayer for a different outcome.

***

Six hours of cramped travel aboard an overcrowded train prevailed before the scene at Victoria Station awakened every soldier to the stark realities of warfare and what lay ahead in trenches of war strewn France and Belgium. Platforms crammed with returning fragments of battle-weary foot soldiers saw them sidestepping lines upon lines of wounded bodies stretched out on blood stained stretchers. Uniformed nurses attempted to care and soothe the neediest, but insufficient numbers portrayed a glaring inadequacy to cope with this disaster. Amputees, fit enough to stand, struggled with crutches, whilst those with two legs either displayed missing arms or hideously bandaged wounds. Twickton Company suffered a similar fate as these soldiers, marching proudly to war one minute only to arrive back home weeks later, decimated in numbers. It was not the wisest arrangement by the hierarchy before confronting the enemy, to coincide raw recruit movement with their witnessing of what war can inflict on the human body.

Mathew barely heard the sergeant bellowing out an order for 102 Company to muster outside the terminal over the din of mayhem resounding round this cathedral-like edifice. Laden with a kitbag, great coat and rifle slung over his shoulder, Mathew hastened from this human flotsam, an obstacle course his fellow troopers hadn't been trained to overcome. Witnessing such terrible injuries only hastened his urgency to relocate somewhere away from the stench of death.

This reality of war to the teenagers of Company 102 issued a stark warning about the longevity of misery inflicted by the general issue weapon slung across their shoulders and those of their enemy. For the macabre amongst them who could write, it would chill the reader of their next letter home.

It was past midnight before the troop carrier pulled out of Victoria Station destined for Folkestone. Packed together similar to tinned sardines, 102 Company shared the journey with an additional eight companies from an assortment of other regiments. Straining to haul the human cargo contained in fourteen carriages, an additional locomotive pushed from the rear to assist the two up front. Despite this great power, progress was painfully slow, as braking was as important as acceleration. On arrival at their destination, there was no welcoming crowd in the early hours. Just an order to rest as best as they could where they sat until daybreak. Dawn would signal the start of a very long day.

CHAPTER 7

At first light, 102 Company mustered, marching in formation towards Folkestone docks. A light dusting of snow fell during the night, softening the sounds of marching boots, but with so much activity within the town, very few took the opportunity to stay in bed and benefit from nature's sound proofer. Adjusting collars snugly round the neck to combat a temperature creeping as low as four below zero, troops obediently followed NCOs to a row of portable huts, erected to feed and water the passing multitude. Having neither drunk nor eaten since the previous evening, a hot mug of tea and sandwich, the filling of which no one could decipher, was gratefully accepted by the thousands passing through.

From Mathew's untrained eye, the dockside appeared a mass of uncontrolled khaki movement of companies seemingly diluted, but as soon as orders rang through the freezing air, the magnitude of personnel shuffled itself into organised formation.

Carrying nothing but high explosives and armaments across the Channel, freighters were allocated a section of the docks furthest away, whilst a quay to the west solely shipped horses on an array of equally ageing merchant ships and barges. Troops, meanwhile, waited on the east breakwater to board overworked steamers, far enough away from an accidental explosion or a flying hoof. Allocated MSV Foxgrove, the smallest ship of the flotila, 102 Company shuffled forward, making up numbers until four hundred boarded. Eight ships of varying sizes formed a convoy outside the harbour walls by mid-morning, between them carrying articles of war and five thousand troops. Assisted by the god Neptune, his good nature assured the raw recruits a winter's flattened sea, enabling the convoy to keep within hailing distance of each other at a steady ten knots. Some faceless bright rating situated on the forecastle began singing but was immediately told to quieten it. In the middle of the Channel, snow fell again. The mood aboard became very sombre.

From three miles out at sea it was obvious their turn to dock wouldn't be immediate. A queue of ships, line astern, waited their turn until a space appeared or could be moored alongside another before proceeding past the harbour breakwater. Enduring seven hours at sea, the Foxgrove's final docking coincided with the temperature dropping further, but thankfully, parting clouds ended the snow fall, allowing a hazy sun to drop onto the horizon. Darkness would soon be upon them.

Once on-shore, similar refreshment tents to those in Folkestone nourished a continual line. Worked by foreign speaking volunteers, complaints about the nondescript food fell on deaf ears. Only a sympathetic smile and a few unintelligible words made up for their inability to understand the plight of the troopers' empty stomachs.

Expecting the same carnage witnessed on the platforms of Victoria Station, nowhere within the harbour walls was there a trace of battle. At last, someone high up in the ranks of Westminster saw the sense to ship the wounded back to England from a different port.

Making friends was never on the agenda when Mathew chose to leave Twickton and trace his brothers' route. Similar to all families in Twickton, most pretended there was great camaraderie amongst the workforce, though a state of underlying selfishness existed where everybody looked after their own; asking no favours from others.

Understanding this basic, unwritten rule, only family bonding existed.

When diverse groups of strangers, such as these, are thrown together, regardless of bad food, bullying NCOs, lack of sleep and respect, Mathew found it strange to be adhering to a band of recruits possessing opposite personalities. Though slow to materialise, each noticed equal survival instincts and techniques in a select few of the group. Confirmation of their newly formed brotherhood surfaced when, in recognition of his sniper skills, Mathew was awarded two stripes, advertising his proficiency. Far from animosity, the others readily accepted this accolade, knowing it wouldn't stand as a barrier. As one of the group pointed out, someone needed to be leader. Confident in their own ability, they were equally adept in their own field as Mathew was in his.

"Hey, Matty. I'm getting worried. Everything looks too quiet round here."

Craning his swan-like neck towards Mathew, George White or Chalky as he was fondly named, gave his first impression of France.

"What do you mean by 'quiet' Chalky?" responded Mathew, as at least six thousand troops milled around Dunkirk's harbour walls.

"There's supposed to be a bleeding battle going on somewhere around here, 'aint there? But I can't hear a bleeding thing." Chalky's voice tapered off, indicating his concern with a raised chin pointing in a southerly direction.

"You have no idea of distance have you matey?"

Mathew offered an educated view. "The wind's coming from the north; the wrong direction to hear anything coming from the south where it's all going on sixty odd miles away."

Chalky looked to the sky, sucking his bottom lip. Since joining he'd mastered the art of signing his name, but it was his prowess with the improved Lewis light machine gun that stood him out from the crowd. Strange, but all the machine gunners' surnames appeared to begin with a 'W'.

"I'm starting to worry."

Keith Mortimer warily brought his opinion into the conversation, joining the other five sheltering from the biting wind on the leeward side of a double-decker bus brought across as a troop carrier.

"What are you worried about, Ginger?" Mathew enquired turning to ruffle his red, uncombed hair. "You saw what we left behind at Victoria, so don't start getting pissed off now 'cos it's too bloody late."

Ginger looked to Chalky for support but received only a toothy, nervous grin.

"Right you morons. As I'm wearing two stripes, I suppose we'd better find where the others are."

Though taken as a suggestion, Mathew's first order prompted the others to follow. Separated from 102 Company during their refreshment break, it proved no easy task to re-join the others. Seemingly everyone in close proximity spoke with a southern accent. Wandering around aimlessly but pretending to know precisely where to go, Mathew's entourage kept in close attendance.

"Oh shit."

Mathew's voice sank to a whisper, stopped in his tracks abruptly, causing a concertina-like pile up behind.

"What's up, corp?" Chalky asked troubled by Mathew's cloak and dagger antics.

"Do you see that bastard of a colour sergeant up front?" Burying his voice further into his chest, Mathew pointed in the direction of an NCOs uniform obstructing their path. "I don't really want to meet him. No, I'll rephrase that. I don't want him to see me. We have, what some might say, a dislike for each other."

"Oh, why go to the frontline and get fucked when you can end it all right here? You don't 'arf pick 'em. Get out the way you stupid bastard and let me lead."

Private Moses Rafferty, the shortest amongst the unit, ushered Mathew to the rear and took on the disillusioned mantle of wearing the stripes, relying mostly on guesswork as strategy of what to do next. Confidence was one thing Moses didn't lack.

"I don't know what you did to him, but I'll want to know all the devious details as soon as we get to the other side of that big bastard."

No one bothered to ask why this Dublin born kid got tangled up with the war effort because no one really cared, but this son of an Irish importer of dubious goods somehow got stuck with the nickname McJew. Allowing him into their tight circle wasn't an accident, apart from being the eldest of the unit at twenty-one, he possessed an uncanny knack for obtaining any type of provisions when no one else could. Obviously a family trait.

Displaying uncanny skills inherited by a poaching uncle, McJew kept the group in close formation, outflanking the adversary with a neat piece of manoeuvring to coincide their arrival back to where 102 Company mustered during the onset of darkness.

"Glad you lot could make it," Company Sergeant Andrews sarcastically greeted their presence from the front of the column, a hurricane lamp in hand picking out his not too pleased facial features. "If you wanted a little more time for sightseeing, why didn't you ask? I would have gladly arranged a mademoiselle to take care of it." Waiting for laughter to fade, he left no one in any doubt who was in charge. "Get in line, you motley crew." Allowing reaction time, another order swiftly followed. "By the right. Quick march." His screamed order reached an ear-splitting level of decibels, unfortunate for those up front.

Sergeant Andrews might have relayed the order, but Major Church led 102 Company, marching out of the docks, his NCOs in close proximity behind. During the following twenty minutes, the company of two hundred men, five abreast, kept up an unrelenting pace, reaching the outskirts of Dunkirk, where, in a boggy field strewn with tyre-gripping hay, buses of all shapes and sizes, advertising everything from soap to chocolate, waited to transport them to their final destination. Avoiding what could become a logistical nightmare, Major Church's no-nonsense approach commandeered seven empty vehicles despite remonstrations from drivers, ordered to remain stationary by a 'no-where to be seen' higher ranking officer. Ignoring continuing protests, Mathew's unit filled the last available seats in the last bus to leave the compound.

Private Allen Broadfoot, alias Kicker, refused to be denied access to the empty seat next to McJew. His attribute to be allowed to join the six was a skill of throwing a cricket ball twice as far as any of the others. Useful when the ball is replaced with a hand grenade.

"How long are we going to be on this thing, eh Corp? He asked, turning to Mathew.

"Shut up and put your head down."

It wasn't the answer he wanted.

CHAPTER 8

An hour into their passage, the first sounds of heavy artillery disturbed any thoughts of continuing with much needed sleep.

"Who do those guns belong to, eh Corp?"

The sixth member, Pat Brickman or 'Bricky' to his friends, questioned Mathew, his voice just audible over the straining engine. He was about to get an answer when McJew, seated behind, leant over his shoulder.

"How the bleeding hell is he supposed to know?"

A trained ear might distinguish the differences between friendly and enemy artillery, but to these novices, one bang sounded very much the same as the next one.

An alteration in wind direction fooled the troopers into thinking they were closer to the action than they really were, as it would take a further two hours of slow headway over unlit terrain to thread the convoy through an increasingly battered landscape to reach their destination, a derelict small farm house, recognisable as just a heap of rubble. Though assumed to be a strategically safe area five miles behind the front line, a row of Howitzer artillery guns fired deafening salvoes from an adjoining field, filling the air with dense smoke and a choking smell of cordite. Any verbal command was drowned out with the incessant barrage, but 102 Company moved forward, each soldier instinctively attaching himself to a trooper in front as a guide.

Marching out of the dim light produced by a few scattered oil filled lamps into darkness, the night sky erringly accompanied the artillery 'orchestra' playing in the rear, whilst an ensemble of sudden flashes and shells fizzed through the air toward the enemy. Occasionally one didn't fit the pattern of the others by coming from the opposite direction, exploding somewhere behind them. Though told what to expect, no form of training simulated this sudden introduction to warfare.

The further they marched, the more their ears became accustomed to the din. Though deafening, the powerful edge appeared to soften sufficiently for the troopers to compare their anxieties. Officers' orders to remain silent were lost in the cacophony of sound.

"Bloody hell. Chalky. I don't like the bloody look of this lot." Ginger shouted to his left-hand marching partner.

"I suppose you think I do," he replied.

Kicker looked back over his shoulder and smiled, a smile individually created.

"What do you mean? It's bloody marvellous. Reminds me of a Saturday night back home when it's throwing out time at the Roxy. You should know how twelve pints down your gullet can add inches to your height when dealing with an arsehole of a doorman."

Not one in the rear heard the order to 'Halt' though their reactions coincided with the man in front. Outside a makeshift, submerged, Regimental Headquarters, Major Church left 102 Company at ease, striding off into the lower reaches of the dugout for directions and orders to where they should go next. Believing to be undetectable under the camouflage of mayhem, a few managed to light a roll-up and successfully take deep lung-fulls of smoke before an eagle-eyed sergeant barked out a stern warning to those partaking in this small pleasure.

"Put those bloody things out. The next I catch smoking will get the full force of my boot up his arse."

***

Word filtered through to muster in a semi-circle around the commanding officer. Flanked by NCOs, confronting his company, the major stood on a pile of rubble.

"Right," he nervously began. "Well, men. This appears to be it. We have orders to by-pass the holding camp and reserve trenches and go straight to the front line. Our Battalion appears to have taken a bit of a pounding, leaving it short of personnel."

From under his breath, Bricky spoke, knowing only those in close proximity could comprehend.

"Short of personnel, my arse. They're all dead."

Attempting to soften the obvious repercussions of such a directive, Major Church added a possible redeemer.

"Don't worry chaps. Reserves are on their way and shall relieve us in a couple of days. Just think, you can tell your grandchildren you were there when we finally defeated the Bosch."

A murmur spread throughout the ranks.

"What are they saying?" The major turned to an aid. "I can't make out what they are saying, Sergeant."

"Putting it into language that won't offend, Sir. They are telling you to go forth and multiply."

The sergeant smiled at his commanding officer, but privately thought the troopers were not far from the truth in their assessment. Turning to face the company, he silently mouthed the same profanity then lambasted the closest with a verbal screech.

"Get in line and form a Company."

***

At a pace of quick march, they reached the holding camp within twenty minutes, but instead of witnessing soldiers relaxing, having done their stint at the sharp end, they saw a scene reminiscent of Victoria Station, with injured, dying and the dead covering an area of frozen ground far exceeding the vision of a naked eye in the dark. Small fires illuminated the macabre picture of what was left of the Regiment huddled together amongst carcasses of dead horses, totally demoralised and unfit to return to the front line. No one appeared from the chilling background to welcome their arrival.

The ground beneath their boots broke up into a frozen mush, causing an even greater hardship accompanying the growing din of battle. Enduring underfoot conditions more similar to a ploughed cow field in the middle of Antarctica, their once proud formation broke, resembling a crowd coming out of a football stadium after they'd witnessed their team loose. For many, fatigue was taking its toll, but finally they reached the reserve trenches, a location initially thought to be their resting place. They continued to trudge past. 102 Company were the reserves.

Up front, frantic activity fragmented the company into a single line organised by a single colour sergeant. Mathew couldn't hear what was causing the verbal commotion because he was so far back but sensed orders were being given. Ensuring his trusty five kept close, Mathew traced a corporal in front, edging closer to the NCO screaming abuse at every conscript being man-handled into man-made trenches. Suddenly, Mathew stood frozen to the spot. What he saw necessitated leaving an ever increasing gap between him and the man in front.

"What's up, Corp?" Ginger questioned, stumbling into Mathew's back.

"It's that bloody Colour Sergeant Higgins again. He's bound to notice me. What can I do?"

"Keep walking. You'll bring more attention to yourself if you don't catch up. He'll never recognise you in uniform and under a tin hat."

Not having the luxury to decide an alternative plan, Mathew confronted his adversary in the hope his face would melt in with the many indiscriminate faces. From fifteen yards away, Mathew picked out Higgins's familiar raucous scream.

"Come on you bastards, hurry up."

There were just four in front of Mathew before his turn came to be physically propelled down into the trench. Lowering his chin to meet his chest as a final attempt to mask his identity, he moulded his body to the one in front.

"Hold it, scum bag."

Mathew felt the webbing of his backpack grabbed, separating his torso from the protection of the body in front, instantly bringing his momentum to a grinding standstill.

"I know this fucking face."

"Come on, Serg," Chalky wailed from the back, trying to divert Higgins's attention. "If I stand here much longer, Jerry will have me in his sights and my mum won't be too pleased with you if he has."

"Button it, you little ball-bag."

Higgin's vocal cords stretched to snapping in conjunction with dragging Mathew half way down the trench, followed by five others cowering under their own protective arms.

"I know you. You're the bastard who asked how tall I am. Well, pay-back time you little shit. I've got the best position for you, especially reserved to guarantee a bullet through those lovely, fucking blue eyes of yours. Red Section 4. Now piss off and woe betide you if you're not there when I come round later. I'll put a bullet in your fucking head myself if you disobey my order."

Throwing Mathew like garbage to the bottom of the trench, Higgins's uncontrolled temper turned to inflict the same on anyone in close proximity, but they'd slipped past his attention and stealthily tracked their corporal.

"Hey, you lot. You don't want to go where I'm going. Peel off into one of these other trenches and keep your heads down."

It was advice not an order.

"No chance, mate. All for one and one for all, and all that bollocks," McJew shouted, his soft Irish brogue confirming how they felt. Their forced friendship, moulded back at Catterick Barracks, had grown in a short space of time into a strong bond.

Crouching through a labyrinth of twisting trenches, each no more than six yards long to counteract a direct hit's shrapnel spreading, Mathew led the way past tired soldiers billeted in holes shared by mud, lice and vermin. These short, cul-de-sac type mini villages made of anything to hand that might support crudely built trenches up to eight feet deep, could be a trooper's home for months.

Troops of all ranks, from major down to private, nodded a welcome as the group squeezed their way through. Stopping to enquire if they were on the right track for Red Section 4 prompted an intake of breath or laughter from those fortunate enough to be stationed behind the aptly nick-named, Coffin Box Section.

"Where has that bastard Higgins sent us?" Kicker asked, exaggerating his movements to keep his head way below the ridge.

"We'll soon find out. By my reckoning it's just round the next corner."

Mathew was correct with his navigation. Some past humorous inhabitant had pinned a skull and crossbones pendant to a buttress above a scrawled sign indicating they'd reached their objective. Being the last to enter, McJew studied the lettering, but lost his nerve to ask a squatting trooper if paint or blood was used by the sign writer.

"So, it's you who's drawn the short straw, Hobbs," Major Peter Church welcomed the new arrivals.

"Fraid so, Sir. How come you got this little bit of paradise?"

Mathew's salute acknowledged his superior officer.

"Oh. I was the last CO to arrive, so they gave me the only vacant position. How many are in your party, Corporal?"

"Myself and five others, Sir."

"Just enough to relieve these poor chaps who have been here for god knows how long without a break. I've been told we might get some relief ourselves later tomorrow, but I wouldn't count on it. As we're the foremost trench nearest the enemy, you'd better get a periscope up in the middle to scan the horizon. We don't want the bastards creeping up on us in the middle of the night, now do we? Get the Lewis Gun positioned over there and for your skills, Hobbs, in the other corner someone has conveniently stacked a turret of sandbags, ideal protection for what you've been trained to do and you never know, you might get a chance, sooner rather than later, to put your skills to good use as at 2200 hours we are ceasing our artillery bombardment. So I've been informed, this might make the Bosch believe we are going over the top and in doing so, they come out of their hidey-holes and wait for our charge. Of course we'll do nothing of the kind, but it might catch them unawares out in the open before the artillery boys think they deserve another pounding. Who knows, Hobbs? You might just be able to make out a shape and be the first of 102 Company to rub one of them out. It would be great for moral if you could bump one of them off. It must be nearly time, so get into position and wait for my signal. I'll inform the others what to expect."

Acknowledging Church's order, Mathew took the eloquently delivered suggestion, sliding between sodden sandbags, the width of which barely accommodated his body whilst the other five shook the hands of the squaddies they relieved and filled up their relinquished positions. Each saw the same thankful look in the eyes of the liberated.

***

Darkness entombed the trench apart from a glimmer emitted by two heavily shielded hurricane lamps. Smoking was forbidden, not to give a trooper's lungs a rest, but to save a life from alert snipers, focusing telescopic sights two hundred yards away on the look-out for glowing cigarette ends where lips will be attached to a head.

Tension grew as the minute hand approached the hour. Though the temperature continued to drop, Mathew felt beads of anticipating sweat form under his armpits. Positioned only a few feet away from his commanding officer, he could barely make out the shape of Major Church holding a periscope to his eye, scanning no-man's-land over the ridge for the slightest movement. Lost in darkness, the other five were only picked out when a shell exploded too close for comfort, lighting faint silhouettes. Lying flat on his stomach, legs sprayed behind, Mathew inserted a 303-calibre shell, taught over many hours of training to be second nature, into the well-oiled breach before slipping the bolt back quietly, engaging the bullet in his Lee Enfield sniper's rifle. Surreal under the canopy of sound, he threaded the end of the barrel through a small opening in the sandbags and placed his right eye over the felt rimmed sight. Apprehension was in abundance, but nervousness deserted him when he felt the way the gun-stock rested rock steady against his shoulder.

As if a giant conductor had directed his baton to halt the orchestra playing in mid symphony, the overhead overture stopped in unison. The powerful sound of sudden silence overwhelmed the trenches on both sides, but all Mathew heard was a ringing in his ears and the scurrying of rats around his feet. Kicking one unfortunate beast fully in the stomach, he hoped it would find an old corpse to feed on rather than wait around for a fresh one. For what seemed an eternity, nothing appeared to move along the corridor separating the two armies, but slowly, as the still darkness began to play its tricks, ghostly shadows darted through Mathew's eyepiece. Every time he tried to follow one, another seemed to zip past in the opposite direction.

"Major, is there something out there?" he whispered to his commanding officer.

"Steady Hobbs. Wait."

In their panic but true to the plan, the enemy fired phosphorus flares from their positions, illuminating the sky into a dark orange glow over the entire area below.

"Wait for it, Hobbs. They've taken the bait. The stupid bastards have made it easier for us to see them."

Through his magnified sight, Mathew saw frantic movement over two hundred yards away in the opposite trench. No definite shape was discernible, but the odd glimpse of a German helmet hurrying along their trench line confirmed he might get a clear shot if the head it belonged to remained stationary for long enough.

"There Hobbs. Near enough right in front of you. To the right of those two burnt tree stumps, next to that hillock with a pillbox on top. He's looking straight over here but must think he's hidden. Can you see him?"

Tracking Church's directions with the point of the barrel, Mathew's eye focused on the hillock, roaming each side of the gun emplacement for the figure pinpointed by the major.

"Jesus!" Mathew screeched, pulling the gun-sight away from his eye. "I can see him."

"Don't give me a running commentary. Shoot the bastard," Church yelled back.

Without thinking of the consequences, Mathew replaced the sight to his eye and found his prey in the same spot. A lone, loud crack broke the silent night air, echoing along the trenches. Lifting the barrel six inches, the recoil masked his effort to witness the result.

"Bloody good shot, Hobbs. Now let's find you another one."

From a trench behind, Mathew heard an unfamiliar voice break the eerie silence.

"Nice one, mate."

He'd just killed a man and everyone congratulated him. Slowly allowing the gun to rest on the ridge, he sprayed out tense fingers. Training taught him to kill but he never thought he would be so calm when it came to the real thing. Should he write home and tell his mother that her eighteen year old son was the first of the company to register a kill?

"Hobbs, there's another in exactly the same place as the last one. Looks as though he's gone to help your last victim. Quickly, he's getting away."

Another shot rang out, but this time, Mathew countered the recoil and witnessed the body flying backwards. Through his telescopic sight the image became ten times closer giving an explicit picture of where the bullet hit. Vomit spewed from his mouth, covering his weapon. Unable to remove his eye from the prone body, instinct pulled the bolt back discharging the spent cartridge case in less than two seconds. Mathew wanted more, revenge for his two brothers and the rest of Twickton Company. He wanted the mothers of Germany to feel what it's like to suffer the loss of loved ones.

Swivelling his sight along a never decreasing line, he allowed his focus on the opposite ridge to travel further than taught in training. Feeling a gooey mess accumulate round his chin dripping down onto his trigger hand didn't dissuade his determination to find his next victim. Though artillery bombardment was in its fifth minute of silence, frantic activity opposite continued giving short lived opportunities for a shot but nothing remained static. A twinkle of light reflected off a bayonet offered some hope, but it wasn't until he ventured fully half a mile down the line that he made out the clear shape of a spiked helmet.

Mathew's heart raced for the first time. He needed one of these badly and he wanted the major to witness the result.

"Major. How many points do I get for an officer?"

"Where is he?"

"He thinks he can't be seen, but I can see him standing there so fucking proud of himself way down on your left with what looks like half a tree with something waving about in the branches poking out in front of him."

Disregarding the danger of a German sniper mimicking Mathew, Church discarded the periscope and scanned the horizon with binoculars above the ridge.

"He's too far away. Leave him for one of our chaps further down the line."

Regarding the order once again as a suggestion, Mathew deftly squeezed the trigger.

"Bloody hell, Hobbs. You got the bastard. Excellent shot."

***

As suddenly as silence descended ten minutes earlier, artillery shell bombardment restarted, signalling Mathew's first taste of war to come to an end as quickly as it began.

"Okay lads," Church bellowed above the explosions erupting from the German line, fired from the wastelands behind. "Stand down."

Not content with what they'd just seen, the wide-eyed unit remained at their post afraid they might miss a piece of action. This was the war they'd read about and trained for. And at this moment, adrenalin running high, they couldn't understand why this war hadn't been won already. Only one of the unit dared remove his eyes from the hammering the horizon was taking. Sliding out from within his allocated cubby-hole, descending the side of the frozen trench, Mathew peered down to his soiled uniform covered in a mixture of Belgium mud and British vomit.

"You appear to be a bit of a mess, Hobbs. Couldn't keep your dinner down, eh?"

"With respect, Sir. None of us have had a bite to eat since this morning."

Using rank as a privilege, Church requisitioned the solitary chair, a sole surviving relic found by earlier trench inhabitants in the ruins of a shelled out café. Church beckoned Mathew to sit opposite on an empty wooden box; once containing canned peaches when food was plentiful on the frontline.

"Have you ever killed anyone before, Sir?" the sniper asked, disregarding protocol to speak before permission was granted.

"No, not physically, Hobbs." Church paused, trying to pick out the features on Mathew's face in the shielded light. "But there have been times in my life when I'd dearly love to rub one or two out."

Socially a million miles apart, the manner in which Mathew reacted to the major's order to kill dissipated any class divide.

"I believe I understand what you must be feeling. Don't feel so bad, Hobbs. As I gave the order, I feel as much as a murderer as you must feel. You've stopped three of those bastards from killing some of our chaps."

Comforting words, maybe, but Church covered his face with open hands, attempting to mask his despair at trying to rationalise the order to kill. This wasn't a hardened soldier he was talking to; he was once, not long ago, an innocent teenager.

"I think you have got it wrong, Sir. I don't feel any remorse for those bastards. I'm just paying back the suffering they caused my family."

Mathew related the time his brother's marched out of Twickton and the subsequent massacre.

"You do surprise me, Hobbs. There was I, endeavouring to do my best to ease your conscience, when

78

all the time you're probably more like me than I first thought. If you remove your place of work and replace it with my mundane office job, I was just like you six weeks ago, doing nothing better to fill the hours of a working day than reading about what was going on over here. My father got me the office vacancy in the civil service before the war, but when it started, he was near enough calling me a coward for not volunteering. So, to appease him, I agreed to join up with help from his 'old-boy-network'. It certainly worked because here I am, a commissioned major, never fired a gun in anger in my life and put in charge of a company facing the enemy. All in six weeks. Bit of a bloody joke, don't you think?"

Seven years older with qualifications and social connections far outweighing anything Mathew could muster, Church showed he was honest enough to be fully aware of his failures and capabilities. Witnessing an eighteen year old with only a smattering of education reacting to an order without hesitation justified a spewing aftermath. He wondered, if the tables were turned, would he have the nerve to kill on demand and be as calm as this boy sitting opposite.

"You being commissioned a joke? No, I don't think so, Sir. Someone has to be in charge and with all due respect, Sir, that person is you. We're all in this together. I heard you shout out and I fired. The first one was easy, I didn't see him go down, but the second was different. I saw where the bullet hit and the mess it made. What was left in my guts just came up. Can I light up, Sir?"

"Of course you can, Hobbs, but keep your head down. You did a good job tonight, especially with the third victim."

Any other officer might have taken what Mathew said as insubordination, but Church smiled, glancing back to see Mathew light a half smoked roll-up. Chalky and Ginger, their initial shot of adrenalin now diluted, joined the small gathering to confirm if they could do likewise. Unlike the major and corporal, the only available option was to squat their backsides on mud encrusted wooden duck-boards. Too intent on the action going on in the distance, the other three remained at their posts.

"Bricky!" Church shouted. "Use the periscope, you fool. Don't keep poking your head over the top, otherwise, someone over there who is as skilled as our Corporal will have it off in seconds."

"So, there you are, you little bastard."

Startled by a voice coming out the murk, Colour Sergeant Higgins stirred everyone to their feet - that is, all except Church. Those on watch turned to see what interrupted their viewing

"What's your name, you little shit?" Higgins roared, directing his venom toward Mathew. "And who the hell said you could smoke?"

"Colour Sergeant," barked Church from the darkness, catching Higgins by surprise; causing him to turn to where the voice originated.

"Who the bloody hell do you think you are, Sergeant? Striding in here without first acknowledging me as your superior officer. And then you have the audacity to undermine my order without consulting me first. If we weren't in this position, I'd frog march you down to HQ with a bayonet up your arse and have those stripes ripped off your arm. Do you hear me?"

Anger festered. Never, in Higgins' entire life in the force, had his authority been questioned. Recognising the major's insignia, he resisted his natural instinct to verbally or physically attack. The squaddies openly smiled, but he knew he could do nothing except to do what he was good at, leave a trailing line of abuse.

"Fuck you bastards and that includes you, Sir. I'll be back with something that'll really make you smile."

Rising from his chair, Church's attempt to confront the colour sergeant disintegrated with his disappearance.

"I don't think he likes us."

A smiled creased Church's lips whilst ushering the troops to retake their original positions.

"What on earth did you do to that man, Hobbs?"

Relating the story brought laughter from Church and the others. McJew understood the reasoning as to why he took the lead way back at Folkestone.

"Don't worry, Hobbs. I don't think we'll be seeing too much of him again," Church confidently assured Mathew.

"Oh, I wouldn't be too sure about that, Sir. With respect, you made him look like a right old prick in front of us and he didn't like it."

CHAPTER 9

Shelling finally ceased at precisely 0200 hours the next morning. Having fooled the enemy once, they weren't about to make the same error, preferring instead to stay firmly ensconced inside relatively safe shelters. McJew and Kicker stayed alert at their posts, but for the first time since the unit's arrival, all appeared quiet, satisfying Church to order the others to get some sleep wherever they found a spot out of reach of scurrying rats.

It was maybe an hour later when, without warning to break the blissful silence, Higgins reappeared. Rapping his knuckles on a buttress supporting the dugout where Church slept, the figure stood at attention, saluting only when the major appeared.

"Orders, Sir, from HQ."

Keeping dialogue to a minimum, he handed over a folded piece of paper. Warily accepting the note, Church read the written order by the light of a struck match.

"Is there any reply, Sir?"

Higgins played everything by the rule book; standing bolt upright as a mark of respect at the same time freely displaying he enjoyed the moment.

"Yes, there is Colour Sergeant. If I live to see this evening, I will personally arrest you and have pleasure of giving evidence at a Court-Martial. I will personally see you swing for this. Do I make myself clear?"

Higgins didn't move but his smile broadened.

"As clear as shit, Sir. You and your six little bastards won't be alive much longer after 0800 hours, so I don't think I have to worry much about that. Will that be all, Sir?"

Not bothering to wait for an answer, Higgins marched away without the customary salute.

Awakened by the commotion, those dozing quickly gathered where Higgins once stood.

"What's up, Sir?"

With corporal's prerogative, Mathew enquired, knowing something was not at all right. Unable to make eye contact with his unit, Church fully understood the gravity of the order and the repercussions such an action would have on his men.

"At 0700 hours, we have been ordered to fix bayonets and go over the top. As we are the nearest to enemy lines, we will in essence, lead the attack. I don't have to say much more, do I? We'll be the first group the Krauts see and so take the brunt of their... fire."

His words quietly tapered off, words the whole group dreaded hearing.

"I knew we hadn't heard the last of that bastard," Mathew muttered for all to hear.

"Well, we have three hours."

Church's feeling contradicted his smile, thinking this was exactly what his father wanted. The bragging rights about a son who led the line as an officer but unfortunately got killed whilst attempting a suicide attack on the enemy.

"Ginger, get the burner on and we'll have a brew. Bugger orders about no naked flames. Smoke if you wish but keep your heads down and while you're doing that, I think it's a good time to write a letter home."

Unaware only two in the party were literate, Church tried to keep up a cheery banter, knowing it was highly likely, and he included himself in this analogy, that no one would see their homeland again.

"And when you've finished your chores, I think we'll have a game of cards. There's a pack in my dugout someone conveniently left behind."

Taking his tin mug, Chalky relieved McJew. Bricky did likewise to Ginger. Little conversation took place as each focused on what lay ahead. Mathew cleaned his rifle whilst Kicker arranged grenades neatly in a waist pouch, only to take them out and try an alternative formation. Mathew listened to what Ginger wanted to say in a letter, then wrote down every word, even signing it on his behalf. McJew busied himself writing for the others, leaving his own letter to last.

"Right you lot, we're going to play some poker. Dawn's a long way off, so gather round," Church announced not to everyone's pleasure.

"Sir, what are we going to gamble with? I've only got a couple of bob and I'm sure the others aren't too flush, neither." Chalky's toothy, nervous grin appeared, accompanied by his chin rubbing trademark.

"I like your style, Chalky. I didn't think of playing for money, but now you've suggested it, come on lads, let's see what you have in your pockets."

Attempting to try and dissuade the major of this diversionary plan, Mathew suggested resting would be time better spent.

"Nonsense, Hobbs. If we get out of this in one piece, we have all our lives to rest, now, what's in your pocket doesn't have to be money. Anything of value will do."

Leaving Kicker as solitary lookout, the remaining five squatted as comfortably as the duck-boards allowed to watch Church expertly shuffle the pack, each card showing effects of being well thumbed. Whilst dealing, Church gave a running commentary on the rules of poker, for most it was too much to comprehend. Having seen his father play in the local drinking hole, Mathew possessed a faint idea on what a winning hand should look like, but apart from

McJew, the others only participated because they were ordered.

Only pennies changed hands during the next hour, but the less knowledgeable began to enjoy the banter and the chance to win something, especially off the major. Taking turns to deal, time slipped away unnoticed until the first signs of dawn filtered through an overcast, grey sky.

"Well lads, it looks as though this will be our last hand, so let's make it a good one. You can't take a pocket full of coins over the top, 'cos it'll hinder your progress and only weigh you down."

Church dealt before studying his hand.

"There you go, everything I've got on me."

Church placed a handful of copper and fragments of silver in Chalky's forage cap, used as a pot to contain the wagers. To everyone's astonishment, he threw a crisp, white five pound note in amongst the coins. Apart from Church, none had ever seen so much money in one place. Bricky leant forward to retrieve it; announcing he'd never handled one before, whilst Chalky rubbed his chin and McJew's eyes widened.

"Come on you lot. Everything out of your pockets."

Unmistakably, this was an order. One by one, handfuls of small change joined Church's money. Intrigue grabbed the players, each attempting to improve their hand by discarding one or two unhelpful cards. Sitting back, enjoying the intensity on their faces, Church issued the cards they hoped would win the pot. Church's smile broadened when each in turn displayed their chances with a verity of facial expressions. But one in the group didn't react or give any sign to the quality of what he held.

"If I think I have the winning hand by putting something of value in the cap, does it mean everyone else has to do the same before we see who's won?" Knowing only one in the group understood the rules, Mathew directed his question to Church.

"You're getting the idea, Hobbs. Yes, whatever you put in, we all have to match your wager to continue, that is unless you throw your hand in because you think you can't win." Church pondered what Mathew had in mind.

"Well, I've got this gold Saint Christopher, it was my grandmother's. I don't think I have much use for it, but it's worth a few quid."

Unfastening the top button of his tunic, Mathew unclipped his heirloom.

Unable to follow, each one of the unit dropped out disappointedly until the bid reached Church.

"Okay, Hobbs. I'll go along with you. That looks like an expensive piece of jewellery, so it'll have to be something of equal value."

Sitting back in his elevated position above the others, Church smiled but admired the guile of the young corporal. He didn't possess a watch or any trinkets and his pockets were empty. Removing a pencil stump from a breast pocket, he scribbled a note on the reverse side of the order-form Higgins personally delivered, before placing it in the 'pot' alongside Mathew's necklace.

"I have a young mare stabled near Ripon. She's a fine animal and is worthy of your wager. I've written the address where she's stabled, also a disclaimer of my ownership should you win."

Mathew looked at Church unsure, then to the others sitting transfixed.

"Alright, Hobbs. Let's see what you have."

Daring not to breath, Mathew turned and showed his cards.

"You cheeky sod," Church blurted out, pushing forward in his chair to confirm what he thought he first saw. "You put everything you own on a pair of threes?"

Mathew kept his eyes firmly planted on Church's.

"You deserve to win. Go on, pick up your winnings."

Destroying the evidence showing he held the winning hand of three queens, Church replaced his hand back into the middle of the pack.

A resemblance of a smile broke across Mathew's lips whilst scooping up his winnings, placing both notes in his breast pocket, watched by envious eyes. Chalky complained, without sympathy from the others, that he should have stayed in the competition with two pairs, whilst McJew discreetly asked if he could borrow a couple of quid if he got through the next twenty-four hours.

As each minute passed, daylight grew stronger and though no one possessed a watch, they knew the second they all dreaded was creeping nearer. Confirming their worst thoughts, a squaddie ran through the trench announcing ten minutes to go before the whistle would sound to indicate it was time to go over the top.

"Right lads. Fasten your bayonets and make sure you have a cartridge up the spout."

Urging his troops to be ready, Church shook each of their hands before positioning himself in the middle of the group, commandeering solo rights to the ladder, denying any of the others to be first over the top whilst they in turn scrambled to find convenient footholds.

"Make me proud of you, boys, and Hobbs; you take care of that horse."

Heart rates tripling, they were the last words spoken before a shrill whistle rang through the still, cold morning air.

***

Straightening his body once clearing the ridge, Mathew arched his body, running half a yard behind Church. The five others fanned out three strides behind. Remaining in their trenches, the rest of 102 Company either didn't react to the whistle, or were ordered to wait until thirty seconds later when a second whistle sounded leaving seven lone soldiers fully fifty yards ahead into their charge.

The first German salvoes skidded off frozen mud from a machine gun emplacement yet to find its range to their left. Wayward single shots fared no better. Head down and running for all he's worth, Mathew saw activity ahead meaning it was only a matter of seconds before the full force of the enemy's fire-power would be aimed at them.

"Fire from the hip, lads. Let the bastards have it."

A short volley rang out but Mathew couldn't make out whose shot caused a body to slump in the trench ahead. Screaming continuous abuse as he advanced, turmoil dictated he ran as fast as possible and to keep within touching distance of the major. The first mortar shells landed in a spasmodic pattern but unhindered, the charge tried staying together to draw gunfire away from the main body of 102 Company now making progress in staggered lines behind them. There was no time to think as red-hot shells whistling past their bodies, exploding into the massed line behind.

Five yards to Mathew's left, Chalky was first to be taken out of action. Hit in the chest and by the way his forward momentum was reversed, Mathew knew he wouldn't be getting to his feet. Never stop to attend a fallen friend, he remembered the order drummed into every recruit. With so much lead flying through the air, every second alive counted as a bonus.

Mathew didn't see the next victim fall, Smoke erupting from the fierce shelling masked anything further than five yards away. Losing all sense of distance and ignorant of his position, Mathew didn't realise he was so far behind Church until he sprawled over his prone body, pumping blood skywards from hideous leg wounds. Landing face down but lying in an ideal firing position, Mathew expertly loaded, aimed and fired but the bayonet unbalanced his shot, wasting precious killing time. Discarding the steel offender in manic haste, reloading and firing in one fluid movement took seconds, but the density of the swirling smoke made identity of a positive result impossible. The shape of decimated 102 Company appeared bravely advancing out of the fog behind, but soon their decreasing numbers would dictate a withdrawal. Fearlessly determined to retaliate and sure there was another cartridge in the breech, Mathew struggled to stand. No sooner had he risen when a stinging pain in his right leg spun his body, lifting his torso into the air, landing in a crumpled heap next to Church.

"Oh, Jesus."

Screaming, Mathew grabbed the wound. The inflicting shell landed some fifteen yards away, but razor edged shards of white hot shrapnel exploded in every direction. Fortunate to have missed larger pieces, a small fragment passed through Mathew's thigh at the speed of a bullet galvanising excruciating pain to pollute his entire body. Only pumping adrenalin kept him conscious.

"Medics," Mathew screamed, but his words fell short, mixed indecipherable amongst a cocktail of noise. "Medics," he screamed again.

"Is that you, Hobbs?"

Semi-concussed, Mathew eased his head off a lump of frozen mud, focusing on Church straining to crawl to where he lay.

"Don't move, Sir. There'll be a medic over here shortly."

"Oh, God."

Incoherently, Church pleaded for heavenly intervention.

Racked in agony, Mathew dragged his injuries towards Church. Bad as his own might have been, Mathew's injuries didn't compare with the horrific mess inflicted on what was left of the major's legs. The most effective anaesthetic might have been a bullet to the temple, but disregarding persistent bombardment whistling past their prone bodies, Mathew rested the major's head in his lap. Unhitching his water bottle, Mathew fed Church a few drops only for it to dribble back out.

"That bastard Higgins," Church gurgled, passing in and out of consciousness.

The battle continued raging in the distance but near enough for attending medics to be hit whilst searching amongst the dead for the treatable wounded.

"Hang on, Sir. They'll be here any minute."

Scanning for help through clouds of wafting smoke, a figure appeared in the distance. Mathew shouted again, but it didn't hear. As the breeze strengthened, three stripes and coloured epaulettes became decipherable on a static figure spying the action from back at the trenches. Ignoring danger of making himself a larger target, Mathew painfully eased into a sitting position, every small movement instigating electric shocks. Replacing the need to wait for medics with bravado, he lifted his rifle; confirming the identity through the telescopic sight.

"Sir, can you hear me?" Mathew bent to put his mouth close to Church's ear. A deep, guttural croak responded as acknowledgement. "Higgins never went over the top with the rest of us. He's standing not a hundred yards away looking at the action through binoculars."

"He's not only a bastard, he's also a fucking coward," Church groaned, attempting to raise his body. "And do you know what the army does to cowards. Hobbs?"

Shuffling closer, Church used Mathew for support.

"Er, no Sir. I don't."

"Well let me inform you for future reference, my dear friend. They stick them up against a brick wall and shoot them. As we haven't got a wall handy, I'm ordering you to shoot the bastard, now."

"I can't do that. He's one of ours. They'd shoot me for murder if they found out."

90

Increasing pain created muddled interpretations of the true meaning to Church's words.

"I'm giving you an order, Corporal Hobbs. And as I'm the only one who knows what that order is, then nobody is going to find out amongst all this fucking mayhem. Do it."

Mathew tried reasoning, But Church shouted him down.

"Do it. Do it now."

Replacing the sight back to his eye, Mathew's loaded rifle confirmed the target hadn't moved from its original position. He squeezed the trigger. Amongst the explosions and gunfire, Mathew's perfect head-shot melted, undistinguishable from other noises.

"Well Hobbs. Give me some good news and by Christ, I need some."

Mathew stared at the slumped body, not daring to remove the telescopic sight for fear it might move.

"He hasn't moved, Sir."

"Where did you hit him?"

"In the head."

"Well, I've witnessed what your rifle can do, so I can safely go to my maker knowing the bastard's dead. I only hope the fucker isn't going to the same place I'm going."

Lungs struggling to take shallow breaths thwarted Church's attempt to laugh. Suddenly his body convulsed, lurching to one side in a vain effort to witness Higgins death only to collapse over Mathew's blood saturated legs. Amongst so much scattered human destruction, Mathew's personal fight for life became dependent on the medics shifting through the carnage. Enemy snipers picking off stretcher bearers as easy as shooting fish in a barrel diminished their chances, but the longer he stayed awake, the odds on survival lengthened.

Their saviour in the form of a strengthening breeze scattered what was left of the smokescreen, signalling to those behind friendly lines to continue another ear-splitting bombardment. Sending the enemy scurrying back into their dugouts, hordes of medics safely entered the battlefield. Soon, four surrounded Mathew and Church.

"He's going to be alright, isn't he?" Mathew pleaded to the nearest. "He's not dead. Please, tell me he's not dead."

"No, son, he's not dead, but if we don't get a move on, he might be very soon. Now, don't worry about him, think for yourself. And if I'm any judge, it looks like 'Blighty One' for you, you lucky sod."

The corporal at the head of Mathew's stretcher continued his vocal barrage, endeavouring to keep Mathew alert and not let him fall asleep. He joked and swore, occasionally spitting in Mathew's face, anything to keep his eyes open, recognising the symptoms of losing a patient's personal battle with so much blood pumping from a serious leg wound. Urging his stretcher partner to quicken his paces, the corporal continued his unconventional survival technique in the ambulance. If he survived this tirade and the bone-shaking journey, he was confident Mathew would have an even money chance.

Recovering from under the surgeon's knife and patch-work skills for two hours in the confines of a canvas field operating theatre, Mathew finally opened his eyes in a state of weakness and excruciating pain. Panicked by a loss of feeling below his waist, he tentatively felt under the blood stained sheet for proof of legs and genital equipment. Retrieving a relieved hand confirming everything was in its rightful place, he broadened his smile when recollecting the corporal's mention of 'Blighty One'. If Mathew's prognosis of the maxim was correct, his war was over and only after one day on the frontline. Many thousands of troopers spent years in the same position, wallowing in mud and starved of nutritious food, only to die. At worse, the length of recuperation on this side of the channel would decide when he would be fit enough to return to England.

***

"I'm glad to see you're awake. How do you feel?"

Mathew hazily traced the voice to the end of his bed and found an angelic, white uniformed figure standing, smiling, her outstretched hand holding a thermometer. Such beauty he'd never seen before. Possibly a few years older, her blue eyes accentuated finely honed facial features encased in a flawless complexion. Enduring all the prevalent filth and misery, Mathew stared at the vision of cleanliness, her belt pulled tight, emphasising her perfectly proportioned body under an oversized, starched white apron.

"I've felt better in my time, but you're placed better to tell me. Will I walk again? What's your name? How long will I be in here for?"

"Oh, so many questions. Now let me see if I can answer them in the correct order. You're fine, yes, Mary and the last one depends on you. Now, open your mouth."

Smiling broadly, the distance between her body and Mathew shortened, aiming the thermometer towards an open target.

"Don't try to talk. Just nod your head if I have the correct information about you."

She read out his name, serial number, company and regimental details. Mathew nodded, attempting to garble a few words.

"Shush, wait until I take a reading. Then you can talk."

Replacing a clipboard to the end of his bed, she replaced the thermometer in a tumbler on a cabinet by his side.

"Now, what is it I can do for you?" she asked, pouring a glass of water.

"Major Church. Major Peter Church. He was my company commander. He was badly injured alongside me. Is he alright? Could you find out?"

"I'll try, Mathew, but there are so many coming back from the front line to so many hospitals, it will take time. It's possible you'll get moved on before I get word."

"Please. I have to know."

Mathew's fingers brushed against hers taking a glass of water. She smiled, understanding his concern and promised to try.

Laying in the same position for six days, Mathew witnessed corpses removed only for another soul to fill the same bed. On a daily basis, it was not unusual for more than one death to occupy the same bed. There would be no regimental letter sent to his parents describing Mathew's heroics before his untimely death. He would be one of the lucky ones going home alive.

Twice a day, Mary changed his dressing and as his pain subsided, solids in the form of better rations than those issued on the front line, indicated progress. Word filtered through, telling of weakening German resistance succumbing to superior allied advances, but still no word about Church. Believing positive information was better than none; Mary disturbed him from an afternoon sleep.

"I've got some good news for you, Mathew. The doctor confirms you're strong enough to travel. You're moving out tomorrow morning and do you know who's going with you?"

Mathew's face lit up, anticipating what Mary would say. The major was not as badly hurt as it first appeared.

"Me." She saw immediate disappointment. "I'm sorry, Mathew. I thought you'd be pleased to know you're on your way home, back to England. I'm still trying to find out about what happened to Major Church and there's still another day. I've spread the word to some friends to keep a lookout for him. Look, I've got to go to Brigade HQ this afternoon. I'll ask there as well."

"I'm sorry, Mary. It'll be great to have you coming along with me. Thanks. Thanks for everything."

She lightly squeezed his hand, bringing a rare smile to his face.

"When we get back to Blighty, will you come out with me and have a drink?"

"Of course I will, Mathew."

She lied, having been propositioned so many times in the past; giving the same positive answer knowing it was highly unlikely they'd ever meet again. Her feminine response gave the injured something other than wounds and war to think about. Mathew was to be no exception. It was cheap therapy and in most cases, a promise of female company responds better than medicine might achieve.

※ ※ ※

Locating rips in the canvas marquee, sharp rays of morning sunlight transformed the grey interior of the field hospital where twenty patients lay, each suffering degrees of differing injuries. A number, similarly injured as Mathew, consumed breakfast made up of marmalade sandwiches and a mug of tea, but most of his fellow bed-pals lay unconscious, groaning or grieving over lost limbs. It was during Mathew's attempt to have his mug refilled when two medics entered, heading straight towards where he lay propped up.

"Time for you to go home, my lad."

A sharp pain, caused by voice recognition, resonated through Mathew's thigh. He vaguely remembered one of the faces, but from where, he couldn't place.

"Haven't I seen you somewhere before?" Mathew's enquiry only broadened the smile on the medic's face.

"Should do. I was the bugger who dragged you off the front line," the corporal confirmed their first meeting. "See, I knew I was right about you going back to Blighty." His contagious smile reassured.

Aided by his partner holding Mathew under his armpits, they lifted him onto a canvas stretcher.

Dressed in a navy-blue raincoat covering her uniform, Mary entered the ward, her face carrying a worried look. She didn't speak until they boarded the ambulance.

"I have news of Major Church, and I'm afraid it's not good. To save his life, both legs required amputation and I don't know if he survived the trauma. A friend of mine assisted the surgeon. That's all I can tell you. I'm so sorry."

The effect was evident on Mathew's face. It wasn't unusual for soldiers to cry, she had seen it on many occasions, but this time it brought a tear to her own eye.

***

They travelled through war-ravaged countryside in silence; occasionally she interrupted Mathew's grief by lifting his head to offer water. Monotonously slow, the bone shaking journey drifted into oblivion until finally coming to a halt by the sea, the ambulance parking adjacent to a steam ship. Though Mary joined other nurses to tender the numerous injured aboard, most of her time she sat with Mathew. Similar to Major Church's background, she knew hers was opposite to Mathew's. Just another brave soldier. She had lost count of how many drifted into her life and left either on a stretcher or in the direction of the cemetery. They all carved their own indelible scar on her emotions, but unlike the others, she wouldn't forget Mathew. It wasn't until the cross-channel steamer entered Ramsgate Harbour that their silence broke.

"You've been asleep a long time, Mathew. It's the best medicine to recuperate and what's more, I've just been informed where you're going to stay until you're fit enough to leave. Here in Ramsgate, right on the seafront. Won't that be nice? With all this sea air, you'll be up and about in no time."

Her enthusiasm wasn't infectious.

"Are you billeted in Ramsgate?" Mathew spoke his first words since leaving Belgium.

"No, I'm afraid not. I have to report back to London, but we'll keep in touch," she lied again.

Situated on the town's seafront, the military hospital, converted from a vaudeville theatre, housed eighty beds split between two wards. Daily exercises for mostly young recruits prompted quick recovery, especially if capable of walking unaided or comfortable with crutches. The chronically infirmed requiring intensive care arrived at the same port, but were segregated to specialist hospitals. Compared to these unfortunates, Mathew's wounds were considered superficial, though a ten-inch scar down his right thigh might confirm he'd done his fair share in the face of the enemy, resulting in his country having no further use for him. There was always a 'Chalky White' or 'Kicker Broadfoot' to fill his boots.

***

Time boringly drifted by. Prognosis concerning his injury was that it would heal in time and a full recovery could be expected. Fortunately, the shrapnel missed his thigh-bone but the muscle took the full brunt of the intrusion. Under strict doctor's orders, Mathew spent days resting, writing letters home from his clean, crisp sheeted bed.

He wasted sheets of paper attempting to describe the nightmare of fighting a war without belittling the bravery of the common soldier. How do you describe a trooper's reaction to an order when there is no choice but to obey? If you didn't attack when told, there was a good chance of being shot for cowardice, so running blindly towards blazing guns was the only option. Cowards and heroes ran side by side into the Germanic organised lottery. If your number was up, too bad, the bullet didn't discriminate.

Instead he chose to write about Church, the game of poker and his close allegiance to Chalky, McJew and the others, not forgetting a beautiful nurse. His mother needn't know how Ginger was killed, the only friend he witnessed dying. He knew his father would be proud when he described the feeling of revenge, but one subject he failed to mention was Higgins. It was a secret, and if Major Peter Church had died, then he would carry the story to his deathbed.

In danger of getting bedsores after a week of bed-sheet internment, the doctors diagnosed exercise, though having lain on his back for so long, the muscle in his good leg sympathised with the injury through lack of use. Only his upper body strength and an art for controlling crutches allowed progress for morning sorties along the promenade. Dressed in a new uniform and determined to go a little further every day, the town's folk grew to recognise him and brighten his spirits with a smile or a 'well done, lad'. The younger ones even halted his progress. Seemingly oblivious to his injury, they meekly asked for advice on how to evade military service. A helping hand was never far away when climbing steps and offers of free ale continued whenever he felt in need of civilian company in a local public house. Southern beer, so it seemed, tasted much more palatable than the swill up north. Maybe he had grown up in the last two months. It was a far cry from the horrors of the front and life in Twickton. He would return home one day, but not before his body and mind healed.

Every passing day saw an improvement. So much so, that the matron bent the rules by allowing Mathew to sit by his bed instead of laying in it. Not to abuse her trust, Mathew sat quietly looking out to sea, a windowed view he never tired of.

To brighten the ward, junior nurses hung paper-chains as a gesture to celebrate Christmas, only a few days away. Mathew's mind drifted to past celebrations, a time of anticipating presents, a mother turning meagre provisions into a festive feast and the 'men' of the family sneaking out into the darkness to steal a tree. The giggles and laughter when trying to hide swaying branches from prying eyes on the four-mile trek home from the forest. The obligatory glass of father's whisky offered on a successful return. They were happy times. How he wished he could turn the clock back. Having nothing to celebrate, Mathew pondered on memories from past years.

As hospital life was free, money was not important, but soon there would be a time when fending for himself would be an issue. Mathew knew he wasn't penniless - his winnings from the poker game confirmed this assumption - but the amount he won remained a mystery. Curiosity replaced boredom.

Sure of not being overlooked, Mathew bent to his bedside locker and removed a handful of assorted coins. Counting them diligently into pound piles, he replaced them back on top of the cabinet. Reaching to retrieve what was left, a searching hand found a few more, a Saint Christopher, a five pound note and a piece of folded paper.

Never imagining he'd ever see the medallion again, Mathew put it to his lips in remembrance to his grandmother and replaced it round his neck. Next, he counted the piles of coins alongside the five pounds. Quite a tidy sum for a teenager only into his eighteenth year by two months, but what troubled him was the discarded piece of bloodstained paper nestling by the money. It wasn't Church's IOU bothering Mathew, though he wasn't sure how he would react on seeing his handwriting. It was what was written on the back of the order handled by Higgins. His first inclination was to destroy any reminder of that fateful day, but that would ruin proof of why only his unit of seven men reacted to a whistle and charged the entire German line alone. Something went terribly wrong on that morning and the piece of paper might throw up some clues. Unfolding the evidence, a thousand vivid pictures flashed before Mathew relating to a few minutes between the whistle sounding and the abortive sprint towards volleys of molten lead.

Reading it carefully, then again, it confirmed his initial surprise of so many spelling mistakes. Even to Mathew's eye the handwriting appeared naive, with punctuation marks conspicuous by their absence. Allowing the paper to flutter into his lap, Mathew raised his head, his stare settling on panoramic scenes from the open window. Masking this idyllic view was the image of Church having insufficient time to verify the written order from HQ and threatening Higgins with a court-martial. What followed were the colour sergeant's profanities towards the major, as though he knew there would be no repercussions. Something went drastically wrong.

From the multitude of images, Mathew selected one from his stockpile, the graphic picture of that morning's charge. He remembered two whistles, the second being louder than the first. Conjuring conflicting scenarios, just one kept returning. Why was their unit so far in front before 102 Company went over the top? It all began to become clear.

There could only be one solution. From a trench nearby, directly behind theirs, someone blew a whistle before the official time of 0700 hours. It might have been only thirty seconds or so early, but it had the desired effect to initiate their charge before 102 Company reacted to the correct time, blown by their commanding officer. Who possessed such hatred against Church? Mathew didn't have to ponder for too long. Adding his own run-in with Higgins to the equation, it could only have been him. Mathew found him guilty, but needed to be sure of the verdict. If Higgins were to have lived, it would be a hanging offence if proved.

Church's life in the army had been no longer than Mathew's and Higgins gambled on the major being ignorant of commanding officer procedure. Buried in The Book of Regulations, protocol demands each CO to initiate their own platoon's ordered attack by blowing a whistle at the correct time. Had Church owned a timepiece, it would have gone into the poker-pot instead of an IOU. Such a stupid, small mistake to respond to the first whistle, but big enough to guarantee a time difference and subsequence slaughter.

Mathew wished the major's suspicions were passed down the ranks. It might have been possible, as corporal, to persuade the major to take caution. Knowing what he knew now, it wouldn't have needed an order from Church to shoot Higgins. Regaining a clear conscience, Mathew's smile returned broadly. His eyes refocused on the view of Ramsgate seafront.

CHAPTER 10

"Well, Corporal Hobbs. It's time for you to leave us. Your wound has healed nicely, although you'll limp for a while, but you'll be pleased to know I have signed you off further duty. No one can say you haven't done your bit for king and country. You probably won't get a medal, but you have a scar to prove it. From this moment you are officially out of the army and free to do whatever you like. So get dressed and gather your belongings. There's a staff sergeant from the pay corp. outside waiting to come in with your demob forms and reimbursement for monies owed. So, Mister Hobbs, have a good Christmas and good luck for the future."

Shaking hands, Mathew thanked the doctor and waited for the sergeant. A few minutes passed, before the large twin doors separated, pushed aside by a burly soldier in full uniform holding a leather briefcase under his arm. Standing to attention by his bed, Mathew instinctively saluted.

"You should know better than that, Corporal. No hat, no salute." His thick Yorkshire accent boomed across the ward for all to hear.

Disengaging his hand from his forehead, Mathew saw the stranger's face and readily recognised the craggy features.

"It's Jack Fowler, isn't it?"

Mathew held out a hand to be shaken, but saw no reciprocal response.

"How do you know my name, Corporal? Have we served together?"

Quickly realising, when Fowler left to go to war with Robert Noble he was little more than a boy. Time had moved on since then and hadn't been kind to Fowler. He appeared aged, far more than the years he'd been away and during that time Mathew had grown into a man.

"I'm Mathew Hobbs, George's youngest boy."

Fowler stood bemused, looking down at Mathew from a height of six feet two. Nothing registered. But slowly, the shape of eye recognition gave it away. Creased at the edges showing his pleasure, Fowler removed his cap and engulfed the son of his best friend.

"Oh, Jesus. It's good to see you. I saw the name but never put two and two together. Thank God you're alright."

Those conscious within the ward who were unprivileged to know the reason why two men in uniform should be hugging, found it quite amusing. Fowler pushed Mathew away, holding the young soldier by the shoulders, inspecting him at arm's length.

"You're a fine figure of a man, Mathew, and by what I've read in your report, saw a bit of action." Fowler smiled, knowing it to be an understatement.

"You could say that, Jack."

"Come on, son. Get your coat and let's get out of here. We can do all the paperwork in a pub. This calls for a drink."

Curbing an instinct to march off at regulation speed, Fowler appeared awkward keeping pace with a man reliant on crutches. Fighting pain inflicted by walking the furthest since his operation, they arrived at Fowler's chosen watering hole and though only eleven in the morning, the place was crowded with customers, none of whom wore a uniform. All eyes turned to the new arrivals, especially following the progress of the injured one, to a vacant table and chairs positioned by a window whilst the other stranger deviated to the bar. Returning minutes later carrying a pint in each hand to where Mathew sat, Fowler chose a spot in the shadows, out of the glare of low winter sun shining through frosted glass.

"Well Matty. Tell me all about it."

Time slipped away unnoticed as Mathew related his tale from the beginning when Noble led his company out of Twickton. For reasons of his own, Fowler never returned to Twickton since the day he left, but wanted to know everything about his family and how the mine managed with diminished labour. He told Mathew he wrote home every month, but Mathew was unsure of his frankness. Why was he so interested with what Mathew related if in constant touch with his wife? It was his problem and Mathew wasn't going to allow mind-games to interfere with his first day of freedom.

Leaving Twickton illiterate, the army taught Fowler how a pen could change his life. Fortunately for the home coming hero, an opportunity materialised in the form of a direct route into the Pay Corp., a non-physical, non-combat arm of a London based regiment. Just as Mathew brought his story up to date, Fowler continued with his own. Though it appeared their companies' time on the front was similar, Mathew listened intently to Fowler's description of how Noble died.

Resembling Mathew's closeness to his major, Fowler endeavoured to do the same with Captain Noble, but unlike Church's injury, Noble received a direct hit in the face, taking the back of his head off. Fowler went on to describe how Twickton Company took the immediate German line after fierce hand-to-hand fighting, only to be left holding the position without reinforcement. Despite runners sent back to muster support, an hour after their glorious victory, the Germans, in the guise of a fresh, fully manned company, reclaimed their lost territory. Badly decimated in their first attack, within ten minutes of the second, most of what was left of Twickton Company lay dead in the

German trench. Fowler's strength attributed to his escape, carrying a wounded trooper across his shoulder over no-man's-land, making it back to his own line miraculously without a scratch on his body.

Hailed as a hero by the lads in the trenches, Fowler's bravery was mentioned in dispatches and subsequently awarded a medal. Taking advantage of a four-day pass to spend time recuperating in a small town fifteen miles behind enemy lines, and relatively untouched by the ravages of war, Fowler passed his time with a glass of wine or two in a small bar specially catering for high ranking officers whose intention was to go nowhere near the enemy. Unfortunately, Fowler's time at the bar coincided with that of a drunken brigadier. Accusing Fowler of using the rescued private as protection against enemy gunfire resulted in the superior officer skidding across the wooden floor on his backside with a broken nose. The subsequent court-martial was conveniently cancelled, as was the medal ceremony. Compromise agreed; the scandal was buried. 'Broken nose' accepted an office job back at Whitehall with all expenses paid, whilst the Pay Corps found a post for the other.

"I didn't want a piece of bleeding tin stuck on my chest in the first place. Laying that bastard out flat was far more fun."

Recalling the incident with satisfaction brought laughter from Fowler prompting Mathew, encouraged by alcohol, to share his personal altercation. Beckoning Fowler closer so his lowered voice could not be overheard, he knew he could share a secret with this man, a secret once promised only he and Church would be privy to.

"My Major ordered me to shoot our own Colour Sergeant."

"Well, that's different and a much better story than mine. But did you do it? That makes the story even better."

"Yes I did."

Revisiting his childhood, Mathew giggled like a naughty schoolboy, but Fowler wasn't surprised by this admission. From what he'd witnessed during his own campaign in action, it would have been a bigger surprise if it never happened.

"All I can say is, if he was anything like my brigadier, he must have deserved it. There are a lot of shits on our side who would have been more comfortable on the other side of the fence."

They looked at each other wide eyed, open mouthed and shocked at the admission. Twin choruses of raucous laughter broke the hushed surrounds. Each couldn't believe what the other had just confessed.

"You and I have got a hell of a lot in common, Matty boy."

Fowler grabbed Mathew's hand, shaking it vigorously before returning to the bar.

"Landlord, get this hero another pint and whilst you're doing that, pour this hero one as well."

Drinking went on past midday into the afternoon, stopping only when the barman called 'time'. Standing when sober was difficult for Mathew, but with untold pints of ale in his enlarged belly, found it nigh impossible. Relieving his bladder required two customers to help, but the bar now being empty, any thought about moving demanded postponement. Fowler attempted the same exercise but succeeded with only two steps before succumbing to gravity. Watching these antics from the safety of distance, the amused landlord decided discretion was the better part of valour by leaving them where they slept, knowing from past experience, it was more than it was worth to try and remove two inebriated servicemen. Judging by the quantity of alcohol, he confidently wagered they'd be in the same position when he reopened in the evening. His mistake in judgement would later cost him the price of two over large whiskeys.

***

Awoken first, recognition of surrounds took time. A throbbing head and desert-like mouth confirmed the quantity of ale consumed. From his vantage point, Mathew scanned the darkening bar for the whereabouts of Fowler, recalling him passing out with a bone shaking crunch against the bar. Deciphering a pair of boots from out of the gloom on the other side of the floor, his eyes travelled over the prone body, noticing it hadn't moved from the time it hit the floor, though a puddle spreading out from around his darkened crutch wasn't there before.

"Jack," Mathew called, getting little response apart from a rasping, guttural groan. "Jack. Get up here and give me a hand, you drunken bastard."

Mathew heard a familiar laugh heralding slow leg movements.

"Oh, shit. I've pissed myself. I'm soaked. What time is it?"

A wall clock, illuminated by weak gas light shining from the pavement outside through an adjacent window, suggested the time.

"It's coming up to six o'clock."

"Oh, bugger."

Struggling to sit, propped up against the bar, Fowler exercised his full vocabulary of swear words.

"Fuck it. I was supposed to be back at HQ by four. Oh bugger it. Sod it. What can they do to me that they haven't already done? If it hadn't been for that fucking brigadier, I'd be considered a fucking hero. I bet that arsehole doesn't have to report back after he's had a skin-full."

Unable to be of any assistance, Mathew's glazed eyes focused on Fowler's pathetic figure, but couldn't restrain from laughing. It was easy from where he sat to admire Fowler's contempt for authority, but it wasn't Mathew who would face a charge of being 'absent without leave', he'd been discharged from further duty that day and possessed papers to prove it. According to English Army Law, this automatically meant a spell in the 'glasshouse' for Fowler, or if he was on the front line, the firing squad.

Mathew wished he could have gone to war with Twickton Company and seen, at first hand, Fowler's handling of officers, Captain Noble excluded. It would have made a good story for the folks back home if it was Fowler who carried him to safety on his back.

"Come on, Matty. Time to get the hell out of here, but not before, my little bumpkin, we help ourselves to a drink. We'd better make it sharpish 'cos the governor will be back any minute."

Leaving Mathew rummaging the floor in search of crutches, Fowler poured two tumbler-full measures from a whiskey bottle found hidden behind the cash register. It wasn't the quickest exit Fowler planned but their timing was perfect. Disappeared out the back door, the landlord unlocked the front. A cold winter's breeze greeted their not-so-swift getaway along Ramsgate's deserted seafront.

"We've got to find somewhere to get out of this bloody wind. I've still not given you your pay, so let's find another pub so you can sign these bleeding demob papers and then I can get the fuck out of here."

Giving Mathew an opportunity to catch up, Fowler's intention was obvious by the direction he pointed towards another watering hole.

"Please Jack. Your last train must have gone by now, so let's just find somewhere to sleep tonight. We can have another drink tomorrow and do all the signing. I'm whacked."

CHAPTER 11

Mathew woke early the following morning. Manoeuvring around the small bedroom proved awkward, but the narrow hallway leading to the bathroom suggested he left the crutches hanging on the back of the bedroom door. Though offering only basic facilities, it was worth every penny for Mathew to experience, for the first time, the luxury of washing behind a locked door and in the privacy of a proper hotel. To the affluent it might be considered a boarding house, but to Mathew it contained style. Long ago in the past and never to happen again, were days when he squatted in a tin bath surrounded by his family, his mother trying to prepare something to eat whilst his father sat by the open fire.

Whilst the other hotel guests slept, Mathew wallowed in the extravagance, especially viewing his image in a full length mirror, the first time he'd seen his body in its entirety instead of just a head and shoulders reflection. Brushing away incriminating evidence from the previous night's antics, Mathew posed at attention, saluted and liked what he saw.

Quietly vacating his bedroom so as not to disturb the other guests, Mathew carried his crutches, hopping along the corridor; his raincoat thrown over a shoulder. Adapting the same formula for a staircase descent, using the banister rail to carry most of his weight, Mathew negotiated the obstacle to the ground floor where a small room to the right containing a few clothed tables and chairs greeted his arrival.

"Would you like a cup of tea, love?"

Interrupting Mathew's concentration to remain upright with a minimum of noise, Mathew turned to see who owned the voice. A plump, middle-aged greying woman dressed similar to his mother was already pouring steaming liquid from a large brown teapot into a white mug.

"Thank you. Just what I could do with."

"With that accent of yours, you must be a long way from home," the landlady enquired, aiding his progress over to the window by removing a couple of chairs from his path. "Badly injured were you, love? Shame. Still, you look as though you're on the mend." She relieved him of his coat and pulled out a chair ready for him to sit. "It's a nice place to sit for your first cup of the day. Much nicer, I'll bet, than the place you've been, eh son? If you want anything else, just holler out, I'll be in the back."

Relishing tranquillity, he rolled his first cigarette of the day only for Fowler's appearance to fragment the moment.

"A nice cuppa. Just what I could do with. Where did you get it?" Announcing his untimely arrival, Fowler pointed at the solitary steaming mug on Mathew's table.

"There's a pot of it on the sideboard."

Showing no trace of a hangover or incriminating stains caused by an inability to distinguish the difference between an oak floor and a urinal, Fowler appeared as smartly as when Mathew first saw him the previous morning.

"Here's the money the army owes you." Pushing a brown envelope across the table, Fowler extracted two official forms from his briefcase. "And all you have to do is sign. There, you're free as a bird, you lucky sod."

"Lucky sod, my arse. I nearly died on that bleeding stretch of French mud and all for what. A few measly quid. I should have listened to my old man when he tried to give me some good advice."

"Actually Matty, its Belgian mud where you nearly got your balls blown off." Wearing a false smile, witnessing

Mathew sign the forms only emphasised who got the best deal. What service his country received for so little reward. "What are you going to do now, Matty? It's Christmas Eve tomorrow."

Mathew scanned the grey landscape, his line of sight settling on a flock of seagulls foraging for breakfast. Though full of parked army vehicles, the promenade stood deserted. Even soldiers, so it appeared, didn't get up this early in Ramsgate.

"Well, there's one thing for sure. I'm not going back to Twickton."

Reflecting on the circumstances, it wasn't time to offer advice. Fowler held his mug between both hands, a cigarette dangling from his bottom lip. As the closest person he had as a friend, he felt Mathew wanted to talk and clear a backlog of gremlins niggling his conscience, but decided to wait. Only when he lit a second cigarette did Mathew break the silence.

"I've got a nice few quid in my pocket, so the first thing to do is get rid of this uniform and buy some decent clobber. Then I'll go to London and find a place for a few days over Christmas. I want to see the place as a regular bloke instead of what a soldier saw. I want to see it as I've read about and not with bodies lying around in pools of blood. There are so many terrible pictures in my head but I want to try and bury them deep so that one day I'll wake up and they'll be blurred, not so crystal clear. I don't want to see death anymore. I want to see people enjoying life. I want to enjoy life and get rid of these fucking crutches before I step out of this door."

Fowler saw a look of meaning and determination in Mathew's face.

"Then, I'm going to follow this up."

Mathew threw the piece of folded paper across the table.

"Is this what I think it is? The gift from God you won in a game of poker? What will you do with it if you find where it's stabled? Your money won't last you that long, so you'll probably have to sell it or eat it."

Fowler's laughter wasn't reciprocated.

"I'm skint apart from what I've got on me, so I might sell it. Anything the Major owned must be worth a few bob."

"Well, Matty. I haven't got time to sit here and chat all day. I've got to get back to Ashford and face the music, so why not travel up to London together. The train goes through Ashford on its way, so it'll give us time to have a drink until we meet again and if you're thinking of buying new clothes, London's the place."

Mathew was about to struggle to his feet, preparing to leave, when the landlady shyly entered the room from the rear of the building.

"Before you go, love. I couldn't help but hear what you were saying. If you want to get rid of your crutches, help yourself to a walking stick in the stand by the front door. I don't know who they belong to. People come and go and just leave their stick behind. You can leave the crutches behind if you like, who knows, I may get a visitor who needs a pair."

Fowler looked indignantly at the old lady for eavesdropping, but Mathew smiled, hobbled to where she meekly stood and kissed her cheek.

"Thanks misses. You've made my first wish come true. Happy Christmas to you."

Appearing blissfully pleased with her offer, she returned to the back room. Feeling a lack of sympathy brought on by the old lady's generosity, Fowler rummaged around in the bottom of his briefcase and withdraws a handful of pink dockets.

"Before I forget, you might as well have these railway passes as I don't think I'll be going anywhere for the next couple of months after I get back to HQ."

**

It was mid-afternoon on a bright December day when Mathew stepped onto the platform. Similar to the last visit, army personnel filled Victoria Station, but on this occasion everyone moved under their own steam without a hint of an injury or prone bodies lying on stained stretchers. Carrying no belongings, only a limp slowed his progress towards the exit. How he wished his parents could see him with straightened back and pride in his two striped uniform mingling with a multitude of other faceless heroes. Though his impairment was obvious, the walking stick allowed his left arm to swing in rhythm with a diminished stride towards Victoria Street, where he intended to leave Corporal Hobbs, number 2774394, 102 Company, behind as a memory and reclaim Mathew Hobbs, private citizen.

Knowing what he was looking for, it wasn't too far before a shop window attracted his attention displaying accessories a young man required. He'd selfishly ignored father's advice, instead answered his calling to fight. He'd taken revenge for his brothers' deaths and nearly got killed in the process. It was the right time to leave the war for others to fight.

"Good afternoon, Sir. May I be of assistance?"

Eyeing Mathew's uniform, the shop assistant immediately noticed no pips of rank on Mathew's epaulettes; only two stripes on a coat sleeve. Standing firm, blocking further progress into the shop, the assistant belligerently glared at Mathew. Neither greased strands of hair combed to disguise receding baldness, nor an ageing morning suit reflecting light due to over-pressing persuaded Mathew from taking the hint of not being welcome.

"Yes, you can. I would like to try on the grey suit you have in the window and that pair of shoes."

Pointing to his requirements, Mathew reeled off a shopping list of items, but his selections fell on deaf ears.

"May I stop you there, Sir?" a condescending south London accent broke across Mathew's Yorkshire dialect. "With all due respect. Our goods are tailored for the discerning gentleman with an eye for quality. This, of course is reflected in the price. Need I continue, Sir?"

Planting his feet apart, steadying his stance, Mathew hooked the salesman round the neck with the wrong end of his walking stick, not unlike how a shepherd snags a sheep. Surprised and unable to resist, Mathew pulled so only the length of their noses separated their faces.

"Listen here, you pompous little shit. I didn't nearly lose my life on the front line for arseholes like you to decide if I'm a gentleman or not. If I couldn't afford it, I wouldn't come into your poxy shop. So, shall we start again?"

Sensing a disturbance, the manager emerged from the rear.

"What's going on here, Jacobs?"

"This gentleman wishes to inspect our range, Sir." Jacobs spluttered meekly, rubbing his neck where the stick left a ring of red flesh.

"Well man, get on with it and treat our brave soldier to the highest degree of service."

Chastising Jacobs in front of a customer might have been a show, but, due to the war, profits were at rock bottom and any sale, no matter how small, would ring the cash register's bell for the first time that day. Long gone were the days when trade was brisk and profits high. Turning to entice his first customer to purchase some stock, Jacobs transformed his face with a sickly smile.

"I'm sure we can offer a little bit of discount. Would you like to take a seat, Sir?"

It was possible someone might have witnessed a soldier entering the shop, but they would have missed his departure. Attired in a grey suit, stiff collared white shirt and tie, matching overcoat, brogue shoes and a black trilby hat, the transformation from lowly ranked trooper to a visibly acceptable member of London's social set was complete.

***

Recognising the young man heading across Euston Station towards a newspaper stand would be difficult. Albeit limping and reliant on a walking stick, Mathew's demeanour and appearance demanded respect as confirmed by the paperboy's reaction on receiving a penny tip for his service of selling Mathew a copy of *The Times*. Not surprisingly, being the day after Boxing Day, few passengers boarded the northbound train. Time was at Mathew's mercy and with so much of it in hand, Mathew meandered the platform looking for an unoccupied, second-class department of his choice. Selecting a window seat, he sat alone, wrapped in his new coat, his other purchases packed in a new case above in the luggage rack; new brogues resting on the seat opposite. Fearing nothing but the haunting of Higgins' ghost, Mathew pulled the rim of his trilby over his eyes contemplating a future without cash. He'd tasted the wealthy lifestyle over Christmas, but it only endorsed his decision to escape Twickton, regardless of extravagances seriously damaging his savings.

The freezing weather covering Yorkshire in late November returned with a vengeance. The further the train travelled north, the deeper the covering of snow. Though the temperature inside wobbled higher than that outside, Mathew pulled his collar higher and settled back, staring at the bleak, white landscape flashing past through a soot encrusted window. The colourless vista forced him to look away as too many dark, vivid memories replaced the mesmerising view. In need of artificial stimulation, his eyes settled on the rolled newspaper he tossed on the seat earlier as the train approached Watford Junction.

Beginning with the headlines, it appeared from an experienced war correspondent that the allied advance was reaping rewards, but similar articles on inside pages reflected a not too subtly written difference of opinion, warning of future battles around the Passchendaele area. Acquired first-hand experience of how the Germans fight convinced Mathew that this war was far from over.

The privacy he searched for at Euston broke as the train slowly pulled out of Huntingdon, caused by the door of his compartment sliding open. Mathew looked up at the stranger, a railway ticket inspector, understanding full well that Fowler's travel permits only covered army personnel. The way Mathew was dressed bore no resemblance to a serviceman.

"On leave, are we Sir?" the inspector questioned, assuming this smart young man to be an off duty officer.

"Yes, my good man. Taking some time out to visit my parents, don't you know?"

Gone was the lad from Twickton, Yorkshire. In his place was someone speaking with an accent extraordinarily similar to the officer he'd just served under.

"Very well, Sir. All correct. Have a good day." Backing into the corridor, a sloppy salute signalled his departure.

"Close the door, that's a good man," Mathew cringed, thinking he might have gone over the top with his impersonation.

There was still a long track in front to travel before needing to change trains at Northallerton, but deteriorating weather convinced Mathew his final destination, his dream, was in jeopardy of ever being reached. Resigning his fate to whatever barrier lay ahead; Mathew folded his jacket neatly, assuring to flatten creases before donning his coat.

Tilting his hat down over his face, the corner seat accepted his body. He couldn't remember closing his eyes.

Shunting carriages at York belied any fears he might have had of sleeping through his connection. Worsening snow falls caused timetables to be decimated, resulting in a motionless train alongside a station platform, a scant white expansive void of people in darkness, except for the station clock glowing ominously alone showing he'd been travelling for eleven hours. Mathew was in no doubt, there was to be no further progress along this line for the foreseeable future.

Through continuous smoke clouds bellowed from the stationary locomotive, a distant voice grew in strength, informing passengers of their predicament and strongly advising them to stay aboard until a snow plough cleared the way. Spending the night aboard a warm train appealed more than spending the night shivering in a draughty, station waiting room.

Finally, by the following lunchtime, Mathew's train lumbered into Leyburn station, a few miles short of where hopefully he would find the horse stabled in a farm on the edge of the Yorkshire Dales. The snow-laden grey sky preceded the north bound train for many miles finally exhausting itself from adding depth to underfoot deposits. But a weak image of its former self hovered low over the town. Black brogues, a smart combination of suit, overcoat and trilby, proved totally unsuitable for conditions akin to Arctic exploration. Considering the surroundings as another obstacle purposely placed to question his fortitude, Mathew began questioning the notion of whether owning a horse was worth all this effort. Not known for his theologian thoughts, Fowler's rare passage of succinct words about the horse being a gift from God and a saleable commodity, spurred him on. In the comfort of having money, thoughts about returning to Twickton never entered his head, but now it was different. Money spent on appearance wasn't going to feed him and the experience of a few days living the high life over Christmas in London convinced Mathew he wanted more, but it might only continue as a memory. Before him lay a life of continual decisions, to be made by what, a dreaming teenager or a sensible adult? An adult would use the few pennies left to travel the thirty odd miles back home and continue with a life where he already knew what the outcome would be, but then there was the teenage way, pulling for the unexpected. Was it a fantasy to think of the horse as his passport to better things? What could happen if he chose to chase the dream?

He was so close to the stable housing his fantasy at Spennithorne, but it might well have been a million miles away having no visible means of transport outside the station capable of transporting him through deep snow.

Mathew squatted on his upturned case, pondering his next move. Cold and tired, the large coal, warming fire constantly maintained by his mother during winter days sprang to mind and tempted a weaker side of his nature, as did her food. Casting these mirages aside, Mathew looked for a taxi; he could just about afford one, but needn't have bothered. Marooned in this desolate, white outback, five pounds wouldn't solve the problem of getting to the farm. Squeezing positivity out of disillusionment accelerated confusion until a timely distraction appeared in the shape of a lone figure approaching.

"No good hanging about here if it's a train you're after. The only one running today was the one you got off."

The affable stranger stood looking down at the shivering youngster, dressed for the city and not for rural orienteering. "You're not from round these parts, are you son?"

"No. My family lives in Twickton." Mathew's voice, constricted by cold, squeaks between chattering teeth.

"Well, you're miles away from home. Why did you get off at this station?"

"I'm trying to get to George Pinkerton's farm near Spennithorne. Is it anywhere near here?"

As sole employee of the station, the accolade of Station Master meant little to Arthur, but despite meagre wages, the work gave him the security of a small tied cottage where he lived with his wife for the past sixteen years.

"Well, sonny. I don't know for the life of me how you're going to get there in this stuff and especially dressed in those clothes. You'll freeze to death. Come on, pick that case up and come and get warm."

Mathew gladly followed the Samaritan, treading in footprints left by size ten boots, into the welcoming arms of a ticket-office where a fire roared from an open grate, its heat effective as the door swung shut.

"Sit yourself down and get warm, lad. Bet you could do with a cuppa?"

Getting to know the train drivers as he had over the many years, Arthur was convinced none of them would dare risk being marooned miles away from anywhere, but more importantly, their home. Assuming his analogy of the situation to be correct, then his working day was over, albeit to sit and share the heat with Mathew. Situated on a grill above the flames, a tarnished kettle simmered, constantly affording a steady flow of tea on tap. Thawing nicely, Mathew removed his coat and settled down to what could be a long wait in the hospitality of Arthur, a man comfortable with his own companionship but attempting to nurture friendship by instigating conversation on a subject Mathew wanted to forget. Refusing to satisfy Arthur's well intended but inquisitive nature; the young stranger subtly turned the banter towards Arthur's life with an astonishing coincidental outcome. Living on land adjacent to the farm of George Pinkerton, Arthur suggested he accompany Mathew to reach his goal, but the prospect of this happening decreased rapidly when announcing he wasn't sure when his relief would manage to get through with so much lying snow. Darkening clouds suggesting further downfalls increased the likelihood of them both spending the night in the ticket office.

***

"Ay op. lad. I'd know that whistle anywhere. It's got to be Charlie. You know what that means don't you? If he's got here to relieve me from where he lives, he's found transport."

Arthur's face lit up, having voluntary inherited Mathew's problems.

Raising their backsides in unison off fireside chairs, the duo headed towards the exit in perfect shoulder to shoulder formation, Mathew's limp handicapping his speed to counteract Arthur's age. The laws of probability guaranteed failure for one to get through in this pattern as Mathew found to his expense, his damaged leg succumbing to superior body weight.

"What are you doing down there, sonny? Come on, get off your arse."

Arthur laughed excitedly, the unexpected situation relieving the everyday boredom even it was to last only a few hours. By the time Mathew got to his feet and mustered propulsion, Arthur was off the platform, scurrying towards where the shrill notes originated on the station forecourt. Charlie's arrival was met by Arthur's joyous, outstretched arms greeting his workmate as a long lost friend. Mathew's dishevelled materialisation coincided with Arthur's infectious laughter, crowning the moment of victory, proudly turning to point towards their mode of escape.

"There you go. All is not lost."

Spiralling plumes of steam from a large black dray indicated its exertions to pull a snow covered cart through a foot of snow. Perched aboard, expertly muffled against whatever the weather threw at him, Charlie appeared confused why his arrival should be the cause of so much commotion. Standing in unison, jacketless and coatless, instigating hunched shoulders due to falling body temperature, Mathew's frozen hand managed a response to Arthur's thumbs-up sign.

"Where did you get that from, Charlie?" Arthur eagerly questioned his relief pointing to the horse and cart.

"Borrowed it from George Pinkerton. Told him you'd return it on your way home."

"George Pinkerton," Mathew blurted, unable to disguise his relief. "Bloody hell. I am going to get there after all."

CHAPTER 12

Steering a path off the lane, Arthur allowed the ageing gelding its first breather after an hour's struggle of pulling a burdened cart through deep snow. George Pinkerton observed their arrival from inside the warmth of his farmhouse but didn't recognise one of the figures aboard. By the time it took Arthur to negotiate the route hidden beneath a thick covering of snow, farmer Pinkerton and a black and white collie stood to greet them.

"Hallo George."

"Hallo Arthur. Who's that with you?"

Before Arthur could exchange niceties, Mathew interrupted. It took maybe a second or two for Pinkerton to register where he'd heard the name.

"Oh yes. I've been expecting you. But I didn't think I'd see you this side of New Year. Get yourself down and come inside out of the cold. Arthur, can you see to Billy? Put him in the long barn and rub him down. It's nice and warm in there with fresh hay. The 'ol fella deserves a bit of pampering after all the work he's just done."

Together, Arthur and Billy had achieved what was beginning to appear impossible. A mere 'thank you' was insufficient for Arthur's assistance and a pat on Billy's neck seemed an insult for all his effort. Assisted back onto terra firma, Mathew watched as Billy was led away for a comfortable rest, his needs coming before those of Arthur's. This consideration for his livestock might have been the reason why the major chose Pinkerton to care for his equine property. Mathew was pleased to be back where his accent wasn't frowned upon as an impediment.

"Get that coat off, lad, and sit yourself down by the fire. You must be stark raving mad or very impatient to come out here in this bloody awful weather."

A widower of seven years, sixty year old George Pinkerton resembled everything Mathew thought a Yorkshire farmer should resemble with a robust, ruddy complexion and a refusal to remove his cap once inside his home. Baggy corduroy trousers, whose knees had long lost the 'cord', were kept aloft by a regimental tie, contrasting against a check shirt and sheepskin jerkin held together by the one button refusing to succumb to a spreading waistline.

"I received a letter on Christmas Eve informing me of your pending visit."

"Who from?"

"Why, Major Peter Church, of course."

Unable to believe his ears, Mathew asked it to be repeated.

"You're saying he's alive?"

Pinkerton saw shock, relief and pleasure in a split second cross Mathew's face.

"Well, if he isn't alive, I don't know who wrote the bleeding letter,"

"I thought he was dead. Oh, my God. He's alive."

Turning away, masking eruptive emotions, Mathew's chin dropped to his chest. For so long he'd assumed survival was negligible but now there was concrete proof to the contrary.

"Here, son. Take a dram of this. It'll cheer you up and banish the cold out of your body." Pinkerton stuck out a hand holding a glass containing a large malt whiskey.

"I'm not sad, George. It's the best news I've had since I signed up. You must give me his address. I must see him."

Taking the offered glass, Mathew sank the contents in one gulp.

"Hey, steady on there, lad. Not so fast. That whiskey that's just disappeared down your throat is the finest there is in these parts and should be savoured, not woofed down in one go." Disbelieving the sacrilege bestowed upon his treasured tipple, Pinkerton returned to the serious subject of the major. "I'm sorry; it's in the terms and conditions contained in his letter. I can't tell you where he lives. He's very poorly after losing both legs but he's still maintains his pride. It's going to take plenty of time before he gets use to the idea of living in a wheelchair for the rest of his life. Still, after all he's been through, he must think a hell-of-a-lot about you."

"Why do you say that, George?"

The sudden effects of Highland malt whiskey reacting to an empty stomach prompted eyes to bulge and brought an alert reaction.

"Well, I can only see it from my point of view. Thinking what state his body and mind must be in at the present, one of the first priorities is to write and inform me the mare has a new owner. Ever since he bought that animal, some very rich people have tried to buy it off him; offering a small fortune, but he's refused them all. When he bought her from Ireland, he was sure she was a gooden; even though there's a chance she might turn out to be an expensive flop like so many others. The right breeding doesn't always mean a horse can run fast. It's like a professor having a son who won't do his schoolwork. With all the kid's pedigree, it's a cert he becomes a scientist. Wrong, he turns out to be a bricklayer. You get the picture."

Standing, his back facing the fire, Pinkerton causes a long shadow to cross the low beamed lounge whilst keeping a firm grip on the whiskey bottle. Champ, the sheepdog, curls up on the hearth mat, close by his master's feet.

"He says in his letter, you were in the trenches together. The way he wrote, it seems he knew he wasn't going to come through unscathed. You must be a special person for him to give away his beloved mare. There must have been something you did, but he didn't say, so if you want to tell me, I'll listen."

Similar to Arthur's prompting; Pinkerton attempted to pump for information, but received a stony silence. It's obvious; whatever the major and Mathew shared would remain their secret.

"Okay, have another drink and after you've shaken off the chill, we'll go and see your new property. There's a spare pair of gumboots by the door you can use. Don't want to ruin those nice shoes of yours."

His arrival at the farmhouse couldn't have been timed better. Had Arthur had reason to delay their departure from the station any longer, Mathew doubted Billy's ability could have pulled the cart through the accumulating snow. Practiced in the art of following embedded footprints, Mathew traced Pinkerton's trail to the rear of the long barn where a fenced, open paddock sprawled. Brushing snow aside, Mathew's arms rested on the top rung allowing his eyes to wander in the direction of Pinkerton's pointing finger, indicating a dark shape sheltering under a wooden lean-to.

"Stay there, Matty. I'll call her over." Forming a funnel with cupped hands, Pinkerton hollered, his words allowing a large plume of vapour to escape. "Come on girl. Over here beautiful."

Waving a tantalising fistful of hay in her direction, the shape slowly emerged from its hideaway and sauntered over to where they stood.

"Should she be out in this weather?"

Knowing nothing other than what humans prefer, Mathew questioned Pinkerton on his ideas concerning animal welfare and in return received his first lesson accompanied by a wry look.

"Contrary to how it looks, it would be cruel to keep a race horse in all day. She's nicely rugged and loves to stretch her legs, even in snow. She's not stupid and knows how to look after herself. I'm right in thinking, aren't I, that you know nothing about horses?"

In her own, seemingly languid way, she closed in on the two spectators standing on the other side of the five bar fence. Through ignorant eyes, Mathew saw why Pinkerton called her beautiful. A long, loping stride gracefully brought her across the snow, stopping no more than three feet away to accept Pinkerton's gift.

"Well, Matty. What do think of her?"

Mathew stood silent, mesmerised by the mare as she searched for another titbit, taking a pace forward to nuzzle Pinkerton's empty hand, turning to search Mathew for replenishment. Slowly, Mathew's hand raised, feeling velvet soft nostrils and warm breath. A community called Twickton became a distant memory.

"What's her name?"

"She hasn't got one yet. Peter Church didn't have time to come up with anything, so it's down to you to think of one."

Allowing time for this special moment to mature, Pinkerton stood aside watching Mathew nurture a fledgling relationship.

"You said she's a racehorse?"

"Yeh, she's a five year old mare with a great pedigree but I've already told you that can mean nothing. She had a foal last year back in Ireland, but it's yet to be seen if she knows how to run and jump."

Slowly, without her noticing, Pinkerton eases a leading rein through the halter and guides her to the gate.

"Come on girl, let's put you to bed for the night." Obediently, without the rein tightening, she followed as if understanding his soothing words. "Once I've given her a brush down and made sure she's okay for the night, we'll go back inside and have another dram. Now you've seen her, I've got a proposition to put to you."

Escorting the mare, Mathew noticed the difference in care in comparison with the pit-pony handlers back at Twickton. Through no fault of their own, the handlers believed every animal worked to exist, often inducing brutality if the animal faltered. Ponies below ground rarely surfaced to witness daylight and existed purely on their ability to haul loaded wagons. Only the hardiest animals survived the criteria of constant slave-like work, little nourishment and an existence of breathing contaminated air.

"Kick those boots off, Matty and get yourself over to the fire. Here, put this down you."

Pinkerton offered another goblet of whiskey, but on this occasion the measure was treble that of the first.

"Don't get me wrong, George, but I've got this funny feeling you're buttering me up for something."

"I'm not doing anything of the sort," the farmer bristled, feeling his intentions questioned. "Since I received Peter's letter, I've been thinking of an idea that might be of interest to you. As you know, Peter bestowed the ownership of the mare into your hands and describes you as a young man with an old head on his shoulders. He also informed me of your background. Now, I know Peter's background and I know he can afford to buy a racehorse and all expenses accrued when owning such animals. Then I look at you and know, apart from what you have in your pocket, you're probably skint. So, what do we do, I ask myself? There's already a small bill owing. Horses don't eat for free, you know, well not on this farm they don't."

Pausing to allow the ramifications of what he said to be absorbed, Pinkerton was about to continue when Mathew cut him short.

"Alright, George. I understand where you're coming from and you're right, I'm skint, but before I got here, I had every intention to make a quick profit and sell her. But now I've seen her, spoken to you and know how much Peter thinks of her, I can't do it. I want to keep the mare, but I don't know how. Maybe you could help me George?"

Inwardly, Pinkerton breathed a sigh of relief. Given instructions, by way of letter, he saw Mathew's qualities described by Peter Church. He also saw similar characteristics to his only son who perished on the frontline about the same time as the Twickton Company suffered at Ypres. Church's directions were not to try and persuade Mathew, but allow him to choose for himself. He needed to hear sincere reasons why Mathew should keep the mare. Unbeknown to Mathew and regardless of the outcome, a private agreement between Church and Pinkerton had already been put into place. If Mathew decided to keep the animal, then Church would finance the expenditure.

"Look, Matty, this is the deal I'm offering. I've got thirty head of cattle and all need milking twice a day. As soon as the weather changes, there's more acreage than I care to count requiring tilling, as well as forty odd sheep soon to be lambing. I've got nobody else to help me apart from a young girl who comes in everyday to give me a hand with the evening milking. You obviously have nowhere to stay so you can live here in the loft. I'll feed and shelter the mare but I'm not doing it for nought. She's as fat as a sow at the moment and needs plenty of exercise before we can think about putting her into training. This is where you'll earn your corn."

Brought up never to expect free handouts, especially from a Yorkshire man, Mathew appreciated Pinkerton's frankness, but there was one part of the deal Pinkerton hadn't accounted for, Mathew's inability to ride. Mathew tried to interrupt, to inform him of this deficiency, but Pinkerton brushed this feeble excuse aside, continuing to outline Mathew's proposed working roster.

"This snow will be lying around for weeks yet, which gives us plenty of time for you to learn how to ride in one of the barns. You are the one who will get her fit, 'cos I haven't got the time. Don't worry, it's roadwork she needs and plenty of it to get rid of those pounds round her belly. I'll get all the paperwork done to register new racing colours and you as the new owner. There's one redeeming factor about this weather, there won't be any racing this side of February, possibly March, and with the war going on it could be a while longer. Plenty of time to get her into proper training. And all I ask for this is a handshake and a gentleman's agreement. If I believe she's fit enough to race and win money, I get forty percent of the purse. What do you say?"

Mathew sat facing the shadowed figure of Pinkerton, his silhouette picked out by the fire burning behind. Such a huge decision and nobody around to ask advice. How he wished for his father's wisdom to confirm he wasn't being taken for the proverbial ride. His suit might be creased especially below the knees where he stuffed his trousers down the necks of gumboots, and he felt ridiculous wearing such clothing in these surroundings.

Trying to find negatives where there weren't any angered Mathew, as Pinkerton's words sounded genuine, but a nagging doubt rang loud in his head, 'if you're going to make a mistake, make sure it's a small one'.

Mathew's passport to a better life lay stabled in the outside barn, but without the financial clout and knowledge to fulfil the mare's true ability, he might just as well have been given a rocking horse. He'd known Pinkerton for less than two hours, but couldn't visualise an alternative offer appearing from the snowbound landscape.

"It's a deal."

A nod of the head, a shake of the hand and refilled whiskey glasses cemented them as partners, but Mathew added a proviso of his own to the agreement.

"When she starts racing, I want you to lend me enough money so as I can have a decent wager on her. That's until I've got enough to lay my own bet."

Pinkerton accepted, smiling reassuringly. He knew Mathew chose his only option.

"We'll start work tomorrow. Don't worry, she won't hurt you, she's a true Christian. It's a sort of blessing in disguise with all this snow lying around. It'll allow us time for her to get to know you. We'll spend the next week inside the long barn, should be enough time to teach you to sit on a horse without falling off and breaking your neck. When the snow melts, all you have to do is trot her round the country lanes at an even pace. Nothing fast, just enough to get her lungs working and with the right food, she'll shed those pounds with no trouble. Not only will it get her fit, your leg will benefit from it as well."

Feeling pleased with himself, Mathew stretched out in his armchair, permitting the heat to mingle alongside the whiskey warming his body.

"I'll have to go into town to get some working gear."

"No need for that. My son was about your size. All his stuff is packed away in the attic. I knew it would come in handy one day."

Unaware of Pinkerton's son demise, Mathew felt humbled by his gesture. It was a terrible thought for Mathew to consider, but the best thing to happen to him was when a piece of shrapnel got wedged in his leg. Coinciding with the emptying of the whiskey bottle, conversation became more lucid. Pinkerton finally informed Mathew of his son's death and enticed his partner to relive his own experiences of what it was like to be surrounded by death, but Mathew fell short of the grisly details, the bits Pinkerton wanted to hear. He made this mistake the last time he was drunk, but knew with Fowler his darker secrets were safe.

Darkness had long descended over the countryside, extenuating a warm, cosy glow from the only illumination emanating from burning embers. Pinkerton suggested they retire early, adding a cheery warning about the volume of work he intended to get through the next day.

"Tomorrow is going to be a long day."

Similar words Mathew had heard before, but this time, there would be no going over the top to face a barrage of gunfire.

CHAPTER 13

The attic where Mathew slept was swathed in darkness when a knock on the door startled him out of his dream filled slumber.

"Mathew, are you awake? Time to get up, lad."

Seemingly in the middle of the night, Mathew uncovered his aching head from under warm blankets and saw Pinkerton's unmistakable shape approaching, picked out by the moonlight shining through a small eyelid window in the rafters. In one hand he held a bundle of clothing, in the other a steaming mug of tea.

"Got a sore head, have we? I've brought you some of my son's old riding gear. Should fit, though on second thoughts, he was a bit bigger than you."

He placed the mug on the floor and spread out a worn pair of jodhpurs, sweater and riding boots on the bedside chair.

"By the time you come downstairs, I'll have some eggs and bacon on the go, one of the privileges of living in the country." Pinkerton winked, letting Mathew into his secret of retaining small luxuries from those less fortunate. "As soon as the sun comes up, I want to get started in the long barn."

***

Snowfall relented during the night to herald a morning canopied in a blue sky. A freezing wind blew across The Dales, welcoming their protectively dressed reappearance outside the farmhouse. Champ, finally unleashed from his housebound restraints, showed his exuberance and liking for deep snow. It wasn't the interior warmth of the barn that first struck Mathew; the sweet smell of hay mingling with an earthy scent of animals hit his nostrils the second the door closed behind them. On hearing human activity, every sheep responded, poking their heads through balustrades surrounding the pen, seeking attention and food. Seemingly knowing each by name, Pinkerton calmly poured forty portions of 'breakfast' as they bayed in unison. Ignoring Mathew, he began a conversation with those more determined to reach the trough, chastising the perpetrators as a father would scold unruly children. Quite how he could stomach taking them to the slaughter house made Mathew wonder. Encouraging this farmyard cacophony, Champ sprinted along the line, snapping at any head daring to protrude more than the others. This was his domain and he belligerently showed who was in command.

For Pinkerton, this daily faffing ritual gave him the most pleasure, leaving Billy as the penultimate receiver of half a bucket of oats. When satisfied all were fed, Pinkerton's world of reality returned, indicating the moment for Mathew to meet the mare once again. From the second they entered, Mathew saw her looking towards them from the half walled stable at the far end of the barn. Calmly waiting her turn, having got used to the fact that she was always last on Pinkerton's feeding roster, she knew she was the one to receive singular attention.

"As I said, Matty. She's not stupid. Look at those big brown eyes. Don't they just melt your very soul? She's something special and she knows it."

Easing the mare to one side of her box, Pinkerton flicked strands of bedding off her backside whilst a wall mounted manger enticed her snout. There was no rush.

"Come in, Matty. She won't hurt you. Allow her time to get used to your smell."

Apprehension didn't hit Mathew immediately, but being so close to such a large animal made him aware of the damage she could cause if she didn't care for his aroma. Cautiously, under Pinkerton's discreet watchful eye, Mathew entered and sidled up to her side. Whilst her lowered head concentrated on eating, his hand felt the soft hair running down to her withers.

"Well, have you thought of a name for her yet?" Pinkerton enquired, throwing a saddlecloth across her back

"No, I haven't. I don't want to rush into it. It's got to be something special."

"You're right, Matt. No hurry. Now go to the tack room and fetch me the saddle and while you're there, bring the bridle hanging above it".

Tentatively, with guidance from his mentor, she obligingly opened her mouth, accepting Mathew's efforts to insert the steel bit between her teeth. Displaying the same nonchalance, the mare didn't flicker when the bridle was placed over her head by fumbling fingers. Pleased with his progress, Mathew buckled the girth, but Pinkerton's stern rebuke brought him back to reality over its tightness.

"She's just eaten, Matt. She's full of air. Lead her out and let her walk around for a few minutes. Then you can tighten it a notch. No, not on that side, lead her on the near side. Her left."

Standing in the centre of the large barn, Pinkerton watched Mathew walk the mare round the perimeter of the indoor paddock.

"This place must have cost you a few bob to put up," Mathew casually questioned from the furthest corner.

"Mind your own bloody business." The rebuke resounded loudly across the sawdust floor. "Another two circuits should do it."

A rising sun filtered light with every passing minute, shining in from highly placed windows circling the barn, bringing not only light, but raising the indoor temperature.

"Lead her into the middle, and let's get you mounted."

Obediently the mare followed Mathew to where Pinkerton stood supervising.

"Now, stand here to the left of her head, take the reins in your left hand and turn your back to her head. Place your left foot in the iron and grab the pommel on top of the saddle with your left hand. That's right. Now pull yourself up so your left leg is straight and then throw your injured leg over her back. Good, that wasn't so bad, was it? You're a natural."

Pinkerton lied, but his enthusiasm prompted Mathew to appear more confident than he was five minutes before.

"How does it feel?" Leading the mare back to the edge, Pinkerton looks up to Mathew sitting stiffly.

"High, isn't it?" Mathew's words didn't come easily. Concentration became his first priority.

"Yeh, it is and remember, it's a bloody sight longer coming down, so keep falling off to a minimum, 'cos it might hurt." Pinkerton laughed, but Mathew felt only danger. "Don't keep waving your hands around like an idiot, rest them on her neck; elbows in and slacken the rein."

Pushing Mathew's heel in, Pinkerton moved the stirrup so it rested under the ball of his foot. Ensuring he mimicked the position with his other foot, Pinkerton started to jog by the side of the mare, cajoling her to break into a trot.

"Oh, my God."

Mathew's jolting voice broke the calmness each time his backside collided with the saddle out of sync with the mare's stride.

"Come on Mathew, concentrate. One-two-one-two. I can't hear you. Count." Pinkerton shouted his orders. "On every second step she takes, lift your arse, boy."

Mathew understood what was being called out, but putting it into practice was a different matter. Each time he thought he'd cracked it, the mare stops in her tracks.

"What do you think you are doing? Kick her on."

Pinkerton bellows from the middle of the barn, having exhausted his stamina after one circuit, allowing Mathew full control of an animal when he had no idea where the brake or accelerator was situated.

"I'm trying. I'm bloody trying. It's impossible. I'll never get the hang of it." Anger replaced Mathew's excitement.

"I say you're trying. You're trying my bloody patience. Do it properly 'cos there's only one thing in the world that I'll accept as impossible."

Mathew looked pleadingly to the centre where Pinkerton stood, amused.

"What's that, George?"

"Juggling custard. Now get your head out of your arse and do it properly. Come on, Matt. Do it."

Nearing the moment when Mathew would willingly capitulate with the devil if it would ease the agony, his bottom hit the saddle softly on the right beat sending him up to bounce again on the right leg.

"That's it, Matt. You've got it. Told you it was easy. Now straighten your back."

Pinkerton's method of teaching wasn't out of a textbook, but in this case it appeared to be working.

"I'm still concentrating on one-two. Straighten your own bleeding back."

It took less than an hour for Mathew's humour to return - Pinkerton knew his plan was going to work out fine.

***

Every morning, just before sunrise, the same ritual took precedence after milking cows, but not before the livestock's breakfast. Safely negotiating the first day's exertions, Mathew's war injury appeared to melt into oblivion compared to the excruciating pain erupting around his buttocks, but a week into this crash course of equestrian education, natural synchronisation of rear parts coinciding with the rhythm of a rising saddle progressed to a slow canter without too much verbal persuasion erupting from his teacher. Each suggestion for improvement was achieved with confidence and a modicum of style.

Laying snow dictated the length of training, but with rising temperatures, a thaw allowed the cows out to safely pasture and the sheep to wander. Champ's impatience at not being allowed to do his job after the enforced winter holiday evaporated once permitted to do what Welsh Collies do best. Racing freely, snapping at any animal stupid enough to disobey, Champ herded the flock exactly to his master's instruction. The end of Mathew's training coincided with the farm getting back into full operation.

In this glorious part of the English countryside, it was easy for Mathew to forget the ravages of war continuing on the continent; and with the Americans joining the allies eight months earlier, the prospect of beating the Bosch had improved.

Woodrow Wilson, the US President, proclaimed a peace settlement, but it fell on deaf ears. Mathew wondered if any of his old platoon were still alive to fight. If the reports in the national press were anything to go by, the Germans still fought to win. It all appeared to be so futile when Mathew read about the loss of life each advance was costing only for the gain to be reversed the following day with more losses. How he wished someone with a modicum of common sense, regardless of which side of the fence he sat, would be brave enough to stand up and call it a draw.

As the sun started to drop out of the sky to end another day, Mathew and Pinkerton walked back to the farmhouse after ushering the cows back into the barn, ready for their second, daily milking. The girl from the village started work again after the lanes became passable, relieving Pinkerton of his more mundane duties, but when asked if Mathew would like to try extracting milk from an udder, the answer was as expected. Even so, Pinkerton trusted the girl, allowing her freedom on most occasions without his guiding influence. She appreciated the responsibility, enjoying the time to invite her boyfriend along for a helping hand. On these particular evenings, it wasn't unusual for Pinkerton to see the two walking home hand-in-hand, later than they should have been after their duties, her back covered in strands of hay.

"You go and wash up, George, while I get dinner ready."

Guided by his mother's ability to rustle up a nourishing meal out of scraps encouraged Mathew to test his skills, as long as the fare didn't go beyond the use of a frying pan.

"Don't worry about that, Matt. We're going into the village for a pint or two. I think we deserve it. Don't get yourself all dolled up, 'cos Billy's taking us. If we get too pissed, he knows his own way back home."

By mid-February, the sun had melted most of the snow, leaving only frosted lumps in sheltered hollows. Graduating from a complete novice into a competent rider, together with Mathew's confidence being fully restored, encircling the surrounding lanes every morning became a daily routine. The pair began with short distances, the mare's fitness barometer dictating the length, but as she progressed the mileage grew. Correct with his assumption, when Pinkerton said not only would the mare's muscle tone return, Mathew's injured leg strengthened to a degree where he no longer limped or felt pain. Arriving back at the farm each morning, Mathew diligently washed the sweat from her coat, grooming it back to its previous velvet-like touch, ready for Pinkerton's inspection. In time, there would be no need to double check Mathew's work.

"You have got to come up with a name for her soon, Matt. I'm waiting to send in the forms for her registration."

Though the daytime temperature rose as the year progressed, the nights still bore a heavy ground frost, instigating the need to keep a roaring fire in the grate. Pinkerton's love of whisky and the need to warm his backside in front of the hearth hadn't changed since the day Mathew arrived. They were becoming close friends despite their age differences.

"You're right, George. Give me a few minutes and I'll come up with a name for her."

Looking down at his fingers, becoming expert at rolling a cigarette, a tinge of pride showed on Mathew's face. Not only was he mastering the art of not dropping tobacco, but blisters, caused by continual rubbing of reins, formed on hard skin. Adding the regained feeling to his backside and the ability to walk without a sign of a limp, he smiled contentedly, feeling very comfortable.

"What you so happy about?" Pinkerton questioned, positioning the whisky glasses for a refill.

"You will never know how good I feel and it's all down to you and the Major." Hardly finishing his impromptu tribute, the mare's future name suddenly flashes across Mathew's eyes. "We'll call her Salvation."

"Yeh, I can see where you're coming from. It's an apt and good name."

Pinkerton passed a goblet full of the amber liquid over to Mathew and raised his own glass.

"Here's to Salvation, and may she have a long and successful life."

Mathew stood, offering up his glass in unison with Pinkerton's. A minute passed in silence with each man pondering on past memories. With true Yorkshire, manly spirit, Pinkerton broke the indulgent interlude before either could sink further into remorseful memories.

"I went to see John Brooks today; he's got the farm in the next valley. Not only is he offering us his horsebox when we need to travel to courses, but his son wants to ride Salvation when she has her first race." Pinkerton's news didn't excite Mathew. "Come on, Matt. He's been riding ever since he was a small kid and is a bloody good amateur for his age. There are not too many jockeys left to pick from, you know? Most have gone to the front and I doubt if we'll be seeing many coming back. Only last week I read Fred Arrowsmith was killed, he won the last running of The Grand National, you know. You're a good rider, Matt, and you have learnt a lot, but this seventeen year old has been riding over jumps for years. Nobody knows him, except the people round here, so when Salvation goes to the course, not only is the mare an unknown quantity, so is the jockey. Don't get me wrong, Matty. What you have done with her has been bloody marvellous, are you getting my drift? We'll get a good price with the bookies. All we have to do is make sure she's fit and good enough and by what I've seen, I believe she is."

Mathew regrettably understood Pinkerton's reasoning, but it did no harm to dream of riding Salvation to her first victory whilst astride her back around the country lanes. In reality he knew his expertise fell way short of what was needed to ride a race.

"You're right, George. It's just..." Mathew couldn't finish the sentence. Pinkerton understood.

February came and went with days getting longer and nights shorter. Pinkerton, taking advantage of the spring like weather, began the laborious effort of tilling his land, leaving Mathew his one and only task of exercising Salvation. Apart from when they met for breakfast, the two lived separate lives until dusk. Some evenings, Pinkerton continued ploughing into the night. Following weak beams of tractor headlights, he worked on, confident in knowing his only paid help was looking after the milking. Though the farm was too big for two people to manage properly, Pinkerton and the girl formed a remarkable team during these war torn years of inaccessible labour

Many miles of continuous roadwork began to reap benefits. Displaying tight muscles, the leather girth around Salvation's stomach required six notches less than when she started. Wallowing in warm sunshine and fed on Pinkerton's special diet, she showed a spring in her step that wasn't there before. After eight weeks of solid, mundane exercise, her transformation was nearly complete. She was resembling a racehorse.

CHAPTER 14

A strange sensation of being in bed with sunlight streaming into his attic bedroom irritated Mathew's eyes from behind closed lids. Regaining consciousness from another alcohol induced sleep, the realisation of where he was and where he should be startled the lethargy from his body, instigating an immediate reaction to sit bolt upright. Since his first night under Pinkerton's roof, regardless of previous evening's indulgences, Pinkerton roused him before dawn. Fear shook his body. Throwing the bedclothes to one side, Mathew leapt out of bed, nearly falling over the solitary chair in his haste to confirm the hour by looking out the small window. The sun was certainly quite high, eight o'clock as near as he could judge, but activity in the closest paddock drew his attention. From his elevated position it appeared Pinkerton was transporting six bales of hay out of the smaller barn with the aid of a trailer and dumping them in a straight line across the grass. Apart from the usual ritual of not being woken before dawn, everything else in the farm appeared normal, with the sheep and cows grazing happily in the distance and Pinkerton whistling a nondescript tune, a sure sign he was in a good mood. Mathew's anxiety was unfounded until Pinkerton noticed his naked torso standing at the attic window.

"Morning, Matty. Enjoy your lay in? Cover yourself up, lad, you'll scare the animals. Get your clobber on and get down here and give me a hand."

There wasn't time for embarrassment as it took Mathew three minutes to be standing by Pinkerton's side.

"What are you doing, George?" Mathew questioned, unsure of Pinkerton's motives. He was acting very strangely with a schoolboy grin creasing his face.

"Today, my son, we're going to see just how well Salvation can jump. Johnny Brooks' kid should be here anytime to put her through her paces, so go and saddle her up while I finish putting this fence together. I've been looking forward to this day for a long time." Pinkerton's excitement was infectious.

Salvation greeted Mathew with her ears pricked. Her eyes sparkled as she anticipated the chance to get out in the morning air and stretch her legs.

"Today's your big day, beauty. Show George what you can do. Make me proud of you."

Seeming to understand her importance, she turned and nuzzled Mathew's arm as the saddle landed over her back.

"Come on girl. It's not the day to get all sentimental."

Meticulously scrutinising her tack for any blemish, an oiled cloth removed a speck of dried mud. Until he was satisfied with her appearance, Mathew was not going to present Salvation to strangers. Standing back, he afforded time to admire her condition and his handiwork. Patting himself on the back, he smiled, knowing he didn't have to be an expert to know she looked stunning.

Leading her out on a loose rein into sunlight, her physique became apparent to the new arrivals anticipating her appearance.

"My word, George. Is this the same animal I saw in your paddock before Christmas? Bloody hell, you've given her a lot of work. She looks bloody marvellous. Look at the sheen on her coat and it's still only spring." Brooks announced, running his hand over the mare's quarters.

"Not me, John." Pinkerton rectified. "I can't take any credit for it. This is the man who has done all the hard work. Let me introduce you to Mathew Hobbs. The owner of Salvation"

The strangers shook hands, Brooks somewhat bemused. Remembering the time when Peter Church laughed at his audacious bid to buy the mare for a sizeable amount of money, Brooks wondered how someone so young and visibly working class could have afforded such a heavy price.

"It's a pleasure to meet you, son. You have done a marvellous job on her. This is my boy, Joey."

Mathew felt uneasy to be greeted by someone his own age, doffing a well-worn cloth cap as a mark of respect.

"Now remember, son. This is the owner of this wonderful beast, so you treat Mister Hobbs as you would any employer."

Joey, a fraction over five and a half feet tall and weighing no more than ten stone, donned a home knitted, roll-neck sweater, disguising an upper body physique capable of making a good welterweight boxer. The rest of his attire was how Mathew imagined a working jockey should appear. Fawn jodhpurs, ankle boots and a tweed cheese-cutter type cap complementing the uniform.

"Pleased to meet you, Mister Hobbs."

"And you, Joey, but for god's sake, my name's Mathew, or Matty, as friends like to call me."

Mathew knew in this instance Salvation would be in good hands.

Fascinated to witness a 'professional' horseman at work, Mathew watched Joey shorten the stirrup leathers before turning to accept a hand on his ankle to assist mounting. Once in the saddle, he stood in the irons, judging the balance; then asked for the girth to be tightened. Unlike the way Pinkerton taught Mathew, Joey's posture appears to be one of a compact ball with his knees drawn up higher than Mathew thought possible to stay aboard.

Lightly patting Salvation on the neck, Joey gently pulled her right ear before bending to whisper something in the other. Seeing Salvation's response to this preening agitated Mathew. He was a little jealous. She appeared to like this preening. Instantly responding to a squeeze of Joey's legs, she gracefully walked away from the three men, her head proudly nodding with each stride as Joey steered her in a figure eight pattern before pulling her up to receive orders.

"Canter her round the edge a few times to warm her up, then approach the fence from this side. Don't let her dawdle, but not too fast the first time."

As the registered trainer, Pinkerton gave the orders; brushing Brooks' attempt to muscle in with his own idea on how his son should approach the fence. Acknowledging Pinkerton with a touch of his cap, Joey let out an inch or two of rein. For the first time, Mathew saw Salvation as a spectator, not as a rider. Her sleek black coat glistened as she cantered to the bottom of the paddock, moving effortlessly to Joey's command.

"You look as though you've got a gooden' there, Matty." Brooks muttered, unable to take his eyes off the action. He wasn't the only one impressed with her action.

"God, she's a good mover." Pinkerton adds to the appraisal.

Mathew didn't t possess the trained eye of the others, but he knew this could be the passport to wealth he'd dreamt about. No one dares to look away as Salvation completes two circuits at a gentle canter. Instead of beginning a third, Joey cuts the corner to steer a central path towards the bales of hay. On seeing the obstacle, Salvation pricked her ears but didn't falter with her approach. Joey, without the need to encourage, sat quietly, letting her find her own range before she took off, clearing the fence without touching a twig, to land on the opposite side running.

Any apprehension Mathew had unknowingly stored up inside was released with a shout of encouragement.

"Go on my girl. You bloody beauty."

145

Pinkerton laughed in unison, throwing his cap down onto the grass. It was the first time Mathew saw what lay under it, never realising he was bald.

"Now Joey. Take her round again, but this time approach at a racing pace."

Acknowledging Pinkerton's shouted order with a raised hand, Joey gently squeezed Salvation on to achieve the intended speed. She appeared to do it effortlessly and cruised round the paddock, taking the same, previous course. Joey again remained still in the saddle, allowing her to gallop towards the fence on a free rein. Pricking her ears, she takes to the air, taking off a full stride before her previous departure.

Mathew heard Brooks and Pinkerton take in a large lungful of air as she sails over the obstacle, only letting it out when she lands on the other side, the same distance away from the obstacle from where she took off.

"Bloody hell." It was unlike Pinkerton to swear, but for confirmation of what he saw he turned to Brooks.

"I don't believe it." Brooks mumbled, equally open-mouthed, his complexion not unlike Pinkerton's when he arrived, but now turning ashen white. "We have got to keep her well and truly under wraps. No one must know about this."

"Joey, go round and jump it again." Pinkerton shouted new orders to confirm Salvation's first effort wasn't a fluke.

This time, Joey takes a tighter line and if anything, approaches the hay bales at a faster speed. As if she knew a small, but elite audience was judging her, she accelerated just as she approached her take off point and flew the fence once again.

Mathew couldn't understand why they were so serious. With what he witnessed, he thought they would be at least as happy with her performance as he was. Suddenly,

Pinkerton and Brooks burst out laughing in unison, each doing a sort of arm held jig on the spot.

"We have got to enter her for the Challenge Cup next month." Brooks enthused, unable to control his excitement.

"What's this 'we' business?" Pinkerton similarly had difficulty speaking.

In their euphoria, they completely forgot Mathew was standing next to them.

"Hey, you two. What's all this Challenge Cup?"

Both stood, staring at Mathew with momentary straight faces; astounded that Mathew couldn't understand the relevance of what was being played out before them.

"You don't understand, do you Matt? You are so lucky to have seen something like this at your young age. I've gone a lifetime and I thought I had seen the best, but boy, that performance beats everything I've seen in the past. Not only have you witnessed something so wonderful, you own the bloody thing."

Unable to console himself, Pinkerton wept. Brooks didn't do much better and sat on the grass, his head bowed.

"Will someone please tell me what's going on?" Mathew implored, trying to bring a sense of reasoning into the discussion.

During this emotion upheaval, Salvation returned to the gathering. Pinkerton grabbed the reins and kissed the mare between her nostrils.

"Mathew, Sir. You have got one hell of a horse. I would deem it an honour to ride her. I can tell already, even after such a short exercise, I have never ridden such a good horse."

As taught by his father, Joey kept his emotions together, but was having difficulty.

"You're the only one round here who I can get any sense out of. Are you telling me you think Salvation will make a good racehorse?" Mathew needed an answer from Joey, as the others appeared to be in a world of their own.

"Believe me when I tell you. If she can get three and a half miles, this horse of yours has the potential to win the Cheltenham Gold Cup. She's brilliant and she's only five years old. She can only get better."

Even with Joey's conformation, Mathew wouldn't allow himself to be sucked into their euphoric state of excitement. It wasn't until Brooks and Pinkerton endorsed Joey's appraisals, but with higher accolades, that Mathew began to tingle with anticipation.

"Are we not in danger of exaggeration here?" Mathew pumped the experts for double confirmation.

"Listen here, you stupid, beautiful bastard. There is not enough available money in the racing world to buy such a wonderful animal as that."

Drunk with happiness by letting his heart overprice the mare, Brooks ratified what Mathew needed to know and finally buried any doubts. He didn't mind Brooks questioning his parentage. He knew he wasn't a bastard. He was a lucky bastard.

Before her exhibition of excellence, Mathew would normally be alone to unsaddle and sponge her down, but on this occasion, three happy helpers joined him. Whilst the two elders fussed, ensuring Salvation hadn't over-reached herself, Joey inspected her feet, flicking out the smallest piece of lodged gravel wedged between foot and shoe. The Maître de Hotel at The Savoy couldn't have offered Salvation better service.

"I've got a very nice bottle of malt inside. I think we should put a big dent in it while we decide her future."

Finally replacing his cap, Pinkerton threw a light blanket over her back, but he couldn't disguise a broad smile. Any plans of tending to his land were forgotten for the day; there were more important things on his mind.

"What were you saying about The Challenge Cup, John?" Pinkerton called from the kitchen, whilst preparing a jug of lemonade exclusively for Joey.

"Middleham Point-to-Point have decided to run a meeting at the end of March. It'll be the first they've held since the outbreak of war. Because the Grand National has been moved down south these last couple of years, there will be a lot of interest up here with plenty of good horses running. Fortunately for us, all the good 'uns are three years older than when they were before the war and the break in racing wouldn't have done them any favours. Not to mention there's £250 up for grabs to the winner."

Brooks' enthusiasm clearly showed as he took it upon himself to retrieve three glasses and the bottle of malt from Pinkerton's private liquor cabinet.

"The prize money is all very nice but what's more interesting is the chance to take money off that scum-bag of a book maker, Manny Heanen, and wipe that oily smirk off his face. I never thought I'd be in the position to bankrupt the bastard" Pinkerton returned, taking up his usual stance with his back to the fire even though it remained unlit. "We know Salvation can jump, so all we have to do is tune her up to be able to travel three miles in a race. We've got three weeks to do it in."

Ignoring Mathew's past efforts with Salvation, Pinkerton turned to Joey.

"Starting tomorrow morning, I want you to put in some healthy speed work with the mare. Keep her down in the valley; along the tow path by the river, it's nice and private there. It runs for about two and a half miles, so we should get some idea how fit she is."

Turning to Brooks, Pinkerton mentioned that the mare should be entered for this race only if he keeps his enthusiasm to himself. Any inclination the bookmakers glean about Salvation's ability will seriously bring down her starting price.

"John, you're a good friend, but I know how your mouth can run away with itself when you've had a few drinks down the pub. Now, tell me. Where do I enter her for the Challenge Cup?"

Understanding Pinkerton's reprimand, Brooks promised to keep what he saw in the paddock a secret. Eagerly accepting a glass of malt whiskey, he began to outline a direction they should take with Salvation's future.

"First of all, I've got to thank you and Matty for allowing Joey the chance to ride such a wonderful animal and allowing me to witness a young horse with so much ability. As a way of saying thank you, I'll pay the required twenty guineas entrance fee for The Challenge Cup. Don't get any ideas I'm getting soft, I'm still the same, mean Yorkshire bastard I have always been. I'll get my money back off Manny Heanen when she wins. Don't worry about the paperwork, I'll do it and get it off to the Middleham Treasurer, tomorrow."

The following two weeks were filled with intense activity in the mornings around Pinkerton's farm. Whilst Pinkerton tried, with Champ's help, to block out the anticipation of the impending race whilst tending his other animals, Mathew and Brooks surveyed Salvation's progress. Beginning with long canters she progressed to prolonged gallops along the prescribed route Pinkerton suggested. Appearing to accept her work with relish, Joey urged her to improve each day. Over a measured distance, Brooks recorded her times whilst Mathew viewed her action through binoculars, occasionally swinging his view round to scan surrounding woodlands for any trespasser who might also be witnessing Salvation's progress. Every lunchtime after the mare had been washed down, groomed and let loose in the paddock to roll about in the fertile brown earth, the four met back at the farmhouse to discuss her morning's progress.

The day was fast approaching when Pinkerton would have to give Mathew the information he'd been badgering for since the day he arrived at the farm. A day didn't go by without Mathew bringing up Peter Church's name into conversations, whether it was by relating insignificant incidents in the trenches, or the fact he wished Church was at the farm to be part of the team nurturing the mare into a quality racehorse.

It was during the evening, three days before the big race, when Pinkerton, standing in his favourite place by the fire, called Mathew in from the barn after bedding Salvation down for the night. Confronted with a fresh bottle of malt sitting on a side table with two glass goblets, Mathew knew Pinkerton was preparing himself for either a long drinking session or an announcement of something profound.

"How is she, Matt?" Pinkerton questioned.

"She's in good heart, but I've got a feeling you've got something on your mind other than Salvation's welfare. You haven't said much this afternoon and it's unusual for you to be so quiet. I know you've got something to offload. What is it you want to say, George?"

Mathew sensed Pinkerton's apprehension; watching him go through his familiar ritual of breaking open a fresh bottle and listen to the gurgle of amber liquid pouring. A minute passes before he decides in his mind the order of what he has to say.

"Do you know the big house standing on Trollops Hill? You must have seen it when you took Salvation out across the valley."

Sitting back, relaxing in his usual chair, Mathew acknowledged the question, whilst swirling a fine malt whiskey. Pinkerton paused, smiling to himself. There weren't too many eighteen year olds he knew who liked this precious tipple. It had taken him years to acquire a taste for it, yet this young man appeared to be born to appreciate the finer things in life.

"Unbeknown to you, the person living there has been keeping a close eye on the progress of Salvation. For the last three months he's watched you and the mare through a pair of binoculars."

Before he continued, Mathew's lower lip drops, accompanied with a worrying look.

"Is he a spy you've warned me about?"

Pinkerton's smile broadened at Mathew's response and naivety.

"No Mathew, it's not a spy. The person living there is Peter Church," he waits for the news to sink in. "He and his family own all this land, as far as the eye can see, it all belongs to them. I'm just a tenant farmer. I've been here for the last twenty-six years, in fact the same year as when Peter was born. During that time, we have become good friends rather than me having to treat him as my employer. When you asked about the long barn, saying it must have cost a few bob to build, I thought you might have guessed I couldn't have afforded to put the thing up. I'm sorry to keep this secret from you all this time, but Peter made me swear not to tell you. He doesn't know I'm telling you now, but I think the time is right. It wouldn't be fair, what with Salvation's first race coming up, if he couldn't be part of the fun. He had such high hopes for her; it would be so cruel if he wasn't part of it, after what he's been through."

Mathew's bottom lip drops further as his body tightens, unconsciously shifting his weight so as to sit on the front edge of the armchair oblivious to his loosening grasp of a whiskey glass, tilting to a point where Pinkerton's precious nectar spills onto the rug under his feet. Instinctive, Pinkerton's first reaction was to break Mathew out of his trance, but seeing Mathew's mind was in another dimension, he waited until Mathew returned.

"I think it would be a nice gesture if you invite Peter to the races on Friday. His wounds have healed quite nicely and I think you are the only one who could get him out of the house. Since he arrived home he hasn't been outside once. I do believe you are the therapy he needs to continue improving. That's the reason why I told you all this."

Slowly rising to his feet, Mathew outstretched his hands as though he was about to shake Pinkerton's, but disregarded the reciprocal gesture and bodily hugged his older friend. Taken somewhat by surprise, Pinkerton's first reaction to push Mathew away relented. Instead, he returned his embrace, looking over Mathew's shoulder, confirming that Brooks hasn't returned to witness a softer side that only his departed wife knew he possessed.

"Come on, Mathew. That's enough of that." Pinkerton eased Mathew away, but held his arms. "You're a good man, Matty. Peter doesn't know you're going to visit, but I think, deep down, he would like to see you."

Burying his chin into his chest, Mathew tried to disguise his emotions, unable to wipe his eyes due to Pinkerton persistently holding his upper arms. Champ squirmed around Pinkerton's feet, uneasy at what was happening. He'd never seen his master behave like this with another human being, let alone with another man. He never showed this amount of emotion with his only son. Maybe he was making up for lost time.

"Go and wash your face before you go over to the big house, but before you do, have another dram. I know I need another one."

CHAPTER 15

A few months earlier, walking two miles would have been unthinkable carrying the type of injury Mathew sustained, but largely due to Salvation, he no longer limped or attracted unwanted attention from good Samaritans intent of giving a helping hand or trying to inveigle a first-hand account on what it was like on the frontline. Carrying only a hidden scar as proof of his participation in the war, he pondered on his reactions when seeing Church's visible credentials.

***

A gravel driveway greets Mathew's approach to Church's home, a large Georgian mansion, its appearance not unlike the Nobles' residence back in Twickton. Contrary to his past eagerness to know of the major's health and whereabouts, apprehension stops him from stepping onto Church's property. Unsure whether to proceed, Mathew camouflages his location behind a brick pier supporting a pair of wrought iron gates from any spying eyes from within.

Mathew's mind drifts back to when he woke after surgery, a time when he met Mary and learnt his life was no longer in danger. Secure in that knowledge, nothing was more important than his quest for information concerning the major's health. Ignorant of Church's situation, Mathew feared the worse having witnessed his hideous injuries, with death the likeliest outcome. To survive such trauma would be rare in a city hospital, let alone a battlefield operating theatre. It was later, when Mary traced Church's medical records, that Mathew learnt of the amputations, but not if he survived surgery. From there, the scent went cold until today. Before, Mathew yearned to know if the major lived. This was only verified by Pinkerton on his arrival in Spennithorne, but now, with proof only a matter of yards away behind an oak front door, Mathew felt uneasy at invading Church's self-imposed privacy.

Slowly, as daylight follows the sun over the horizon bringing darkness, Mathew waits, occasionally peering from his concealment for confirmation of residents with the onset of any illumination within the house, but no clues appear from the windows. Excuses on why he should turn and walk away run freely through his mind. The longer he stares at the bleak house, the more he decides it's futile to stay.

Giving in to feeble reasoning, Mathew turns to retrace his journey back to the farm. Looking over his shoulder for one last look at the mansion's darkened silhouette, a flickering light passing a ground floor window stops him in his tracks. It was all so different to how he expected he would feel after getting news of Church's survival.

A large brass knocker in the shape of a ram's head hangs in the centre of the front door. There is still time to turn and walk away.

Just one knock breaks the evening silence, scattering roosting crows hidden in nearby trees. From Mathew's side of the door, he hears approaching footsteps on a stone floor. The door opens slightly, sufficient to decipher a small figure, but the face is masked by darkness. A weak, female voice enquires the caller's identity.

"My name is Mathew Hobbs. If it is convenient, I would like to see Major Peter Church."

Mathew tries but fails to distinguish if there is another person behind this diminutive woman through the small gap left for conversation.

"I'm sorry, he can't see anybody today."

Politely, the door begins to close.

"That's alright Mrs Freeman. Show Mr Hobbs in," a distant familiar voice counteracts the old lady's first decision.

Mathew's heart races when the door opens wider giving sufficient space to pass. Eyeing him conspicuously, Mrs Freeman beckons; a nervous complaint shakes the hand holding a lit candle. Appearing to be in her late sixties, she's a slight woman, no taller than five feet and obviously a trusted member of the household.

"Please follow me," she orders coldly.

With only one light illuminating the darkened entrance hall, Mathew stays close, following a weaving passage past the main staircase, through a network of smaller corridors. Stopping before she reaches a room at the back of the house, she points towards an open door, the extruding light appearing stronger.

"You will find Mr Church is in there."

Being polite but curt, Mrs Freeman abruptly turns and shuffles back into the darkness; leaving behind a strong impression he isn't welcome. Tentatively, Mathew approaches the opening, dreading what degree of hopelessness lay on the other side. His first view is one of an oblong library, flanked on one wall by ceiling to floor windows overlooking spacious gardens. It's a testament of wealth and furnished with an eye for top quality antiques.

"Hallo Mathew."

Obscured by bookcases covering the other three walls, Church's wheelchair is at the end of the room.

"It's good to see you again."

The voice is how Mathew remembered, but the face is gaunt.

Though the distance between them is only thirty feet, it's a long walk for Mathew. Feeling Church eyeing his every movement, he dared not return visual contact for fear of what he saw.

"At last we meet again, dear friend."

Church's voice is chirpy and not at all how Mathew thought it might be. There is no malice or pain in its tone. It sounds genuinely pleased to see him.

"Hallo, Sir."

Blurting out a greeting, Mathew's trembling vocal cords forewarns what is to come. Emotionally stricken, Mathew bursts into tears and drops to his knees, hugging the seated figure, igniting a depressing atmosphere whenever Peter Church's name was mentioned.

Contrary to how his unaffectionate father would view this prostrate, snivelling figure, Church lays a comforting hand on Mathew's shoulder. Understanding this reaction, Church only wished he could spontaneously show the same emotion. Taught by loveless parents to accept adversity and happiness with identical expressions, Church's compassionate gesture would have been totally out of character had it happened before that fateful morning on the wastelands of the Somme. Huddled together in indescribable conditions, the outsider born into wealth witnessed a brotherhood of six young soldiers bonding under his command. What Church witnessed in the cold light of adversity verified his private belief that males can show true affection for another man.

Totally alien to his placid nature, Peter Church reluctantly volunteered to don a uniform. But this appeasement wasn't sufficient to satisfy his belligerent father who continually voiced his embarrassment about having a civilian son whilst his fellow officer's offspring were either commanding officers on the frontline or buried in makeshift graves. Either of these situations was more acceptable to Sir General Cuthbert Church than having a perceived coward for a son. Closely associated with the First Lord of the Admiralty, Winston Churchill, and to those within the tight confines of the War Office, after hearing of his son's injuries, he freely boasted to anyone willing to listen in the elevated circles of which he mixed. Describing amputations as a badge of bravery, privately he would have preferred the bragging rights to describe how his son achieved a posthumous medal. Peter's debt to his father was final. Though the price he paid was high, it guaranteed the family name remained unblemished. Peter Church could start to live the rest of his life without the burden of parental criticism.

"Come on you stupid bugger. Sit down and join me for a drink. Pinkerton informs me you're rather partial to a drop of scotch."

Tapping Mathew gently on his back, Church slowly eases Mathew away. Sheepishly turning to sit uneasily on a chair opposite, Mathew surreptitiously wipes his face with the cuff of his woollen sweater.

"I'm sorry, Sir. I don't know what came over me."

"Mathew, it's alright. If I don't understand, then no one can. And please, don't keep calling me 'Sir'. Those days are over. I'm Peter, remember?"

Comparing the cold blooded soldier who killed to order, to the civilian sitting before him, Church found the differences astonishing and unless he knew better, couldn't believe this eighteen year old could have witnessed so much devastation in such a young life. Conscious of his disabilities, it would be easy to forget how much this youth had also suffered, mentally and physically.

"You have done a really good job with Salvation. I think the name you've chosen is perfect. I'm sorry about all the cloak and dagger antics Pinkerton and I have put you through, but I needed to be certain your intentions about the mare's future were the same as mine. From what I've seen and heard, she should run a good race on Friday. Pinkerton told me about the day you put her over her first jump. I wish I'd been there to see it. It must have been terribly exciting."

Purposely altering the course of conversation away from the direction it was heading, Mathew's face lightens when Church brings Salvation into the conversation.

"You will see her jump, Peter. I'm taking you to the races and I'm not taking no for an answer, so don't even think about objecting."

"Oh, I don't know about that. It's a nice idea, but how on earth do you think you're going to transport me and this contraption I'm sitting in to the races?"

Making light of his disability, Church points to different parts of the chair outlining the difficulties to try and transport the package ten miles to the racecourse.

"No problem. Brooks is lending us his horsebox. It's got room for two horses, so as we are only taking one, you can occupy the vacant space along with the rest of us."

Smiling at the idea, Church knew his father would disapprove the sharing of a compartment with a horse and servants, but how could he object to the mode of transport when given the opportunity to see the mare's first race? When Church bought the horse a year before, he dreamt of this day. Believing the mare was capable is one thing, but proving it quite is different. This opportunity to assess his judgement of horseflesh was too compelling to refuse.

Thinking of more reasons to persuade Church, Mathew waits for an answer, but is surprised to hear a quick acceptance.

"Good on you, Peter. We'll pick you up on the day of the races. We want to make sure we get there on time, so we'll call round about seven on Friday morning. You better be ready and no ducking out at the last moment."

Mathew's apprehension to this first meeting vanished as quickly as it began. The fact that his commanding officer was sitting in a wheelchair, his legs amputated from the knee down, never became a visual problem. Conversation flowed as much as the whiskey with neither having a problem when returning to the topic of their time on the front line, but the shooting of Colour Sergeant Higgins was never mentioned. Each knew it would bring sobriety to what was a happy reunion. Mrs Freeman affords a smile, putting an ear to the door when hearing raucous laughter. Whoever Mr Hobbs might be, she thought, he is certainly doing her master some good.

It's past midnight when Mathew suggests he should leave. Unsteadily getting to his feet, he follows Church in the direction of the front door.

"It's alright for you in that chair. You can drink as much as you like and still manage to steer yourself in a straight line."

Abruptly Mathew stops, placing a steadying hand on the wall, swearing under his breath for bringing Church's disability back into the conversation.

"Oh, I'll swap with you anytime. You can walk off to the toilet while I have to piss down a tube, but you can borrow the contraption to go home if you like, as long as I get it back for the day at the races. I must warn you though, the brakes are bloody awful and there might be a puddle on the seat where my aim wasn't that good."

Church laughs, crunching his face whilst visualising the prospect.

The mundane art of opening the front door, without Mrs Freeman in attendance, proves to be too difficult for Church and impossible for Mathew, wobbling in the rear and unable to release the wall. Infantile giggling replaces swearing whilst each ponders an escape route, but once the door opens and the cold air hits them, it is clear Mathew is unfit to walk the two miles back to the farm. Unperturbed by his self-inflicted alcoholic disability, Mathew staggers onto the gravel, turning to wave a farewell

"Are you sure you can make it back?" Church calls out, watching from the front door as Mathew approaches the gates. "It might be best if you stay here the night. I've got plenty of empty rooms. It's no problem for Mrs Freeman to make up a bed."

"No thanks, Peter. I'll be all right. It'll do me good to take a walk." Slurring his words, Mathew reassuringly answers.

"Thanks for coming over, Matty. It's been good to see you," Church returns the high-pitched banter, a smile etched on his face.

"See you Friday morning. You'd better be ready."

Mathew waves a final farewell, his voice fading into the distance under a quarter moon, dimly lighting his passage back home.

CHAPTER 17

An inability to sleep prompts Mathew to rise early. Night-light still reigns over the countryside when he enters the kitchen, fumbling in the darkness for the kettle to put on a stove smouldering from the night before and only in need of a rake and a shovel of coal to release heat. Disturbed by the sound of activity, Champ appears wagging his tail. Similar to all dogs, he's a creature of habit, viewing Mathew no longer as a stranger, but someone who will readily administer an early morning tummy-rub to accompany his personal bowl of sweet tea.

Pinkerton surfaces soon after, attired in unwashed overalls to bring the cows in from the far meadow ready for milking. Though the girl and her boyfriend are now working full time, Pinkerton's workload hasn't diminished with the lambing season adding to the burden, but his thoughts are elsewhere on this day. Gambling on fine weather and uncomplicated births, he will leave the farm in the competent hands of the youngsters and take the rest of the day off to go to the races.

Preparation for Salvation's big day begins at daybreak. Starting with a brisk canter round the near paddock to get sleep out of her bones, a chilled rinse-down follows to refresh her senses. Adhering to Pinkerton's orders, whilst she consumes a small breakfast, padded bandages are wrapped around each lower leg for protection on her journey. To complement her pampering, a new blanket rests over her back. In the first, bright rays of a spring morning, she looks stunningly beautiful.

The same cannot be said of Pinkerton. Returning from the fields encased in muddied dungarees, he reappears transformed after twenty minutes of preening, standing at Mathew's side wearing his interpretation of how a countryman should be dressed when attending a prestigious point-to-point meeting. Prompting disbelief in its diversity, Mathew ponders on how many years of expert salesmanship it must have taken for Pinkerton to have assembled such an eclectic ensemble within one wardrobe.

The jacket could only be a one off; woven with the entire range of coloured tweed contained in an intricate, unplanned pattern. Even Salvation pricks her ears when she catches sight of the scary kaleidoscope. The light brown shirt would be fine by itself, but put together with a sky blue cravat and cavalry twill trousers, the final picture resembles the effect of what a force ten gale does on novice sailors.

Allowing the cows, after milking, to trace their way back to the meadow, Pinkerton's helpers delay their intended duties of acting shepherds to join the excitement festering in the farmyard. Initially, bewilderment shows on their faces, each unable to decipher Pinkerton's reason for wearing unseen garments. If it's a fancy dress costume, then surely he would win a prize, but the youngsters try to disguise, with well-placed hands, the compulsion to burst into giggles.

"Kids!" Ignoring their antics, Pinkerton shrugs his shoulders.

Mathew only needs to look at Pinkerton to relieve his building anxiety. Choosing everyday riding gear and deciding not to dress for the occasion, Mathew hopes Brooks doesn't arrive clad to outdo his neighbour. Having one clown in the party is bad enough, but two would surely undermine the seriousness of what lay ahead.

At the prearranged time, Brooks arrives behind the wheel of the horse-box, a converted butcher's delivery wagon and thankfully, disembarks soberly dressed. Amusing banter between the two farmers relieves the tension and reinstates a jocular atmosphere, leaving Mathew and Joey to load the precious cargo. Without hesitation, Salvation follows Mathew up the ramp, settling into her stall like an old professional, seemingly oblivious to the building excitement. Closing the rear of the vehicle, Brooks returns behind the wheel to find Pinkerton sitting beside him.

"What you looking at?" Queries Pinkerton.

"Thought you might want to travel in the back with the others?"

"I'm the bloody trainer and sit where I want to sit, so get a bloody move-on."

Without a written sign on the side to indicate its precious cargo, the budding point-to-point champion and her entourage proceed, stopping only to pick up Peter Church.

Helping Church negotiate the wheelchair down the two steps leading from the front door, Mrs Freeman views the vehicle driving through the open gates.

"Morning Mr Church." Greets Brooks, lowering the ramp at the rear of the vehicle. "Good day for winning some money," he continues flippantly, brought on by the earlier sight of Pinkerton's dress ethics.

"Good morning, Mr Brooks. You appear to be in good spirits," Church replies, ignoring the commotion coming from behind caused by Mrs Freeman and Mathew squabbling as to whom should push the wheelchair up the incline. Naturally, Mrs Freeman wins.

"Good spirits? You just wait a moment. There are few things better to get the morning off to a good start than seeing someone making an absolute arse of themselves."

Brooks laughs, pointing towards the oblivious brunt of the morning's entertainment.

"Morning, Peter."

Pinkerton echoes from inside the horsebox, brushing strayed strands of hay away from the bare floorboards so the wheelchair gets a better grip.

"My word, George. That is some jacket."

Church's understatement confirms his high regard for the sublime.

***

When it came to fuelling industrial machinery, farmers and similar essential providers got priority, accounting for the lack of civilian traffic on the narrow, twisting country roads, resulting in an early arrival before the clock had yet to register the ninth-hour of the morning. Unperturbed by the time, Pinkerton withdraws a pewter flask from a hidden pocket and takes a five-second slurp, drowning any possibility of negative thoughts returning. Confronted by the obstacle of padlocked gates, Brooks finally releases a nervous, white-knuckle grip of the steering wheel and willing accepts the offer, partaking in a dose of the amber tranquilliser. Waiting to enter was not on their itinerary.

Common to most officials handed a subordinate's post, a brown overalled, bowler-hatted steward approaches exactly on the hour. Merely doing his job, clearly learnt over past years, he diligently scrutinises their papers and finally allows entry, never once looking up at the faces staring at him from within the cab. A clipboard in one hand, he points with the other to an empty cordoned area in the distance. The flask is emptied before the handbrake is released, injecting Brooks with the spirit required to negotiate his precious cargo across the dry, rutted meadow to a far corner sheltered by woodland. Having six hours to waste before the main event, Pinkerton lowers the ramp, but halts further movement from those inside the horsebox.

"Now don't get me wrong. Peter." Pinkerton's knack of changing moods from joyous to serious took all by surprise. "But it wouldn't be a good idea if the stewards and bookmakers knew of your connection with Salvation. Everybody knows your ability and wealth would only be associated with good animals, so it would be wise if we didn't mix with you outside in public. One whiff of your involvement would send her price spiralling down like a brick in water, so let's wait until just before the 'off' and after we've laid our bet before joining up."

"You have got a very good point there, George."

Church thoughtfully mulls over the suggestion, having enjoyed the most comfortable of journeys, compared to Mathew and Joey who grabbed anything at hand to stop them being thrown around.

"I'll wait until the crowd assembles, then wheel in amongst them. Here, take this."

Relieving an inside pocket of a roll of bank notes, Church offers Pinkerton money.

"Put this on for me. Using your theory, you're right, the price would tumble if I were to get my money on Salvation before you lot could."

Pinkerton counts the cash.

"Fifty pounds! With what Matty, John and I are putting on, the total comes to £300. Might be difficult to place a bet this size in one go. I don't think Heanen would risk taking it all, even if he thought Salvation stood no chance. He knows me as well as he knows you."

"He's never seen me before."

Butting into the conversation, Mathew's determination to take a bigger part in the proceedings counteracts his previous desire to be aboard Salvation.

"What a good idea."

Church confirms, positively brimming with excitement at the thought of a young miner's son confronting the old adversary.

"Oh, I don't know so much."

Turning to Brooks for support, Pinkerton pours scorn on the suggestion, attempting not to appear disagreeable with the man who pays his wages.

"What are the likes of Manny Heanen going to think when a young lad comes up with £300 to stick on a horse? Someone he has never seen before? He's going to smell a rat. That's for sure"

"No George, I disagree. Knowing Manny as I do, he'll think all his birthdays have come at once. He's a greedy man and if I'm not wrong, will take a quick look at the race card, weigh up Salvation's chances against proven animals and take the lot with eager hands."

Reluctantly, without showing disapproval, Pinkerton agrees, allowing Mathew the responsibility of laying the wager.

Leaving Pinkerton and Brooks squabbling about how Mathew should perform in front of Heanen, Church manoeuvres his chair into a corner out of the breeze and settles under a blanket to catch up with lost sleep, confident he'd made the right choice in Mathew's ability. Pinkerton's concern centred on his appearance; appearing too confident would result in only a portion of the wager taken at fugal odds. Brooks endorses this reservation, but as Church sanctioned the move, who were they to argue? Church, on the other hand, sleeps peacefully. He'd witnessed Mathew in action under far worse conditions than those he might find whilst confronting an unscrupulous bookmaker.

***

Where there were once huge crowds attending the national pastimes of football, rugby, cricket or horse racing, the declaration of war demanded all sporting heroes to be treated the same as spectators, thrown together in a quest for victory by participating in a dangerous game on Europe's most competitive playing fields. In the days before hostilities, expertise to control or hit a ball elevated the few out of poverty, but with the working class dying alongside the privileged, memorable sporting events were something of the past.

Starved of competitive sporting action for four years, elongated lines of enthusiastic supporters formed outside the dilapidated grandstand long before the first race. Hungry for visual action, regardless of which sport was to be played out in front of them, the numbers in the crowd far exceeded those estimated by the governing body entrusted by The West Riding Hunt Association. Blessed by spring morning sunshine, the reinstatement of Yorkshire's premier equine country pursuit couldn't wait to get underway.

Away from prying eyes, the solitary figure of Joey is left to walk Salvation in continuous circles whilst Mathew, Pinkerton and Brooks avoid being connected by prying eyes by taking different routes round the course. The elders decide to deviate onto the course and inspect the ground underfoot, whilst Mathew mingles amongst the ever-growing crowd to pinpoint where Manny Heanen has erected his bookmaking pitch. Church, true to his word, is content to sit in the horsebox studying the race card, picking out who might be Salvation's main rival.

After five races containing mediocre equine talent, the last and most important race is only twenty-five minutes away from start-time. Everybody connected to Salvation congregates back at the horsebox. Mathew diligently inspects the mare's bridle and replaces the heavy, travelling blanket with one of a lighter fabric. Away from the limelight of the changing room, where household named jockeys donned their respective racing colours, Joey strips off in the back of the horsebox, replacing work clothes with a roll neck sweater, diligently knitted by Mrs Brooks in a combination of yellow and purple wools. Standing proudly whilst the others compare the jockey's conservative colours to those of Pinkerton's jacket, Joey prepares to go alone to the weighing room, his racing saddle tucked under his arm. Weighing just over ten stone - the leanest of jockeys in the field, Joey's weight-cloth will require a quantity of lead to bring him in line with steward's mandatory conditions that every runner carries twelve stone.

"It's time you went to get our money on, Mathew," Church suggests, winking at his young prodigy.

"Good luck."

Brooks and Pinkerton respond negatively, quietly suggesting after Mathew's departure, that should anything go wrong, they cannot be held responsible.

Growing in number, the crowds restrict Mathew's progress to the line of bookmakers operating on the rails adjacent to the flimsy, corrugated iron-roofed grandstand. By the time he arrives at his chosen spot, a throng of eager punters, six deep, are struggling to get a wager on their chosen fancy. Mathew joins the frenzy, craning his neck, trying to see what price is being offered on Salvation's chances. Though his chosen prey is only five yards away, he scans other bookmaker's assessment of Salvation's chances against her adversaries and notices differing opinions, but his interest is focused on only one chalkboard, the one advertising the odds offered by Manny Heanen.

In the middle of a line where the crowd appears to be the deepest, the arrogant bookmaker entices punters to part with their money with inflated odds on what he considers 'no-hopers' compared to his competitors' odds. Exaggerating his height by standing on a wooden orange-box alongside a flamboyant sign advertising his name, Manny Heanen scowls at his customers, unaware of Mathew roughly pushing aside those barring his path.

Dressed in black and wearing a face more suitable for a funeral, the wizened character in his sixties charms his customers by making them hate him. Time after time they return to the same bookmaker on the premise that one-day their luck will change.

Mathew stands at a safe distance, listening to the odds being offered and taken up by regular punters seeking financial revenge. To aggravate their animosity further, his accent is more in keeping with those living in East London than here in Yorkshire. Instantly, Mathew understands why Pinkerton and Brooks loath him so much.

"Hey, you," Mathew barks, his voice reaching Heanen's ears above the humdrum of the crowd.

"Yeh, what do you want?"

Heanen's eyes converge on Mathew whilst taking cash from eager hands pushing through the mêlée.

"What price are you offering on Salvation?"

"Can't you see for yourself, sonny? Come on, make a bet or piss off. You're stopping me taking money"

Ignoring Mathew, Heanen turns, concentrating on the cascade of small bets eager to be placed.

"Hey, you ignorant piece of crap. I'm talking to you."

Mathew's ploy works. Instantly, Heanen turns on his box, his stare zeroing into the eyes of the person responsible for the confrontation.

"What did you just say?"

Tightening his body, Heanen's face visibly angers.

"I asked you what price are you offering on Salvation?"

"Oh, so you want special service do you, you little prick?"

Focusing solely on Mathew, Heanen leaves his assistant solely in charge to grab wagers from a forest of outstretched hands. Sardonically, Heanen turns to the board for confirmation of the odds and answers.

"Thirty-three to one. Now piss off and give your two bob to some other poor sod down the line who would welcome your business."

For a person who'd seen many more summers than Mathew, he admires this old man's spirit and smiles, but needs to verbally dig deeper to infuriate Heanen further before being in a position to win this personal confrontation. It is imperative for Heanen to feel confident in holding the upper hand.

"Give me forty to one and you can have my money."

Mathew stands his ground, enjoying the challenge.

Rising to the bait, Heanen's attitude changes for the first time. Un-humorous laughter lines spread across his face when directing his condescending reply to an accountant working alongside a small band of sheepish helpers.

"Obviously this little scrotal bag is deaf. I've told him to piss off, but he's still here. Just get rid of him. Give him the forty to one he wants."

Deliberately turning his back would infuriate most docile characters, but Mathew smiles, content to do business with Heanen's assistant whilst the old man deals with the persistent hordes baying for his attention.

"What do you want, son?"

Heanen's helper is sympathetic, having witnessed unforgivable behaviour from his governor on many occasions. If he could find alternative work, he would, but in these barren times of unemployment, he is grateful to earn a wage.

"Three hundred pound at forty-to-one, please, on Salvation to win," Mathew nonchalantly announces, but loud enough to reach Heanen's ears.

"What the bleeding hell are you playing at?"

Mathew's ploy works, turning Heanen's arrogant manner to one of full attention.

"You're a bookmaker and I'm a punter. I want three hundred pound at forty-to-one on Salvation to win the Challenge Cup. You offered the price and I'm accepting it. I'm not playing at anything; I just want a bet."

"I can't take a bet like that."

With a few chosen words, Mathew's gambit to undermine Heanen in front of the crowd starts to reap benefits.

"Oh. So the big Manny Heanen is afraid to take a bet."

Choosing tactics to drive the nail home, Mathew turns his attention to the crowd who are far more interested in the verbal battle going on before them than they are on placing bets.

"I wouldn't bet with this man. If you pick the winner, I don't think he's got the money to pay you out. Place your bet with someone else. I know I am. This man from down south is all mouth and no balls, like so many from his neck of the woods."

Sensing his day's takings are about to fall into his competitor's purses, Heanen splutters to regain the aura that all had grown to despise.

"Don't listen to this prat. I'm the biggest bookmaker in the north; you all know your bets are safe with me. I'm the richest man on the course. If this kid wants to back a no-hoper at forty-to-one, I'll happily take his money."

The crowd, in awe of Mathew's audacity, watch three hundred pounds change hands. Most had never seen so much money let alone witnessed a bet of such proportions.

"I expect you to be still here, Heanen, when I come to collect my winnings. I have a hundred or so witnesses to prove I put the bet on. So no doing a runner."

Having spoken the last word, Mathew turns towards the crowd, parting as he approaches to let him through as though he is a member of the Royal Family, each staring, wondering how someone of his years and dressed in workman's clothes, could accumulate so much money. A few attempt to follow Mathew's lead by having a few shillings on the mare, but Heanen slashed the odds to single figures. Now, to hand Heanen a knockout blow, all Salvation has to do is win.

Heanen also eyes Mathew's passage away into the distance, wondering much the same as the crowd. In thirty years of being a bookmaker, he'd never been financially threatened. Having attended all the big meetings throughout the country, he used his judgement and guile to never get into a position where his personal fortune was in danger of being transferred into a punter's hand. Though they gave him his wealth, he viewed gamblers with disdain, treating them with total disrespect.

Rudely snatching a race card away from an unwary punter, he searches for Salvation's form. Nothing suggests the mare compares in quality to the rest of the field. A wiser man might have off loaded some of the financial responsibility to another bookmaker, but Heanen can see no reason why he should. In his estimation the mare stands no chance of winning.

Confronted by hordes of eager spectators straining to catch a glimpse of their chosen fancies, Mathew scrambles to reach the packed running rail circling the parade ring. All but one of the sixteen runners are reacting in their own way to the cacophony of sport-starved masses making their presence known with vocal support. As one entrant starts bucking, two more copy, giving their handlers anxious moments. Some show signs of sweating whilst most of the remainder tiptoe nervously. Only Salvation appears unfazed, walking peacefully at Pinkerton's side on a loose leading rein. Waiting for Salvation to approach, Mathew ducks under the rail, joining Pinkerton on the other side of the mare's head.

"Well." Pinkerton's excitement is obvious. "Did you manage to get the bet on?"

"Yes, no trouble. I understand why you hate that arsehole so much. It'll be a pleasure to see his face when we go and pick up our winnings. I hope he doesn't slash his wrists before then because I want to see the look on his face when he parts with all that cash."

Pinkerton laughs, hunching his back, rubbing his hands expectantly.

"What price did you get off the old leech?"

When Mathew answers, Pinkerton punches the air excitedly.

Positioned in the centre of the grass covered parading-ring alongside the other owners and trainers, Brooks stands with his son at his side, nervously anticipating the sound of the bell to ring, indicating that the jockeys should mount. Amongst the frantic activity of the crowd endeavouring to find the best viewing position, Church surreptitiously wheels his chair through the massed gathering. Finding a perfect view of the course, close enough to the winner's enclosure, but far enough away so it appears he has no contact with any of the owners, Church waits until he is sure Mathew has laid the wager before joining the others. The day is too perfect to enjoy this excitement alone.

**

Pulses race as the sound of a brass bell indicates jockeys to get mounted. Bending his left leg at the knee, Joey reaches for the saddle waiting for a leg-up. Once aboard, he anxiously fiddles with the buckle of the stirrup leathers, but drops his whip to the floor. Though once begrudging Joey's involvement, Mathew looks up and smiles at the rider, assured in knowing Pinkerton was right to choose Brooks' son as Salvation's pilot. Handing back the enforcer, Mathew encouragingly slaps Joey's boot.

"Relax. It's going to be alright, Joey, just don't fall off the bleeding thing."

Mathew's smile continues to reassure, but Joey's in return doesn't convey confidence. Confusing the jockey further, Pinkerton and Brooks argue about tactics, voicing their opinion voraciously. Though Salvation remains unaffected, Mathew grabs the leading rein from Pinkerton's grasp, leading the mare away from the turmoil onto the racecourse, leaving the two to argue alone in the middle of an emptying parade ring. Exiting the paddock in race-card order, Mathew follows the other runners parading past the enclosure for the spectators to get their final look at the field before being released to turn and canter off to the start. Excitement is building within the crowd, with spectators and horses alike sensing the electricity.

From his elevated position, a pair of eyes watch the proceedings, noticing how quiet and confident a mare appears compared to a number of fractious runners. He hadn't bothered to check the visual fitness of the runners, he rarely did, relying instead on the volume of money from respected gamblers to suggest the likely winner, but he couldn't help but notice the bristling, tight muscled animal bringing up the rear of the parade. Idly letting his eyes wander to its handler, a shiver runs down his back on seeing the same person who'd laid the hefty bet on a no-hoper named Salvation. Though the sun shines in a clear blue sky, there is a nip in the air, but it's insufficient to quell a sweat building up under his black shirt. Sensing he is about to be on the wrong end of a betting coup, Heanen frantically tries to lay the liability off onto neighbouring bookmakers, but like him, they have noticed Salvation and refuse to take a penny.

"Right Joey."

Mathew makes sure the jockey can hear him above the noise of the crowd and understands what is being said.

"Forget what your father and George told you in the parade ring. I'm the owner of the horse so you ride to my instructions. If you sense they are going too fast, hang back.

Remember it's a three-mile race; so don't take too much out of her on the first circuit. We know she can jump and is fit, so use her qualities and keep her wide of the others just in case something falls in front and brings her down. Go and win it, Joey. Good luck."

Confirming he understood, Joey touches the peak of his racing cap with his whip. Allowing an inch of rein to slip through his fingers, Salvation instantly strides into a canter, following the rest of the field down to the start. Mathew is not religious, but standing alone in the middle of the course watching the entire balance of his life trot away, he raises his eyes to the heavens and offers up a silent prayer.

CHAPTER 18

Deeming it safe to leave his unobtrusive position, Church re-joins his friends by the running rail just as the race is about to start. Viewing the runners through binoculars, Church relays the proceedings to his small group, as the crowd shouting in one voice, confirm his information that the competition is under way.

Before the field reaches the first fence, Mathew picks out his colours in mid-field, but more importantly, Joey is heeding his pre-race instructions and settles Salvation on the wide outside.

"What's Joey doing out there?" Brooks shouts.

"Doing precisely what I told him to do," Mathew answers, not daring to take his eyes off the action. "I told Joey to disregard your instructions."

"What did you do that for? You've been in the game for five minutes and you think you bleeding know it all. She can't win from out there; it'll add on another furlong by the end of the race."

Pinkerton echoes Brooks' anxiety.

"I own the horse, so I decide how she runs. Now be quiet and watch the race."

Church hides a smile as the banter goes back and forth above his head. For obvious reasons he understands why Mathew instructed Joey to take this path and it will only be at the end of the race when his instructions will be judged a mistake or a master-stroke

All seventeen runners clear the first obstacle, but the next fence is an open ditch and will test the ability of most of the field. A gasp from the crowd indicate two of the front-runners falling, but a further three followers get tangled up in the melee and are brought down, prompting the crowd to a higher decibel of disbelief. By the time the runners complete the first circuit and two more miles to the finish, another three competitors have failed to negotiate the course and are no longer amongst the field.

"She's going nicely." Pinkerton announces, his head turning to follow the field galloping past for a second circuit. "But why doesn't Joey bring her infield now there aren't so many runners?"

He looks at Mathew for contradiction to his assessment.

"When the time's right, Joey will do what has to be done. It's easy to criticise from here, we're not sitting on Salvation's back."

Inwardly, Mathew is as apprehensive as the others, but outwardly, he's showing calm. Church notices and is impressed.

Keeping wide of the others, the mare moves up to fourth place, galloping freely on the bridle and appearing to have plenty in hand. Behind her, the strong pace the leaders are setting is beginning to take effect on those who hadn't reached the same stage of fitness, or hadn't the ability.

By the time the field pass the grandstand for the second time, only seven runners remain in the race. Apart from Salvation, the other six represent a quality field, with the previous year's point-to-point champion leading the way going into the final circuit. With the race on in earnest, the favourite makes a long run for home. Every race goer knew of his class and expected the gap between him and the rest to widen, but excitement grows as the crowd of knowledgeable spectators witness an unknown mare come out of the pack to chase the champion, but for four onlookers, their fervour falls on deaf ears.

Not daring to take their eyes off the action unfolding, each rides their own hypothetical race. Amongst the vast crowd, only four know of Salvation's ability and aren't surprised by the quality of her performance, but seeing her actually fulfilling her promise and being in with a chance of winning, prompts statue-like figures rooted to the spot, unable to raise a whimper of encouragement.

Attempting to demoralise his closest pursuer with four fences to be jumped, the favourite stretches three lengths clear of Salvation and tries to widen the gap as the leading jockey endeavours to urge his mount on with hefty slaps of his whip down his mount's flanks. Third place becomes insignificant. The crowd's interest is fully focused on the two front-runners pulling clear of the field.

"Why doesn't Joey get after her and close the gap?"

The noise from the crowd intensifies but Brooks is first to break the four's self-imposed, spell binding silence.

Approaching the third last fence, Salvation remains three lengths down, but Joey appears content to track the leader and isn't asking Salvation any questions concerning her effort.

"He knows what he's doing."

Mathew's words go unheard as nobody dares take their eyes off the athletic dual.

The pace seriously quickens from the front, stretching both horses to their full potential, but this is where the mare begins to show her previously unseen class. Similar to how she displayed her natural skill back at the farm when asked to clear the bales of hay, the faster she gallops, the more spectacular her jumping becomes. Three lengths down with two strides to go at the third last open-ditch, becomes half a length when they land on the opposite side of the fence. The crowd gasp approvingly at her disregard for such an awesome obstacle and start to chant her name in unison even though a large portion have laid a wager on the horse battling it out with her.

Two fences left to negotiate and both sensing glory, Salvation appears to be going the easier, though Joey sits lower in the saddle rattling the reins as encouragement. The response is immediate, flattening back her ears to take up the challenge. If at all possible, their speed quickens with neither animal giving in to the other. The quality of how each horse jumps the last two fences will decide which will be victorious.

The pilot aboard the favourite whirls his crop down the side of his mount, disregarding any displeasure the horse is obviously feeling from such an attack. He's an old pro and never expected to be so hard pressed by an animal and rider he'd never seen or heard of before. Mustering all of his experience into his next action, he switches his whip into his left hand a dozen strides before the penultimate fence. Sensing his victory to be in danger, he skilfully steers the favourite so each animal is no more than a foot apart, then strikes Salvation across her nose with a hefty blow of his crop. The effect is instantaneous. From the grandstand, this incident blends in with the frantic whip waving expected when two horses contest a tight finish, but Church, one of only a few amongst the crowd able to afford such a luxury, witnesses the intentional blow through his binoculars.

"The bastard."

His scream hardly audible above the din of the surrounding crowd.

Cowering away from such a ferocious blow, Salvation gave no warning to her involuntary change of direction. Joey shot out the saddle as momentum dictated, his twisting arms and legs unprotected from the forces of gravity. Miraculously, as the turf beckoned his arrival, a hand grabs her mane. Momentarily restrained from a downward spiral, a leg drops across her back but on the wrong side to stay aboard. Visual disaster is inevitable as the penultimate fence looms into Salvation's sight. In a blink of an eye, the crowd's vocal crescendo drops to silence, every single spectator holding their breath. Expecting the race to be over for the gallant challenger, the crowd suddenly exhale in a single breath, gasping at what the jockey and the mare do next.

Anticipating a refusal, Salvation takes to the air diagonally across the face of the fence. Grabbing anything coming to hand, Joey wraps an arm round her neck whilst his legs swing uncontrollably on the same side of the mare. Defying logic, Salvation lands on her hooves on the other side, her rider attached, albeit running in a wide arc forfeiting many lengths, but still in the race. A deafening crescendo of vocal support erupts, acknowledging Joey's acrobatics to swing a leg over her back and regain the reins. Straightening her course and with no time to locate his stirrups, Joey slaps her once down the withers and punches the reins. If possible the noise increases to accompany the approach to the final fence no more than a hundred yards away. But to those watching this epic encounter, her task appears hopeless.

"That horse is so brave."

Mathew hears a sympathetic supporter cry out from nearby.

Swinging his heals in unison with Salvation's stride, Joey sits deep in the saddle, encouraging his mount. Instructive words from his father come flooding back into Joey's brain, if a horse is giving its all, keep it balanced and don't beat the skin of its body with uncaring slashes of a whip.

Under the exertions of trying to beat off the opposition over the last mile, the leader is starting to falter. His stride shortens and though his backside stings from his rider's efforts, he will do well to retain his position. Looking up at his adversary through Salvations ears, Joey recognised the symptoms of fatigue and asks his mount for a final effort.

Replicating her previous jumping display, Salvation clears the last ditch two lengths down, but the result is never in doubt. Sprinting past a brave, but exhausted favourite, Salvation wins by four lengths going away.

Though punters lose money on the beaten foe, the entire gathering salute her courage with many rushing onto the course to chase after the victor cantering a full furlong past the winning post before pulling up. Joey isn't the only one in tears.

Belying his robust figure and age, Pinkerton swirls Brooks around in a crazy dance oblivious to the way their bodies scatter the humoured crowd standing close. Nobody bothers about such antics, as they know they have witnessed something special between two very brave racehorses. For a few fleeting minutes Church forgets his disability and joins in the raucous celebrations as best he can, but Mathew is missing.

Forcing his way through the congratulating hordes to the middle of the course where the victor stands sweating profusely, Mathew confronts hundreds of strangers. A novice racehorse of her standing might have become agitated by this unfamiliar sight, but she greets these congratulations with pricked ears, as if understanding the enormity of her success. Allowing a forest of hands to touch her without flinching, she stands bloodied, her breathing quick and deep, but showing immense pride. Salvation knew she had done something very special.

"Nice one, Joey."

Mathew shouts up above the noise to his jockey staunching tears with a cuff of his racing colours.

"Come on, let's get the hell out of here."

Gathering the reins hanging loosely round Salvation's neck, Mathew's expression leaves the crowd in no doubt that he wants them to part. Her nose is bleeding badly when she reaches the hallowed unsaddling area reserved for the winner, a sign for all those who missed the incident, of what steps were tried to thwart her victory. Having endured dark times over the last four years in this corner of

Yorkshire, this spark of heroics by an equine unknown lifts the congregating crowd's spirits to a level most had forgotten. Enduring persistent backslapping on his way to the weighing room, Joey's feet barely touch the ground; allowing his body, saddle, plus two stone of lead to be carried by strangers whose legs hadn't been wrapped around a horse's belly, jumped eighteen fences and run over three miles of sodden grass. Not only had Salvation made her mark, the jockey appeared to have made his.

"I'll be out as soon as I can," he shouts over his shoulder, knowing Mathew couldn't leave Salvation. "Then you can go and pay Manny a visit."

True to his word, Joey returns to lead Salvation back to the horsebox after weighing out. The bleeding soon stopped, but the cut across her nostrils would leave a scar, a visible reminder of her first great victory.

Within half an hour of Salvation's memorable victory, most of the crowd were either long departed or dispatched around the course in family groups trying to re-enact the dramas of the day's racing by trying to scale the infamous fences, much to the groundsman's displeasure. A few who'd earlier witnessed Mathew's wager scurried back to the bookmaker's enclosure, encircling one particular turf accountant, eager to see the hated man hand over a fortune to the youngster who dared make the bet. Also gathered in a prime position, Pinkerton, Brooks, and Church wait for Mathew's arrival. A whisper ignites round the gathering as an onlooker spots Mathew's approach. Similar to the fabled parting of the Red Sea, a narrow channel opens for Mathew to stroll up to where Heanen stands aloft on his box. Though envious, they don't begrudge Mathew's fortune. They'd waited a long time to see this day when Heanen would for once turn out to be the big loser.

True to his character, Heanen isn't about to hand over any winnings if he can at all help it, even if it means relinquishing the possibility of never returning to this part of the country. In his mind, he wasn't going to let this minor race meeting ruin his life. If he could escape without payment, he would stay in the south where wealthier punters would use his service, unaware of his antics up north by means of paying off the right people to keep it out of the press.

"What do you want?"

Heanen spits in Mathew's path as he approaches backed up by Pinkerton, Brooks and Church in close attendance.

"Don't be silly, Heanen. You owe me money."

"I'm not paying cheats like you a bleeding penny. When the stewards get wind of this, they'll warn you off every course in England. Putting ringers in a race is illegal. Now piss off before I get the police onto you."

The watching crowd stay silent - even those at the back hear Heanen's every word. Anticipation mounts, as they know it isn't going to end so easily. From the corner of his eye, Heanen just manages to duck under a beer bottle, thrown from some distance only to land harmlessly on the grass behind.

"Pay up, you bastard," a lone voice from the crowd shouts. "Or the next one won't miss."

"You have a certain way with people, don't you Heanen?"

Raising a hand to quell what was starting to resemble a hostile situation, Mathew attempts to reason. A rowdy crowd involving the police might have been Heanen's saving grace to wriggle out of his obligation.

"How long do you think you'll last in this business if you welch on winning bets? You're in a rural part of the country where word spreads like wild fire. Believe me, Heanen. If you don't pay up, it'll be me getting the stewards and police, not you. So let's just settle this like gentlemen. Put it down to experience that when a scruffy kid comes up with a wedge of money, take a good look at the animal before taking the piss out of the bloke trying to have a bet. It wasn't me who took the money off you. The horse did all the work."

A few witnesses voice their opinion and hatred, but the situation calls for calm. Heanen too senses the volatile atmosphere. For all his life he played the odds, learning from an early age to quickly calculate risk. Choosing to remain silent brought him extra time.

"Obviously, you don't carry the sort of money I've won, so I'll take what you have in your satchel and escort you back to where you live, where I dare say the rest is safely stashed away somewhere. Believe me, if I offer five pounds to each man, I will able to muster three large blokes in the crowd, champing-at-the-bit, to join me. Do I make myself clear? Or have you a better solution?"

A low murmur spreads through the gathering, closing tighter around the lone bookmaker, each trying to put themselves in the front line to be one of the chosen three. Watching Mathew delicately deal with the hostile crowd whilst manipulating Heanen into a corner, Church is impressed by his diplomacy in the manner he offers Heanen a perceived escape route whilst threatening repercussions should he not accept.

Surveying the menace in their eyes, Heanen knows time is not on his side, at least, not at this moment. Capitulation appeared the clever route to take. There would be a period in the not too distant future when he would sit with a brandy in hand, comfortably ensconced in his plush, London residence planning retribution.

"Alright."

Pausing through experience to weigh up not too many options, Heanen finally submits, unable to disguise a festering anger waiting to explode.

"I have just over a thousand pounds in my bag and if we can get to the bank in the next town before it closes, I'll give you the rest. We'll take my car."

Showing where he lived in London with four thugs in his car was not considered.

A cheer echoes round the crowd, but for some it's a disappointment, as conflict had appeared a genuine possibility.

"Be careful, Mathew. I don't like the way he gave in so quick."

Heeding Church's warning, Pinkerton and Brooks, oblivious to any repercussions, gleefully rub their hands in anticipation of receiving their winnings.

"I know what you're saying, Peter, but I've got to go along with it. There's no other option. Don't worry, I can look after myself."

***

Whilst Joey departed carrying the precious cargo home in the horsebox, Pinkerton, Brooks, and Church arranged to meet Mathew after the transaction at the Farmer's Inn, a hostelry popular with the racing fraternity in Middleton. True to his word and for added insurance, Mathew chose three of the larger bystanders to be his escort. Having never seen a Rolls Royce let alone been a passenger in one, Mathew and his small entourage couldn't help but be impressed, but unlike his three helpers, Mathew looked upon the car as security if all else failed.

Before the Town Hall clock struck three thirty, Heanen, with Mathew in close attendance, entered the bank, as a cashier was about to bolt the main doors shut. Brushing aside his objections, Heanen demanded to see the manager.

At first, Heanen's request to withdraw such a large amount of money was scoffed at, as being a small provincial bank, they only held a fraction of what was required, but after Mathew reluctantly agreed to accept a bankers draft for the residue, the door slammed shut behind them within twenty minutes of their arrival.

Paying off his helpers with a bonus, Mathew smiled, knowing he would be held responsible for the next day's hangovers as he watched the trio walk straight into the nearest pub. Opposite to their pleasure, Heanen's smouldering anger finally erupts when confronted by Mathew, standing alone without a bodyguard. He'd dealt with threatening people in the past, never flinching when injury was a possibility. In his knowledge that a few pounds in certain directions secured sufficient muscle to scare off most persistent creditors, in this case he assumed he'd scare this young thug off, after all, he was only a kid and his muscle had long departed. What could he do without his three henchmen?

"Now we are alone," whispered Heanen from the side of his mouth, scanning around to be sure he wasn't overheard. "Don't think this is the end of it. If you think you're just going to walk off with twelve grand of my money, you're very much mistaken. Keep one eye looking over your shoulder you little scumbag. I'll be back, and when I return you'll feel the full weight of how miserable I can make your poxy, useless little fucking life."

Mathew listened; understandably nodding his head to what he heard and waited for Heanen to finish his unrehearsed tirade. Regardless of the few locals walking past, he grabbed a shocked Heanen by the lapels of his black suit. The lightweight body posed no resistance to Mathew's strength, the wall of the bank coming to Heanen's aid to halt further progress across the pavement. Lifting the lightweight body, Heanen dangles, his highly polished toecaps six inches above ground level.

"Listen to me, Heanen. If your threats ever materialise, you'll be the first person I'll be coming to see. You wouldn't like me when I get annoyed, so think twice before you do anything. I killed a lot of nasty shits on the front line so another won't make any difference to my conscience. Be warned. Don't do anything that might upset me, but if you do, make sure I'm dead before you leave."

As easily as Heanen was hoisted, Mathew releases his grip, allowing the body to crumple on landing. Bruising the ribcage with a well-aimed kick is tempting, but Mathew overcomes this urge, allowing instead for Heanen to get back to his feet.

"Do I make myself understood?"

Heanen saw a look in Mathew's eyes he hadn't seen before. For the first time he knew he wasn't dealing with an ordinary country boy. He saw a menace in Mathew's face that he'd seen only once or twice before on faces belonging to some of London's most notorious criminals. The knowledge he'd gained over fifty years dealing with London's lowlife told him it was not wise to respond. Driving off at speed into the distance, Heanen knew time was on his side. Whatever he planned, it would require the effect of a stiletto plunged deep into the heart to feel vindicated. No-one was getting away with six thousand pounds of cash alongside a bank draft for another six thousand three hundred.

Approaching The Farmer's Inn, the noise of people enjoying themselves became increasingly audible, but suddenly stopped the second he opened the door to the hostelry. Gathered before him stood a sea of unrecognisable faces, silently staring in his direction, until recognition caused an explosion of cheering. One by one, each shook his hand, congratulating him on Salvation's victory. They introduced themselves with names he would never remember, but a smile and a nod in their direction appeared to appease their curiosity about the owner of the new champion. Recognising a few faces of other owners he'd seen earlier in the paddock necessitated a silently mouthed 'sorry' and a smile as he passed on the way to where three familiar, apprehensive looking faces stared seriously into his, unable to decipher Mathew's blank expression.

"I think it's my round."

Just five small words put an end to their anxiety, turning uncertainty in to uncontrollable laughter. For owners and their entourage of popular winners at the local racecourse, the landlord kept a reserve of Champagne stashed away in the cellar, the price of which would never be considered had Salvation failed, but the champion required toasting, not only by the four involved, but by as many as the Champagne would stretch. Sensing a bonanza and drastic increase in profit, the landlord was only too pleased to rummage around his spider webbed cellar to find anything that went pop when opened.

"You've done bloody marvels today, Matty." Pinkerton acknowledged, handing Mathew a bubbling glass. "I must say I wasn't the only one who thought you gave the wrong orders to Joey, but you proved to all of us that you're not as stupid as you look."

Laughing retrospectively to their earlier gibe on the racecourse, Mathew knew this was the nearest he was going to come to an apology. Ignorant to the intricacies of racing tactics, at the time it seemed the sensible thing to do.

"How did it go with Heanen?" Church diverted the party spirit back to a serious subject.

"Oh, he didn't like it one bit, but after I had a quiet word in his ear, he understood he was doing the right thing."

Mathew winked at Church, but didn't laugh. He understood what was required for Mathew to squeeze Heanen into paying up.

"He could be trouble in future," Church reminded, thinking of past enemies.

"I know, but we have ways of dealing with those sorts of people, haven't we, Peter?"

Pinkerton and Brooks wouldn't allow the sobering conversation go any further and readily filled any glass that appeared to be getting empty. Before the party atmosphere could get into full swing, Mathew called the other three into a quieter corner.

"Look, I've got six thousand pounds in cash in my pocket which is making me feel uneasy. So here are your winnings."

Mathew discreetly handed Brooks and Church their share much to their pleasure.

"I'm afraid you'll have to wait until I cash in the banker's draft before you can have yours," he informed Pinkerton. "But don't worry, George. You can have a thousand of it right now."

Feeling safer, after unloading his financial burden, Mathew wrapped his fingers round the thousand pounds in his own pocket. If Heanen arranged for some of his thugs to rob him, at least his close friends would have been paid off.

"What are you going to do with your share?" Pinkerton asked, directing his question to Church.

"Oh, I'll just put it the bank along with my other bundles," he laughed. "How about you, George?"

Before he could answer, Mathew butted in.

"Oh, he'll put it under his bed alongside his other thousands."

Any dark thoughts disappeared under the infectious laughter spreading throughout the Inn.

"As we have no form of transport to get home, we'd better order a taxi for later before we all get too pissed to do a bloody thing. Don't worry, I'll pay the fare."

Brooks volunteered, ignoring looks of surprise from the landlord and friends who knew of his frugality.

"Don't forget, you lot." Brooks announced before they all got too drunk to remember.

"As Salvation won The Challenge Cup, Mathew and his chosen guests, who by the way are us lot, are the only ones who don't require an invitation to attend the Hunt Ball. We've got to go because that's where they hand over the Cup and the prize money. Its tomorrow night at The

190

Tavistock Hotel. Everybody, whose anybody will be there, so if you haven't got a black tie outfit, treat yourself to one. We can all afford it now thanks to Salvation."

CHAPTER 19

The following morning couldn't come quick enough for Mathew. The excitement he felt was the same as he remembered when he was a boy waking up on Christmas morning. There was so much he needed to do and wasn't sure if there were enough hours in the day to fill everything in.

Before Mathew could fill the kettle, Champ greeted him in the kitchen in his usual way, lying flat on his back, legs in the air waiting for his customary tummy-rub. Surprised his hangover wasn't as bad as it should have been, a sharp submerging of his head under the kitchen cold water tap enlivened his appetite to be ready for a busy day.

In contrast, appearing much the worse for wear, Pinkerton, who unusually sat to give Champ his morning greeting, stood, replacing his hand with the sole of his boot but Champ seemed to like it.

"What are you looking so bloody cheerful for?"

An angry grunt slipped painfully out of Pinkerton's mouth, his eyes fully opening when spotting a mug of tea.

"We've got a busy day ahead, and guess what? To get everything done by lunchtime, I'm volunteering to give you a hand. Then, we are going into town to put this cheque into the bank, have a few beers and buy two of the smartest evening suits money can buy. I want those at that Hunt Ball to know who precisely we are, 'cos you and I know Salvation is one of the best racehorses in the country and I want to announce her arrival from the highest hilltops."

"Steady, lad. All you want to do is rub their noses in it," a coherent mumble echoed from the mug's interior, held closely to Pinkerton lips.

"You might be right, George, but Salvation's victory has guaranteed my future. If she carries on the way she won yesterday, you and I are going become very rich. It would be nice if I can get to speak to my dad when we're in town. I know the Nobles have a telephone in one of their offices." Allowing his mind to drift to his folks in Twickton for a second, Mathew startled Pinkerton with rekindled enthusiasm. "And don't forget, we have to order a taxi to pick up Peter and John. We don't want to be seen rolling up with Billy pulling the cart, now do we. We might not be the part yet, but we're certainly going to look like it. Now get that tea down your throat and let's go."

True to Mathew's word, by lunchtime they had completed the essential chores a farmer laboriously but lovingly undertakes daily. Leaving the farm in the care of the girl and her lover, the evening milking and the flock of lambing sheep were in capable hands. Tilling the fields could wait another day. Salvation, appearing none the worse after her exertions, wallowed under the heat of spring sunshine in the paddock. She could wait to be put away for the night after they got back later that afternoon.

Though they wouldn't admit it to each other, the quartet involved with Salvation privately felt a degree of scepticism before the Challenge Cup, but she'd shown her ability over hales bales had been no fluke by replicating her previous efforts in the arena of competition; defeating the best on offer on the day. It might only have been a point-to-point meeting, but the field was a strong one, including past winners. She performed like a seasoned professional, belying her novice status, and with a few more years under her girth would surely improve sufficiently to be considered a serious contender for the Cheltenham Gold Cup, one of the most prestigious races in the British national hunt calendar. Apart from owning the hottest prospect in the equestrian sport, Mathew's finances allowed the hiring of Joey full-time, not only as her personal jockey, but to take over Salvation's daily care. She deserved special attention.

***

At a lazy pace, Pinkerton steered Billy into the forecourt of The Queen's Head, joining nine other working horses and carts within half an hour of setting out from the farm. Turning a blind eye to having these obstructions preventing wealthier customers from parking their automobiles, the landlord, guaranteed good profit and plenty of manure for his wife's tomato plants, was pleased as they discouraged noisy contraptions from scaring prolific egg laying chickens into unprofitable barren Sunday roasts. At heart, the landlord was a farmer

Spennithorne, a small village nestling a further half mile down the road, boasted a butcher, baker, dairy and a post office. Amongst these essentials, the village also bragged about having one of the finest tailors outside of York. Why Lech Bergman elected to move to this location from his native home in Poland, only he knew, but word quickly circulated of his prowess with a needle and soon became known for his quality of workmanship at prices locals could afford. Over the years Pinkerton got to know him well and was sure if he didn't have any ready-made suits to fit, with his artistry it would only take an hour or two to alter one to Mathew's and his own dimensions.

Seeing as Pinkerton possessed a one-off physique, amazingly, Lech produced a perfectly fitting example of his handiwork, but Mathew posed a bigger problem. Having a clientèle of ageing, overweight farmers, making suits for young, athletic bodied customers never crossed his mind. Mathew was the first to enter his shop of this variety who could afford such a garment.

Apart from the trousers requiring lengthening, the tailed jacket necessitated a complete rebuild. Standing before a long length mirror watching Lech's image scramble around his ankles, slashing tailor's chalk across a multitude of inserted pins, Mathew pondered if he was the same magician responsible for convincing Pinkerton to purchase the tweed jacket. Promising a complete rebuild within two hours, Pinkerton chose to allocate the time with a few beers and friends back at The Queen's Head, whilst Mathew attempted to place a telephone call from the post office.

Despite the fact that Mathew constantly wrote to his parents, he couldn't be sure if they ever received the mail. The last time he spoke to his father was on the day he left to join the army. Surprised by his own apprehension having never used the contraption before, the cashier called from behind the counter confirming she'd made a successful connection.

"Hallo, dad?" Tentatively, Mathew shouted in an abrupt, staccato like voice down the mouthpiece of the receiver.

"Hallo, son." George Hobbs replied. "Bloody hell, it's good to hear your voice again."

From his father's vocal frailty, Mathew felt how he must be reacting to having proof of his youngest son being alive and well.

"We received your last letter a couple of days ago. Tell me, what happened to Salvation. Did she win? I managed to get ten bob on her with the local bookie."

Mathew relaxed, thinking it was typical of his father to enquire about something other than wanting an itemised report on how his leg was repairing, or the state of his health.

"She won, dad. And at forty to one, so go and collect your twenty quid."

Representing the equivalent of twelve weeks working down the mine, he knew his father wouldn't be able to keep his good fortune secret from his mother. Mathew intended to send them a couple of hundred pounds, but until then, his windfall would enable them to pay a few debts and buy a luxury or two.

They talked for twenty minutes and not once did either mention the war. There would be plenty of time in the future to reminisce about those times when newspaper headlines concentrated on test match scores rather than quoting numbers of deaths.

"Well, son. I think it's time to get back to work, or the governor might dock my pay if I'm away from it too long. I've enjoyed using this new contraption. I thought it would die a death, but now I've used it, it's a bloody good idea, isn't it?"

Father and son talked as though there had never been a war to split the family and, by what he heard, his mother's relief at hearing of her son's safe return brought happiness back into the household. With vigour in his step, Mathew collected his suit before joining Pinkerton for a glass or two. Everything in life was perfect.

CHAPTER 20

Coinciding with the last chime of the hall clock indicating the hour of seven, an ordered taxi arrived at the farm. Startled by its punctuality, Pinkerton woke from an alcohol induced slumber, a self-inflicted suffering courtesy of The Queen's Head. Erupting from behind a closed, bedroom door, a ten-minute tirade of vitriolic swearing indicated a momentous struggle to fasten a collar stud. Estimating at least a further ten minutes before Pinkerton's titanic battle was either won or lost, Mathew prepared a welcoming bottle of the farmer's finest malt as an appeaser to greet his eventual arrival. Forgiving his mentor's timekeeping, Mathew privately raised a glass to his health. The taxi could wait.

Heavy, laborious footsteps announced Pinkerton's approach before his imminent appearance. Aiming for Mathew's outstretched hand offering the rejuvenating nectar, his persona belied comparison to anything Mathew had witnessed before. Usually covered under a battered cloth cap, Pinkerton had sculptured what little hair remained into a centre parting, each strand appearing to be separately smeared. Resembling a rotund penguin, Pinkerton rigidly stood, holding a glass in his flipper, waiting for comments. Fearful of bursting buttons from his waistcoat, Mathew bit his bottom lip, nodding approvingly. Confusing mischievous brain cells intent on soiling his pants, Mathew gulped a measure of Pinkerton's finest.

"God! Bloody hell, George. You look erm..."

Few appropriate words came to mind that could embellish this vision.

"You don't look too bad, neither, Matty. Lech did us proud with the suits, don't you think?"

"Yes, not bad, but I thought you told me he was reasonably priced. What the hell, we can afford it. He certainly has worked wonders with you, transforming George Pinkerton from a farmer into er...a gentleman."

The local taxi driver, unable to believe his initial image of the 'elder statesman', continued to confirm his vision in the rear view mirror whilst driving to where Brooks lived.

Mathew's anticipation of Brook's ribald comments was immediately squashed when he matched Pinkerton's appearance, apart from an early flowering rose pinned to the lapel. Only Mathew and the driver appreciated the spectacle of two overweight, ageing characters, sitting side by side. Attempting to appear as if it was an everyday occurrence, each lifted their buttocks, folding their coattails neatly over chubby thighs.

Peter Church, on the other hand, couldn't restrain his humour when Brook's, followed by Pinkerton, disembarked outside the mansion. The occasion was given its final seal of approval when Mathew noticed Mrs Freeman surreptitiously conceal a smile behind a well-placed hand.

"My God, am I going to enjoy this evening," Church blurted out from behind a handkerchief, wiping tears from his eyes.

Appearing at ease in such a suit, Church readily accepted helping hands whilst Brooks manoeuvred the wheelchair into the space reserved for luggage.

***

An illuminated exterior signalled their arrival outside The Tavistock Hotel, their taxi joining a queue of large, expensive automobiles waiting their turn to offload occupants, assisted by an army of commissionaires adroitly positioned to open doors. Viewing the spectacle of Yorkshire's male dignitary disembark from the confines of their automobiles, accompanied by lady-folk of all shapes and sizes flouting their refinery, didn't amuse the four onlookers. Humour died when Church spoke and reminded them.

"Looking at this lot, who would think there's a war going on where our boys are still getting killed?"

Peter Church led the quartet, pushed by Mathew, into the large marble floored foyer rapidly filling with new arrivals being offered aperitifs from alert waiters.

"This is the life, eh Matty?" Pinkerton whispered, elbowing Mathew whilst surveying the throng.

"Peter Church, how good to see you!" a rotund ageing military type, sporting a waxed grey moustache bellowed, greeting Church from a short distance, a quantity of medals spread across his evening suit defying the possibility he'd seen so much action and survived.

"General Johnston, nice to see you," Church responds. "Sorry I can't get up."

Only Church laughed, breaking the icy glares and atmosphere that festered as soon as he appeared, being wheeled in amongst old acquaintances of his father.

"I didn't see your name on the invitation list."

Haughtily, the general enquired, pompously addressing Church, whilst attempting to stretch his height above the seated figure before him.

"No, you're right, General. I didn't receive an invitation, but my two friends and I are with the owner of The Challenge Cup winner, so following tradition, we are the honoured guests."

Dissent bristled from the retired army officer.

"You mean to say one of you is the owner of Salvation?"

Unashamedly staring condescendingly at Church's companions, he scanned for the one who could own such a wonderful animal.

"How do you do, Sir?"

Stepping forward unperturbed, Mathew offered an outstretched hand, but Johnston flippantly disregarded the gesture by turning to shakily walk away, an affliction caused not by a war injury, but by alcohol.

"Are they all like that?" Mathew discretely enquired, eyeing the ever-increasing numbers entering through the vast portals of the hotel.

"Yes, I'm afraid most of them are. I'm just pleased my father isn't here to meet you because he'd be even worse. Still, we shan't worry about these bigoted arseholes. I want to see their faces when you get up on the stage to receive the cup. It'll make my night. Come on, wheel me to where we can get a decent drink."

***

Breaking the banal banter from the foyer below, the master of ceremonies announced from the top of the broad, red carpeted staircase, that the festivities were about to commence in the Grand Ballroom. Replicating Pinkerton's cows patiently waiting to fill allotted milking pens, invited guests slowly filtered towards the sound of a ten-piece orchestra striking up a selection of Strauss waltzes, leaving the four friends marooned in the middle of an empty marbled floor. Waiting until the last guest disappeared over the top step, Church indicated it was time for the three to go into action, one on each wheel whilst Mathew balanced the effort by holding the handles. As a team resembling a military operation, they ascend twenty plush steps.

"May I have your name, please sir? Then I shall show you to your table," a waiter enquired. Dressed similarly to those he served, it was difficult for Mathew to discern who worked there and who were there to enjoy the evening.

"Hobbs."

"It doesn't appear your name is on the list, sir."

"Take another look and tell me where the winning owner and guests of The Challenge Cup sit," Mathew suggested.

"Oh that's different, sir, but I count four in your party and only two places are allocated for that person."

"Look, I'm sure you can lay another two places for my friends," Mathew suggested a compromise, placing a five-pound note into the waiter's breast pocket.

"Thank you, sir, but each table only has eight placings, so it is..."

Gently squeezing the waiter's elbow, Mathew directs him behind a marble pillar before rebuking the seating arrangement.

"The last thing I want to do tonight is get annoyed. So please, just humour me. Be a good chap and show us where to sit. You've had a good tip and if you're a good boy, there's another for you at the end of the night. If you get into trouble with your boss, just point him towards me and I'll take the consequences. Tell him the size of tip you got and if he's sensible, I'll double it for him. Enough said?"

Re-joining his party alongside a smiling but wary waiter, Mathew suggested that Pinkerton finds an unoccupied chair and to follow the waiter to their table.

"I'm so sorry to disturb you ladies and gentlemen, but instead of eight on this table, there shall be ten. So if you wouldn't mind all shuffling up together, the good waiter will lay another two places. I thank you for your cooperation."

Mimicking an accent practiced on a ticket collector, Mathew apologises to his fellow dining companions. Whilst the waiter resigns himself to cater for ten instead of eight, the new arrivals take their places at one of the five front tables reserved for benefactors and guests of the Middleham Hunt.

Elevated, on a stage above the multitude of tables seating the majority, the hunt hierarchy sit alongside a decorated table facing their guests, flanked on each side by the Honourable Chairman and guest for the evening, Sir General Johnston.

Unbeknown to Mathew, Johnston's reign as a serving general had been turbulent, ruling those beneath him in peace time with the same unsympathetic iron fist he showed to those he sent unnecessarily to their death during the Boer War. If it hadn't been for Kitchener censoring the news reports filtering back to Fleet Street, Johnston would have been totally disgraced, not to say court-marshalled. Records concerning his diabolical decision making on the battlefield found their way into files marked 'top secret' and were conveniently placed deep within the ministry away from prying eyes. Unperturbed, his reputation remained unblemished and persisted with arrogance, pomposity and a dependence for alcohol, the cause of many frontline errors.

"I don't want to put a dampener on the evening, but I don't believe we are very welcome," Church whispered, noticing tittle-tattle and finger-pointing from the surrounding neighbourhood, especially the top table on stage.

"Let them pucker my transom."

Translating the cryptic message, Church nigh choked, rescuing a mouthful of red wine with a serviette before it could spurt across the entire table.

Outstaring any who dared prolong the contest, Mathew caught Church's eye who recognised the look transmitted as a signal not to make enemies. If Mathew was to become part of the racing fraternity, these were the same people to befriend. Apart from his three companions, no-one knew of Mathew Hobbs or his background, but if questioned, not one would have guessed that less than six months ago this finely tailored young man toiled under the earth's crust for wages that wouldn't buy a bottle of champagne, a luxury so freely quaffed by tonight's elite. Insecurity could never enter the equation. Adamant not to allow a lack of education to hinder his progress, if Church, the heir to probably the richest family represented on this night, accepted him as an equal, there was no reason why others shouldn't do likewise.

"Could I get you something from the wine cellar?"

Posing the question, the same waiter hovered behind Mathew, a note pad and pencil in hand. If he were to receive another five pound note at the end of the evening, Mathew, though the youngest in the party, appeared to be answering for the others in his party.

Handed a wine list, Mathew's eyes blurred when settling on each unpronounceable name alongside exorbitant prices. His eyes drifted past a distant table, its occupants appearing to be in deep conversation, but all except one. Between candlesticks, bobbing heads and wandering floor staff, Mathew saw a face he knew, but couldn't place. She looked straight at him and smiled. Obviously she knew him, but from where, he couldn't place.

"To start the evening we'll begin with three bottles of your finest Champagne and another three put on ice for when we need them."

Placing his order, Mathew turned, disengaging the stranger's eye contact.

"And over dinner I'll trust your choice to be acceptable with whatever is being served."

Very astute, Church thought, seeing Mathew browse the wine list, totally bewildered by the French names and descriptions of château bottled varieties.

"Shall that be the same number of bottles as the Champagne, sir?"

"Yes, why not. If we require more I shall wave you over."

Allowing the waiter to depart, Church nudged his wheelchair closer to Mathew.

"Please, Mathew, drop that bloody stupid accent. It's not you." Jolted back to reality, it was the first time Church said anything resembling an order since their reunion back at the manor house. He was right of course, if people couldn't accept him for what he was, then they were to be the loser. "I can't help but speak the way I do, neither should you, so be proud of it."

Mathew lifted his glass.

"You're right, of course, Peter. Why do I try to ascend to their level, when they have no intention of sinking to mine? Thank you for everything. And to you two, George and John. I thank you for your friendship."

In unison, the four raised their glasses.

"Waiter, would you offer the other occupants of our table a glass of bubbly? I'm sure they would like one."

From one of apprehension, their wariness disappeared when offered free, expensive liquor, smiling their appreciation and readily joining into conversation.

Over the rim of his glass, Mathew's eyes reverted back to the face in the distance. She smiled once again and raised a hand, daintily wiggling her fingers. Before reciprocating, Mathew checked who she was acknowledging, maybe someone seated behind. A glance over his shoulder confirmed he sat between her gaze and a row of marble pillars. Suddenly, he remembered.

"Won't be long, Peter. I've just seen someone I'm going to marry."

Again, Church spluttered, unable to rescue his drink this time, dribbling down the front of his shirt. Though they'd known each other for only a short time, Church believed nothing what Mathew attempted would shock, but he sat open mouth when Mathew stood and walked off, throwing his serviette back to his chair as an afterthought.

"Hallo, Mary. Of all the places to meet, I didn't think it would be up here. Still nursing the wounded?"

"Hallo, Mathew. You're looking really well and no limp I see. I'm surprised to see you here. I wouldn't have thought this is the sort of place to interest you."

Her face was how he remembered, but out of uniform and in a revealing ball gown, she was the one appearing out of place, as the vast majority of females present would be hard-pressed to be described as feminine.

"I'm here to collect my cup."

She noted a sense of pride in his face, but didn't understand his meaning.

"The Challenge Cup," he confirmed, giving the correct title to his prize.

"You're not telling me you own Salvation?" She appeared pleasantly surprised.

"Yes, I own her. Were you at the races to see her win?"

"No, but everyone I know who was there are thrilled at her performance. You must be very proud of her. Where did you get her from?"

"Oh, that's a long story. Look, I better get back to my table as I'm getting in the way of the waiters. Maybe we could have a dance latter?"

Purposefully cutting their conversation short, he stopped himself from asking the waiter to put another place setting on her table.

"Yes, that would be nice."

She smiled as Mathew turned back to his table. Not daring to take his eyes off the encounter on a neighbouring table, Church noticed Mathew's smile was as broad as hers.

"Who is that beautiful woman?" Church demanded when Mathew arrived back to his seat.

"She looked after me in hospital. She's the nurse who tried to find out how you were. Remember, I told you about her?" answered Mathew, peering back to see she continued looking and smiling in his direction.

"What's this about you getting married to her?" Church warily questioned.

"What do you mean?"

"When you got up from the table, you said you've just seen the girl you're going to marry."

"I didn't say that, did I?"

Church needn't answer, but saw their continuance to hold eye contact across the tables.

The quantity of wine freely flowing contributed to the atmosphere mellowing over dinner. Pinkerton and Brooks found themselves in deep conversation with those sharing the table, verbally re-enacting the race though they'd all been at the course to witness it for themselves. Between the two they consumed more than their share of claret and if Church hadn't intervened and stopped the lighting of the largest Havana cigars the waiter could find before the toast to the King, they would have only brought more rebuffs from those who practiced and understood protocol.

If they could get through the evening without attracting more discredit, Church promised himself; he would teach the two farmers the fineries of etiquette, if that was at all possible. Should Salvation start to win bigger races, he thought, the sooner he began the better.

Mathew, on the other hand, was totally different. Church had no idea how he knew which fork to use with fish, or the differences between a wine and a water glass. Every passing day he learnt a little more about the boy he met in the trenches and couldn't help but admire the skill with which he handled diverse occasions. There would soon come a day when he would sit Mathew down and ask questions about how this youngster, with no educational background, knew so much.

"Ladies and Gentlemen. May I have your attention?" the Master of Ceremonies called from behind the Chairman's position on the top table.

"We now come to the highlight of the evening. Sir General Johnston, on behalf of The Middleham Point-to-Point Trust, shall present The Challenge Cup to the winning owner of this year's race."

Once silence descended around the hall, the General got to his feet. Unsteady at first, but realising he held everyone's attention; he puffed out his chest, rolled his moustache and took a large mouthful of cognac.

Mathew wasn't the only one to notice that his complexion had reddened decidedly since their earlier meeting.

"He's pissed," Mathew discreetly whispered out the side of his mouth for Church to pick up.

"I give him six months to live and that's too long for the old bastard," Church covertly returned the exchange.

After a delay permitting a refilled goblet, he consented to finally speak, his accent more akin to Oxford or Cambridge than to the depths of the Yorkshire Dales. He began by toasting the King, only because he felt a large cigar's weight in one hand ideally balanced a filled glass in the other and the sooner he was rid of this ritual, the sooner he could light it.

"And now we come to the reason why we are all here: to award The Challenge Cup."

He exaggeratedly paused, accepting from a neighbouring diner a match to kindle the object protruding from his mouth.

"In previous years, I have personally known the owners of the victorious animals, but this year, mores the pity, the prize goes to an outsider of our circle, a person I have never heard of and I doubt if anyone else has. It doesn't give me any pleasure to see this coveted prize devalued. Perhaps, next year one of my horses shall be good enough to bring it back where it belongs."

A few of similar ilk to the General stand to applaud, but most greet his summery with polite but soundless acclaim. Having heard the General's vitriolic outbursts on different occasions, Church wasn't surprised by his demeanour, but one glance to his right left him in no doubt what Mathew thought of the speech.

"Steady, Mathew. He's just a drunken old man talking through his arse. Don't rise to the bait."

Mathew sat staring at where the words came from. Guiding the General back to his seat, the Master-of-Ceremonies took over the mantle, calling Mathew up to receive the cup and envelope containing the prize money. He was pleased to hear the applause was stronger than that afforded to the speaker, though many were surprised to see someone so young receiving the cup. An acceptance speech was usual and Mathew wasn't about to let his chance of retaliation disappear. Remembering Church's advice, Mathew raised his head and proudly let forth his strong, Yorkshire accent with volume to those sitting at the back of the ballroom could hear as well as those sitting nearby.

"Thank you for this beautiful prize and the money shall come in handy too," he began, bringing muffled laughter from those before him. "I am extremely fortunate to own such a wonderful horse. I would like to take this opportunity to thank my close friends for making this possible. Without them, I would still be dreaming of receiving such a prestigious prize."

Waiting for the more considerate to finish their light hand-clapping, not one of the seated three was in doubt where he was about to direct his following words.

"I feel I haven't been gracious enough to fully deserve to be standing here. It wasn't I who jumped over those fearsome fences and ran three miles, it was a wonderful mare named Salvation. So for the life of me, I can't understand why a retired army officer should talk the way he does."

He let the muffled banter subside before continuing. He wanted everyone to hear.

"The first things my parents taught me were good manners. I didn't have the privilege of going to a good school to know right from wrong; I had that beaten into me. But from what I've heard tonight from someone who had everything given to him, and should know better, only proves to me one thing. Good manners cannot be taught if the worst sort of arrogance has already been installed. Having been to war and witnessed carnage, the like of which I doubt if our illustrious Chairman got near enough to witness for himself, I take umbrage to being criticised by an ex-high-ranking officer without merit. The same officer who displayed his dislike for me obviously cared little for the men under his command. I have witnessed similar ranking officers ordering soldiers, like myself, to their deaths from the comfort of being outside the range of artillery whilst refreshing their brandy glass. I was one of the lucky ones to return in one piece, albeit with a few scars, but ladies and gentlemen, can I remind you there is still a war going on where our lads are being killed every day. I ask one and all of you to lift your glasses, not to the likes of those who are treating this skirmish as sport, but to those lads who are fighting and willing to give their lives for King and Country."

As one body, everyone in the ballroom got to their feet to raise their glasses. That is all except for two people. One possessed good reason for staying seated. The other was too drunk and arrogant to believe he should stand on an underling's suggestion. Instead of reseating themselves when the Master of Ceremonies raised his hands, tumultuous applause echoed around the ballroom accompanied by cheering.

If anything, it grew louder as Mathew lifted the cup and made his way back to where he sat. Looking through the ecstatic crowd of smiling faces, Mathew tried to pick out the one he wanted to see most. Standing on her chair frantically waving her arms, he saw Mary blow him a kiss

"Nicely said, Mathew. I think you have found a new vocation. You should go into politics. Look at the old fart; I believe any minute he's going to explode."

Imagining the spectacle and the ensuing mess, Church sniggered. Never before had he witnessed the likes of this wealthy landowner derided in such a subtle way in front of so many people of his own ilk. His credibility was questioned by an uneducated youth and for once in his life, couldn't judge or carry out punishment on the subordinate.

It was expected, especially in rural England, that the employer's word was final and woe betide anyone who spoke out against it. But, for Mathew, times were changing and after witnessing what these so called 'Lords of the Land' had achieved by ordering the youth of the nation to commit suicide along a fortified, impenetrable line, he took pleasure in questioning the powers of those who demanded respect against those who earned it.

"I've enjoyed the night. It's also taught me a good lesson. Not that I want to be accepted into their circle, I don't, but I know I shall always be considered by what my background tells them. I think it calls for another drink. Care to join me, Peter?"

With his share of the betting coup, Mathew could afford to be independent and decide his own destiny. Due to Salvation, he knew he possessed the tool to increase his wealth by deploying it into safer investments. Knowing Peter Church was available for uncompromising advice, he wasn't worried about the General Johnston's of this world; it would be the likes of Manny Heanen who would pose the bigger dangers.

Showing no signs of terminating, the party continued long after midnight. Surveying Pinkerton and Brooks drifting into drunken oblivion, Church observed the birth of a new relationship from the discomfort of his wheelchair. Fully aware of the social difference between them, he recognised barriers of class being broken down before his eyes on the dancefloor. To an unknowing bystander, they appeared to be a young, good-looking couple, enjoying each other's company in an environment which would have daunted the less confident.

Where Mathew learnt to waltz, Church could only wonder, but he did so with a sureness he'd shown with everything he attempted. Holding Mary tight to his body, she followed Mathew's steps as they glided across the floor, uncaring to the gossip they created.

CHAPTER 21

Unseasonal weather fooled fragile meadow flowers to bloom early, sprouting up alongside the crops benefiting from premature heat. Beside sunshine, fresh optimism grew with news of faltering German advances along the corridor of the Somme. Enforced the year before by American power amalgamating with their Commonwealth allies, the general consensus was that numbers alone would overwhelm the enemy in the near future. Being one of only a few who'd been on the front line and lived to tell the story, Mathew saw the confrontation differently. Guessing both sides were attempting their last throw of the dice, the victor could be as facile as the first to throw a six. Fortunately for the home war effort, their struggles were now bolstered by the dollar, fresh troops, significantly larger artillery and tanks, invented to crush German occupancy where they once held a stranglehold. Where there was once an ensconced, heavily fortified channel of defiance running from the Netherlands to Switzerland, the Hindenburg Line began showing signs of wear, with punctures appearing in strategic spots. Word also had it, especially in *The Times* editorials, of mutinies, not only in the German navy, but also the army.

On occasions, when Mathew took Salvation down the valley to the river, he would think about these imponderables and what his father said about war. He remembered when they brushed off the snow and sat on a flint wall, when he said men in suits created wars. Usually his father was way off the truth with his theories, but, having lived through the hell, he knew he was right about this one. After the last four, calamitous years, he hoped the British public would see what the faceless civil servants achieved in sending his generation of young, innocent men to their deaths and knew it could never happen again. The ten-inch scar down his right thigh remained a constant reminder of how fortunate he'd been compared to the likes of Peter Church, who, although suffered life changing injuries, survived to see another day.

In times like these it was hard to think positively about the future, but he knew the victors would share the spoils of battle with great growth and capitalisation against those who lost. The best they could expect would be urban decay, starvation, and turmoil. The victorious nations would sweep the world with no other dynasty daring to stand in their way.

In this tranquil part of Yorkshire, it was easy to lie back in the long grass and be content to allow the days to drift pass by just looking at Salvation. Unleashed with the sunlight bouncing off her muscular body, she grazed on succulent fodder, occasionally wandering off no more than a few strides to paddle in the waters. But if he were right in his thinking of an allied victory, there would be untold opportunities for those possessing sufficient capital for investment into the rebirth of not only his nation, but also the entire world. Being a survivor of a decimated generation, he knew this was a once in a lifetime opportunity for a man in his position.

***

"Afternoon, Peter. I thought I'd find you here. You should be outside getting some fresh air. I do believe summer has arrived."

Finding Church in the drawing room overlooking The Dales in the distance, without permission, Mathew pushed open the French windows and pushed Church onto the patio, grabbing a bottle of brandy and two glasses on their way past the cocktail cabinet.

"There're some things I want to discuss with you, Peter."

Recognising a serious tone under the camouflage of a weak smile, Church knew it was easier to listen than contribute when Mathew got into one of these moods. Taking an offered glass, he sat back, waiting until Mathew was ready to say what obviously festered in his mind.

"I've got a feeling this war isn't going to last very much longer and going by what I've read, as it looks like we are going to win, the opportunities are going to fall to those who have got a few quid. Now I know I haven't got that much compared to your fortune, but I thought with your brains and my guile, we should join forces in some sort of business venture. The country is on its arse, so I believe we could make quite an impact. What do you say?"

Since Salvation's win, he saw a new confidence in Mathew he never thought possible in one so young. What Mathew said made sense - he'd been thinking along the same lines himself - but as Mathew only had Salvation to lose, and he had given the horse in the first place, he needed to think of his own financial liability.

"What have you got in mind?"

"Oh, I don't know just yet, but if you were to agree then we have got time on our side to think of a project. One thing we are not, Peter, is stupid. I'm not saying give me an answer now, just think about it. I think Pinkerton has got thoughts of running Salvation in a few more races soon, so that will occupy me for a while. Just think about it. After all, with the contacts you have in high places, we couldn't go wrong."

Church didn't respond, just sat, allowing silence to descend over the private gathering. Mathew didn't expect an immediate answer; he spoke his thoughts and was content to let them be mulled over by his companion. Both knew there was no need to rush into anything without further discussion. Church would consider the proposal and would let the subject lie until Mathew brought it back up again.

Financially secure with trust funds and monthly annuities, Church needn't enter the business world, but what Mathew suggested excited his sense of adventure. Confined to a wheelchair for his entire life seriously damaged his outlook for the future, but with Mathew as a friend and partner, he might just regain the will for a new challenge.

"There's something intriguing about you, Mathew." Interrupting the birdsong perched amongst the clematis draping the rear of the building, Church steered Mathew in a different direction after a pause where both pondered on what had been said. "How do you know how to dance?"

"My mother taught me when I was small. When dad and my two brothers were working down the pit, I used to go for walks with her and usually took the same route taking us past the Noble mansion. You remember, I told you about the family who owned the mine. Well, more often than not, especially during summer months, someone inside the house would be playing music on a gramophone. It was always a Strauss waltz. My mother would take me into her arms and dance with me standing on her shoes. It wasn't long before I picked up the steps and could dance around with her without looking down at my feet. It wasn't anything I boasted about in those days, as, if the other boys got wind of it; they would have smacked me around good and proper. When I heard the music being played at the Ball the other night, it brought back so many memories."

"Was she the one who taught you which knife and fork to use and which glass went with what?"

"Yes. It was a sort of game we used to play. It probably relieved her boredom to have me around. She would set out a table setting with anything we had resembling the proper tool and put a scribbled note under each to say what it was and what it should be used for. In this way, not only did I know what to use, I also learnt how to read and write. Quite a clever lady, my mother. She used to work below stairs in a big house before she married my dad."

Noticing a serene calmness drift over Mathew with his halcyon recollections, Church became envious of the love and affection his parents freely bestowed on their family compared to the dearth of recognition he endured during his childhood. During vacation breaks from boarding school, his nanny took the mantle of surrogate mother when at home. His father, continually absent, preferred to be in uniform surrounded by equally high-ranking officers rather than his family. Being the only child, unlike Mathew, he missed the company of other children his age.

"She sounds a nice person, your mother. I would like to meet her one day."

"You shall, Peter, but you'll have to wait until I go back to Twickton. It could be some time as I won't go back until I can offer them an escape route out of the squalor with enough money so as my dad can leave the mine. I've got to do something quickly because I know one day all the shit in his lungs will kill him."

"Have you seen Mary again?"

The mention of her name snapped Mathew out of his nostalgic daydream and turned to face his questioner.

"Yes I have." Mathew smiled. "A few times, actually." Nothing more needed to be said. Church knew his refusal to expound on the subject meant these liaisons could grow into more than a friendship. "George and Johnny Brooks are joining me down at the local pub at seven for a bite to eat, so why don't you join us, Peter?"

CHAPTER 22

By the end of April, the last meetings of the national hunt racing season were fast approaching and if Salvation was to run again this year, Pinkerton would need to quickly decide if it was worth entering her in another race as preparation for an assault on the larger prizes waiting for her during the following season. Due to hostilities overseas, fewer race meetings had been held, leaving the choice of venues limited to local tracks. But even if the war extended into another year, Salvation still had youth on her side unlike many of her intended rivals. As a novice steeplechaser, she'd proved she could take on and beat the best in this area of northern England, so with one more race and a summer of further schooling, she would only improve for the next season, or when racing was given the green light to get back into full swing.

Word of Salvation's ability spread quickly and took Pinkerton, Brooks, and Mathew by surprise whenever they visited the village. Suddenly, the occupants owned a 'star' of their own to talk about and would turn their conversation towards her well-being when anyone connected to the horse was in the vicinity to answer questions. The most intimidating place for them to visit was the local pub, where groups of local drinkers descended around their table suggesting different races and courses where they thought she might be suited. The Cheltenham Gold Cup and The Grand National were high on their list of suitable engagements.

Being very much a racing novice, Mathew's knowledge of these races remained scant, but guessed they might just be overestimating Salvation's ability to run in such exalted company. Still, he thought, whilst these tougher examinations of equine excellence were scheduled to run in the future, it would extend the time he needed to decide if she was good enough to compete with the best whilst considering her alternative value as a brood mare. So much required consideration concerning the future of such a talented animal.

It was fun to discuss with the local folk where they thought Salvation should take on her next challenge, but unlike his recollection of the days before new-year, he was in a financial position to put reality before daydreams. Never realising the enormity of the animal's popularity within this tight, rural circle, Salvation's name was on every one's lips and they expected to know the route Mathew intended to take with their 'star'. She was their champion and being stabled so close, they were prepared to follow her progress with passion.

On the last racing Saturday of the season, Pinkerton, in conjunction with Brooks' reasoning, decided the mare should take her chances in a three-mile chase at Wetherby, a race course fifty miles south of the farm.

As the strategy used for her first race was successful, it was decided to replicate her training schedule. Joey arrived each morning at the same time and diligently kept to a strict regime so as to get Salvation used to a pattern. Now a race had been earmarked for her, the schedule was stepped up to bring her to peak fitness. When schooled over the 'hay bale fences', Pinkerton, Brooks, Church, and Mathew watched from the side of the paddock. It wasn't as though she needed these extra exercises; it was just she gave so much visual pleasure to the four onlookers. Without too much encouragement from Joey, she mastered the art of clearing these obstacles and appeared to enjoy the chance to show off her skill.

On Wednesday morning, three days before the race, Joey arrived with Brooks to put her through her last piece of speed work. Mathew led her out of the barn, whilst Pinkerton stood ready to saddle her. Joey echoed all their thoughts when he said she looked splendid. Twitching her muscles to dislodge the odd fly, she shimmered in the strong sunlight, her coat appearing to be French polished ebony. Whilst standing patiently for the last tightened buckle, she didn't flinch when Mathew offered Joey a leg up into the saddle. Not even a flock of crows swooping low overhead startled her; instead, she pricked her ears and watched them fly off into a distant meadow.

"Take her down to the river and open her up over the six-furlong mark. She's fit enough for more, but I don't want to leave her form on the gallops. Then walk her over to the next valley to give her something different to look at, then bring her home."

Pinkerton's orders were direct, but simple to adhere to.

***

Mathew fidgeted, peering into the distance from where he expected to see Salvation making her way back. It had been over two hours since the group of three watched her walk off in the direction of the river. Estimating the time it would take for her to achieve Pinkerton's work schedule and to walk back via the route suggested, Mathew knew she was at least an hour overdue.

Unable to restrain his apprehension, Mathew rushed into the barn and harnessed Billy to the cart. Though getting on in years, once the old dray was given his head, he pulled the weight with relative ease and sped through the gate leading to where Pinkerton was mending a broken fence in the far corner of the cow pasture. Seeing what caused his herd to scatter, he immediately knew something was wrong and dropped his tools to lessen the distance between him and the oncoming Billy.

Leaning back on the footplate, giving his legs extra leverage to pull Billy up from his frantic sprint, Mathew halted the cart by the side of breathless Pinkerton.

"What's wrong?" Pinkerton shouted, regaining his breath whilst grabbing Billy's bridle.

"Something's not right, George. Joey should have had Salvation back long ago, but he hasn't appeared yet. I'm worried."

Pinkerton saw the look on Mathew's face.

"You've done right to come and get me. Let's go."

Belying a man of his age, Pinkerton leapt up next to Mathew and took the reins. Turning Billy back in the direction he came, shouts of encouragement replicated the dray's previous effort. Resembling a scene out of an old western film, Billy charged past the farmhouse in the direction of the valley where Joey had taken Salvation. Pinkerton, continuing his verbal tirades, slapped the reins over the dray's quarters whilst Mathew hung on. Billy enjoyed himself, but behind him sat two very worried passengers.

Clearing the small copse, Pinkerton steered Billy down to the toe-path, bringing him under a controllable speed. Lacking recent rainfall, the river was low and barely flowing, but apart from this seasonal dilemma, everything appeared to be as tranquil and normal as it always had been. Following visual, fresh hoof prints in the parched earth, they proceeded along the narrow path keeping to the contours of the river. They had gone no more than two hundred yards along the toe-path when Mathew stood and pointed.

"Oh, my God."

In the distance, they saw Salvation lying on her side with Joey, motionless, curled up in a ball some fifteen yards further on. Pinkerton hauled Billy to a standstill a fair distance from the prone bodies, jumping off the cart running. Before they reached Salvation, Pinkerton grabbed Mathew, stopping him from going further.

"The bastards!"

Screaming at the top of his voice, Pinkerton pointed to the reason why they shouldn't continue to rush in blindly. Straddling the path from a sawn off tree stump on the river side to a fully grown elm towering above the undergrowth, a plaited line of wire stretched tightly across, securely fixed some two feet above the ground.

Using very little imagination, Pinkerton knew what he was about to witness. He had seen the wire only at the last moment, so what chance did Joey have to stop Salvation. From the distance between her hoof marks, Pinkerton estimated Salvation was travelling at full speed and with no warning of what was to come, would have run straight into the razor like wire with obvious repercussions.

Slowly, they approached her prone body. The sight made Mathew turn and empty the contents of his stomach into the river. She was still alive, but her off fore leg had been severed just below the knee joint. On both her rear legs, the skin was scraped down to the bone. Leaving Mathew staring down at the mare, Pinkerton ran to Joey. He was alive, but unconscious. Pinkerton didn't have to be a doctor to be able to diagnose a broken right leg. Kneeling by his side, Pinkerton cradled Joey's head, enticing him out of his trance by talking and lightly tapping his cheek, similar to how the medic prolonged Mathew's life.

"It's no good, Mathew. You'd better take Billy back to the farmhouse and get my shotgun. We can't leave Salvation in agony like that," ordered Pinkerton, shouting, to be understood over the distance separating them, but Mathew heard nothing. "Mathew, for God's sake, man. Pull yourself together. Go and fetch my gun."

Recoiling out of his trance, Mathew slowly nodded. His ashen face a blank canvas of emotion.

"How's Joey?" Lacking volume, Mathew's voice was barely audible.

"He's bad, but I think he'll be alright. Now get off to the farm and if Brooks is still there, tell him to get Doctor Clements out here fast. Once you come back, we can take Joey directly to hospital on the cart. It's the only way to get him out of here. An ambulance wouldn't be able to get down, now get going and be quick."

As ordered, Mathew remounted and sent Billy on his way. Fortunately, Brooks was returning to the farm after visiting Church when Mathew brought Billy to a skidding stop.

"Joey's had a terrible accident with Salvation. Get Doctor Clements."

Unable to understand Mathew's cryptic-like message, Brooks held back Billy's intention to bolt off by grabbing the lose reins and asked Mathew to slow down and repeat what he said.

Reaching above the fire mantle, Mathew dislodged the twelve bore shotgun from its holding brackets and scooped up two of the six cartridges Pinkerton always kept neatly lined up next to the whiskey bottles. There was no need to take more.

Everything appeared to be moving in slow motion. He looked to the heavens, cursing the unknowns responsible for causing his dreams to become nightmares and swore a promise, whoever perpetrated this heinous act would suffer the same fate as Salvation. In a cloud of bewilderment, he sat back on the cart waiting for Brooks to return with the doctor. Billy calmly grazed on lush grass after his exertions, whilst the flock of crows Salvation saw earlier, returned to settle on the farmhouse roof.

By the time Mathew returned, Joey had regained consciousness and was sitting up. As best he could whilst

Mathew was away, Pinkerton removed his shirt and tore it in strips, strapping two small branches on each side of the fractured leg. Mathew stood over the doctor as he inspected Pinkerton's handy work, postponing the inevitable next move.

"Would you like me to do it, Matt?"

Putting his arm round Mathew, Pinkerton saw the agonising decision his young friend was confronted by.

"No. Thank you, George. She was my dream. She'll understand."

Mathew slowly peeled away from the small group, the onlooker's attention diverted to his path leading towards the prone body of the mare. Though in agony, her brown eyes focused on Mathew kneeling to say his final farewell. He felt her breath on his face as he placed a kiss on her forehead. As if under an alcoholic stupor, he stood, unlocking the shotgun to place a cartridge down each barrel. Resting the stock to his shoulder, he looked down the sight. It wasn't a German soldier he saw but two pleading eyes of a fallen loved one.

Lowering the gun slowly to the floor, Mathew removed his jacket.

"Sorry," he whispered, placing the garment over her head, darkening her last view of sunlight.

Two simultaneous shots broke the silence, scattering hidden wildlife from overgrown woodland.

CHAPTER 23

News of Salvation's tragic demise spread quickly around the neighbourhood, though the real cause of here death was sworn to secrecy by the few witnesses. Dreadful as it was, in rural surroundings accidents to animals happen regularly especially to racehorses in training, so it was no surprise when no one questioned the revised version of how she died. Though the villagers took the news badly, showing their grief with mourning similarly displayed to that of dire news coming back from the frontline, the largest black cloud descended over the farmhouse.

For Pinkerton, the death of a prized animal was sad, but he accepted these things happened, though he knew Salvation suffered from the cruellest form of euthanasia. He was a farmer and faced this type of trauma continually, whether it was an accident to one of his herd of prized milkers, or the visit of the slaughter man to do his duty on eight-week-old lambs. But, for Mathew, being a town boy, he hadn't the background to accept this type of death.

Sniper trained, Mathew killed targets when ordered. His victims were a product of war and if given the same opportunity, would readily kill again if given the chance, but their deaths weren't personal, unlike Salvation's.

Normality returned to the farm after the halcyon days of stabling a superstar became a fond memory. Pinkerton simply fell back into a routine of tending to the needs of his stock and the mundane drudgery of tilling acres of fertile soil, but Mathew wallowed in depression, worsened by drinking a sizeable proportion of Pinkerton's stock of whiskey. Even visits from Mary couldn't banish the vivid images of Salvation writhing in agony. Teased with a taste for the better life, Mathew wondered if his chance had come and gone

It was the arrival of the second Saturday after they buried Salvation at the bottom of the meadow where she used to shelter herself under the branches of a hanging oak tree, when Mathew awoke to see Pinkerton standing at the bottom of his bed.

"Morning Mathew. I've brought you up a cup of tea."

"Morning, George. What do I owe this pleasure to?" Mathew questioned his suspicious motives, but wasn't prepared for a side of Pinkerton he'd never seen.

"For the last couple of weeks you've stayed confined to your pit, only getting out of the bloody thing to have a piss or drink my whiskey. Its okay by me if you paid for the privilege to be a drunken slob, but it's my bed and my whiskey you're pouring down your throat, so if you don't move your fucking arse, I'll give it a good kicking. You might be a lot younger and fitter than me, but from where I'm standing, I reckon I can get my boot in before you can throw back the covers. Take your choice. You're wasting not only my time but your own sweet life mourning over Salvation. Yes, I'm sad she's gone, but we can't do anything to get her back, so start doing something else with your life. To start with, Peter wants to see you. So take my advice and get your fucking arse over there as quick as your pathetic body will carry you. If nothing else comes of it, the walk will do you good."

Replicating how his father might have motivated Mathew, Pinkerton made a swift exit, removing any possibility of a confrontation or lame excuse. Being fully aware of his behaviour since Salvation's death, Mathew couldn't lose Pinkerton's friendship or respect, resulting from his own selfish, belligerent behaviour.

Looking at how fate could be so cruel through bloodshot eyes at his mirrored image reflected from a half water filled china basin, Mathew's only gratification was the length of bristle sprouting from below his mouth. Placing a comb under his nostrils, he visualised how a moustache might enhance his appearance, but as growth refused to cultivate in this region, the unsightly fluff protruding from below his bottom lip required removing.

Pinkerton's words, ferociously delivered as though coming from his father's mouth, struck a nerve. Thanks to Salvation, a shortage of money was no longer an issue, but, because of Pinkerton's initial arrangement, the thought of paying a fee for board and lodgings never entered his mind. Much as he'd taken Salvation for granted, he'd reciprocated in the same manner to the farmer's hospitality. His adopted father's outburst shamed him back to reality. The agreed contract, endorsed by a handshake, was cancelled the day Salvation died. Free handouts were a thing of the past.

Rising from his self-indulged mental persecution, Mathew disregarded wearing usual working clothes in favour of the suit he bought in London during days when he hobbled on a walking stick. A stark reminder of when all he possessed was a dream scribbled on the flip side of an order form, today he felt good to be alive, out in the fresh air with the sun on his face and the chance to rethink his future. Since his internment, the countryside had uncontrollably blossomed with lush growth, reminding him of nature's circle of life after winter. Unintentionally, his stride lengthened, his back straightened.

"Good day, Mrs Freeman. You look in fine fettle. I understand Peter wishes to see me."

Church's housekeeper smiled sympathetically, ushering Mathew to follow. No words were spoken. She understood grief only too well. Peter Church sat in his favourite place, overlooking expansive gardens from within the study where Mathew first witnessed the major's injuries.

"Hallo, Mathew. Sit down. It's good to see you up and about again," sympathetically, but warily, Church greeted his friend.

"Why don't we go outside, it's a shame to sit in here on such a beautiful day." Mathew's response was instant, without hesitation.

"Good thinking. I'd like that. I can see you're feeling better."

Hailing Mrs Freeman from the depths of her kitchen, Church beckoned her to follow with a liquor trolley, transporting two glasses and a bottle of his special reserve. Choosing part of the patio where he could turn his wheelchair and face the sun, Church remained silent whilst his housekeeper poured whisky into ice filled goblets. Sensing this to be more than a social gathering, Mathew waited for Mrs Freeman to disappear behind closed doors before breaking the silence.

"It's good to see you again, Peter. What's so important you need to send over a messenger to get me over here?"

"It's good to see you haven't changed, direct and to the point as usual, Matty."

Taking time to refill his glass, Church pondered on how he should begin their conversation. They were alone with no need to whisper behind protective hands.

"If I told you who I thought stretched that wire across the path, what would be your first reaction?"

"I'd kill the bastard."

The fact Mathew didn't think to answer told Church exactly how to proceed.

"Much as I thought."

"Okay, is this a ploy to drink all your whisky before you tell me who it was, or is this a devious plot for me to come over there and murder you?"

"I'm pleased you haven't lost your sense of humour, Mathew," Church responded, but Mathew saw no shred of amusement on his face. "What I have to say is serious business. The night before Salvation went down to the river, two strangers from down south called into The Queen's Head for a drink. Nobody had any reason to take any notice of them, except Bernie the landlord, who started to smell a rat when they began asking questions about Salvation. He thought they were trying to spy on how she was doing and after the performance in her last race, you can't really blame them to try and get first-hand information. They told him they worked for a bookmaker. They wanted to know the form of the mare so they could get one over on the others and price her up accordingly. After getting information about where she was stabled and exercised, they dropped four fivers on the counter for Bernie. You can't blame him for that, but after what happened, he's distraught, because he thinks he's responsible in some way for her death. He doesn't know how she died, but feels if he hadn't said anything she might still be alive today. He came over to tell me this himself and asked me not to tell you as he thought you would hold him responsible. I told him you'd do nothing of the kind and not to be so stupid, but thanked him anyway and said we'd be calling in to have a drink just to show there were no hard feelings," Church allowed time for Mathew to digest the information before continuing. "You know what I think, Mathew, and I did say think. I'm pretty sure Manny Heanen sent these heavies up here to get at Salvation. I've known him for years and it's just the sort of low thing he would take pleasure in doing. After we took all that money off him, I should have known he would try and get revenge. It looks as though he succeeded."

Mathew didn't respond, but Church clearly saw his mouth tighten when mentioning Heanen's name.

"Well, when I asked you what would you do if I told you who killed Salvation? Is the answer still the same?"

Mathew didn't reply; Church knew the answer.

228

Getting to his feet to refill his glass, Mathew looked at the view spreading out as far as the eye could see. The last time he stood in the same position, the trees were in bud and hadn't yet leafed. Oh why, he thought, couldn't life be as simple as the seasons when Mother Nature does it with rhythmical ease?

"Why did I push that bastard so far? If I just stood back for a moment after I realised what a nasty piece of crap he was, this wouldn't have happened. I forgot my father's advice and I shouldn't have done."

Appreciating that Mathew's education relied solely on his parents, Church inquisitively probed for this pearl of wisdom. If it was as good as the rest of the job they'd done on Mathew, then he wanted to hear it.

"My father told me, if I was to make a mistake, make sure it's only a small one."

Simple and yet so poignant, Church thought.

Remembering when those words were spoken returned him to the time he sat with his father on a snow covered wall. This memory of their last meeting uncontrollably moistened his eyes; a tear rolled down Mathew's cheek. Graciously allowing Mathew dignity and privacy, Church turned away. Sometime in their life, men need to cry.

"I want you to listen to some words I learnt when I was at university," Church announced, looking out across his vast acreage, his back to Mathew. "It gave me great strength when things weren't going too well and I still recite them to myself when I have one of my bad days. A poet called *Philip Sidney* wrote them in the sixteenth century and I often wonder what was happening in his life when he put pen to paper.

"'He who shoots at the midday sun, though he be sure he shall never hit the mark; is sure he shall shoot higher than he who aims at a bush'." Allowing time for Mathew to ponder over the meaning of the ancient ode, Church refilled both glasses.

"Strong words."

A voice came from behind.

"Indeed they are, but maybe he had you in mind when he wrote them. I have never known such a strong willed person in my life as you, Mathew, and though at this moment you can't see a way out, someday you might just be the one to hit the sun."

Church turned, witnessing Mathew endeavouring to obscure further tears rolling down his face. Quelling an unusual feeling to reciprocate, Church suffocated this desire by downing his measure in one mouthful.

"Now this is what we should do." Counteracting Mathew's visual depression, Church altered the subject of their conversation. "You and I share a dark secret. If it should ever come to light, both of us would be facing the death penalty. Though it was done in the heat of battle, I don't believe a jury could understand our motive as they weren't there to feel the pressure of being ordered to face certain death by an arse of a coward. We have seen hell and fortunately lived to come through the other side, some more intact than others, but we lived. In my book, Heanen deserves the same as we gave to Colour Sergeant Higgins. We can do it in such a way that it would be extremely hard for the police to prove, let alone pin on us. We'll do it down south where nobody knows us and in a very public place."

"You've planned all this long before I got here, haven't you?" Mathew interrupted; the sad eyes replaced with a smile.

"As a matter of fact, I have. When I heard of Salvation's accident, I knew immediately who was responsible but couldn't prove it. After Bernie came to see me, it wasn't too hard to put two and two together."

"I'll do it, what have I got to lose?" Mathew confirmed his earlier decision with conviction, "That bastard took away the only thing in my life that was valuable, so yes, I'll shoot the bastard...Now what's this plan of yours?"

Wheeling his chair closer to Mathew, Church peered over his shoulder, confirming their privacy, knowing that motivation would not be required.

"In my study, under lock and key, I have the identical weapon you used so effectively on the front line. A Lee Enfield snipers rifle with a telescopic sight. Don't ask me where I got it, just say, when you have a bank balance the size of mine, anything can be bought, especially in these hard up days. My spies tell me Heanen has been setting up a book all over racecourses in the south. What we have to do is wait for a big meeting, Sandown or Kempton for example. The more people gathered the better so we can mingle in with the crowd. Then we find a good spot where you can get an unobstructed view of the prey and hey presto, one dead, rotten bastard. Let's face it Mathew, nobody is going to miss the little shit. He has no family, only a dog. And if the word going round his manor is correct, he even kicks the shit out of that little bugger."

"But there's one thing you haven't thought of, Peter. Don't tell me someone isn't going to hear the sound of the rifle going off. Those things make one hell of a bang." Thinking he might have dampened Church's enthusiasm, Mathew was wrong.

"Amongst all those people, and there will be a lot of them, there are bound to be plenty of automobiles. You've heard the way they backfire, just like a rifle going off. After they have heard a few misfires from a Roller or two, nobody will bat an eyelid. The most important thing is to find the ideal spot to do the job."

"How are we going to carry the gun onto the course? It's not the sort of thing we can easily hide."

Repeating the same theme of doubt, Mathew acted as devil's advocate.

"Thought of that. You might have noticed."

Mathew's excitement became visible, accompanying each suggestion why they shouldn't attempt such a risky adventure, Church countered with feasible solutions.

"I'm a cripple and I need a chair to get around. Add a few modifications to the contraption and we can hide the weapon inside. What do you say? Don't worry, I'm quite a dab-hand with a chisel, drill and a bag of screws."

At first it worried Mathew, but a chameleon-like demeanour transformed Church back to when he was in the trenches.

"Okay, but what if..."

Before Mathew raised further doubts, Church grabbed his hand. It was to be the reunion of an officer giving his subordinate a silent order.

"There will be no mistakes. I guarantee it. Time is on our side, so we don't need to rush into making hasty decisions. First of all, I suggest we go down south when the next big meeting is scheduled. We can note if Heanen is there and where he pitches his stall, as they usually stay in the same place for the whole season. Then we scout around for the best vantage point. Apart from all this, we have got plenty of Heanen's money to have a jolly good time."

"You're enjoying this, aren't you?" Mathew interrupted Church's ebullience.

"I say I am. Bugger the Bosch. I get more fun out of killing our own. Some deserve it more than others and if it wasn't Heanen, I can think of another one right now who I'd love to see a bullet between his eyes."

Their covert whispers disintegrated, each rocking with laughter in their respective chairs. To seal the agreement, a further drink was poured. Reasoning returned to their conversation, but it was something Church said that worried Mathew. He knew he wanted the bookmaker assassinated, but who was the other one?

"If they can make their minds up about this bloody war, the first decent meeting next season is scheduled for

September at Sandown Park. We'll go down south and reconnoitre the place."

Mathew looked puzzled, not quite understanding.

"Ah, I've found a word you don't understand. One up to me. It means we'll go and have a good look at the place before we do any killing. But before we do any of that, I have a little surprise for you; we're going on a short holiday. I've written to a friend of the family, Lord Kilbrook. I've just received his reply. He says he'd be only too pleased to see me again for a spot of hunting. Although the season's just finished, he writes to say we are welcome to have a bit of fun; after all, as he reminds me, we are still at war and who's going to complain if we are a little late with our sporting demands? Not Kilbrook, he owns most of the land up there. So, go home and pack a small bag. We are off to Scotland tomorrow morning to shoot us a stag. It's been a little while since you picked up a rifle, so let's see if you've still got what it takes to kill a moving target."

CHAPTER 24

Seemingly perched on top of the world, Mathew visually circumnavigated the landscape spreading across the highlands of Scotland. Entombed to endure twenty-four hours of uninterrupted motorised travel, Yorkshire's beauty paled into insignificance when confronted by the vista stretching beyond his visual capability. Last season's snow, still visible on the peaks, had melted in the glens. For two weary travellers, this majestic vista conjured reasons why artists came for inspiration and insight on how to spread ingeniously mixed kaleidoscopic colours without leaving a resemblance of a join.

Though tedious, they travelled in comfort, care of Laird Kilbrook's *Rolls Royce,* coinciding their arrival to *Bora* with fading afternoon light. Their chauffeur, MacTavish, showed his skill at negotiating high twisting hilltop passes and narrow country lanes were clearly inadequate and probably more suited to having reins than a steering wheel in his hands.

"We'll stay at the inn tonight and take full advantage of what this little town by the North Sea has to offer. It boasts one of the best Tweed manufacturers in Scotland and is just the place to get you kitted out in proper hunting attire. Don't worry, Mathew. You can afford it. If you want to be the part, you have to look it," Church bristled with excitement

Whilst spending many youthful months in the region under the watchful eye of his tutor, Kilbrook, Church became proficient when selecting suitable clothing for the climate, manufactured from Scotland's indigenous woven wool trade. Appreciating the workmanship and quality of *Tweed,* Church became an expert, his love of the fabric coinciding with his first taste of malt whiskey. Administered at an early age by his drinking partner, the Laird, he knew Mathew would enjoy sampling the diverse flavours from Scotland's quality distillers, Kilbrook's cellar housing one of the finest collections.

"We'll stay a day or two, so they can knock you up a jacket and while we're at it, you might as well get some shirts, plus fours and boots. The weather up here can change drastically in the space of a few minutes, so you have to be ready and dressed for any inconvenience. Once wet and cold, you stay wet and cold and that spells danger. We'll forget about a kilt. We want to attract animals, not scare the buggers away."

***

As Church predicted, Mathew left *Bora* equipped to endure any changeable climate indicated on a mercury barometer, compensating the weight of an additional suitcase against the lightness of his wallet. Backtracking from *Bora,* fierce combustion explosions manufactured from an overworked engine alerted their host of their imminent arrival at the hunting lodge on the shores of *Loch Buidhe.* Any animal foolish enough to have wandered into the vicinity had long been scared off. Whilst MacTavish laboriously unloaded their luggage, Mathew, Church and the Laird retired to the spacious baronial living quarters, a cathedral sized window encapsulating the arena where Mathew's victim roamed, unaware of its fate. Uncoiling from the MacTavish induced tension, they sat, relaxing in front of a blazing log fire, sampling a welcoming dram of Kilbrook's finest.

"Nice to meet you, Mathew. It's good to put a face to the person Peter wrote about. Looks as though you two saw a bit of action together, eh. I know he must have shown his appreciation, but may I add my thanks for getting him off the battlefield alive. It must have been pretty hairy out there."

Mathew's picture of Kilbrook before they met was different to reality. His accent was southern, possibly from London and younger than the image Church painted. University educated, Kilbrook inherited the title from his deceased father a few years earlier, the death coinciding with his escape from mandatory conscription. Burying himself in an inhospitable wilderness exhausted the most diligent hunter hell-bent on conscripting him at the nearest barracks, not that he shunned serving his country. Cocooned in comfort, the castle-like edifice offered sanctuary from those believing his past service record depicting a surviving captain in the Boer War didn't excuse him from further duty. Inheriting wealth, Kilbrook believed his dying on some far flung ravaged battlefield would be such a waste.

"I can see you have spent some time in *Bora*." Kilbrook continued, indicating Mathew's Tweed jacket. "Good pattern. It was one of my father's favourites. I suspect Peter might have been instrumental in helping you with your choice," he smiled, appreciating the gesture of wearing a morsel reminding him of his benefactor.

Dinner was a sumptuous affair, prepared with delicate precision by MacTavish's wife. Clear evidence of Kilbrook's lifestyle in this outpost of colonial Britain contradicted the shortages suffered by most of the Empire's population.

"I hope you can shoot, Mathew, because the last thing we want is leaving a wounded animal on the uplands dying a slow death."

Kilbrook directed the conversation to why they made their journey. Anticipating trench warfare stories were about to enter after dinner banter, Church rescued Mathew's obvious reticence to answer.

"Oh, you don't have to worry about that, Hamish. He can shoot all right. I've witnessed what he can do with a rifle."

Surprised at Church's ability to continue recalling without remorse, the damage a sniper's bullet can inflict on the human body, the conversation drifted swiftly onto more macabre recollections, these verbal, vivid descriptions conflicting with the agreement Mathew made with Church to never discuss glorifying death. Images ripped from Mathew's memory for use as decadent laughter prompted a question of why killings were being treated in the same way as a humorous music-hall variety act. Considering Church's injuries, Mathew failed to understand why he continually made light of tragedy. A psychiatrist's report analysing Church's behaviour would make interesting bedtime reading, but maybe in an uncomplicated way, these trivialisations of carnage simply disguised his demons.

"And I don't have to ask you if you can ride. Peter described you as a natural horseman. Shame about Salvation, but you must have had a lot of fun with her while it lasted. Tomorrow, we'll set out on an animal a little slower than what you're used to, Mathew. My ponies might be sedate, but they are strong as an ox and sure-footed. Don't worry, Peter, I haven't forgotten you. Just because you haven't got legs doesn't mean you're not coming with us. I've had one of my saddles specially adapted. Even if we have to strap you in the bloody thing, you're coming with us."

Laughter resounded, but Mathew couldn't comprehend their incessant preoccupation with morbidity. He'd seen superior officers on the front line do exactly the same thing.

Maybe, he thought, it was an upper class affliction to make light of other's misery.

A forgotten aroma, similar to frying bacon, wafted under Mathew's nostrils when awakening, enlivening his senses from the pounded they received the night before when emptying the port decanter before moving onto the malt. Attired in newly woven Scottish wool, Mathew inspected his mirrored image. Somewhat smug, but satisfied, he traced the wafting invitation drifting up the staircase from the kitchen below.

"Morning, Mathew!" Kilbrook's raucous greeting bellowed from the opposite side of a large kitchen table, the site of their previous night's debauchery but now cleared of all incriminating evidence. "Sit yourself down."

Church acknowledged Mathew's presence by raising his face from a plateful of fried deer liver. "These are wonderful, Mathew. You must try them. I'd forgotten how good they taste."

Utilising every minute of daylight, their departure was timed with the sun's appearance over the eastern end of the loch. Two of Kilbrook's stalkers hoisted Church aboard his adapted saddle before mounting to form a line of five riders leading a sixth unsaddled pony at the rear, supposedly to shoulder the weight of a dead carcass back to the lodge. Kilbrook was adamant, there would be a kill.

Adapting the low sun to be their compass, the party headed towards *Beinn Domhnaill,* a protrusion predominately rising in an area of the Highlands Kilbrook and his stalkers knew well. Sure of a downwind approach to the moorland glen, the head stalker scanned distant heather with binoculars for signs of movement.

"I believe we're getting close," Church whispered, encouraging his mount to draw alongside Mathew.

Casually, trained to keep sudden movements to a minimum, the lead rider held up his hand, gesturing for the party to quietly dismount. The party, mimicking the stalkers, silently slid from their mounts, leaving Church aloft until conformation of a stag's harem on the upper slopes could be confirmed.

"Hey, you," Church hissed at the nearest stalker. "Get me down from here. I don't want to miss any of this."

"Come over here, Mathew, and take your choice." Kilbrook beckoned quietly, unfastening a leather rifle case containing three weapons strapped to the side of his pony. Releasing one at a time, Mathew judged the weight of each before putting his eye to the sight. He chose the Lee Enfield, before selecting an appropriate cartridge from a smiling Laird's open hand. "I thought you might choose that rifle; a proper sniper's weapon. Here, take a few more shells. You might need them."

Ignoring the offer, Mathew traced the head stalkers footsteps, covertly following the direction whilst Church, straddling a stalker's back, brought up the rear towards a bracken covered ridge. The flora, complementing the shades of their woollen jackets into perfect camouflage, performed as a perfect mattress for five spanned out bodies, lying flat on their stomachs in a straight line. Whilst Church and the two stalkers studied the target through binoculars, Kilbrook sidled up to Mathew's side. ,

"Unwisely, you decided not to take more shells and personally, I believe you've made a juvenile mistake with just the one. Maybe you're trying to impress me, I don't know, but I'm not a forgiving person. If I have to grab your gun and finish off your botched handiwork, I won't be pleased. I've heard Peter describe you as an expert shot, but I'm yet to be convinced a youth from your background can achieve such skill. I'd say it's damn near impossible"

Wary of Kilbrook's sycophantic praise from their first meeting, his derogatory warning, out of Church's earshot, confirming a wariness of his concealed, nasty demeanour. Whether Kilbrook purposely tried to disillusion Church by undermining Mathew's ability, hoping nervousness might affect his trigger finger, only time would tell. The kinship between Church and Kilbrook was not as it appeared to be. Something wasn't right.

***

Oblivious to the hidden party's intentions, a herd numbering seven females grazed on the opposite side of the glen. Mathew placed the single shell in the breach, allowing the well-oiled bolt to silently position the bullet in place, ready for firing. Exonerating the novice hunter from the dilemma of choosing the target, four experienced heads huddled together; corroborating whispered words with pointing fingers, unanimously indicating which sanctioned animal was destined for a dinner plate. Covertly vacating his position, leaving the debating society to find their chosen viewing slot, Kilbrook sidled through the dense bracken to inform the marksman of their chosen target.

"Now Mathew, listen carefully. Aim at the heart. It's located just above the foreleg, six inches above the shoulder. Hitting the target with the velocity of the bullet should instantly floor her. Kenny has chosen a lame doe hanging back from the others who appear to be ostracising her. Unlike the battlefield when one of your chums gets injured, in the animal world your so called mates leave you behind to die." Kilbrook turned to his master stalker.

"Kenny, estimate how far away she is."

Looking through binoculars, the head stalker didn't rush his judgement. Cannily assessing an air of competition between his paymaster and the young lad, his valuation would be vital to ensure an even playing field.

"I would estimate a little over a thousand yards, but there is also a fluctuating breeze cutting across the glen from left to right. It's a very difficult shot. I think it might be better if we get closer, 'cos I don't want to be chasing an injured animal all day just to put her out of her misery. The beast deserves better than that."

After assessment from his most trusted hunter, Kilbrook looked at Mathew, his expression questioning if Mathew wanted to continue. Clearly reluctant to permit a shot taken from this distance, the stalkers had witnessed Kilbrook's acquaintances in the past wound targets from much closer range, only to be left to clear up the mess long after the hierarchy departed back to the comfort and warmth of the lodge. They looked upon Mathew as yet another youthful sibling descendent from a rich, southern family. Unaware of the truth, the stalker's consensus was to move closer, but Mathew shook his head. Being under examination from accomplished hunters he appreciated the difficulty of making a perfect kill, but they'd not witnessed him dismantle a brain under duress from nearly twice the distance.

To Mathew's left, Church lay close. Obscured by lush undergrowth, his discreet arm folded over Mathew's shoulders, his mouth an inch away from Mathew's ear.

"Just pretend that deer is that fucking Heanen." Church's whisper, as if an order, sanctioned the kill. Not wanting to miss the spectacle Church replaced his binoculars.

Ripping out a few strands of heather, Mathew allowed the breeze to waft them from his hand, indicating its direction. Adjusting the telescopic-sight a fraction of a turn to compensate, the rehearsed ritual of taking two breaths before placing his eye over the velvet covered eyepiece dictated his accuracy. Church's description of how he decimated a German's brain to the tunes of laughter the night before resonated inside Mathew's conscience, but this assassination wouldn't regurgitate guilty pangs in the future. Replicating the scenario he'd been taught so many times in training, Mathew diligently searched for the animal with an eye concentrating on placing it exactly between the same cross hairs of his telescopic sight responsible for decimating the head of a soldier adorning a spiked helmet. The animal died before she heard the shot.

"Bloody hell, Mathew. I'm impressed," the Laird announced, leaping to his feet, confirming what he saw.
The two stalkers didn't say a word, their facial expressions confirming they'd witnessed something special. Church looked at Mathew and winked. Witnessing the kill confirmed Mathew's skill wouldn't be wasted. His mind focused on more important targets.

"This calls for a wee dram," Kilbrook's enthusiasm continued, returning from his pony with a flask and a stack of metal, thimble sized goblets. "You can't be taught that skill. You are a natural, Mathew, an artist with a lethal weapon. I'm proud to know you. Tonight we'll eat and drink like kings. You want to keep hold of this lad, Peter. He's a gooden'. If you don't want him, leave him up here with me."

Church stared at the floor, embarrassed by the Laird's remark and the tone it was made in. Brushing aside Mathew's need for confirmation as to its meaning, Church proposed Kilbrook might be jealous of his skill and not to read anything into it.

"I know I should feel honoured to be here. There can't be too many eighteen year olds with my background mixing with such exalting company, but I don't trust or like your friend, Kilbrook. The quicker we get out of this place, the better I'll feel."

CHAPTER 25

Summer in the Yorkshire countryside is a joyous place when the sun shines. The intensity of Salvation's traumatic death faded to a memory, reinstating smiles and occasional laughter where there was once sadness. Constant blue skies combined with the occasional overnight soaking guaranteed Pinkerton's crops flourishing to a degree of exaggerated proportions. Stripped to the waist from morning to dusk, Mathew's torso turned a dark shade of mahogany before July was out. Emphasising the infectious mood, Pinkerton removed his shirt, rolling the sleeves of his under-vest above the elbows. Work was hard and continuous during daylight, but breaking the laborious monotony, enjoyment prevailed in the guise of The Queen's Head evening hospitality.

On occasions, Church would invite the selected quartet of Mathew, Pinkerton, Brooks and Joey, able to walk again albeit with a stick, to dinner parties within the walls of his secluded patio. Drunkenly chatting into the small hours, much to Mrs Freeman's disgust, she knew it would be the following morning before she could clear away the ensuing debris these get-togethers manufactured. The union between the farm girl and her boyfriend grew stronger, if the size of her stomach was anything to go by and with overnight visits from Mary becoming regular, the Germans being driven back to the Siegfried Line and the short break in Scotland, Mathew viewed his life in a different light than that on the afternoon of Salvation's death.

Returning to Twickton saw him treated as a hero, not only by the peoples of the community, but by the Noble's invitation for him and his parents to dine at the manor house. His efforts to persuade his parents to live elsewhere fell on deaf ears. They belonged to this area, and could never envisage living any other life. Before leaving Twickton, Mathew promised Sir Richard Noble he would return on the day the memorial to the community's dead soldiers was unveiled, a stone edifice already built but unfinished due to further names being frequently added. In alphabetical order under their commanding officer, Captain Robert Noble, Mathew's brothers took their rightful place, a reminder to Mathew of his fortune not to be engraved amongst them.

Privacy was fast becoming an important issue with Mathew, especially when Mary stayed overnight. Not that he wasn't grateful for Pinkerton's hospitality and generosity, but to spare further embarrassment, space and soundproofing became an urgent commodity, especially at bedtime. Fortunately for all concerned, a small cottage nestling within two acres of land came up for sale just outside the village. Though he would never admit it, Pinkerton's relief to return to the way he lived before Mathew's arrival was only noticed by Champ.

Church, baffled as to how Mathew sustained his patience whilst living with Pinkerton, congratulated Mathew on his first choice of real-estate. On the second night of his residency, Mathew held a party for close friends, but in this part of the world, when a free drink is offered, Mathew wasn't surprised to find half the village turn up to toast his new acquisition. Throughout the evening, Mary kept close to his side, dissuading him from drinking too much by leaving him in no doubt, with marauding hands, what she expected once they got to bed that night. Much to her annoyance, the sun came up over the horizon before the last stragglers drifted off home.

August went out as it came in with constant daily sunshine. As with the children getting ready to return to school after their holidays, Pinkerton prepared to harvest a wonderful crop. Church hadn't forgotten either, a promised short break planned for a date together at Sandown Park. The biggest news concerning the war quoted Hindenburg apparently showing signs of waving a white flag when Bulgaria chose to quit their alliance with Germany.

Diminishing confidence and a lack of fresh blood to bolster crumbling lines couldn't dissuade Hindenburg's wrong assessment of judging that victory was still within his grasp. The stench of defeat before it reached his nostrils was perfumed by disillusioned, suicidal generals intent on retaining privileged power over a broken, starving state. Hindenburg searched for a miracle.

During the late summer political mayhem, Mathew and Church concentrated on modifications to shield a four-foot rifle in a wheelchair. Surprised by Church's dexterity skills with a saw and screwdriver, Mathew tested the finished article's strength by negotiating an improvised obstacle course in the manor's garden designed to unearth imperfections. Sweating in the heat manufactured by a noonday sun, Mathew's attempts failed, as expected by Church, viewing the exertions in the shade of a parasol, sipping a glass of cool ale. Accepting the craft as stable, Mathew's only reservation was the elongated headrest, but this was flippantly dismissed. There was no possible clue to what lay hidden inside.

Synonymous with this part of the county, hunting and the sound of shotguns never raised suspicion. Blending with social pastimes, Mathew practiced his art with a replica of the one used in Kilbrook's collection. For all Mathew knew, it might have been the same weapon. This might explain why they travelled all those miles. He remembered, when Church suggested he hid the rifle under lock and key, Mathew trusted his friend but didn't actually see it. Judging it wise to omit Kilbrook's name from further conversation, Mathew didn't ask if he was correct in his assumption.

Adjusting the telescopic sight, he demolished the target over half a mile away, as Pinkerton's scarecrow could testify. He was happy with the result and appeared ignorant when Pinkerton complained of some maniac on the loose, but as with the deer, he knew his target might be on the move.

Agreeing the trip down south by train would be a practice run, Church insisted they packed the rifle in its hiding place. Being a perfectionist, he argued it would be better to get over any pit falls the modified chair might create in transit, rather than find themselves in embarrassing situations when it mattered. He knew Mathew would be unable to manage a laden chair alone, necessitating a third party getting extremely close to an illegal weapon. Church's obsession for detail required assurance that they weren't leaving anything to chance.

As predicted, boarding the train at *Leyburn* the morning before the Saturday meeting at *Sandown Park* required a third person, but the chair reacted perfectly to all the manhandling, especially when they arrived some five hours later in London. Whether by luck or judgement, the chair just squeezed into the space reserved for luggage in a London taxi.

"Dorchester Hotel, please cabby," Church called to the driver through the open glass partition.

"Bit over the top, don't you think?"

"Nonsense, Mathew. We're on a journey of discovery, so why not enjoy ourselves and spend some more of the money Heanen was so against parting with."

This act of indulgence, they managed with aplomb. Overlooking Hyde Park, they dined and drank into the early hours, confirming the exalted hotel's reputation for being one of the most stylish and expensive hotels in London.

Just one worry remained; to be awake and sufficiently sober in good time the following day to reach the racecourse before the first race. Miraculously, their intentions materialised, albeit with sore heads, their taxi joining the traffic queue of excited race goers nearing the course. The attendance was also how Church predicted, their automobiles filling the car park with luxuries only the affluent could afford. Powering these magnificent thirsty beasts posed many a question with petrol being in such short supply. Created by amateur chemists for irreverent owners of such luxury, all types of magical potions were conjured up from illicit liquids, resulting in complaining engines exploding at regular intervals. Church smugly chuckled at these choruses of deafening crescendos echoing around the enclosure.

"Music to my ears," he was heard to say, knowing only Mathew understood his jocular meaning.

Mingling unnoticed with owners of these expensive novelties in the Member's Enclosure, the view of bookmakers lining the rail in Tattersalls appeared unobstructed from their elevated position in the bar under the grandstand. One by one, Church picked out each face through binoculars, travelling down the line discounting unknowns until abruptly stopping, focusing the lens on a familiar figure.

"Our friend has graced us with his presence," he uttered nonchalantly, though a pumping heart accelerated with confirmation of the target's arrival.

"Good, your theory was correct, Peter. Let's hope he comes back for the next meeting." Mathew continued to play-out the charade in case a neighbouring table overheard their conversation. In times like these, it was easy to become paranoid.

"Why don't you push me round to the back of the grandstand? The first race will be off shortly, so most of the crowd will be out here in the open, watching the action. It'll give us an opportunity to find a good spot boasting a private, uninterrupted view," Church whispered, picking up Mathew's mistrust of those in close proximity.

Against the flow of late-arrivals entering, Church directed Mathew to a position he remembered from previous visits to the course.

"Stop here. Do you see those locked gates?" Church waited for confirmation. "The stairs behind are used by maintenance men when the roof needs repair." It was obvious Church's knowledge of the course was extensive. "If you go to the top, you'll find yourself on the roof and all alone with a great view. Why not try it?"

Mathew appeared dubious, for the first time feeling apprehensive. Should he be caught half way up the staircase, what would be his excuse for being in such a spot?

"Oh, I don't know about that. Anyway, there's a bloody great big lock and chain holding those gates together. Make a reference note for future, we'll need a fair sized jemmy to break that lot." Mathew's attempt to sound positive fell on deaf ears.

"Look inside my secret compartment, my boy. There, I think you'll find something adequate," Church teased with humour. "Don't worry, Mathew, I'll sit here and guard the place while you pop up and have a look."

Flipping open the hinged lid, cunningly disguised in the back of the chair, Mathew withdrew a steel lock breaker nestling alongside the Lee Enfield. Spying for human movement, Mathew hurried, spurred on by Church's encouragement. Nervous of interruption, Mathew wedged the forked end of the instrument under the arched arm of the lock and forced it down, adding body weight to strength. Appearing rusty and locked for years, Mathew expected more resistance, but it sprang open sending Mathew tumbling to the floor and the jemmy flying off at a right angle.

"Well, don't just sit there. Get that chain unravelled and get your arse up those stairs."

The major and corporal situation was resurrected. Untangling the crusty chain, Mathew afforded a final look for witnesses before opening one of the gates sufficiently for him to squeeze through.

"Go on, take these and get going. I'll close it behind you," Church offered his binoculars, whilst manoeuvring his chair closer to the barrier.

Taking four strides to clear the first flight of stairs, Mathew was out of sight as he turned to take the next. Barely used, confirmed by the amount of dirt and debris covering each tread, making a distinct footprint worried Mathew, but as it was unlikely for him to be followed, he continued. Reaching the top, Mathew stood bent at the waist, hands on knees, deeply inhaling to inflate empty deflated lungs. From a crouched position, he stared up at an obstruction not accounted for in Church's reckoning. A trap door, secured by a bolt from the inside refused to surrender; only grudgingly capitulating when rapidly thumped by the heel of his left shoe. Easing open the weather worn hinge, Mathew opened the timber hindrance, heralding an elevated view across miles of Surrey countryside. Below lay the sprawling layout of the course, but concentrating on generated, pre-race action along a line of bookmakers, Mathew lifted Church's field-glasses to his eyes. Scrutinising every foreign face until recognising features of his prey, the view of this scrawny image quickened his pulse. As before, during their Challenge Cup's verbal barrage, Heanen stood aloft on stacked boxes, his upper torso fully exposed above the crowd. Mathew might have then momentarily dented his ego, but fully restored, he continued his loathing for surrounding punters, unaware that his desire to be seen afforded an easy target.

Confirmed, Mathew scurried back down, stopping briefly to close the gate and scan for evidence of strangers.

"Well, did you see him?" Church burbled, excitement plainly evident on his face.

"Yes, as clear as the view across the course. It would be easy to pick him off."

"Then why don't you do it, now?"

"That wasn't the plan, Peter. I haven't prepared myself." Surrounded by solitude and appearing to have no need for caution, Mathew continued whispering.

"It's an ideal opportunity which we might not get again. The first race is about to start in five minutes. When the horses are running, everyone's attention will be looking out in that direction and not behind them, including that bastard Heanen. We have the gun and the timing is right. Wait until just before the finish of the race when the crowd will be at its noisiest. Then blow him away. We'll be out of here a few minutes later, long before anyone realises what's happened."

Church waited patiently for a response, his fingers tapping the armrest in anticipation, but he knew not to push. He watched Mathew mentally enact the scenario. The time and place were perfect for an assassination. They might not get another opportunity as good as this one. He was mentally pleading with a youth who still hadn't reached his nineteenth birthday to commit murder.

"Okay, I'll do it."

Withdrawing the rifle from its hiding place together with a shell, Mathew headed back up the staircase, his head reappearing through the trapdoor as the tape went up to start the first race. The burden of two miles and eight hurdles confronted the runners, allowing Mathew time to settle into a familiar position before the field approached the home straight. Perched where Mathew last saw him, Heanen remained on his rostrum, clearly visible. Mimicking the crowd, he stood facing the action. Resting his elbows on the trapdoor frame, Mathew loaded one cartridge and locked the bolt. His breathing deep but restrained, he brought the telescopic lens up to his eye, zeroing his sight on the black suited figure's head. Wiping a sweaty palm down a trousered thigh, his preparation coincided with the front runners nearing home. Noise rumbled from the stand below, growing louder as the horses approached the last obstacle. Encouraging their mounts to respond with only a hundred yards of running left to decide the victor, the jockeys' actions spurred on the crowds' vocal response.

Heanen would never know which horse won. Re-enacting past disciplines, Mathew's conscious was clear; the victim deserved to be killed. Cushioning the recoil, Mathew clearly witnessed the execution.

The cartridge hit Heanen in the back of his scull; completely blowing the front of his face off. Creating a forward momentum, the impact shot him off his feet, leaving a prone body, face down amongst the crowd. Nobody noticed the sudden crack of the shot, or the cadaver lying on the grass. Everyone's attention focused on the ensuing result of the race. Leaving the spent cartridge case in the breech, Mathew calmly shut the trap door and descended the stairs, two at a time. Within three minutes, Mathew unhurriedly pushed Church through a straggle of oncoming latecomers to the road outside.

Nothing was said until they were in the safe confines of a taxi heading back to central London.

"You are a calm bugger, Mathew."

Church studied his subdued accomplice, impressed by this youth who could murder in cold blood and yet appear so unruffled. He smiled, but inwardly shivered at the thought of being on the wrong side of Mathew's ability.

CHAPTER 26

As most sporting events attract huge crowds, especially during these hard times, Sandown Park wasn't the exception in catering for the drinker who couldn't hold their liquor which accounted for why Heanen's state of health lay undetected until after the horses returned to the unsaddling enclosure. It was a race goer, collecting his winnings from a neighbouring bookmaker, who saw the seriousness of the Heanen's injuries. Many gave the 'drunk' a wide berth, but for this unfortunate winner, stepping into a pool of blood signified it was more than alcohol poisoning causing the body to lie so still.

The macabre find created hysterical pandemonium, resulting in scattering the race goers to far corners of the course, leaving a huge void in the middle of Tattersalls. Only an off duty nurse remained kneeling with the corpse, her cries for help seemingly going unheard. It took an hour for the local constabulary to arrive, but by this time any thoughts the stewards had to continue racing were diminished by the disappearance of the crowd, bookmakers, and horses. Those close to the incident could see the state of the head wound and with word of the shooting spreading, fears of a crazed gunman running lose prompted an immediate exodus from the course.

This was not the ideal situation for Detective Inspector Vaughan when called to head the murder inquiry from Scotland Yard. His initial reaction was one of despair, as most, if not all of his witnesses, had long since departed. Unable to a trace their whereabouts, it would be impossible to get statements of what they might have seen. One redeeming factor to come out of this fiasco was apparent; there was no need to muster a bigger police presence to clear the murder scene of prying eyes. Apart from a few stragglers insisting on taking advantage of the afternoon drinking extension, the rest of the area remained deserted.

Back at the Yard, Vaughan had very little to go on, apart from the corpse's identity. From the few who decided a murder was not a good enough reason to vacate the bar, it became obvious by their statements that Heanen was not popular. From early inquiries, there were a multitude of punters who despised the man so much that his death was considered a blessing. In fact, most of those he spoke to raised their glasses to the assassin.

***

"Sergeant Boyce."

From behind his desk situated in an office on the first floor overlooking the River Thames, Vaughan called out through a glass panelled open door.

"Get a few of the lads in here for a chat."

Vaughan's detection methods were different from those employed by equally high ranking officers within The Metropolitan Police when confronting a crime scene considered too big for the local police force. The officers under his command admired his leadership qualities and enjoyed the challenge of the responsibility he gave them, unlike his compatriot head of departments, who treated subordinate officers simply as order takers.

Having Vaughan at the helm of a team, his ratio of arrests far outnumbered those of his contemporaries. Though his superiors were far from happy with his methods, in their eyes he was a star, but to officers of equal rank, he represented a threat. He held the benchmark for promotion. The criteria to join Vaughan's team was simple;

they needed ability to think laterally and work unsupervised.

"Right, Boyce. Have you updated the lads with what we are faced with?"

Vaughan began the meeting with six of his team sitting on anything they could find in his not so spacious office. Getting a positive nod from his number two, Vaughan continued.

"As you know, a bookmaker was murdered at Sandown Park race course yesterday afternoon. Now, with so little to go on, it appears the victim was not liked, which only broadens the net of who might have been responsible. It's not helpful. But, if we look at how it was done, I think we can narrow it down to the sort of person with the ability to do such a crime. As Heanen was an ugly bastard, I cannot see this was a crime of passion, so let's go along the lines that money was probably the motive." A ripple of laughter interrupted Vaughan's dialogue. "This wasn't a mad man going round popping off a gun, as the morning papers would like us to believe, this was a calculated assassination. We'll have to wait for the coroner's report for confirmation, but, by going by what I saw, the victim was hit by a high velocity bullet in the back of his head. Not a handgun, but a rifle. I might be wrong, but I didn't see any evidence of powder burns to indicate a close shot. Now, with so little to go on, let's have a few suggestions on where to start…Hughes, what do you think?"

Vaughan pointed to an old but trusted detective constable, a member of his team for the past six years.

"Well, Guv. If it wasn't a handgun, then we are talking about a rifle. To take a shot with one of those he'd have to be somewhere where he was sure he wouldn't be seen, but have a good sight of the victim."

"Very good, Hughes, but you're automatically thinking it was a man responsible. That's okay. Joblin, what are your thoughts?"

From the most experienced, Vaughan chose his newest recruit.

"If Hughes is correct with his assumption, then the culprit has to be a very good marksman and confident his shot isn't going to go astray and hit innocents."

Coming directly into the force from his privileged background of public school and university, his accent differed from those in the office.

"I agree. Anyone else?"

Vaughan looked at faces surrounding him for volunteers to further their assumptions.

"Carrying on with Joblin's theory, do you think it's a coincidence that we are looking for someone who has the skill with a high powered rifle to do the job and we are still at war?"

"Ah, now we are getting somewhere. Thanks Shepherd, good thinking. Right, what I want you lot to do, starting tomorrow morning, is to get down to the course and find out where our sharpshooter fired his gun. You might find an empty cartridge case, but I doubt it. I believe our man is a professional who wouldn't be as careless as that. Don't come back here until we can build on what little we have. Good hunting."

By eight o'clock the next morning, Sandown Park racecourse was cordoned off from the general public. Apart from Vaughan's squad of seven detectives, another twenty constables, brought in from neighbouring forces, helped in the search and kept out the prying eyes of the press. Within the hour, Joblin came across a coiled chain dislodged from a set of rusting gates.

"Sergeant Boyce," he called to his superior officer. "I believe I've found what we might be looking for."

Together they mounted the staircase, following the scuffed footprints to the top of the stairwell. What was once a rusty bolt on the trapdoor proved easily to slide open.

"I think you're right, son," the Sergeant confirmed. "Look there. The dust has been brushed away. The view from here is perfect, but as the Governor suggested, can you see an empty shell-case anywhere? We'd better get the finger print boys up here, but I doubt if they'll find anything."

"There's something else I want to show you." Joblin suggested, descending back to ground level. "It might not be anything, but I think it's worth a look." Outside the gates, Joblin pointed down to the parched earth. "See what I mean, Sarge? There are faint marks that look like a perambulator has been wheeled around. They must be quite fresh, as it rained on Friday night and they haven't been disturbed. Just a thought, Sarge."

His sergeant smiled, liking his enthusiasm, but, for the moment couldn't see any relevance in his discovery.

Receiving orders to stand down the hunting party, a lone police officer stood guarding the area around the gates, just in case it was necessary to return to the scene of the crime. Boyce, having been caught out once before for not conforming to Vaughan's insistence to preserve evidence, played it safe.

Back at the Yard, a scheduled midday meeting in Vaughan's office for all officers concerned with the case, started exactly on the hour.

"What have you got, Boyce?" the head of department questioned, taking only minutes to be brought up to date with their findings. "Good, we're progressing. Now, with what we know, have we more thoughts on who might be the one we're looking for…Staines, over to you."

"Well, Sir. With what little evidence we have, I think the killer could have been in the army and somehow kept his gun from being requisitioned. When I was in Africa, certain kids who shot better than others were weeded out and trained for that purpose. Seeing as we haven't had a killing like this in the past, well not in my recollection, isn't it safe to say this isn't going to be someone we have come across before, so no criminal record of him will probably exist. I believe our friend is new to the game and to us."

"Good, it appears we're all on the same train of thought. While you lot have been sunning yourselves down in Surrey, I've been over to the War Office to ask for records of their sharpshooters, or snipers, as they are better known, who returned home alive. It's going to take time for them to get the information together; as it's not only this war I've asked records for. If our fellow served in Africa, he could still be as young as thirty-five."

During the following weeks, progress on the investigation dragged on, unearthing no proof or visible leads, other than the group's assumption of how and who could be the culprit, but with no names attached. Everyone pinned their hopes on the war records to kick-start their enthusiasm and give identities to personnel so they could finally do some real detective work. On the day all waited for, a War Office courier delivered six boxes to Vaughan's office containing names of twenty-three thousand soldiers of all ranks who received sniper training. Most did not achieve the grade in real action, but the records never mentioned this, nor did they say if they were still alive, or mentally fit to be interrogated. It was an impossible task for seven officers to filter all this information. Vaughan re-gathered his own small, disheartened army in his office.

"As you can see, lads. We think we may have come up with an answer, but all we get is a bigger problem. We're back to where we began. With no word coming in from off the streets and no witnesses, this is one crime we'll have to put on the shelf and get on with other work, that is unless, any of you have got anything to say."

Vaughan didn't expect volunteers until Joblin tentatively put his hand into the air. He appeared sheepish, but his eyes kept nervously reverting to Sergeant Boyce.

"What is it, boy?"

Regardless of age, Vaughan treated all newcomers with a derogatory title, though detectives within the group saw through this façade and agreed that Joblin was one of Vaughan's favourites. Jealousy contributed to the way the majority thought, but at twenty-five years old, they saw this person as a promotion chaser who would go far, either as Chief Constable or up the political ladder.

"On the day Sergeant Boyce and myself found the position where the culprit fired the rifle, I pointed out to the sergeant fresh tyre marks in the earth below. Did he not tell you, Sir? I put it in my report."

Vaughan's eyes zeroed into Boyce's and kept them there when he asked Joblin to expound on what he saw. After the junior detective gave his verbal report, Vaughan got to his feet from sitting on the front edge of his desk.

"Boyce, why didn't you tell me about this? With so little to go on, this evidence might make all the difference. You've done it before to me and now you've done it again. One more time and you're out of here; back in uniform. Do you hear me, Sergeant?"

Boyce nodded. Looking down to the floor, he wondered how he could get even and dent Joblin's reputation.

"Right, gang. We have perambulator type tyre tracks by the scene. Does that mean we are looking for a mother pushing her baby? An accomplice? Somewhere to hide the rifle? It makes good sense to me. Let's face it; a four-foot gun is not the easiest thing to hide."

Joblin shifted uneasily in his chair, not daring to volunteer further comment for fear of further reprisals from Boyce.

"You got something else to say, Joblin, or do you want to go to the toilet?"

It brought a laugh from the group, but Vaughan quickly quietened the gathering. This was not a time for humour.

"Yes, Sir. I have. If we think the sniper is ex-army, then why not the accomplice."

"What, using a kid to carry the ammo. He must have been in the 'infantry'," a muffled voice from the back sniggers.

"Travis, if I hear your bleeding voice again, I'll put my boot up your arse. Carry on, Joblin."

Silence regained, they all saw this wasn't a day when Vaughan was going to join in with their laughter.

"As I say, Sir. If we think the sniper is ex-army, then it's also reasonable to think his partner is also. That is, of course, if he had a partner. We are thinking at the moment the tracks were made by a perambulator, but what if they were made by a wheelchair. If you can hide a gun in a perambulator, you can hide one in a wheelchair. Thousands came back from both wars without legs. What better business to set up for two retired soldiers who know nothing better than how to kill? I suggest we look into Heanen's business accounts and see who has lost a lot of money to him. Then we might find out who hired these two."

"Joblin, are you after my job?" Vaughan questioned, but this time, due to there being another very plausible theory to work on, his humour returned, prompting the rest to follow suit.

"Yes, Sir. I am."

Unprepared for the answer, Vaughan burst into laughter, much to the others' relief.

Deciding to concentrate on disabled soldiers returning alive from the front line, together with Heanen's business accounts, they shifted through page after page of records from the War Office. As no similar assassinations had been recorded over the last nineteen years, they gambled to disregard records dating back to the Boer War. Though flimsy, this was all they could to go on, given a time limit of only six weeks by Vaughan's superiors to come up with hard facts before they dropped the case. The team were determined to track down the cripple and his partner.

During the fourth week of investigations, an order came in for Vaughan to report to his Commander. This was an unusual occurrence, as they usually only met after a case was solved, or when the bottle came out at Christmas. He wasn't unduly worried, as the case was going far better than he thought possible with so little evidence to begin with.

"Come in, Vaughan," a raucous, educated voice bellowed from inside the plush inner sanctum suite of offices.

"I want to introduce you to Sir Rodney Fawcett-Upham, a trusted friend and member of the War Cabinet. Unbeknown to you, after we asked the War Office for help, he has been keeping a close eye on the case you are working on. Are there any new developments in the pipeline?"

Not offered a chair on entry, Vaughan stood, giving his minimalist verbal report on how far they had got in tracing the culprit to the two overweight seated figures.

"By what you're saying, Vaughan, you haven't got very much to go on... Shame." Fawcett-Upham spluttered, choking on the fumes of a large cigar.

"No, Sir. We are as much in the dark as when we began the enquiry." Vaughan replied, breathing in the heavy, hanging aftermath of exhaled Cuban tobacco.

"Okay, Vaughan. That will be all. We'll give it another week and if there is no improvement, we'll call it a day. Put it on the shelf and get on with something we can solve."

CHAPTER 27

Turkey and Austria-Hungary, appearing to have thrown in the towel to protect their own failing economies, further endorsed the earlier assumptions about Germany's ability to prolong the fight. Endeavouring to save himself from utter humiliation, Hindenburg called for an armistice. His right wing theology, responsible for so many needless deaths over the past four years, dictated the self-imposed Field Marshal and Supreme Commander to believe he could play statesman once more by disguising what at one time would be an unheard of defeat. Continuing control of his humiliated country was imperative. Sipping brandy with those he considered enemies in plush surroundings, far removed from the threat of a high velocity shell landing on their heads, he brazenly suggested a draw, knowing his strong-armed tactics responsible for a European war had backfired.

Mathew's anger grew when he read of the allies' capitulation to this request instead of finishing the argument, once and for all, on the battlefield. If they could iron out their differences around a table, he thought, then why couldn't Hindenburg have done it before hostilities took place? Before there were rumours, now there was reported proof of their huge military and naval mutinies. Mathew wanted to see a crushing defeat on the tyrant's empire, an aggressor from the very first day of hostilities. Similar to so many bullies chronicled in history before his regime, when defeat loomed, Hindenburg wanted his name to be etched in marble as the peacemaker. Most, like

Mathew, who fought and were fortunate to return alive, wanted to see him and his army suffer total humiliation. But at least, Twickton's engraver could finally put away his chisel.

Newspapers predicting peace coincided with the last of the harvest, transforming life on the farm from either hard graft to a place for parties. Though there were no visible differences to village life, nearly every family counted the cost of war by losing a loved one or neighbour. Where there was once tears, celebration reared its joyous face, contributing to a feeling of not daring to be left out. Fine weather continued as late summer drifted into autumn, encouraging festivities to begin though peace hadn't yet been officially declared, but the enemy, being in so much disarray, prompted the home nation to believe the end was nigh and could never be restarted.

Little was written in the newspapers concerning Heanen's death outside of London, but for those who did know him, they celebrated the end of the war in the same fashion as those who drank to the assassin. Church and Mathew never talked about the trip down south and rarely, when they were alone in each other's company, was Heanen's name brought into conversation. To them, it was a job well done, and now, as war appeared to be coming to an end, they were satisfied to live in a better world without the likes of Hindenburg, Higgins or Heanen.

"Darling, there's a knock on the door. Can you get it? I'm up to my elbows peeling potatoes."

Mary called from the kitchen to Mathew in the garden, collecting carrots before a frost ruined his last crop.

"Okay, I'll get it."

Bypassing the direct route to the front door wearing muddied boots to spare Mary's polished floor, Mathew took the garden path round the side of the cottage to confront his two good friends, Church and Pinkerton, both smiling and both holding bottles up high, indicating their intention. Mathew opened the front door, calling through to the kitchen.

"You'd better put a few more spuds in the pot, sweetheart, we have another two for supper."

Mary fitted in easily with Mathew's social life, getting on well with his friends, even enjoying the odd night in The Queens Head, chatting to locals as though she was one herself. It was a far cry from the turmoil of having to work in an environment of pain and death her occupation demanded. She enjoyed the difference between the bustles of London to the tranquillity of the Yorkshire Dales, though it meant spending hours travelling. The five-year difference in their ages didn't bother her, as Mathew belied his youth, appearing older in stature and behaviour. Though they'd not long been together, she sensed there was more to this relationship than just friendship. Never doubting her loyalty and believing she was the female responsible for relieving him of his virginity, Mary accepted that this man might someday, if asked, also walk her to the altar.

"Is this your lamb we're eating, George?" Church posed the question, lifting a slice with a knife for inspection.

"I don't know, is it, Mathew?" Pinkerton answered, replicating Church's tactics for clues he might recognise from an animal reared elsewhere.

"Of course it is. I went down to the farm and killed me one whilst you were out on your tractor."

Pinkerton refused to see the humour, prompting the others to hide their smiles behind raised napkins.

"Of course it's not, you stupid beggar. It's from the local butcher," Mathew eased Pinkerton's concern. "Anyway, much as we like you two for company, is there a reason for your visit, or don't you like your own cooking?"

"Well, as Mary's in town, we knew she would be in the kitchen tonight. So we thought, we'd kill two birds with one stone. You and I have been invited to the Regimental shindig next Friday week. It's the old boy's reunion for the lucky ones who came back," Church announced sounding enthusiastic, expecting Mathew to feel the same about meeting old comrades.

"I'm not sure I want to go, Peter. Don't get me wrong, when I joined the Regiment, it was probably the proudest day of my life, but after what I saw on the front and the way they treated us like this piece of meat you're eating, my allegiance to those in command is somewhat tainted. I'm not sure how I would react meeting the 'big brass' again, now I no longer have to salute the bastards. Anyway, I gave away my uniform."

It wasn't the reply Church wanted to hear.

"Come on, Mathew. It'll be fun. I don't mind if you tell them what you think. They can't have you for insubordination, or throw you in the glasshouse. You're a free agent, remember?" Using a little persuasion, Church hoped his young protégée would change his mind. "Think about it. It's not important, but I'd like you to come. After all, who else have I got to wheel me around? If you're wondering how we will get there? Don't worry; I'll pay for a taxi to Catterick and back again. It's the least I can offer."

Exercising honed persuasive skills, Church pricked Mathew's conscience without appearing to be making his decisions.

***

The taxi called first at Mathew's cottage before picking Church up from his mansion. Mary decided not to journey up this particular weekend, saying she would leave Mathew to enjoy himself, as she hated waking up the next morning knowing she had to pamper a walking hangover all day. Mathew relished her weekly visits and missed her ability to knot his bow tie on occasions when evening-wear was a requisite.

Dressed in a freshly starched white apron, Mrs Freeman stood proudly behind Church's wheelchair when the cab pulled up outside the manor's front door. Her face, a picture of happiness, was so different to when Mathew first met her. Her manufactured stern look melted as she got to know Mathew, knowing he became a good confident and the person most responsible for giving life back to Church.

"Afternoon, Master Mathew," she called her greeting. "Looks quite splendid, doesn't he?" she said, pointing to Church sitting in full, major's dress uniform. "And you don't look too bad you're self," she continued, bestowing a rare smile.

"Thanks, Mrs 'F'."

The idea to travel to Catterick during daylight hours was Church's suggestion, adding the benefit of time to talk en-route. Since their London trip, the euphoria resulting in the armistice being called drastically reduced chances to discuss the murder frequently revisited by the national press. It was important to find a quiet spot away from preying ears and Church's choice of an isolated roadside public house appeared to the perfect venue.

Though the story of Heanen's death was big news in the south, interest in northern editions consisted of a few column inches, but the written consensus of opinion from both areas quoted the police had a fair idea who was responsible, but none the wiser when it came to naming the culprits. Calculating this risk when drawing up the plans to eliminate Heanen, Church knew it wouldn't take the best detective to fathom out army personnel involvement. In his guise as a major, he knew approximately the numbers of enlisted men trained to use a rifle more proficiently than the ordinary foot soldier and gambled on neither Mathew nor himself ever being traced and interviewed. It was a remote possibility, but if this investigation reached that stage, hundreds of police officers would be required and even then, their names might never appear on top of the pile.

"Well Matty, finally we are alone to talk." Seated at a desolate table, Church greeted Mathew's return from the bar carrying two large scotches.

"Yeah, London seems a long time ago."

"It doesn't look as if the police have any idea, apart from knowing an ex-squaddie was responsible. Still, we better be on guard, as I believe there might be some representation at the reunion tonight from the local constabulary asking questions."

Prematurely airing his warning, Church knew Mathew would handle the situation if confronted by an inquisitive policeman.

"Quite honestly, Peter. I can't see how they can pin this on us. The only incriminate evidence is the rifle. Talking about that, what have you done with the thing?"

"Back where no one can find it. You never know, we might have to use it again one day," Church raised his eyebrows, prolonging a left eyed wink.

Timing and luck played a large part in the success of the operation, but suggesting they repeat the action startled Mathew. Lowering his voice further, Mathew needed confirmation of what Church meant.

"What are you trying to tell me, Peter? Have you got something else planned you're not telling me about?"

"Not really. It's just I remember what you said to me a little while ago about going into business together. We have both got keys to each other's skeleton cupboard, which means we make the ideal business partners. Do you think we could have done what we did if we didn't trust each other? I don't think so."

For the first time since they met, Mathew was unsure of Church's thinking. This wasn't the time or place to enquire.

"Don't worry, Mathew. They could pull the mansion down brick by brick, and still they wouldn't find it."

***

The familiar sight of the barracks sent a cold shiver down Mathew's back. It was here, by the gates, where he first met Colour Sergeant Higgins. Ensuing remarks made that day were tantamount to reasons leading to why he shot him. It seemed to be an age ago, but as Mathew vividly remembered, it was less than a year.

Before the gates opened to allow entry, all ranks massed outside, waiting for sentries to inspect invitations. Whilst most wore their appropriate uniform, Mathew watched, disgusted by frontline conditioned privates saluting officers, many of which never saw action, but Church enjoyed the experience, constantly lifting his right arm whilst being afforded the luxury of remaining seated whilst the rest, acknowledging his rank, came to attention.

Being one of only a few attending in an evening suit, Mathew couldn't help but notice others arriving out of uniform, dressed as smartly as their wardrobe allowed. They were young men, like him, but who hadn't fared as well, suited in clothes bearing signs of wear and the tell-tale smell of coal dust. Many bore crutches or, indicating a lost arm, a jacket sleeve wedged in a pocket. Looking around the ensemble, Mathew saw many affected by disability in some shape or form, caused by war.

Mathew hoped he might be reunited with some of his old buddies from his unit, but no familiar face shone through the bleakness of the crowd. Presumably, only he and the major from his unit got out alive.

Unlike the time when he was here before, the training hall was festooned with bunting and regimental regalia. New recruits, playing at being waiters, busily offered an array of drinks from oversized, balanced trays. The numbers swelled, gathering below a long table set up on an elevated stage for the arrival of the hierarchy to enjoy more space than those on the floor below. Reminiscent of the evening at The Tavistock Hotel, Mathew envisaged the likes of Sir General Johnston and his cronies, ignorantly taking refreshment from poisoned chalices. Oh how he wished.

Wheeling Church to near the front, they joined a group of officers, most of whom trained with the major and to his relief, a few survived their terms unscathed in the trenches. Blasting musical cords from a far corner, a military band made conversation difficult, which didn't hinder Mathew, as he was more intent on grabbing a glass from a passing tray than making small talk with people he didn't know. Eavesdropping the occasional conversation confirmed the vanity of some higher ranked officer's interpretation of action they witnessed on the frontline. Disregarding the youth's smirk as insolence, they turned their back on one of a few who could so easily discredit their story, but Mathew refrained, knowing Church wouldn't thank him. Watching an overweight, red faced band master raise his baton to bring the entertainment to a halt, Mathew's curiosity switched his attention to wonder why loud cheers, instead of blown raspberries, greeted the high ranking officers appearing from a side door, heading for the raised stage. One by one, in Indian file, they sat on a row of chairs, conveniently arranged so that the Colonel in Chief sat in the middle.

Speeches began, each officer standing to vocally praise the bravery of their Regiment, bringing further cheers each time this repetitive message was announced. General.B.Scarrow, the last of the officers to address the enthusiastic hordes, repeated the same message but over a longer period. Wondering just how much action he saw, Mathew remembered the name as the General who sent the order for the original Twickton Company to be mustered all those years before. Every officer who spoke wore a chest full of medals and appeared to be able bodied, which didn't tally with the percentage of cripples in the audience. Mathew's father's words came flooding back to haunt.

"You see the old farts barking out orders, but none of them ever goes near the bleedin' front line".

Scarrow approached the end of his whiskey-enhanced speech, but not before he introduced the last speaker, a guest and a man whom the Regiment should honour for his sterling performance in the War Cabinet, Sir Rodney Fawcett-Upham.

Another assault on eardrums greeted the figure mimicking the General's uniformed appearance, approaching from the side door accompanied by his aid-de-camp. Beginning his speech, quoting the same congratulations and the debt the country owed to the Regiment, he continued to lavish praise, but by the time he finished, most had heard enough and were taking advantage of free beverages offered by 'waiters' circling the masses. Even to the most loyal soldier, the past hour appeared to contain a re-run of the same recording six times over.

One by one, the Generals and other high-ranking officers descended the stairs to mingle with men they never got near to when it really mattered. Mathew thought it strange, that now the job of war was completed, they consented to fraternize, unlike before, when they treated their rank as a barrier between them and the troops they commanded. Should they have replicated this gesture then, they might have earned more respect in his eyes of those who carried out their orders.

Mathew stood outside Church's circle. Devoid of a uniform, he appeared to be Church's helper and was ignored even by the lowest of ranks. Realising his dress code appeared to single him out to be as wealthy as those Church befriended, Mathew was content to remain on the perimeter and listen to conversations, preconditioned by Church not to air his own opinion. He smiled, listening to their heroics, but wondered just how much action they actually saw. Not one could question Church's credentials, as visible proof prompted Sir General Rodney Fawcett-Upham to be first of the 'dignitaries' to pay this group a visit, accompanied closely by his leech-like aid.

"Good evening, lads. Excellent showing tonight. I wager there are some good stories being bantered around this little group, eh, what?" Directing his speech down to Church, he continued to hold the centre of the circle. "We owe you a big debt, Major. May I ask where it happened, if it's not too painful?"

"No, I can talk about it, Sir. It happened at Ypres. I was one of the lucky ones. We left a hell-of a-lot more behind than got out. It wasn't a day I'll easily forget."

"What's your name, Major?"

"Church, Sir. Major Church."

"I don't suppose you're related to Sir General Cuthbert Church?"

Expecting a negative response, he was surprised, as were those surrounding him including Mathew, when he answered.

"Yes, actually he's my father."

"Good God. What a coincidence. I know him very well. He will be surprised when I tell him I've met you."

Church thought otherwise, having had little contact with his father since he was a boy and even less since he joined the army. Sir General Cuthbert Church boasted about his son's injuries, but saw no reason why he should be reunited with him.

"Look, Church. Why not join me in the officer's mess? It's quieter in there; we can have a chat. Get your man to wheel you through the crowd and I'll join you in a few minutes after I've shown myself around. It wouldn't do just to leave them the minute I got here, now would it?"

"Now you know why I hate people of your class."

Lowering his mouth to Church's ear, Mathew whispered whilst watching Fawcett-Upham leave the confines of the circle, putting his overbearing presence onto some other poor and unassuming souls

"Come on, man servant. Wheel me to the officer's mess."

From the outset of the night's proceedings, Church noticed Mathew's reluctance to associate with his fellow comrades. He didn't appear to dislike them; it was an unwillingness to accept he was part of an atrocity he had no control over. The decorated uniforms making inane small talk with people they would, in different circumstances, rather not be seen with dictated his actions. To them, the whole campaign had been used as a vehicle to further their reputations and careers, but to the ones who saw the real action, they were left to make good their mistakes and get on as best as they could with the devastating memory.

"Don't sink down to their level, Peter. Why not go and ask Sir bleeding General Fawcett-Upham for your legs back, 'cos that's one of the bastards who took them away from you."

The humour Church tried to bring into the evening suddenly disintegrated. He knew Mathew was right about his assessment and realised he was starting to act exactly how his father would want him to. For a few minutes he chose to forget the day of the battle. He knew it was a mistake to come to the gala and a bigger one in convincing Mathew he should attend.

"Sorry, Mathew. You're right; we shouldn't really be here. The last thing I intended to do was get constant reminders of what we have been through. I should have known better."

Mathew saw Church's head drop. Was there a tear being shed, or was he play-acting? Mathew couldn't tell.

"Come on, mate. You need a pick-me-up. Hold on tight. We're going to have a drink with the 'big knobs'."

Only minutes before, the thought of mixing socially with Fawcett-Upham repulsed him, but with Church seemingly returning from the wilderness of depression, Mathew wanted to take this invited opportunity to see into the mind of what actually made the likes of a War Cabinet Minister tick.

"Good evening, Corporal. We've been invited by Sir Fawcett-Upham for a drink," Mathew announced to the sentry guarding the officer's mess door.

Church regained a smile hearing humour return to Mathew's micky-taking, upper class voice.

"Ah, Church. Come over and meet some of my friends." Fawcett-Upham beckoned from the bar. His intended time mixing with the troops was cut short by the lure of free alcohol.

"Whatever you do, Peter. Don't tell them I was in the army with you. Let's go along with his assumption that I'm your man servant."

Mathew's efforts as a whispering ventriloquist humoured Church. Only a cough camouflaged his need to laugh.

"Sir Rodney, so good of you to invite me. Yes, a scotch would be fine."

Mathew listened to the banter of the group, their speech slurring with the passing of time. He stood in close attendance, but was never offered a drink. He knew Church was playing their game and readily accepted the acting role of servant. Vacating the bar, the invited party gradually assembled into an area where they slouched into a circle of armchairs. Where they went, Mathew pushed Church. It was a game he was starting to enjoy watching unfold. When the first in the group unbuttoned his tunic without a rebuke from his superiors, mass loosening of belts and jackets followed as alcohol took effect. Unanimously thinking they were amongst friends, one by one their verbal guard began to slip.

"My job is not all about war or making life or death decisions, you know, Frobisher." Sir Rodney slurred to a captain, slumped opposite. "No, I've been following the murder case of that bloody bookmaker at Sandown Park racecourse."

Suddenly, Mathew's eyes darted onto Church to see if he caught the topic of conversation over the inane chatter of the other officers. To those present, it appeared Church had been drinking, drink for drink with the others, but, surreptitiously, Mathew replaced each full glass of scotch with one of beer. It wouldn't help his bladder, he knew, but it certainly would keep his brain in order. Church acted the part well in appearing to be as drunk as those sitting opposite and though he didn't appear to be listening, he heard Fawcett-Upham's statement.

"Oh, really, Sir Rodney. That must come as light relief for you," Church magically slurred, perfectly mimicking the others in his party.

"Yes. Bloody clever who ever did it and a bloody good shot. We know it was someone in the army who was responsible and he wasn't acting alone, but it's nigh impossible to track down the thousands who have the capability."

From the shadows, a figure quickly approached Fawcett-Upham, quietly talking behind a protective hand.

"Oh, shut up, Joblin. I'm amongst brothers in arms. I don't have to be wary what I say in front of them. They're not going to spill the beans and inform the press that we haven't got the foggiest bloody idea who was responsible."

Joblin stood back, not wanting to jeopardise his short-lived but profitable career move after getting a promotion from being a detective constable within Scotland Yard, to Fawcett-Upham's personal assistant.

"That's interesting, Sir Rodney. So you believe there were two of them?" Church put the question casually.

"We know there were two," he boasted.

"It's not what they say in the newspapers."

This time, another major joined the conversation, taking on the onus of question master.

"Ah, if we told everything we know to the press, we'd show our hand and that would not be a wise thing to do. We believe one of them was in a wheelchair, just like you, Church," confided Fawcett-Upham.

"Oh, come now," Church bravely cut in without hesitation.

"It's true, isn't it Joblin. Tell them. You were on the case."

Joblin muttered a few words, confirming his master's direction.

"It's a shame we can't find the scallywags. I might have been able to use their skills on another matter," Sir Rodney drunkenly announced, causing Joblin to cringe.

The barracks clock struck a late hour as two lone shadowed figures proceeded in silence across the deserted parade ground to waken their patient taxi-driver, a sprightly seventy year old who from past experiences, willingly endured waiting seven hours knowing at the end of his shift, he'd collect the equivalent of a week's wages for one night's work. If need be, he'd wait all night to earn these type of earnings, as proved when Salvation won The Challenge Cup.

It being wiser to remain silent during their journey home, they didn't speak until ensconced in Church's favourite living space overlooking an expansive garden, lit by the full moon. Keeping the volume of their conversation down to a minimum, Mathew poured a nightcap from a chosen bottle, arranged earlier by Mrs Freeman before retiring to bed.

"Well, you're a dark horse," Mathew began, offering Church a glass. Having self-imposed a regime to remain practically 'dry' during the reunion, especially in the officers' mess, Mathew poured unhealthy measures as compensation. "You never mentioned your father is Sir General Cuthbert Church. I can understand why you didn't if he's anything like what you've said about him. He must be a pompous arsehole just like the others who climbed the promotional ladder without getting a spot of mud on their pristine, medal infested uniforms. Someday, you'll have to let me into the secret of reaching the top without getting my hands dirty."

Church swayed in his wheelchair, laughing at the description of his father, unable to control an agreeing, nodding head.

"Of all the people I know who would understand my hatred for my father, I should have known it would be you."

For the first time in his life, Church felt comfortable about offloading his thoughts concerning his father to an understanding listener.

"And, what about being so close to the enemy, eh? Sir Rodney Fucking Fawcett-Upham, I mean?" Mathew recalled their encounter with the Minister overseeing the Heanen murder.

"I know, scary, isn't it?" Joining in with the mockery of a member of the War Cabinet, Church relived a cringe when hearing he was a good friend of his father. "Still, I wonder what he meant about wanting to meet the culprits. By what I gathered and if I can read between the lines, he wants someone bumped off."

Humour disappeared as fast as it started. Mathew tried to catch Church's eye, but he gazed out through the study window.

"Peter, look at me. I'm beginning to know exactly how you're thinking. Don't you get any ideas about asking Fawcett-Upham about what he meant when he said he'd like to meet the culprits who murdered Heanen. Don't put us in the position where this could seriously get us into trouble, more trouble than we are in right now. Remember what my dad said about making mistakes."

Mathew purposely allowed the question to answer itself.

"Alright Mathew. You're right, but it was fun talking about it."

Finally turning to face Mathew, Church answered, freeing Mathew's anxiety, permitting Mathew to walk to the sideboard and refill their glasses, thinking the subject was closed. It was late, and drink began to influence his thoughts, but Church wouldn't allow this opportunity to pass. The last time he felt adrenalin pumping through his body at this speed was the second before shrapnel mutilated his legs.

"We are very good at what we do." He paused, waiting for a forcible rebuke, but nothing came. "If what Fawcett-Upham said was true and concerned a covert Government operation, then there would mean big money involved. Come on Mathew, if the Prime Minister is giving the orders and we decide to take them on, then our past crimes can only be absolved. We've got to be the cunning bastards they're looking for otherwise why did Fawcett-Upham mention he'd like to meet someone with our skills? Think about it, Mathew. You did say we should look out for a business venture. Well, I'm an excellent planner and you are brilliant at putting them into action. What more could you ask for in a successful partnership?"

"You're bloody mad, do you know that? They know one of the culprits was in a wheelchair. It wouldn't take Sherlock bleeding Holmes to fathom out what I did in the war if they got wind of your intention. What was his name...Joblin, the aid? He's no mug. He's just left Scotland Yard. His last case was trying to find us. Well, you're near enough giving us up to the law if you go ahead with this hair-brained scheme of yours. Forget about it,

Peter. I'm not going along with this one, it's not personal enough."

"Shame, I thought you might be interested in making lots of money, very easily and quickly."

"Forget it, Peter. I'm not doing it."

CHAPTER 28

"Come," Fawcett-Upham called from inside his improvised office within Catterick barracks when a knock on the door interrupted his paperwork. "Ah, Joblin. What is it?"

"I have a message from Major Church. He asks if you would consider having lunch with him at his home before we travel back to London."

"That's very thoughtful of him. What have we got on for today? Can anything be cancelled? If his wine cellar is as good as his father's, then it's worth paying a visit."

Joblin read out his appointment book. There was nothing significant to warrant a refusal.

"Get the Rolls ready for five past."

Being Fawcett-Upham's aid meant more than being a parliamentary assistant, as Joblin found out. His skills were soon put to the test when called upon to be a chauffeur, butler, or general dogsbody to a man who never married, but inherited a fortune from ancestors dating back to an illegitimate son conceived during Henry VIII's courting days with a lady-in-waiting, who fortunately, remained single with her head intact. Joblin's apparent promotion appeared to be anything but that, but he knew if he could bite his lip and withstand the minister's foibles, a fast track into politics via a winnable seat at the next general election was realistically attainable.

Mrs Freeman stood fraily alone, greeting the Rolls Royce as it glided to a halt over the gravel driveway opposite the manor's front door.

"Good afternoon, Sir."

She addressed the guest, curtsying with a stiff knee as she would to Church's father. Working within the family household since her twenties, Mrs Freeman and a butler heading ten staff were employed in those early days when Sir General Cuthbert Church utilised the mansion as his main abode, but since his move south, taking up residence in one of London's most fashionable boroughs, she remained as the sole survivor from those halcyon days to care for Peter Church.

"If you would just follow me, Major Church is in the dining room awaiting your arrival."

"Good to see you again, old chap." Fawcett-Upham gushed, striding towards Church with an outstretched hand.

"Sorry, I can't get up."

Church jested, noticing the minister hadn't grabbed the gist of his humour, but joined the light hearted laughter as a courtesy to his host.

"Hope you don't mind, old boy, but I've brought Joblin here with me. Says in his employment remit, he mustn't leave my side from nine until five - anyway, that's what he keeps telling me. So, what a grand house you live in, Peter. It must be a lovely place to while away the days."

"Thank you, Sir Rodney. I'm pleased you like it. An aperitif before we eat?"

"Oh, yes. That would go down nicely. Would you like me to pour, or will your manservant do us the honours? Where is he? Damn it. They're never around when you need them the most. I've got one similar back in London."

Making his exit towards the dining room door, Church stopped Fawcett-Upham before he made a fool of himself by calling for a non-existent servant down a deserted corridor.

"I gave him the afternoon off as I didn't want the two of us to be disturbed. Forgive me, Sir Rodney, but I think we are capable of pouring a twenty-five year-old Bordeaux without the aid of a servant"

The prospect of tasting such a fine wine, Fawcett-Upham returned to where the decanted vintage waited to be drunk.

"He's a good lad and I try to help him whenever I can. I promised his parents I'd look after him." If only Mathew could be present, hearing him lie. Church concealed a smirk on Fawcett-Upham's return to the table, salivating over the grandest wines France produced. "So, a good white to start with, I believe, and then we'll move onto the reds. How does that sound, Sir Rodney?"

Knowledge of Fawcett-Upham's love of the grape made the process of directing the Minister towards Church's lines of conversation easier than if he were tea-total. Similar to a lubricant, Church discovered wine to be the ideal means of torture when convincing people to give up secrets, especially when threatened with another bottle. Joblin remained silent during the courses Mrs Freeman placed in front of the three diners. His short tenure with Sir Rodney Fawcett-Upham taught him not to give an opinion or appear to take an interest in subjects discussed in private over a dinner table, especially the ones Church was cunningly bringing into conversation. It was after the cheese course, in conjunction with his guest's consumption of the best part of three bottles of Bordeaux's finest red wine, when Church brought up the subject of the Sandown Park murder over brandy and coffee.

"I was very intrigued, Sir Rodney, about what you were saying back at the officer's mess last night concerning the race course murder. You interested me when you said one of the culprits involved appears to be in a wheelchair. I thought about it last night after I got home and wondered if someone in the same position as myself could have the tenacity to do such a daring thing."

Sir Rodney listened, his inebriation clear to the others seated at the table. Feeling no apprehension in his state, Fawcett-Upham was clearly prepared to discuss the matter without coercion until Joblin, similarly to how he interrupted the previous night's discussion, cut off their over-the-table chat.

"Sir, I must object. This case is still on going. With privy information you share with Scotland Yard, I'm afraid to say Major Church; I cannot allow this conversation to continue in my presence."

"Well, Joblin. I suggest you go and take a walk round the garden. Take a glass of brandy with you and leave the Major and I to talk in peace."

To object further would be futile. Joblin, having learnt on a few previous occasions, took his superior's advice as an order and vacated the table, heading for the outdoors with a look on his face reminiscent of being scolded by a headmaster.

"Now, getting back to what we were talking about. Peter"

How easy it was to instigate a situation, Church thought, as he watched Joblin reluctantly pick up his glass and proceed into the walled-off vegetable garden. Without Joblin as a constant reminder of what could and couldn't be divulged, Church could talk to Sir Rodney without fear of a witness.

"It wasn't so much the crime I was interested in, Sir Rodney, it was what you said about wanting to meet the culprit. By the tone of your voice, I suspect you secretly admire his professionalism."

"You're right, Peter. The way he planned and executed it, I do admire the person. With those skills, especially now, he could come in very handy to my Government if given the right direction."

Void of an inclination to where the conversation was leading, Fawcett-Upham opened the way for Church to probe deeper.

"I want you to promise, Sir Rodney, now we are alone. What I say next shall go no further than between you and I and these four walls. If you hear something you're uneasy with, I don't want Joblin called in to rescue you. With the trust of my family knowing yours for such a long time, I need your word on complete discretion that you shall not repeat what I have to say to a third person. Do I have your word? If you are prepared to give it, I do believe I can help you and your Government. All I need is your word of honour on this matter."

Church sat relaxed in his chair, waiting to stir Fawcett-Upham's inquisitive nature. Though inebriated, the Minister recognised a piece of delicate information was there to be heard if he agreed. Showing interest by squarely placing his elbows on the table to angle his body closer to his luncheon partner in case the information delivered was in a whisper, Fawcett-Upham didn't have to answer. Peter Church knew the Minister was totally captivated.

"Oh, I do like these bits of intrigue," Sir Rodney excitedly responded, replacing his wine glass back on the table. "Go on, I agree. Whatever is said shall go no further than just between you and I."

His mouth drooled, as if looking at a prostrate naked female body sprawled out before him. His debauched mind automatically led him to believe he was about to hear some sexual scandal involving people in high places, but never thought for one moment he was about to hear something totally unconnected and holding dangerous ramifications for both parties.

"Should you repeat what I have to say, I'll deny this conversation ever took place, but that would only lead us both into a regrettable, embarrassing situation. Do I make myself clear, Sir Rodney?"

"Get on with it, man."

Whilst in the privacy of his own company, Church lost count of the times he mulled over in his mind the consequences a full confession could have on his life. Knowing Mathew's disapproval, he was prepared to go behind his back and lay their liberty, or even life on the line. If he were wrong in his assessment of the biggest gamble of his life, this is exactly what they would lose.

"I know who killed the bookmaker at the racecourse."

A few seconds passed before a reaction registered on Fawcett-Upham.

"You're not telling me you were the person in the wheelchair?"

"Yes, I was."

Digesting this random piece of information, Sir Rodney slowly sat back in his chair, picking up his brandy glass, studying Church more closely.

"O...k...a...y"

Sudden sobriety steadied his drunken body. Good as the secret was, he was somewhat disappointed, as it had nothing to do with what he hoped to hear. A nice, juicy piece of gossip guaranteed dinner invitations for weeks, but this confession would have to be kept secret.

"So, you're telling me you murdered the bookmaker?"

"No, I didn't actually pull the trigger. I was with the person who did. I planned the operation."

For the next five minutes, Fawcett-Upham sat spellbound as Church related the reason why it happened. Not once was Mathew's name mentioned.

"So, Peter. What do you want me to do? Here I am sitting having lunch with the son of a good friend of mine, a man of great importance to the country in these times, but because of our friendship you expect me to do nothing after you admit to being part of the biggest case Scotland Yard has had since the outbreak of war. Who was your accomplice?"

"I will never divulge his name. As I said, Sir Rodney. If you wish to arrest me, you can, but think of the consequences. It won't do you or my father any good."

Pouring a large brandy from the decanter placed in the middle of the table, the Minister smiled at the confessor and was about to speak when Joblin reappeared through the doors leading from the garden.

"Piss off!" Sir Rodney shouted, not looking at the figure re-entering the dining room; his attention firmly fixed on the person sitting in the wheelchair opposite.

"But, Sir..."

"Didn't you hear me? Piss off around the garden again."

"I take it from your reaction to your aid, you are interested in what I have to say?"

Church's confidence only whetted Fawcett-Upham's appetite to hear more.

"I could have you hanged for what you just admitted to me."

"Ah, but you won't, because I'm gambling you can use my expertise."

"There's more to it than that. You're getting a kick out of it. It's the excitement, isn't it?" Fawcett-Upham began to get equally aroused.

"True, I must admit it felt good, but you're probably wondering why a man in my position would risk putting my good family name and its wealth in jeopardy. It was quite an easy decision, actually. When I came round from the anaesthetic and found I had no further use of my expensive, Bond Street brogues, I felt suicidal. I wondered what possible use I could be to man or beast. But when I got this idea of retribution, everything slotted into place. I might not have legs, but my mind is as sharp as it was before. I pitted my wits against the best detective brains in the country and still they are no closer to finding the culprit. If I hadn't told you, I doubt very much if I would ever be accused. So you understand the faith I am putting on your silence."

Heavy cigar smoke wafted across the table, finalising the decadent luncheon scene. The cost of such a spread would have fed a mining family for a year, but to the likes of the two diners, especially Fawcett-Upham, it was commonplace. Church spoke as an equal, not as an underling and Fawcett-Upham knew it. There stood a kinship between such families and Sir Rodney was not about to ruin it, or their reputations, by blowing the whistle over a murder of a working class bookmaker.

"Your secret is safe with me, Peter. In actual fact, in a way I'm pleased you told me, because now if I think Scotland Yard are getting too close to you, I can feed them a red herring to get them off your trail. I don't want them getting in the way of your next job."

This was exactly what Church wanted to hear. By what Church read between the lines of their previous conversation, he knew something of this kind was in the offering. Now Fawcett-Upham possessed the tool, Church knew it was only a matter of time before he was going to be let in on the secret.

"Similar to the confidence you have in me, I must ask for the same with what I'm about to tell you. Actually, this is all working out splendidly," Sir Rodney announced, returning to the brandy decanter to top-up his goblet. "It'll make blackmail out of the question."

He laughed, but Church thought he did have a point. Once he'd heard Fawcett-Upham's confession, he knew he could never be arrested for the crime he and Mathew committed.

"Look, Peter," Fawcett-Upham beckoned Church closer, glancing through the window to be sure Joblin wasn't about to announce his presence once again. "The French are taking control of the armistice as they believe they have suffered the most from the German onslaught.

It's a lot of bollocks, because, as we know, if it hadn't been for the allied troops, France would have been swamped, losing their entire population to the German regime. Okay, agreed, they lost a generation of young men, but it has become very political. Hindenburg realises his advances have gone as far as they can. Thank God the Americans have come in to overwhelm any advantage he thought he might have. Unlike the Commonwealth, the Germans have no other resources to call upon as their friends have all pissed off behind their own borders. So he's playing his only remaining trump card by saying, 'I'm willing to talk as long as I keep control of my country.' Regardless of the fact that while Hindenburg is responsible for millions of deaths, the 'Sorry, but I made a big mistake to think I could get away with it' speech, is not going down too well in certain quarters, as you would expect. Well, we in the Government also agree that the man needs to learn a personal lesson. The fact we reminded the French that we bailed them out has also not gone down well after their demand to take over negotiations was refused."

As an afterthought, Fawcett-Upham steered away from the topic and threw into the conversation an additional diversion.

"It really is quite ironic. After what you have said to me, I find it is quite incestuous to inform you your father is to join the allied negotiation party as Britain's ambassador at the armistice meeting with the enemy."

Church's surprise wasn't noticed as Fawcett-Upham continued, back on track, outlining his plan.

"A stationary, solitary railway carriage at the end-of-the line in a place named Compiegne, a small god-forsaken place some fifty miles northeast of Paris, has been chosen to entertain these agreements. It is our intention to put the wind up the Germans and to make the hierarchy of the French Generals understand their own frailties, by assassinating one of the German superiors at the moment they are about to board the train. We have not yet been informed which of the German High Command will be their representative, but it would be ideal if Hindenburg or his sidekick Von Ludendorff turned up. A bullet in one of their heads would certainly rock the fragile German foundations. We intend to tell the Germans the war isn't over until they sign on the dotted line and that anybody is fair game until they do. That should rubbish Hindenburg's pathetic demands. If they don't like it, we'll invite them back to the battlefield and kill the rest of their nation, but we also have to keep the French in check. They have begun to think it was their efforts that brought Hindenburg to his knees. If we can rub out a senior German minister, the French will think we can do same to one of theirs. When it comes down to it, Allied Supreme Commander Ferdinand bloody Foch wants to protect what he's got without the risk of his country getting hurt any more. It's obvious Foch has eyes on the victor's spoils, regardless of the fact none of his generals put themselves anywhere near the front-line. They gave all their orders from plush chateaus a million miles behind the action. Little does he know we intend to remain the supreme power in Europe together with our friends from America. With so much turmoil going on, our two countries will spread this threat across the whole of the world. Woe betide any tin-pot regime taking us on in the future. It's up to you, Church. Decide to do it and you can name your own price."

The insecurity Church felt in confessing to a murder disappeared into insignificance compared to future repercussions, should he take on this directive from a member of the War Cabinet. What the voice of the British Government wanted, was to alter the face of history. In time, children would read about his actions at school, similar to the murders of Thomas Becket, or Caesar, but he was doubtful if the name Church would be credited for his actions, as he had no intention of being caught. In his euphoria, Church forgot he needed to convince a teenager to go along with this hair brained idea.

"How long do I have to put a plan into action?" Church questioned, confirming his acceptance to the assignment.

"There's talk of the meeting happening sometime around the 10th, 11th, or 12th of November, so we haven't got much time. As I understand, the railway line terminates in dense woodland, so finding a perfect spot for your sharpshooter shouldn't be a problem. But should you get caught, Peter, I can't guarantee your safety. We will, of course, deny any involvement, so it is up to you how you do it and how you mean to get away. What I ask would be extremely difficult and dangerous for able bodied men to achieve, so I emphasise Peter, if you believe this is beyond your capacity, please let me know soon and we'll put your skills to something else we might have planned. If you're happy with the arrangement, then I'll brief you with all the information I have, targets, photos, that sort of stuff, but if it goes wrong, you do realise it's likely you'll be shot on the spot."

Church listened intently to Sir Rodney's plan, but remained unruffled by its complexity. All he was thinking about was confirming his intent and the fee he was about to charge.

"We're going Sir Rodney and let that be final." Consolidating his position, Church admired Fawcett-Upham's candour. "But we haven't discussed money yet, Sir Rodney."

After itemising all the reasons why Church shouldn't take on the task, Fawcett-Upham wasn't surprised by Church's mercenary angle. He knew anything short of a realistic figure could ruin a devious but dangerous plan.

"What have you got in mind, Peter?"

Replacing the onus back onto Church, Sir Rodney mulled over the thought he might even quote a figure less than the one he had in mind, but he doubted it. Fully aware of its enormity, the price needed to reflect its importance.

There was Mathew's future to think about. What sort of figure would be sufficient to give him quality of life?

"Five hundred thousand pounds."

Expecting Fawcett-Upham to scoff at the idea of such a ludicrous amount, Church was pleasantly surprised to see it was greeted with a nod and a handshake. Sir Rodney was surprised at Church's quote. He was prepared to pay double.

"I believe we have a deal, Peter, but now you are privy to my Government's plan and I know your dark secret, both our families' good names are in jeopardy should this arrangement be leaked to a third party. As no agreement shall be written, only my solemn word can be given as a guarantee to keep my side of the bargain. For the sake of our families, I must insist on your word for complete discretion." Fawcett-Upham waited for the Church's all-important nod of approval. "Right, let's get this show on the road. I'll be on my way back to London tonight, so first thing tomorrow morning, I'll gather all the information and photographs to date and have the package expressly couriered up to you."

Only minutes before, Fawcett-Upham showed obvious signs of drunkenness, but now his bodily functions belied the amount of alcohol consumed. With precision, he continued to outline his ministerial effort to aid this covert operation.

"Here's a special direct telephone number into my office. Only Joblin or I have authority to use it, so think of a code name in case Joblin answers before I can reach the receiver."

"Salvation."

The name immediately came to mind.

"Quite appropriate, I like it. Okay, Salvation it is."

Taking this to mean the end of their luncheon, Fawcett-Upham stood, calling Joblin in from the garden.

"Just one more thing, Peter." Sir Rodney turned to Church before Joblin returned. "You overlooked one thing at Sandown Park. Those tyre tracks you left behind. I noticed Joblin taking note of the tread you have on your wheelchair. If you hadn't confessed to me, I'm sure Joblin would have put your name up as someone to look into. He's not as dumb as he looks, you know. And, who knows where that would have led? As it is, I can stifle any further inquiries."

Church led Fawcett-Upham and Joblin back to the front door.

"Okay, Joblin. You go and start her up, I just need to say a few more words to Major Church."

He waited until the engine drowned out any possibility of being overheard by Joblin. "The money shall be deposited in a bank, the particulars of which will also be sent to you by the same courier. Should anything go wrong, I'd deny this meeting ever took place, for that matter, so will Joblin. He will have to be eventually informed, but not of your Sandown caper, though, I'd be surprised if he hasn't already picked up the connection. He's a good man and someone not to be underestimated. He's also very trustworthy; so don't worry if he contacts you on my behalf at a later stage. I'll say cheerio for now, but I doubt if we shall meet again before the assignment. I don't have to say to you, the less people who know about this the better."

They shook hands, knowing each possessed a secret powerful enough to destroy the other person. Church gambled on whether Fawcett-Upham wanted the services of an assassin more than the capture of a murderer. Fortunately, similar to those who knew Heanen well, he couldn't care less whether the culprit was caught or not. Both parties appeared to be very satisfied with each other's offer of assistance.

Watching the Rolls Royce drive out of the gates, Church wondered how he was going to convince Mathew to go along with the next assignment.

CHAPTER 29

Tuesday morning arrived accompanied with climate conditions usually associated with the oncoming of autumn. A vicious weather front streaming in from the east, deepened over Europe, dropping its contents into a gale force wind over Yorkshire. Unaware of this forthcoming torrential rainfall, villagers woke to find holes in their roofs that weren't there in the spring. Trench coats, tucked away in wardrobes, reappeared covered in mildew. Typically of weather patterns in northern Britain, seasons changed dramatically from day to day.

Viewing his arrival from the confines of a taxi parked outside Mathew's cottage, Church saw his presence might not be welcome. Drenched to the skin, struggling to hammer down a flapping, makeshift waterproof tarpaulin whilst perched near the top rung of a precariously placed ladder, Mathew noticed a smiling face peering out in his direction from below, its identity not obscured by a rain splattered window, and offered a cheery wave back in recognition.

In the comfort of his dry interior, Church watched Mathew appearing to be enjoying his battle against the elements. Thrashing an array of erratic hand signals, Church judged the semaphore to mean Mathew would be down the ladder after fixing two more nails.

"What a change in the weather, still, Pinkerton's probably pleased," Mathew managed to splutter, manoeuvring Church's wheelchair across the pathway strewn with broken roof tiles, into the tranquillity and dryness of his cottage. Church, wrapped in oilskins, remained relatively unscathed by the elements, but Mathew resembled someone emerging from a swimming pool fully dressed. "Won't be long, Peter. I'll just get out of these wet things. Wheel yourself into the kitchen and get rid of that fisherman's outfit you're wearing. I'll be down in a minute."

A kettle boiled on the burner and a bottle of brandy stood opened on the kitchen table when Mathew returned.

"Looks as though you could do with a nip or two of this," Church greeted, holding the bottle ready to pour.

"Yes, it's been a hectic morning. Woke up last night with drips coming through the ceiling directly over my bed. Still, I think I've fixed it until I can get a man in to mend it properly. What brings you out on a day like this? Must be important. You're not going to tell me it has something to do with what you were talking about the last time we spoke, are you?"

Church's silence confirmed Mathew's worse fear.

"It is, isn't it?"

"You know me too well, Mathew. Yes, you're right. But before you go off into one of your tantrums, hear what I have to say first. Fawcett-Upham came to lunch yesterday." Church saw Mathew roll his eyes skywards with the mention of his name. "Let me finish, Mathew. I told him everything about Heanen, but never once did your name come up in the conversation. He asked for it, but I refused. We came to an agreement after we talked that if Scotland Yard start sniffing around, he has the authority to hush things up. It was just as well we did talk as it seems his aide, Joblin, was getting suspicious about me. Putting two and two together and coming to four after taking a look at the tread on my wheelchair tyres. Now it's out in the open, so to speak, we can't be charged. That is, of course, if we do this job for him."

Anticipating a verbal barrage of expletives, pouring two large brandies seemed the only way to occupy time before it eventually started, but silence uncomfortably remained.

"Aren't you going to ask me why?" Church broke first, his patience inferior to that of Mathew's.

"No, because whatever I say will have no bearing on what you have already planned, with or without my consent. So why waste my breath?"

Sensing this might be easier than first thought, Church paused, swilling a cocktail of tea and brandy around the inside of his mouth.

"Okay." Looking directly into Mathew's eyes, Church blurted out, itemising the contents of his conversation with Fawcett-Upham. "The price we have to pay for his silence is to do another assignment. I promise it will be the last, but afterwards, you'll be a rich man. A very, very rich man."

Once Church began, his excitement quickened his delivery, describing the plan by saying though the target hadn't yet been decided upon, the location was known to be just north of Paris. All the relevant information would arrive any day by courier and the need to be ready to leave at a minute's notice was essential if it was to work. Whilst he talked, he noticed Mathew sitting calmly on the opposite side of the kitchen table, not at all agitated by what he heard.

"Well, Peter. You have been busy. I knew, after we spoke, you couldn't leave this matter alone. With the fact that we seem to be very good at rubbing out scum-bags, it was only a matter of time before you'd be calling round with some crazy, hare-brained idea someday. But this sounds really dangerous. The place will be crawling with military police and with all due respect to your physical ability, I'm dying to know how you intend to make a quick getaway. There's very little time to reconnoitre the place, so we'll have to rely on Fawcett-Upham's intelligence, which you know as well as I do, is not a clever thing to do when dealing with the army, 'cos a pound to a pinch of shit, you know it's going to be wrong. There's also the fact that, we melted into the background then. We had the mayhem of battle going on around us, with bodies lying everywhere. The second saw thousands of race goers giving cover. This one is not going to be so easy. But, knowing you, you wouldn't have come over here to suggest it if you hadn't already devised some way of getting us in and out."

"Ah, I believe you are beginning to respect my genius."

Feeling relieved, Church smiled, as Mathew appeared to be going along with the plan. Intricacy and danger intrigued Mathew as much as it did him and playing to these strengths, would eventually overcome any reluctance by his partner to participate. The one possible stumbling block would be if Mathew wouldn't believe there was a way of getting out alive.

What Church had in mind was brilliant with its simplicity and daring. Over the following hour of refilled glasses, the disappearance of a cheddar cheese wedge and the emptying of a pickle jar, Mathew listened intently to Church's art for the theatrical, admitting after his monologue, that they might just get away with it. It was foolish, but it needed to be. A daring plan like this could only succeed with unconventional imagination.

"I like it, Peter. You've convinced me. Can't wait."

Whether it was the liquid contents of this unconventional lunch responsible for persuading Mathew, Church could only ponder, but seeing his rekindled enthusiasm not only confirmed his loyalty, but dispelled any insecurity he might have felt.

"And the good thing about your plan is we don't have to lug loads of props across the Channel. We should be able to get everything we need over in France," Mathew enthused.

"Precisely," Church confirmed, offering a raised glass. "For convenience, it would save time and effort if you came back to stay with me until we go. It would also be nice to have some good company. I not saying Mrs Freeman is boring, but our conversations never appear to last longer than a 'good morning' or a 'good night' with very little said in-between. "

Once the euphoria of their discussion subsided and sobriety reinstated, waiting for the 'green light' dampened their humour, but not their enthusiasm. Similar to preparation for the Sandown Park campaign, Mathew broke down the Lee Enfield, cleaning it meticulously before reassembling for a spot of target practice in the manor's garden. Again, the Pinkerton's renewed scarecrow took the brunt of Mathew's expertise. Studying army ordinance survey maps for three suitable positions, should one or more be undesirable due to heavy presence of military surveillance, Church's meticulous organisational skills would not permit an innocuous oversight to ruin their chances. Nothing would stop him from succeeding.

The sun was just about to rise on Wednesday, 6th November, when startling the light sleepers, a raucous engine heralded the arrival of the courier. The sound only sent shivers through Mathew's body when remembering, years before, a similar noise arriving at the mine to summon Twickton Company to war.

Riding overnight, the dispatch courier, on Fawcett-Upham's direct orders, delivered a package no bigger than a large envelope, containing the death penalty for one of those attending the armistice. Gratefully accepting a cooked breakfast, the courier sat at Mrs Freeman's kitchen table oblivious to the fact he carried indicting evidence that could, in the wrong hands, see both the protagonists dangle from the end of a rope.

Scouring each snippet of carefully grafted information, Church slowly thumbed through the pages, studying photographs and maps with precision, keeping Mathew at a distance and far enough away to be unable to eye-ball anything printed. Somewhat puzzled by this action, Mathew accepted the theory that if caught carrying such damning documents, his role as an insubordinate accomplice might see him charged on a lesser offence. Viewing this as a military operation, Church assumed the mantle of the responsible senior officer should anything go wrong.

Boarding the noon train from Leyburn, their itinerary directed them to catch their London connection at Northallerton. Meticulously contained within Church's leather holdall, specific details and photographs of where and when the armistice would be signed on Monday, 11th November at 5am, never left Church's clutched hands. Also enclosed was a thick bundle of French Franc bank notes, sufficient to bribe even the most honest of Frenchman.

Masking their movements so as not to leave a trail, they purchased tickets with cash instead of travel documents and travelled in civilian clothes. Conspicuous only by accepting help to board the remodelled wheelchair into the carriage, this previously practiced performance projected the image of a wealthy disabled gent taking an outing with his trusty manservant. Not a common sight in these parts, but one readily accepted.

The scene at Folkestone the following morning was as frantic as Mathew remembered when encountering his initial crossing of the English Channel. If possible, there was greater troop movement, but on this occasion, they appeared to be returning from France. Seemingly many more able bodied than injured disembarked from crowded jetties. Proving to be an unforeseen problem, their route through a uniformed barricade moving in the opposite direction obscured any clues as to where civilians might be able to board.

Shouting to those in front who might hinder their forward progress, Church treated all who dared enquire of their non-military reasons for a boarding a ship with total disdain. For the port workers, turning a blind eye to rid themselves of this persistent, irritating problem was conscientiously more favourable than combining them into the existing turmoil. Military procedure scrapped, it was not the time to adhere to the rule book with so much movement of army personnel bereft of officer direction. Who was there to notice if a belligerent crippled ex-major wanted to travel on an empty ship in the opposite direction to the general flow of personnel?

Finally arriving, the tramp steamer docked two hours later at Calais. Disembarking, Mathew couldn't believe Church's first instruction was to find time to relax in a venue where they might have lunch. Obviously, Mathew surmised, installed within Church's timetable - a schedule he couldn't rationalise coming from a working class background – was the desire of the rich to take a noonday break for refreshments even though they had done nothing during the morning to warrant them.

The town's total disruption, so vividly described in the English press, appeared to be ignored by Church who expected the French to keep local spirits alive with what little alcohol they could beg, borrow, or steal. Benefiting from allied protection, he was sure within the confines of Calais and bereft from the ravages of war, there would be a small place capable of catering to his requirements. Off the beaten track, in an unused side road leading from the harbour, they found what Church expected to be there.

***

"Bonjour."

A shocked bar owner, unable to believe his eyes, saw his first Englishman in four years not wearing a uniform and sitting in a wheelchair, enter his bar.

"Bonjour," he replied, his uncertainty of this insane Englishman's motives prompting two local customers to swing round in disbelief of what they witnessed. "What do you want?" he demanded, his thick Gallic accent attempting to speak Church's language.

"Oh, good. You speak English," Church responded, surprised.

"Mon dieu!" Reverting to his mother's tongue, his disbelief brought a rare smile to his weather beaten, war torn features. "Yes, I speak English. What can I do for you?"

"Well, my good friend. First of all, what have you got to eat?"

"Monsieur, do you know there is war taking place not seventy kilometres from 'ere? Give France a week or two to clean up the mess, then we might be ready to welcome tourists, but not just yet."

Church laughed at French sarcasm, but dismissed his objection.

"Oh, I'm sure you can rustle something up. Eggs, bacon, bread, something in that nature. A bottle of red maybe, even coffee."

"Coffee, he says." Looking round to his locals, the owner of the bar hunches his shoulders in dismay as French inherently do so nonchalantly. "Do you know how long it 'as been since I drank coffee? How do you say? Three bloody years." Though initially rattled by Church's ignorance, his humour remained. "Okay, my mad Englishman. You sit at zee table and I see what I 'av."

Left alone to settle round a corner table, they mull over ideas about how they should progress south to Paris, unaware of the locals' continuous, open-mouthed staring.

After twenty minutes of improvised planning, the bar keeper reappeared carrying two plates.

"Dis is all I 'av. I 'ope it is okay."

Placing his efforts on the table, he stands aside, admiring his creation.

"Looks splendid. You have done wonders. Thank you."

The aroma of fried bacon, eggs and bread was one of long forgotten, better times memories. Fresh crusty bread wiping all traces of food from the china plate brought a broad smile from each participant to this culinary delight. Reminiscing of happier times, the dangers lying ahead were put aside for a moment by further complementing their enlivened taste buds with an unlabelled bottle of red.

"Monsieur."

Sitting amongst his regulars, discussing the eccentricity of the British, the bar owner looked across to where Church called. "May I talk privately with you?"

Grateful for enlivening a dull day, he approached the strangers with an extra bottle and sat on a spare chair.

"What can I do for you?" he enquired, refilling empty glasses.

"We have a small problem. You see, we need a few items and I was wondering if you could maybe help us acquire them."

Church discreetly placed a wedge of French Francs on the table in front of the innkeeper. Immediately his eyes widened, settling on the notes before silently whistling to himself. He didn't care about the amount. From where he sat, it looked a lot.

"What is it you want? If I can 'elp, of course I will."

Temptation could not be ignored during these fugal times.

Church's wary glance towards the locals didn't go unnoticed.

"Do not worry about zem, Monsieur, zey do not speak your language. Zey can 'ardly speak French," he laughed, putting a glass to his mouth, but found it empty.

"I need a British field ambulance with a big red cross on each side and an English army uniform, the rank of private will do, with a Red Cross armband, large enough to fit my friend here. A stick of dynamite and a short fuse. And the last thing we need is a container of fresh blood, preferably taken from an animal."

Puzzled, the bar keeper studied each pair of eyes stationed on the opposite side of the table. If there wasn't such a large amount of cash positioned so close to his grasp, he would have thrown them out onto the pavement, regardless of the wheelchair. Attention reverted to refilling his glass, he took a mouthful and lit a foul smelling cigarette whilst pondering the possibility of supplying their bizarre shopping list.

"Bon. Yes, I tink I can 'elp you, mon amies. It might take a little while, but I am sure I can 'elp."

"Can you get them by tomorrow?"

"Oui, I tink zat is possible. But you will 'av to trust me with some money."

"That is no problem. How much do you need?"

The owner scooped up what was on the table.

"Ca va." Discreetly thumbing each note, he declared. "Zis will do, nicely."

"Should you manage to get it all, there will be a bonus of the same amount."

Church whispered, hoping this promise would act as an incentive for him not run off with what was already being stuffed in pockets.

"Tres bon, Monsieur. I will 'av everything out zee back by tomorrow. If you wish, you can stay 'ere the night. Zis one will be on me, as you say."

Cementing the deal with shaken hands, they watched their future by-pass the bar and walk out of the front door in determined mode.

Thinking of Twickton, the frontline and being hunted by Scotland Yard they knew there were worse places to be on a cold, drab afternoon than sitting in a bar, enjoying the hospitality shown by the owner's wife's persistence to keep their glasses filled. Local customers came and went, enjoying a quick glass of wine until darkness began to fall, provoking the landlady to light a few scattered oil lamps, an expensive commodity but bringing a cosy, welcoming ambiance to the atmospheric bar. During the third shared bottle, Church suggested it might be wise to make it last a little longer than the first two as both showed signs of their effect.

As quickly as he disappeared that morning, the owner reappeared from behind the bar, displaying a sign of raised thumbs and a big smile.

"Come," he beckoned.

Standing unsteadily, Mathew followed, leaving Church to ponder on the owner's success. In the low light of an autumn evening, parked under a large khaki sheet of tent canvas, Mathew saw a Red Cross ambulance, exactly as ordered.

"See what I 'av in zee back."

Opening one of its rear doors, the bar keeper pointed proudly to a British uniform equipped with an armband, then redirected his finger to a short fused single stick of dynamite strapped safely to one of the stretcher frames

"Voila," he boasted, an even bigger smile creasing his face.

"Brilliant. Let's go back inside and give my friend the good news."

Returning, Church joined the backslapping after hearing Mathew's news. Having the best pay-day the barkeeper could remember, he toasted the Englishmen, whilst they in turn, toasted the Frenchman for his ability to relieve them of a possible headache. Unable to refuse French hospitality, they resigned themselves to an evening of drinking and eating, the food being a kind of which they knew existed, but had never tasted. Mathew wasn't sure if the amount of wine drunk was responsible for finding snails very tasty, but knew they would wake the following morning with heavy heads. Having time on their side, they could afford to enjoy this brief interlude of indulgence and put to the back of their minds the seriousness of what lay ahead.

CHAPTER 30

Forecasting the inevitable, Friday morning arrived heralding two alcohol induced sore heads. Accompanying his cockerel's warning of imminent sunrise, the landlord's day began before dawn, collecting freshly laid eggs. Reminiscent of Pinkerton's reveille, the familiar chorus stirred both guests from their heavy slumber. Wedging pillows against the headboard for support, Mathew trawled his memory of the previous evening. Blurred recollections of an ambulance appeared, but try as he might, couldn't remember how Church climbed the stairs to the neighbouring bedroom, that's if it was him he heard snoring through the thin plaster walls. Contained in a large white bowl, he fragilely peered onto the surface of ice-cold water, reflecting a drawn, tousled haired image. Gritting teeth under tight lips, he gently lowered his head towards the glass-like surface, feeling needles of pain shoot through his brain the second his nose touched the surface. Confusing his brain, the sudden numbing remedy achieved the objective. Hurriedly dressing before his face regained blood temperature, he went in search of Church.

"Ah, bonjour, Monsieur. Your friend still asleep, no?" Freddie, the bar owner, greeted the sight of Mathew descending the staircase.

"I wouldn't think so by the noise your bird in the back yard is making. How did he get upstairs last night?"

Mathew questioned but unlike Freddie, appearing fresh and unaffected by the previous night's indulgence, felt facial normality returning to reignite his hangover.

"Oh, no problem. I carry 'im. 'Ere, I 'av coffee today. Take a cup while I go and get your friend. It's good for your 'ead." Pointing to his mop of jet black hair, Freddie sympathised with Mathew's pain.

Comparable to the fried breakfast the morning before; the aroma of brewing, freshly ground coffee was one Mathew had long forgotten. He'd drunk it on rare occasions, but the flavour was unmistakable.

"Is that coffee I can smell?"

Tracing the direction of the voice, Church descended the stairs, straddling Freddie's back. For a man appearing to be little bigger than Joey, the Frenchman showed extraordinary strength.

"So, that's how you got upstairs."

Similar to Freddie, Church's persona reflected the Frenchman's, showing no evidence of the previous night's consumption.

"Every cripple's home should have one of these."

In good humour, Freddie replaced Church back into his wheelchair.

"Now that is what I call coffee," Church continued, removing the large bowl from his lips.

"As I 'ave enough money now for small luxuries, I treat you." Freddie joined the conversation. "And when victory is ours, you celebrate with one of these."

Expanding his chest with typical Gallic pride, he placed a large cigar in each of their breast pockets. The kindness Freddie bestowed on the two strangers affected them both.

"When this war is over, we must come back and do this all over again. I must thank you and your wife for everything you have done for my friend and me. You have been absolutely bloody marvellous."

In typical, accented English, Church's words embarrassed Freddie. His arms and hands wafted in unison with a bobbing head, but try as he could; no words came from moving lips.

"Monsieur, it is me who must thank you," he finally uttered, choking his words. "Without your money, it would 'av been very 'ard to carry on 'ere. Now we 'ave a good chance to get to the end of these terrible times."

"Thank you, Freddie. I'm glad we could help you in the same way as you helped all our lads in uniform, but we must be off soon. We have a long way to go. One thing I have to ask, Freddie. Is there petrol in the ambulance?"

"Oui, Monsieur. I, er…'ow do you say? Took it from the gendarme wagon when they no looking." His laugh was infectious.

"Oh, I nearly forgot. Did you manage to get the blood?" Church brought sobriety back to the proceedings.

"Oh, yes. My friend killed 'is pig this morning, ready for the big victory celebration. ''Ere I 'ave it in 'zis container."

Handling the glass, screw top glass jam-jar, turned Mathew's stomach when feeling the warmth and weight of the quantity extracted from the butchered carcass only twenty minutes before. It wasn't a remedy to cure a raging head.

***

Continuing to be an able assistant, whilst Mathew stowed the wheelchair in the back of the ambulance, Freddie carried Church to the passenger seat. Appearing bewildered, Mathew occupied the only other seat available behind the steering wheel. Protruding knobs, levers and circular dials of all shapes and sizes stared back at him.

"Okay, Freddie. Turn her over," Church called from inside the cab.

The barkeeper's bent knees in readiness whilst his hands gripped the starting handle.

"Well, Mathew. What are you waiting for? Turn the petrol on and give her a bit of choke. Come on, let's go."

306

Transfixed, Mathew's feet brushed against pedals of which he had no idea what use they were made for. For reasons why Mathew didn't react to his order, Church immediately recognised his vacant look.

"Oh, my god. You can't drive, can you?"

"No, I can't. I never thought I'd be the one to drive. I automatically thought, as you planned everything, you would be doing it."

"What, with no bloody legs, you fucking imbecile?" Shattering his usually calm demeanour, Church cursed this simple oversight. "Oh, bugger."

Squatting in front of the ambulance's radiator, Freddie wondered why nothing happened after his first strenuous efforts at swinging the crank handle.

"Right. Whether you like it or not, as you are the only one in this partnership with feet and believe me you need them to make this thing move, you are going to drive this fucking vehicle."

Calming himself, Church assessed the hopeless situation, quickly realising he was left with no other options.

"I've never sat in the front of an automobile before, let alone driven one. Even in Heanen's Rolls Royce I sat in the back," Mathew lamely excused his lack of skills.

"Well, there's no time like the present to learn. Now, turn on the petrol and slide that button on the steering wheel...No, not that one, on the steering wheel, you buffoon...Yes, that one, good."

The sudden grinding noise of hand driven pistons made Mathew jump back in his seat.

"Again, but this time keep your finger on the button until I tell you to release it back." Unamused by this folly, Church's attempts to temper his anger by suggesting a calm assurance, failed miserably.

As ordered, Mathew kept his finger pressing hard. The whole superstructure rocked in unison with the stubborn engine and Freddie's frantic efforts, but it still refused to fire.

"Give it some more choke, here, let me do it." Leaning across Mathew, Church slid his finger all the way round the dial. "Keep your foot away from the accelerator; otherwise you'll flood the bloody carburettor. Now Freddie, try again."

Unable to understand a word of Church's mechanical jargon, it didn't explain why Freddie's next effort prompted the four cylinders to fire into action, aggravating Mathew's initial fear with the sound of grumbling pistons. Sitting rigidly upright, a position caused by this unexpected confrontation, he felt physically and mentally unable to cope with what was expected.

"Push the clutch down all the way to the floor," Church demanded, pointing to a pedal in the middle of a group of three.

"Now remember Mathew, it is very important. The pedal to the left is the brake and the one to the right is the accelerator. Please don't forget or get them muddled up," stressed the apprehensive passenger.

"Now relax and place your hands on the steering wheel. To start the thing rolling, we'll use the choke instead of the accelerator." Beginning his instruction, Church forced an unconvincing smile. "I'll change the gears, while all you have to do is steer and brake and when I shout 'clutch'; you press the left pedal down to the floor. CLUTCH!" Church yelled. "There, easy, isn't it? Now gently raise your foot, letting the clutch slowly rise. When you feel it bite and we begin to move, take your foot right off and concentrate on steering us out of this yard and onto the road in one piece."

Needlessly using the entire thigh muscle strength to depress the clutch, his leg began to wilt under the intensity of the weight, but whilst understanding the order to slowly release the pedal, his mind spun in turmoil with coordination.

"Think, Mathew," Church whispered. "Get your thoughts together. Slowly lift your foot."

As directed, Mathew's boot lifted, slowing the racing engine to allow the gear to grab the correct cog. Miraculously, the engine didn't stall but initiated the vehicle to move.

"That's it. Now, release your foot altogether and steer round this corner. You're doing well, Mathew."

Looking on in amazement, Freddie stood open mouthed.

First gear achieved a distance of fifteen yards, but Church couldn't see them getting further than the outskirts of town before the engine overheated. Shaking his head in disbelief, Freddie waved a final farewell and mouthed a silent prayer.

"Good, we're on our way. Get over to the right, Mathew; we're in France and the French do things differently to us English. They drive on the other side of the road? Now press the clutch again. CLUTCH!"

A commodity rarely used by Church, sarcasm appeared to be having the desired effect on the unsuspecting driver. His fear waned and noticeably anger started to fester

Slamming his foot down preceded a grinding crunch when Church strong-armed the gear lever into second; increasing the speed.

"This is easy," Mathew laughed.

"Not so bloody confident, and keep your eyes on the road. We have got another hundred miles to go. We're lucky, there's no traffic around this time of day. Just as well."

The speedometer needle flickered onto ten as Church ordered 'clutch'. Achieving more revolutions, the change to third slipped in without effort.

"That's better. We're getting quite good at it."

Hoping he hadn't spoken too soon, Church's relief was apparent.

Encountering fewer traumas than expected, they reached the open road heading south. Travelling at a speed of twenty-five miles an hour was as fast as Church felt safe but there wasn't a lot more the engine could give, the horsepower under the bonnet wasn't calibrated to go much faster. Travelling six miles before road conditions dictated slowing down eased Mathew's anxiety, but Church worried about running into army vehicles moving north.

"Do you see those trees up ahead? Pull in there. Start braking slowly, not so much, let her glide. That's better. 'Clutch'. Now we're in neutral she won't stall. Just concentrate on the brake."

Steering off the road at the designated spot, they came to an abrupt stop.

"Very good, Mathew. For the first time behind a wheel, that wasn't a bad effort. Right, we've got to get changed into uniform. These civvies we're wearing are out of place."

Anyone approaching the seated figure of Church from his side of the cab would have difficulty noticing his legs had been amputated below the knee, a map draped across his thighs obscuring his old uniform trousers freely dangling down to the floor. Demoted to private, Mathew's peaked cap more than compensated with its visual importance.

"Now, whatever happens we don't stop. If someone waves us down, we don't stop. If there is a blockage in the way, we don't stop. We go round it. We are an ambulance attending an emergency. Don't forget."

Not wanting to get into a situation where Mathew's driving skills could be judged, or his own disability noticed, Church repeating the same routine as when leaving Freddie's bar. Re-joining the road with more confidence than before, with luck on their side, Church could see them actually pulling this off.

CHAPTER 31

They travelled fifteen miles of uninterrupted progress when evidence of war became increasingly apparent. What began with the odd dead horse carcass lying by the roadside soon manifested itself into a vision Mathew and Church remembered from their short stay on the frontline. Manoeuvring through each desolate village, the buildings began to show signs of battle until they got to a stage where no structure remained intact. Scattered masonry covered the ground, alongside a multitude of dead horses and discarded vehicles of all descriptions, obliterating the road. They lost count of the number of inverted rifles pushed into the sodden ground. Only a helmet balanced on the butt of the weapon suggested it was where a fallen soldier lay buried.

Living how they did in Yorkshire, untouched by war, it would be impossible to relate to those back home the amount of destruction and suffering the French endured. It was difficult for Mathew to think how any sanity could return from the mess he witnessed, or how the French could ever afford to rebuild whilst forgiving a neighbouring enemy.

Continuing south unnoticed, they unwittingly stumbled into *Arras,* a town where hundreds of troops from a multitude of nations crowded the streets, their pride appearing to be battered. Long forgotten was their desire to march into battle in tight formation. In its place, under no visible command, finding refuge was the order of the day but at their own pace. Seeing a scared, ageing civilian attempting to steer a horse and cart filled with his family and last possessions through the carnage of what was once the pride of British fighting forces, Church urged Mathew on through the rubble of human flotsam and told him not to apply the brakes. It was difficult for the youth not to stop and tender aid, but Church's insistence relieved his conscious from making a choice.

"We have to get off this main road," Church implored, breaking the silence this vision of despair caused.

"Don't you think I bloody well want to? There's no bloody road signs," Mathew chastised his partner for stating the obvious, seeing the predicament they were in.

"The sensible thing to do would be to head for Paris, but I think if we do that we could run into more of what we have left behind. I would like to approach Compiegne from the north, but the further we go south; the more likely the bridges over the Oise will have been destroyed. Take the next turning to the left at these crossroads. We must be going in the right direction." Sounding confident, Church was fully aware of their predicament whilst studying his road map.

Heavy artillery fire, just audible half an hour before, grew louder, but they managed to find a track with a decent surface offering few obstructions before they needed to confront defence lines. Mathew's driving skills improved enormously, attempting solo gear changes when Church's attention was diverted to decipher the name of an uninhabited pile of rubble. Once a docile farming village before the war, it now represented a forgotten strategic position fought over at all cost. Gleaning nothing as a reference to prove their direction, Church relied more on where shadows fell to calibrate east from west and all points between.

The sun rapidly fell from the sky indicating they'd spent most of the day travelling just sixty miles. Both agreed it would be foolish continuing in the dark. The place to spend the night chose itself as they approached a small wood to their left, amazingly relatively untouched by shell or mortar fire and neatly situated about a hundred yards off the track they'd followed for the past hour.

The robust ambulance tyres made light of the uneven terrain, gripping the sodden earth until an umbrella of branches enveloped the entire vehicle, making any visible contact from the road impossible. It was the ideal spot where they could safely light an oil lamp, whilst bedding down under hospital blankets on two raised, metal framed stretcher-bearers. Both needed sleep, especially as their previous night's efforts to relax were heavily induced by alcohol.

Mathew woke first the next morning, peering out onto the misty, tree covered landscape.

"What's the weather like?"

"Oh, you're awake, Peter. Not bad, misty, but the rain looks as though it's stopped. Bloody cold, though," Mathew replied, settling back under his warm covers.

"What's that box under your stretcher?" Church pointing under Mathew's makeshift bed.

"Don't know."

Pushing his blankets down sufficiently to bend at the waist, Mathew swung his hands down to the described article. Flipping the lid open, two sets of inquisitive eyes looked down at the contents with gratitude.

"Bloody hell. One day we will have to go back and thank Freddie."

Neatly arranged, bread and cheese wrapped in a white napkin protected two bottles of red wine.

"Breakfast is served."

Church smiled, humorously knotting the napkin round his neck.

Staying within the warmth of their blankets, they ate where they lay. Between mouthfuls, Church spoke of how he intended the day should be planned. It wasn't so much a discussion; it was more of a way of thinking out loud. It

313

was the morning of the 9th November. Although they were in front of the clock, he knew it wouldn't take much to put them behind time. If they could make the same sort of headway they achieved the day before, it would leave them ample time to consolidate and spy on the whereabouts of the security forces he knew would be stationed around the Forest of Compiegne.

Leaving the wheelchair camouflaged beneath the blankets, Mathew carried Church back to his passenger seat before taking his position to crank the engine whilst Church adjusted the choke from inside the cab. It took a few turns for Mathew to get used to the kickback, but as Freddie succeeded, two more efforts brought the engine back to life. Retracing tyre tracks to the road, Mathew swung the ambulance round into their desired direction with noticeably more panache than when he started the day before.

For reasons unknown, gunfire had been quenched, leaving an eerie silence to the morning. Swirling mist caused visibility to vary from ten yards to two hundred, making time to adjust to a driving error more of a lottery than skill. Church knew he should warn Mathew of his speed, but hung on to a piece of webbing dangling from the roof. There was very little to crash into as everything in their passing vicinity was decimated should the ambulance slide off the beaten track. In private thoughts, he believed speed was probably the better option than to take caution.

Suddenly, Mathew slammed his foot down hard on the brake, followed quickly by a manual effort on the handbrake. The wheels locked, careering the ambulance down a muddied incline before stopping forty yards on. Being correct with his analogy didn't compensate a racing heart-rate.

"What the bloody hell's all that about?" Church screamed, having no idea why Mathew performed such a drastic action without warning.

"Look, down there in the field."

Church followed Mathew's pointing finger.

"What is it?" Church queried.

"It's what we have been looking for. A sign post."

Scrambling out of his seat, Mathew approached the half hidden piece of wood. Scraping away encrusted earth, an eight feet long road sign emerged from under the grime. Felled by the allied army to confuse the enemy should they pass this way, Mathew replaced it in its rightful, up-right position.

"Peter. What was the name of that place we went through yesterday?"

"Arras, why?"

"Is it anywhere near Amiens?" Mathew questioned, looking at an array of names engraved above his head.

"No. Amiens is in the opposite direction to where we want to go," Church negatively replied scanning his map.

"In that case, we are heading towards St Quentin. Is that any good to us?"

Church ran his finger over the place names, searching for clues.

"Yes, that'll do us fine. From there we can approach from the north. I'm still worried about intact bridges, though."

Friendly or enemy bombardment, they weren't sure which, began its remorseful pounding, but coming from behind them in the distant north. Though never far from decaying equine carcasses or discarded military hardware, there appeared to be less structural damage in these parts. Some resemblance of life showed in the small settlements they passed, though nobody appeared to welcome an army ambulance driving through, regardless of its nationality.

On the stroke of midday they cautiously entered St Quentin, an ancient fortified town sculptured from a by gone age. As they'd witnessed in Arras, sheltering amongst the backdrop of medieval stoneware, shattered soldiers, many lying wounded on improvised stretchers, waited their turn for attention by overworked nursing staff attempting to work miracles in the confines of the commandeered *Hotel de Ville*. From a distance they saw doctors frantically waving at them to stop and give assistance, but they drove past, fully aware of being frauds using a medical vehicle for their own convenience, but in professional hands, might save a life or two. They witnessed the troopers' morale. It would be unreasonable to order the able bodied amongst the wounded back to the front line. Appearing disheartened and completely spent, their wounds were mental and they were in no fit state to resume fighting. If this conflict was to continue, where were the next generation of fighters going to be trawled from?

"Mathew, don't go any further. Stop right here," Church ordered, slapping his hand onto the dashboard, startling Mathew back to reality.

Up ahead, a roadblock crossed their intended route out of town. Manned by a unit of burly British military police, Church thought quickly as they'd witnessed the approaching ambulance. Any false movement or U-turns would only make them suspicious.

"What shall we do? Turn round to find another way?"

"No, they've seen us. We go for it."

Unsure what Church planned, Mathew watched his partner remove a thin pad of papers from his tunic breast pocket.

"I was given these by General Scarrow's office in the days before our company went to France. All commanding officers were issued these forms to give written orders should there be a breakdown in communications between HQ and the front line. The date is a bit old, but not to worry, I can alter that. It's the signature of the bastard that's important. I can write out my own order and it will be up to the MP to decide if it's genuine. As I know Scarrow is still back at Catterick, the MP will have to decide its authenticity or waste time by trying to trace its originality. My bet is his communications are as buggered as when we were on the front line, so hopefully, he'll wave us through. With all this mayhem going on, the last thing he'll want to do is contact HQ."

"What are you writing down?"

"I've written we've been ordered to attend a French General's pregnant wife who's just about to give birth in the village called Bierancourt. It's a small place over the River Oise ideally situated outside the forest, so let's give it a try, but, for god's sake, leave all the talking to me."

Whilst the engine idled, Mathew's choice of gear slotted in quietly, prompting the ambulance to slowly roll up to the barrier crossing the main thoroughfare. On seeing the vehicle approach, the sergeant stood firm in the middle of the obstruction, his hand held high as an order to stop.

"Afternoon, Sir."

A strong London accent boomed across the cab from Church's side, his salute well-rehearsed.

"Afternoon, Sergeant," Church nonchalantly answered, returning the Sergeant's acknowledgement. As he spoke, Church handed over his hastily scribbled order form for inspection.

"Some bloody Frog General has pulled strings to get individual attention for his sprog. Bloody cheek, I call it, taking us away from our real duties."

The Sergeant studied the order. From his frown, Mathew wasn't sure if he could read, as he appeared to be slowly mouthing the written word.

"We've had orders to be careful who we let through, 'cause there's an important get together with all the big knobs from both sides in Compiegne on Monday."

The Sergeant informed Church, standing back, offering a further salute as he ordered the barrier to be raised.

"Foster," he shouted to a private idly sitting astride a Royal Enfield courier's motorbike. "Give the Major here an escort down to Bierancourt."

Turning his attention back to Church, he advised in a lowered voice, the outrider would save them time going through the other checkpoints they would encounter en route.

"Thank you, Sergeant, very thoughtful of you."

Concealing his smile, Mathew knew if he looked at Church, he might spoil the illusion.

Following the escort under the barrier, Mathew kept close to the courier's back wheel. As the Sergeant predicted, within four miles they came across another checkpoint, but allowing the outrider to do all the explaining, a salute was sufficient for them to pass.

"This is certainly our lucky day, Mathew. We won't even have to try and find a bridge, he'll do it for us," Church smugly announced, rubbing his hands in anticipation.

Maintaining the luxury of the escort for the duration of the journey, they reached their destination before nightfall. Indicating they'd arrived on the outskirts of Bierancourt, the outrider raised his thumb, turned his bike and rode off in the direction back to his unit.

"Well, Mathew. That couldn't have been easier. Mind you, I don't go much on their security. The way it's handled, I wouldn't be at all surprised if there wasn't another half dozen snipers hiding in the undergrowth when we arrive."

He laughed, not so much as to what he said, but in relief to have got this far, a distance seemingly impossible two days before with the advent of Mathew's initial inability to drive.

"We can't stay here in the middle of the road all night. Drive through the village and find some cover. When it's dark, you can slip out and have a look round. It's not far to the forest. You might be able to find a good spot; well hidden, but with an uninterrupted sight," Church offered advice.

On the other side of town, the lush growth of the distant woodland, darkened by the blackening skyline, offered the desired cover to park up for the night.

CHAPTER 32

Assuming the sentries would be at their least alert, midnight was the time Church suggested as an ideal time for Mathew to slip out into the darkness. Cold, wet mists descended to further mask his movements, cushioning his footsteps on previously brittle, underfoot foliage. Keeping crouched whilst foraging through the undergrowth, Mathew kept the treeless clearing of the road to his right.

Having been out in the open no more than half an hour, Mathew encountered his first obstacle. Up ahead, penetrating the darkness, a warming glow took his attention. Granting the obstacle respect, Mathew gave it a wide sweep and skulked round his protective tree cover to close in on where a lone private sat on a log pile, warming his hands over a well-lit brazier. The illuminated surroundings gave Mathew a clear view of a small hut, probably housing a small unit of MP's off watch and asleep. To his left, possibly a hundred yards away, another lit brazier illuminated a similar hut. Through the trees, he saw similar units, each one appearing to be equally spaced apart.

Taking advantage of crackling, burning logs, he crawled through the invisible security line unobserved to continue south. From what he could ascertain, the entire area was circled with these small units, but once inside their cordon, there were no further obstructions until he came to a wide opening where a single railway line dissected the area. Gaslights, erected on twenty feet high poles, circled a solitary Pullman car, creating a surreal image penetrated by artificial flood lighting playing tricks with swirling mist.

To improve the picture in his mind, he needed to be on the other side of the carriage as it was there where the delegation would embark.

Keeping low under cover, Mathew circled the perimeter of the clearing searching for the right spot. Trying to visualise the scene he would encounter on Tuesday morning, he knelt next to a pine tree and brought an imaginary rifle up to his shoulder. Peering through cupped hands he moved in an arc, calculating the expanse of time required to identify the target, aim and be successful. This position was as good as any he found and with the nearest security post more than a hundred and fifty yards away behind, it would allow sufficient time to instigate their prearranged getaway plan.

Delicately using a sheaf knife, he stripped a portion of bark from the nearest tree, not noticeable in this light, but findable when searching for this spot again in the morning darkness. Back tracking through the woods, he duplicated the mark every twenty yards on another tree until he reached the road. Needing more than just a strip of bark as a marker to indicate the entrance back into the forest, Mathew dragged a fallen branch into the clearing and placed it on the verge. Any vehicle passing would hopefully disregard its importance, but to Mathew, it would act as a beacon when travelling at twenty miles an hour with only moonbeams as an illumination. He had no intention of heralding their arrival using headlamps.

Judging the chances of being apprehended by a foot patrol, Mathew decided it was worth the gamble to walk back along the roadside to where Church was hiding rather than concealing his presence back in woodland. Conscious to take a mental picture of the route, he muffled his footsteps by keeping to the grass verge, arriving back at the ambulance without contacting those who would ask for reasons of his whereabouts. His successful scouting mission took little under two hours to complete.

"Saved you the last of the wine. I bet you could do with it," Church offered, whilst Mathew shut out a cold blast blowing through the open rear door. "Everything go okay?" he continued.

Mathew related his findings, recalling everything from the staggered units in the woods to the registration number on the Pullman car, 2419D. Impressed by the detail, Church immediately got an image of what Mathew saw.

"Very good, Mathew. You should have been in intelligence with your memory, but instead, you opted to become an assassin. Somewhat ironic, don't you think?"

Puzzled by the terminology, he wondered if he was receiving a complement or being pigeon-holed into a profession he was beginning to wish he left behind on the battlefield. Mathew sat huddled in a blanket and finished the wine, leaving the thinking to someone who was better at it than him.

Wrapped in his own blanket, Church thumbed through scattered pieces of typed paper, none of which held any clues as to their originality. If they were to be caught, the War Office made sure its office could not be associated with this mission.

"According to Fawcett-Upham's intelligence, the first cars in the entourage arrive at 0450 hours. So it says, the French shall be first, followed by representatives from the allies. The German party are due to board the carriage at precisely 0500 hours. So we'll get into position at the same time the French get there. That means parking the ambulance by the wood, no later than 0445 hours. We only hope there isn't a nosey patrol driving around in the fifteen minutes it'll take to do the job and get away. We have a good place here to lie low for a day. Apart from my rumbling stomach, I feel fine, so what do you say to just sit tight for twenty-four hours?"

The feasibility of the plan sounded fine to Mathew, but it was the length of time Church suggested they sat tight that worried him. If stumbled upon by a patrol, it would take a lot of explaining as to why a crippled major with a customised wheelchair containing a sniper's rifle was parked in woodland not two miles away from where history was about to be made.

"Look, Mathew. It's going to be a long night, so you get some shut-eye first. I think it might be sensible if one of us takes a watch. I've got plenty to do. My trousers need burning off from the knee down and I've got to make it look authentic. So it'll take me some time."

Mathew sensed Church getting agitated. He'd never rambled on in so much detail about a subject he would normally think about to himself. Ducking his head below a blanket, Mathew smiled, content to finally prove Church was human after all. Strangely, he felt easier knowing his associate suffered from the same apprehensions as his own.

Waking at first light, Mathew saw the outline of his good friend silhouetted against a side window, the view showing a misty dawn enveloping the forest canopy.

"What do you see out there?"

Even on a mundane mental plane, any person would have flinched when suddenly disturbed from an inert daydream when hearing a voice breaking the silence, but considering the situation and the time he sat in silence with his own thoughts, Church spoke calmly, as though he'd been in a continuous, two-way conversation throughout the night.

"Oh, I'm looking at life, and death, and wondering which one of these freaks wants me the most. There is such a thin line dividing them. I've been sitting here wondering which one of the two I would be happy to settle for at this moment in time. Everything appears to be right or wrong, black or white, but there must be a third option, a way out for people who can't accept the rulebook. Why are my needs so different to those people who can't hear my screams? Don't think I'm the only one in this position, Mathew, there are many others out there who would also like to scream and be heard, but they, like me, are gagged by laws and protocol. Sadly, Mathew, you're not one of us. So just listen and advise me if you consider I should see a specialist who truly understands mental anguish? Your opinion really matters."

Mathew stared at the back of Church's head. He hadn't turned, but Mathew saw the reflection of his face in the glass. It was drawn and void of its usual ruddy complexion gained over months of sitting in a Yorkshire garden. His voice no longer held its usual rhyme, or depth. Instead it was hollow and frail.

"Before I went to war, I had what most people would call the ideal life. Due to no effort of my own, I'm wealthy and in a position in the community to warrant lesser mortals to doff their cap. Unlike my father, I never needed or wanted their subservience, but from an early age they directed this unwanted accolade upon my young shoulders. Having no personal target to aim for, my days were constantly filled with nonsense, resulting in the smallest mistakes erupting into full-blown headaches. I had no friends to talk to, or a relationship to nurture. I wasn't even allowed to keep a dog. I was slowly dying under the burden of the privileges handed to me due to my birth right, but nobody bothered to listen, or understand what I really wanted. Even when I joined up, I was given the rank of major within six weeks without consultation. It was all done on the assumption I could lead men. All of a sudden, there I was sitting on the front line in charge of a unit of soldiers, little more than boys and expected to do the right thing once again, but this time, instead of giving orders to butlers or housemaids, I was expected to obey them with authority to kill. My whole life changed that night in the trench. Nothing prepared me for that whiff of excitement in my nostrils and not knowing what was going to happen next. Suddenly, the mundane boredom of what was expected, disappeared. It was the first time my life I didn't have to follow a script. You have no idea what sort of burden was lifted off my shoulders on that night. I was free to decide for myself. And then, Mathew, I met you in that hell-hole. The first time we met, I knew you were special. I couldn't believe you were only eighteen. You were so calm, confidant and a million miles away from how I felt. I knew then you were not only a companion, but also someone I needed to be with. For the first time in my life, my mind was at ease with itself. I knew what I wanted and regardless of what my father thought; I wasn't going to let you go. In those few short hours, most of the feelings I needed to suppress in the past were eager to surface, and I would let them go in whatever direction they wanted without a care about what people would say."

Mathew wasn't ignorant that there were men who found male companionship preferable to that of females, having a sex life to match. He heard of such men being ridiculed and totally ostracised in communities where male manual workers dominated everyday life, but having never witnessed this sort of union, he never imagined for one moment he could be drawn by another man's affection, or be attractive to one. Not for one moment did Mathew suspect Church's friendship to be anything more than just that, but now, he needed to confirm Church's true meaning.

"Hey, Peter. Turn round, and look at me."

Swinging his legs down from the stretcher, Mathew broke the chill atmosphere with a humourless laugh.

"Here, I've found a little bit of wine left in the bottom of the bottle. Take a mouthful."

Picking up each stump to follow his body, Church turned. Mathew saw a stranger. His eyes had become watery slits and somehow appeared to be nearer to his nose. His hair no longer appeared smart, but was stacked up in an array of unruly spikes. Taking the offered bottle, he placed the opening to his lips, letting the remnants of liquid disappear down his throat.

"I need to have a piss, Mathew. Help me?"

In the past, this plea for assistance would be given without a second thought, but Mathew held back. After what was just said, he was unsure about his next move.

"Mathew, for Christ's sake, give me a hand to get out of here so I can have a piss."

Sensing Mathew's split second of indecision, Church knew their friendship would never be quite the same.

"Sure, yes, of course."

Placing Church on the grass by the side of the ambulance, Mathew retreated, giving Church privacy when he unbuttoned his trousers.

"Give me a shout when you've finished."

Not a word was said once back inside the confines of the vehicle. Mathew found it hard to look at Church in the eye. It wasn't embarrassment, just a foreign feeling of not being able to understand the meaning of why Church opened up his personal life, now of all times.

"Look. I've been thinking, Peter. We don't have to do this job. We could go back to England, tell them we weren't good enough and give back their money. Nobody harmed and all forgotten about within six months. What do you say? Fawcett-Upham won't reopen the Heanen case, because we've got too much on him. So, let's call it a day and go home."

Mathew posed the question calmly, repressing the temptation to scream. If he was right about Church's motives, there was no possibility of being included in his plans for the future other than being a good friend, but the more he thought about their situation, the less he was inclined to put his life at risk and go along with this suicidal plan. There were no half measures with Church, as with everything in his life, it was a case of all or nothing. It was a trait of his upbringing he would never be able to shake off. If need be and it was starting to look likely, to save embarrassment for both parties, Mathew would end their friendship here and now. It began to look extremely likely their differences might result in them both getting killed and Mathew wasn't prepared to go along with this interpretation even if Church wasn't prepared for this eventuality.

Sensing he'd administered a self-inflicted wedge between their friendship and trust, Church knew he had to act fast to stem the widening rift from increasing, only if to regain Mathew's confidence. He wouldn't permit all his meticulous planning to come to no avail.

"No, we can't do that. I've given my word. I have been sent to do a job and whether you do it with me or not, it shall be done."

Turning his gaze away from Mathew's inquisitive eyes, Church gambled on Mathew not leaving him to attempt the assassination alone. The odds of success without Mathew diminished to suicidal. Church needed Mathew. Hoping their friendship retained strength, he cursed himself for putting it under jeopardy.

"I'm not saying I won't be with you, Peter. It just might be one job too many. If I'm going to die, I rather it was back in Yorkshire with a whiskey bottle close at hand. Why don't you get some sleep? You look all in. We'll talk about it again after we get some sleep. "

Trying to reason with Church in this mood appeared hopeless. If he was listening to Mathew, he showed no signs. Mathew laid back in his stretcher, looking at Church pressing his nose to the glass, his right hand spread flat against the pane; his index finger lightly tapping a remorseful rhyme. Having seen Church as the backbone of their partnership, he now saw a liability. In fact, he thought, if need be, he could do the job without him and still have a better chance of getting them both away. Mathew knew their roles were reversed with him now being the stronger in terms of having not only the success of the mission on his mind, but also their escape. This, so it appeared, Church was willing to forfeit. He would need all his wits about him to cajole Church to do it his way. He must remember to be sympathetic; Mathew fell asleep.

Starkly woken by shaken shoulders, Mathew opened his eyes seeing the face of his friend directly above his, his eyes wide open and manic.

"Quickly, Mathew. We have to go."

A sudden adrenalin shock rocked his body, pushing Church to one side in his rush to look out from where Church stared through the window. Though the light was darkening once more, he saw nothing. He tried the opposite window, but saw only trees.

"What is it, Peter?"

"I've just been told. We have to go now."

"Who told you?"

"I've got voices in my head. They keep talking, but now they say we have to move."

Mathew shrugged Church's hands off his shoulders, and reassuringly replacing his own on Church's.

"Peter, look at me damn you. Snap out of it. We are waiting here for another twelve hours. You have to be strong and let me help you. Now, I want you to show me the photograph of the target. It's about time I got to know the face I'm about to kill"

This sudden reversal of aggression was exactly how Church assumed Mathew would react to his improvised insanity. If there was one thing Church excelled at, it was the art of being able to change his persona to fit any scene. Whilst at university, he became the star of the amateur dramatic society and so good was he at it, he thought seriously about taking up the challenge of the stage professionally. With these natural skills, he could switch his personality to fit into any given scenario, a skill performed daily with the ease of a chameleon to screen his true sexual preference.

As Church gambled, his performance worked and Mathew was back in line and prepared to go through with the plan. He would hear no more talk of skulking away back to England before the job was completed. He wouldn't allow it.

"Alright, calm down."

Church responded, pushing Mathew away as if irritated by being manhandled.

The sudden change in Church scared Mathew. The manic look, previously so glaringly obvious in his eye, was replaced with usual composure. Stretching out in a relaxed posture on his improvised bed rang alarm bells in Mathew's head.

"Right, you want to see the target. Well this is it."

Authority regained, Church fumbled inside his briefcase in search of the photograph of their intended assassination.

"I don't recognise him. For all I know, it could be Lord Kitchener, the old fart..." Mathew held the image at arm's length, simulating his identity at a distance. "Do we know his name?"

"I'll let you know after the job. It's more fun with a bit of intrigue involved. Just think of the turmoil it will create in the German and French camps. Fawcett-Upham is a devious bastard for coming up with such a plan. It's brilliant. Can you image how nervous they'll be after a General is knocked off? They'll be shitting themselves. If an assassin can get that close, then not one of them is safe. The Germans will sign anything and the French will keep their heads down thinking one of them could be next."

From speaking earlier with what appeared to be a mouthful of marbles, Church regained his old, charismatic ways. The transformation worried Mathew still further.

"I'm pleased we have got a few minutes to talk to each other now you've seen the target. In case something goes badly wrong, before we left England, I rewrote my last will and testament. I did it just to piss my father off. I used his solicitor to guarantee my decision got back to him before we came away."

Mathew saw a genuine smile on Church's face. He was as calm as he'd ever seen him, without a trace of irrationality.

"Don't be silly, Peter. You're not going anywhere. We have been through worse than this and lived to tell the tale," Mathew interrupted.

"I think I'll take that suggestion of yours and have a nap."

Watching Church pull a blanket over his body, Mathew never dreamt there was such a thing as a soul until today; he'd seen Church's. Every behavioural change for a mortal to harbour was on full display that evening.

Mathew let him sleep while he checked and re-cleaned the Lee Enfield. All around was quiet. A glance behind the curtains told him it was freezing outside by the amount of frost gathering. He sat waiting for Church to wake. There were a few hours to go before going 'over the top'.

***

"Peter, wake up. It's nearly time."

"Okay, Mathew. Let's do it."

Pushing his torso into a sitting position, Church slid his improvised trousers over his bare thighs. The effort made to burn the lower leg of the garment quite impressed, sending out the right illusion. His tunic followed together with shoulder straps and cap. The last and most important piece of clothing waited till last, the MP armband. Above the waist he appeared to be every inch a military police major.

"O425 hours, Mathew. I think we should go."

In readiness to be lifted to the front of the ambulance. Church lifted his arms

"If we should get out of this in one piece, you have to promise me this will be the last job we do."

Church saw passion in Mathew's eyes. Trust had returned.

"I promise, Mathew. This will be the last job, now let's go and do it."

From past experience, each knew their position to start the engine. Waiting for Church's signal, Mathew swung the crank hoping for a swift response. The low, metronome-like throbbing engine spluttered into life, its noise seemingly louder.

Being so quiet, he was sure the drone would travel over the crisp ground, alerting those huddled in huts further down the road. There was no time to think of repercussions. Leaving the handle swinging in its place, Mathew quickly squeezed into the driver's seat. Fumbling to find first gear in the dark only added the racket to their anxiety of being discovered.

Keeping the engine revolutions down to minimum, Mathew allowed the vehicle run on choke, rolling through the intricate path of planted trees using only the moonlight as a means of illumination. He saw Church check his watch, but said nothing, resurrecting his horse-riding skills as a preference, cushioning the blows erupting from worn-out shock absorbers unable to cope with frozen ruts and occasional blind potholes.

Once on an even surface, Mathew released the choke allowing pistons to idle, then cautiously persuaded cogs to accept second gear. Fully accustomed to the dark, his eyes picked out mentally noted objects registered from his scouting mission. It felt more like an hour to walk, but within ten minutes, Mathew identified the shape of the broken branch on the side of the road, some fifty yards ahead. Booting the clutch pedal to the floor engaging neutral, the ambulance glided silently to the chosen grassy spot, its engine ticking over.

"What's the time?" Mathew whispered.

"Don't worry about that, we have plenty."

Squeezing out from his position, Mathew scrambled to the rear, hastily grabbing the rifle, a stick of dynamite, and the jam-jar full of cold pig's blood. Slinging the weapon over his shoulder he hastily returned to Church, impatiently waiting to be hoisted onto Mathew's back.

"Here, take these."

Pushing the jar of blood into Church's grasp and jamming the explosives into a breast pocket, Mathew required both hands to assure a firm grip on what remained of Church's legs. Even minus significant portions of his body, Church weighed substantially more than a kitbag, making movement awkward when crouching to enter the forest by the tree with a square foot of bark missing. Up ahead, Church noted the glow of floodlights over Mathew's bobbing shoulders.

"Steady, Mathew. Let's not bugger it up now we're so close," Church whispered.

Relieved to hear Church back to his confident self, Mathew edged closer to the clearing. Voices became audible, not the contents of their conversation, but if they could hear them, they could hear Church and Mathew. Treating his burden as a piece of bone china, Mathew delicately lowered Church to the grass, making sure their position was adjacent to the tell-tale scar on the pine tree to their left. Mathew watched Church unscrew the jar and slowly pour the congealed contents over his trousers, stumps and body, ensuring the surrounding area of scrubland received an adequate covering. Only when satisfied with the effect did he then remove the stick of explosives from his breast pocket, along with a box of vestas.

Adrenalin kicked in knowing the time was close. Shielding his mouth, Church whispered.

"Right, Mathew. Get into your position. We have only a couple of minutes before the allied party arrives. Remember, once I've lit the fuse you have only four seconds to aim and fire precisely at the same time as the explosion goes off. So, good luck and remember, we have only got the one chance, so shoot at the head of the arsehole in the photograph and no one else."

On all fours next to the prone body of his accomplice, Mathew encircled his arms round Church's neck. Nothing needed to be said.

Scampering low across the bracken as he'd been taught so many times during training, Mathew reached his position thirty yards behind Church, but with an unobstructed view of the railway carriage and the path leading to its elevated door. There was plenty of movement from all nationalities in uniform under the glare of the lights, but nothing appeared to be moving in the forest near where he lay. The units of MP sentries stayed within their own boundaries and hadn't strayed. Too interested in witnessing history unfold in front of them, none bothered to glance to their side. Even if they did, it was highly unlikely they would be able to spot two bodies lying flat on their stomachs, hidden amongst the long grass.

Attaching the telescopic sight to his eye, Mathew settled in a comfortable position, his legs sprayed out behind. Slowly, covering an arc from the forest edge to the carriage, he counted seventeen figures, but none bore a resemblance to his target. In deep concentration, Church put his binoculars to use. Keeping Church in constant visual contact, Mathew's actions would be decided on his partner's decision to light the fuse. Droplets of sweat formed under his uniform. He would have only four seconds to deliver the killing blow.

The sound of powerful automobiles broke the inane chatter coming from the clearing, causing conversations to stop and turn to their direction of approach. A Rolls Royce, festooned in camouflaged livery, led the entourage, coming to a stop where a line of French commissioned officers stood to attention whilst a solo uniform positioned itself to open rear doors. Mathew looked straight down the sight to see who would be first to exit.

A large shape of an officer emerged wearing an unrecognisable uniform. Unsure of his nationality, but appearing French, Mathew looked hard at the General before switching his sight to the next occupant. Slowly a second figure uncurled, but masked by the door. Nationality and uniform confused by the figure wearing a fawn trench-coat, the facial features under his cap resembled those in the photograph, but Mathew needed confirmation. Just a glimpse in Church's direction, preparing to light the fuse, assured his identity.

After introductory handshakes, the officers set off at a dawdling pace, talking as they walked side-by-side the fifty yards towards the wooden steps of the carriage.

Mathew didn't have to see the lit fuse, the struck match was sufficient to replace his eye to the telescopic sight and watch the fizzing stick of dynamite flying through the air some fifteen yards from Church's throwing hand. In his mind, he counted. One; line the officer's head directly between the cross-hairs. Two; hold your breath in preparation for an explosion. Three; there is no going back. Four...

CHAPTER 33

Simultaneously, as a blinding flash broke the tranquillity, Mathew squeezed the trigger. Through the smoke, Mathew confirmed the kill as every other eye in the compound turned away from where the officer slumped. Their vision focused on the spot where the forest burst into flames after a thunderous explosion. Achieving the objective of attracting every eye, the target lay unattended. Under the cover of mayhem, Mathew sprinted back into the undergrowth, depositing the rifle in the ambulance under a pile of folded blankets. The only sounds coming from the forest above the turmoil of raised voices was Church's theatrical scream of a man in agony.

"Oh, my God. It's blown the poor bastards legs off, quick, someone get an ambulance. Get a medic out here, fast."

Over raucous confusion, Mathew made out the accent of the first to arrive at the devastated sight. A Scottish military police sergeant shouted orders to those approaching.

Mathew faltered, impatiently waiting for the planned thirty seconds before rushing in to announce his arrival.

"I heard an explosion, is everybody alright?"

Mathew announced his arrived at the scene, visibly breathless compared to four others mustered over the writhing, screaming body. In unison their eyes zeroed in on Mathew's Red Cross armband.

"Hey, man. Can you do something for this poor guy?" the sergeant implored.

"Quick, give me a hand. I've got an ambulance just over there. Here, you." Mathew took control, directing his order to the sergeant. "Take his arms, while I grab his legs, or what's left of them. Quick."

Numbers grew as the entire gathering ran towards the dramatic scene being played out before an audience of unsuspecting military officers. Nobody noticed the body lying flat under the floodlights with a high calibre shell hole in the middle of his forehead.

"Hurry up, he's bleeding to death."

Mathew shouted to the sergeant carrying most of the weight on the other end of Church's body.

Screaming hysterically, Church's eyes remained on Mathew. They held a surreptitious smile, knowing, if luck remained on their side, they were just a few seconds away from pulling off this most dastardly deception.

"Quick, help me put him on a stretcher," Mathew ordered, opening the rear doors before bundling Church aboard.

A crowd of MP's and officers followed through the wood, not so much as helpers, but curious bystanders. None questioned why the major was there, nor how there came to be a landmine in the area. They accepted an awful accident had occurred during the last minutes of hostility, causing one of their own to be seriously injured.

"If I can get back to St Quentin in time, they might be able to save him" Mathew called over his shoulder to a sea of faces watching him scramble behind the steering wheel.

Inhaling deeply, he stamps hard on the clutch and crunches first gear. Pumping the accelerator with one foot, he raises the clutch with the other. It was not the time to stall, he prayed. Abruptly, the vehicle jumped forward with shuddering momentum but kept rolling to the tune of a screaming engine. Mathew's persistence to achieve maximum speed out of first gear startled the crowd watching his erratic departure. Their piercing eyes only hastened his desire for more speed, knowing he only had seconds before all hell would break loose on the discovery of the corpse. Forbidding the pounding pistons to drop below frantic revolutions, forcing the stick into second brought groans from the troubled gearbox, but initiated instant acceleration.

Disappearing into the blanket of darkness with dawn at least an hour away, Mathew grabbed the opportunity to put distance between him and the pursuers. Purposely letting it be known where he intended to take Church, especially to the sergeant, he knew they would eventually come after him. The chasers, hopefully, would take that track.

In the rear of the vehicle, his navigator wasn't helpful, but by retracing the route he'd driven forty-eight hours earlier, Mathew was confident of reaching the River Oise. From there he could choose any one of four different directions.

Fifteen minutes into their escape, Mathew safely manoeuvred the ambulance into Ribecourt, the village by the bridge. He couldn't go left at the crossroads as that would take him back south, albeit on the other side of the river, but too close from where they'd escaped. Dangerously, he kept to the main St Quentin road. From the rear he heard movement, but didn't dare pull over to bring Church up front, knowing a significant stop of thirty seconds could mean disaster if the cavalry were closer than estimated. He drove, with very little light coming from his lamps, as though the whole British army was bearing down on his tail. Just when he thought he saw lights in his rear-view mirrors, his distracted attention focused on a turning off to the right.

Slamming the foot brake down to the floor, the back wheels lock, initiating the rear of the vehicle to violently carousel on the frosty surface. Careering broadside, Church's hidden scream resounded from the other side of the partition, but this scream wasn't play-acting. The steering wheel in novice hands took on its own direction, narrowly missing a stone wall, to run off the road onto the muddied verge. Speed dictated, had they been going faster, momentum would have taken them into a deep ditch. Shuddered safely to a stop, muffled deranged screams from the rear grew weaker.

"Get me out of here," pleading, Church timidly aired frustration by punching the interior bodywork

Racing to the rear, the back doors were already open displaying Church, ashen faced, lying prone on the floor as a result of being thrown about like a solitary pea in a tin can.

"Get me out of here," he screamed again, unperturbed that a raised voice could indicate to pursuers their whereabouts.

Indignantly dragged through long grass and shaken to a near unconscious state in the back of the ambulance, the pig's blood appeared everywhere, covering his face and most of his body. If Mathew didn't know better, Church looked as though he was only minutes away from death.

"Come on mate. You look like shit. Let me get you up front. I've stalled the bloody engine, so you'll have to play around with the bloody gadgets whilst I crank the sodding handle again."

Whether it was adrenalin pumped from a racing heart, transferring Church to his place in front proved easier, but speed was imperative. It wasn't the time to be stranded in the middle of a hostile country with dawn just about crack open another day. Ignorant of knowing hot engines start without the aid of the choke, Mathew waited impatiently for Church to signal him the sign to start swinging, but he sat stationary, smiling.

"Bugger you, Church. You mad bastard."

In desperation, Mathew swung. Immediately, four cylinders turned over in unison.

"Thank Jesus for that. Now, let's get the hell out of here."

Once off the main road, tension subsided, but neither spoke during fifteen minutes it took to be far enough along their newly chosen route to feel safer from the chasing hordes. Self-satisfied with his performance, Mathew afforded the luxury to slow down to a speed he was confident he could control.

"I think we might just have got away with it, Peter," Mathew finally announced, breaking the silence.

Brought on by their farcical escape, a film of sweat froze on his face caused by onrushing, sub-zero morning air rushing through an unprotected windscreen, but try as he might to concentrate, out the corner of his eye he felt a piercing stare. Confirming it wasn't imagination; Mathew turned unprepared for the sight of Church in the cold light of morning.

Beneath the defiled major's tunic, his skulking torso appeared three sizes smaller and twisted to fit a ruffled khaki uniform, having rolled sausage-like around his neck. Under the camouflage of self-imposed desperation, his congealed pigs blood stained face couldn't hide a satisfied smirk.

"Hey, Peter. Are you alright? Bloody hell, you look terrible."

"I'm feeling great. Why shouldn't I? As a team, we've done the nigh, bloody impossible. It's such a beautiful morning, why don't you pull over and stop for a while so as we can get our breath back? Don't worry about those scallywags behind us. They haven't the foggiest idea where we are."

In manic haste, Mathew tore the innards out the engine for twenty miles, defying logic as to why it kept spewing power to reach the summit of a long drawn out gradient. Crawling to a standstill, Mathew sympathetically applied the handbrake, resisting temptation as steam gushed from a boiling radiator, to roll back down again. Similar to a true thoroughbred, the workhorse sweetly ticked over, obliged for a rest but ready when the foot hit the accelerator to continue pumping pistons. Church relaxed, thinking how good a brandy might taste, whilst Mathew's thoughts concentrated on a cigarette as light appeared over distant hills.

"I wonder if they'll go through with signing the armistice. I'm sure the French will demand it. After all, what's another dead soldier worth when the lives of countless other thousands are at stake? Now that bastard's dead, it's probably the only worthwhile thing he attempted to do in the whole campaign and fully expected another medal to go with all the other bogus awards for so-called bravery, poor sod. Maybe, someday, when this war is just a memory, the British public will view all those generals weighed down with tin objects on their chest as phonies, just like we do. The real heroes are those who never got back to England and are lying in peace with their conscience under three feet of foreign soil." Saliva dripped from the corner of his mouth, but Church spoke with clarity and calmness.

This first morning of peace in four years appeared cloudless without the sound of an exploding shell and from where Mathew parked the ambulance, the view across the open countryside, albeit horrifically scarred, opened out under the disappearance of night mist.

"Could you get my wheelchair out of the back? I'd like to go up to the top of that hill."

Church pointed to a piece of raised land a hundred yards to their left.

"Sure, won't be a minute. I wish we had something to drink. I bet Pinkerton has got something special out of his cabinet if he's heard the news."

Reaching into the cab, Mathew gently eased his friend out of the ambulance. All previous thoughts about bodily contact never entered his mind as he manhandled his body back into the contraption. Sympathetically, Mathew guided the chair over the moist earth, reaching the top of the shell-holed, grassless expanse of land where in past years it entertained harvested crops.

"Reminds me of back home, with the flatlands and hills in the distance."

Following Church's gaze, Mathew surveyed the landscape.

"Yes, you might be right, Peter, but Yorkshire air smells sweeter and hasn't got the crap of war everywhere you look."

Church smiled - unlike him, Mathew didn't possess the art of being a romantic.

"It's good to be alive, isn't it Mathew? It's the first time since I was a kid that I feel free of all the burdens I've accumulated in my useless time on this planet. Do you realise, we have changed a bit of history today? One day, when you're old and grey and when nobody cares a damn about what happened just down the road, you'll be able to tell your grandchildren your side of the story. They probably won't believe you, because they'll think you're a sick old man who's lost his marbles, like old folks do. Still, we'll know the truth, you and I."

Church's ability to see into his future amused Mathew.

"Yeah, I wonder what the 'Dear Lord' has got planned for us next. If he gets in touch with you and asks us to bump off the Pope; tell him to piss-off."

The sudden outburst of laughter catapulted Church's head forward, disguising a distant crack of a rifle shot. Continuing his forward momentum, scattering his wheelchair on its side as he tumbled to land face down in the rutted earth, Mathew continued laughing, unable to comprehend his friend's out of character sense of humour.

"Peter, what's wrong."

Expecting to be asked for assistance, Mathew stood over the prone body.

"Peter, for God's sake. Talk to me."

Humour vanished as quickly as it began. Dropping to cradle his head in his lap, memories of carnage, agonising cries for help and choking smoke, flashed through his mind when he remembered the time he replicated this manoeuvre on the battlefield. But unlike before, Church's face showed no pain. Just a small hole oozing blood showed where the bullet entered. Seeping from the wound, Mathew felt a warmness spreading across his thighs. Struck with fear, a scarlet stain spread across his khaki trousers. On this occasion, his screams for help went unheeded.

"No."

Like a wolf eerily silhouetted on a hill, his head pointed to the heavens whilst his screech echoed across the barren landscape. Howling his vengeance to the unseen who dared to take the life of his best friend, Mathew stood daring the marksman to take another shot.

A further bullet winged past, ruffling his hair but hit the earth behind. Unable to control tears flooding down his cheeks, Mathew dropped the body in a crumpled heap and faced the direction from whence the missile came.

"You bastard. Don't you know the bleeding war's over?"

Screaming in defiance, a third bullet whistles past his temple.

Crucial milliseconds elapsed, converting time into action. Throwing himself below the shell-hole ridge where he once stood, Mathew raises an enraged eye but spies nothing in the distance between him and possible cover the sniper might chose to hide his existence. If he were a civilian, his next move would probably be his last. But, like his unseen adversary, training taught him to subdue natural emotions and consider options. The enemy sniper had obviously considered his by killing Church, but wasn't clinical with his other target. Mathew believed this to be a failing. Stealthily re-emerging in a different position, his eyes slowly covered an arc of ground, returning to the spot where Church lay next to the overturned wheelchair.

"God bless you, Peter," he whispers, wiping away unwanted tears with the back of his hand.

The lid of the hiding place where Church covertly stowed the rifle had flipped open revealing the butt of the weapon, surrounded by half a dozen cartridges scattered closely. Regardless of his apparent manic state during their hectic departure, Church managed to hide the evidence of their exploits back into its hiding place whilst being thrown about in the rear of the ambulance. Mathew could only wonder how he achieved this, but silently thanked his partner for making the effort. If he could get his hands on the gun, the odds would no longer be in the other sniper's favour. Given three free shots to kill without hitting the target, Mathew knew his nemesis' skill level was inferior to his own.

Crouching in the crater, though unarmed, the speed of his pulse drastically reduced knowing he no longer represented the hunted. Assuming his prey wasn't wounded, an experienced sniper would wait all day if need be, hidden under camouflage for one direct shot when the bunny chose to show its head out of its warren when confident the coast was clear. Mathew wasn't prepared to play the part of a rabbit. Timing his countdown from five to one, Mathew took a deep breath and without warning sprinted over the ridge and dived, grabbing a wheel as he flew past the chair, dragging the whole contraption on top of him into an adjacent artificially made indentation.

Replicating a movement practiced hundreds of times; he withdrew the *Lee Enfield* and bolted a 303 cartridge in the breach. Placing the telescopic sight firmly against his eye, the distance between him and his undetected target reduced drastically. There was no need to make concessions for wind, unlike the conditions on the Scottish Moors. If Mathew could just find the prey, this would be easier than killing the deer. Unlike his previous encounter with a German when the devil and his brother conducted a cacophony of indescribable noise above, there was no battle to distract. It was just Mathew and a fellow hunter stalking each other.

Slowly creeping higher in the morning sky, the sun cast shortening shadows from anything left protruding after previous bombardments. The objects were few and far between, but the odd broken tree trunk, bereft of branches, offered a false shield. So many deviations in height at ground level convinced Mathew his foe couldn't have fired his shots from a shell-hole or whilst lying flat on his belly, so gambled on him kneeling, if not standing behind one of the burnt tree stumps.

He was in no rush, time was on his side, if need be he would wait all day for his chance, unlike the opposition. Suddenly patience paid dividends. As planet Earth slowly curved its orbit round the sun, in the distance, some three hundred yards to his right, a bare tree trunk cast two shadows where an hour before showed only one.

"Gotcha. Go on mate. Stick your little head round and see if you can see me, you bastard."

There was no need to whisper his warning.

Patience is a sniper's best friend, but his target hadn't been taught from the same text book. Appearing through Mathew's sight to be no more than fifty yards away, the recognisable shape and colour of a German helmet slowly separated itself from its protection. Only the merest fragment edged away from the stump, but as he grew in confidence, the enemy, a renegade unaware the war was over, began to show too much for a professional opponent to miss.

As the deer fell to her death before she heard the crack of the shot, Mathew saw the distant body fly backwards as though knocked senseless by an aggressive uppercut. There was no need to confirm the kill.

His state of euphoria evaporated with the sight of a pool of blood encircling Church's hidden face. In the space of seconds, he experienced complete opposites of emotion. Looking down at Church's twisted body, Mathew realised there was more than a common male bond connecting them. Church's words about how he felt became understandable, but at the time they were said, Mathew dismissed such crudity, unable to go beyond his naivety when thinking about the meaning of love. It was only now, seeing his prostrate, lifeless form that he began to understand the volume of compassion Church bestowed on him without asking for it to be returned. Whether it was youth or his preoccupation about the mission, he was unable to accept the love of another man when Church needed it most.

Blinkered by loving parent's attitudes, taught to them by their own uneducated parents, Mathew's upbringing totally depended on their directives, unlike Church, whose father, highly educated, disowned and ridiculed his only son in favour of wealth and position. Notwithstanding his feelings for Mary, now Church was gone, he realised he could never rekindle the same relationship with either a man or a woman again. Experiencing Salvation's death plunged Mathew into uncharted depths of grief, but nothing that happened that day could compare to the cavern of despair burdened within a juvenile brain. Too late in translation to understand the meaning of Church's bubbled words of affection, Mathew would never be able to reciprocate by telling Church in his own words that he felt the same.

The strain of trying to reason with a corpse evaporated all willpower to remain standing. Falling to his knees, Mathew offered a last prayer to whichever god listened. Struggling for divine intervention, no-one above appeared to be interested about what he should do with the corpse. Reality demanded he leave the body where it lay. In time, he hoped it would be retrieved and placed amongst the other fallen heroes who gave their lives in the belief that their efforts made the difference between keeping a free world to that of being ruled by some crazed despot.

***

In this day when mechanised warfare replaced the bygone theory that a battle lasts no more than a day in a field usually chosen by a defender, the outcome of-which depended on superior manoeuvres or jingoistic momentum created by an onrushing cavalry charge, why do Field Marshals today keep insisting the war continues for over four years instead of admitting they made drastic errors in their assumptions? In future, these events will confirm when two heavily fortified lines confront each other, the likely outcome would be catastrophic numbers of deaths on both sides. Declaring a draw, as the armistice agrees, shall be considered a gross miscalculation. Not ridding Europe of an uncontrollable despot by demanding complete surrender might result in revitalised aggression by the same ideology in not too many years to come. Maybe a shell or bomb, powerful enough to dissuade an enemy advancing, shall be invented to thwart future aggressor's intentions.

As there was evidence of inadequacy from high-ranking officers when it came to planning confrontational assault, it was a wonder how lessons from previous disastrous confrontations went unheeded but continued the suicidal trend of ordering massed numbers to advance into certain mortal jeopardy. This attitude of suicidal advance relieved Mathew of any misgivings he might have felt about his last paid assassination.

The Germans on the other hand, must have wondered whom these crazy people were who accepted an order to walk, not run, into red-hot gunfire spewing out from overworked weapons. After the war, someone should ask why the enemy never attempted the same tactical manoeuvre. Maybe, their commanders had more compassion than they were afforded.

***

From his position, deep in the shell hole, Mathew couldn't see them, but heard voices heading in his direction from the valley below. Too far away to discern their conversation, he panicked, guessing they could be the group of chasing military police. It was useless to try and hide or play dead, so he reacted like a wild animal about to be caged.

Ripping the MP's armband off Church's tunic, together with his own Red Cross insignia, he stuffed the incriminating evidence into the wheel chair's secret compartment before throwing the whole contraption into a neighbouring shell hole. This was all he could manage before voices, clearly audible and speaking English, appeared over the crest of the crater.

"Hey, mate. Heard some gunfire from up around these parts. Thought we'd come up and take a look. You probably haven't heard, but the war is over."

An officer with an unfamiliar accent and uniform, called down, striding towards where Mathew stood.

"Yeah, I've heard the news, but our friend the German sniper didn't. He's over there. I'm afraid the only way he'll be going back home will be in a wooden box."

Mathew brought laughter to the group circling the ridge sculpted by a heavy calibre artillery shell.

"Never mind. If I had my way, I'd never leave here until every single one of the bastards was dead. Are you wounded, son?" the officer enquired, looking down at Mathew's blood stained trousers.

"No Sir."

The temptation to cry built in Mathew's throat.

"It's his blood. I've been rolling around with him to try and get out of the way of that bastard's bullets."

A sympathetic hand slapped Mathew's shoulder, whilst his other removed a fat cigar stub from his lips.

"Was he with you?" he continued, pointing to Church's body.

"No, he wasn't."

Mathew regrettably lied, thinking if they were on the lookout for assassins, they might associate their partnership.

"He must have been hit by the shell that made this bloody great big hole. Poor bastard. Still, doesn't look as though he knew much about it. Look at all that blood over him." Masking his true emotions, Mathew kept up the banter, putting on a jovial face.

"Well, we can't leave him like that. I'll get the boys to bury him. We'll have a look round to see if we can't find the rest of him, but I doubt if there's anything left of his legs. It's the least we can do," the officer offered.

Mathew stood by whilst the unit buried Church with little reverence.

"We'll leave his tags on for when they come along to give him a proper funeral. But I'll take his name and number to report his death."

Void of feeling after seeing so much carnage, the officer wrote down Church's particulars in a dog-eared notebook.

"His family probably won't thank me for it, but it's better they know the truth and get it over with, rather than get a telegraph saying 'missing in action'."

It would have been a poignant statement had it been anyone other than Church lying dead in the ground, but the officer's motives were sincere. Continually witnessing the cheapness of death, why should the officer bestow any favours onto someone he had never met?

In the eyes of the officer, this is how he would expect Mathew to react, so any emotions he might unconsciously emit would only draw attention. Silently, he said his final farewell before driving the barrel of his rifle into the sodden earth. It would represent his version of the Holy Trinity. The reason why they met, the tool used for Salvation's retribution and the cause of Church's death. A fitting memorial.

"You might as well join us. It's probably safer coming with us than going it alone," the officer suggested, mustering his unit together in readiness to move on after their burial duties.

"There might be one or two of those bastards still out there waiting to take a pot shot at us. It's safer in numbers."

His heart told him to stay, but Mathew knew it would be a mistake.

"Yeah, okay. I'm right behind you," Mathew confirmed as the unit made their way back towards the road. Suddenly, he saw it, the ambulance, and remembered Fawcett-Upham's notes.

"What the hell," Mathew thought, walking past the open rear doors. With so much war debris lying discarded in ditches lining the route, who would bother to take any notice if he disappeared from view for a second or two? The one sheet of paper with a bank number worth half a million pound obliterated the risk it might take to retrieve it. The war was over and there was nothing else left to incriminate him hidden amongst the other pages. Whoever found the battered briefcase would have no idea the instigator of the assassination lay buried not a hundred yards away.

"Tell me," Mathew said, slightly out of breath after his exertions to catch up with the officer. "What regiment are you with?"

Without hesitation, the officer pumped his chest with visible pride and answered.

"We're the Texas Rangers, the finest outfit in the United States of America. God bless her. My name's Major John Armstrong, or 'Duke' to my friends. What's yours, son?"

Intrigued with the whole concept of Armstrong's accent and indisputable confidence, Mathew quickly offered the information before turning the conversation back to the American.

"Why do they call you Duke?"

Armstrong laughed, whilst twiddling the unlit cigar between in his lip.

"Well son, that's a good question. It's probably because people look at me and believe, how would you say it here in England? I'm lord and master of my domain back home in the States. You see, my family own quite a bit of land and have done pretty well since they settled fifty odd years ago. There was nothing there then, just one big expanse of land. The only thing to worry about was killing the Indians before they killed us. But now, I suppose we have some five thousand head of cattle to help feed the nation with the livestock number growing every year. The biggest bonus though, and this is where I think we'll make real big bucks, is the fact we have found oil under our land. Believe me, Mathew, with the advent of the piston engine, oil will be the next best thing to gold in the future."

Mathew consumed every word, mesmerised by Armstrong's faith for the future. They walked no more than a mile when other straggling troopers from an assortment of regiments joined the march, but their attempts to make conversation went unnoticed as Mathew pumped Armstrong for more information about this wonderful country called America.

Mathew's ignorance to his country amused Armstrong.

"America is the land of opportunity. You could land there with nothing, but if you've got balls, in a year you could be a rich man. You should think about coming over, because your country is going to be suffering for a long time and not the place for a young lad like you to try and better himself."

Everything the American said lodged in Mathew's brain.

"What if you had money? What would you do?"

"Matt, I've got money, and the way things are going back home, I'll have a lot more very soon."

"No, I mean. What if I had money?"

The answer came true and how Mathew expected.

"If you have got money..." the American smiled at this seemingly hypothetical question. "I'd get on the next boat across the Atlantic."

CHAPTER 34

Any resemblance to an organised retreat was hopeless as thousands of troops of all ranks gathered in villages and towns across the whole district of northern France. Wearing a uniform from one of the allied armies guaranteed no questions asked, but they all had one thing in common, each was thankful to be alive and going back home.

Caused by such a huge number of personnel moving in the same direction, each piece of transport capable of starting an engine overflowed with wounded, or those fortunate enough to hitch a ride. The majority of fit Commonwealth and American forces formed lines to foot slog it back to the nearest port where they would wait their chance to board one of the many requisitioned boats transporting a 'first come first served' policy back across the English Channel. For the French, they were left to clear up the mess and the unenviable task of burying the many dead.

Though de-mobbed a year before, Mathew blended in spiritually with his khaki surroundings. Sleeping wherever he could find adequate cover and feeding on scrounged scraps, Mathew wearily approached the outskirts of Calais after six days of forced walking through every element the weather threw at him. Amongst fellow troopers, time offered the luxury to daydream during those monotonous hours of following the rear view of the soldier in front. But, unlike the majority of those around whose future would be bleak, Mathew was confident about his.

Constantly, 'Duke's' words entered his equations. Mathew's only apprehension was his return to Yorkshire and the confrontation with those who had become his second family. How they would react now Church was dead, he would have to wait and see.

CHAPTER 35

Sheets of rain descended from the heavens on the eighth night after Church's death, but it helped, together with the cover of darkness, to conceal Mathew's arrival back to his Yorkshire cottage.

Whilst the rest of the homecoming horde from the continent brought the flimsy railway system to a standstill, Mathew bribed a staff driver with twenty pounds to forsake his duty as chauffeur to a Major General. Privy to witnessing Church convincing the unwilling to do favours with his undoubted acting ability, Mathew emulated his tutor. He was surprised how easy he succeeded once pound notes were waved in the face of someone who already guessed his fate was one of zero prospects, accompanying long term unemployment or prison. His final words to the driver as he pulled the handbrake on outside Mathew's front door were that he should take the staff car, have it resprayed black and sell it. England was in so much disarray with tons of accumulated army scrap metal scattered across Europe, who was going to search for a missing car? It was something the driver pondered on as Mathew watched him disappear into the darkness.

Closing the world out from behind a locked door, Mathew felt his way along the familiar hallway to the kitchen in the rear of the cottage. Knowing there was likely to be no one braving the weather in the vicinity, Mathew confidently lit an oil lamp. A warm, welcoming glow emitted a feeling of sanctuary, but also illuminated an unopened bottle of Pinkerton's finest malt whisky, standing where he left it on the pine dining table. For a second or two he felt good, pouring an over generous measure, but this waned when he caught a glimpse of his image reflecting back from the grubby windowpanes. Dressed in the same uniform without the use of a bar of soap for the past twelve days, the sight was not a pretty one. Comfortably protected under a roof from the howling wind and lashing rain, the stillness encouraged pungent odours to percolate from unwashed flesh. As all his homeward bound buddies smelt the same, he hadn't noticed his own aroma. Alone and amongst clean surroundings, the stench was quite unbearable, though the growth around his chin quite impressed for a youth of nineteen. He didn't care; he would bathe and shave tomorrow. Tonight, his first priority was to put a big dent in the whisky.

***

For three days Mathew kept a low profile from the outside world, living off whisky and baked potatoes dug freshly from his allotment. He tried to put off the inevitable, but knew the day would come when he would have to face the boys back at the farm, Mrs Freeman, and Mary.

The last of those named would be the hardest. Understanding her dedication to her profession and background differences, before his mission to France he thought he might love her and she felt the same, maybe looking upon him as a husband, but did he want marriage just yet? It was a hard decision. For the first time in his life, Mathew felt selfish.

It finally stopped raining on the fourth morning after his return. The luxury of hot water and clean clothes lost their novelty after a few days. Long were the days when a clean shirt lasted for two weeks before being washed.

Wealth retrieved from a bank's safety deposit bank guaranteed a life of luxury and cleanliness.

Dressed smartly in a grey suit, white shirt and tie, waistcoat and trilby hat, Mathew confronted the morning breeze blowing with a hint of oncoming winter. It was a long walk to the mansion, but he didn't mind; it was time to stretch his legs again even though he had walked a hundred miles the previous week.

Arriving at the familiar manor gates within an hour of setting out, he stopped, taking in the sight, knowing Church wouldn't be on the other side of the door when it opened. How he would react when it did, he didn't know. It took two resounding knocks before a gap slowly appeared with Mrs Freeman's familiar voice coming from behind.

"Hallo, Mrs Freeman? It's me, Mathew."

Slowly, the door opened further showing the frail figure of the woman who took on the mantle of Church's mother in later life.

"Oh, Master Mathew. It *is* you." She clasped her hands to her face, covering her mouth in shock. "We all thought you had perished alongside Master Peter." She burst into tears.

"Come on, Mrs 'F'. It's all right. I'm safe, and sound. It's good to be home."

Mathew reached, putting a consoling arm around her small, frail shoulders. Turning to close the door, he gently led her through to the back, to a room he knew well. The house seemingly holding on to Church's spirit, Mathew fully expected to see him sitting in his favourite position when entering, but of course, he couldn't be there.

Instead, a large, rotund, grey haired middle-aged gent stood facing the garden, resplendent in a tailed, black suit. For an instant, the sight of such a figure shocked Mathew, but facing the new arrival, any beliefs he might have held concerning the supernatural, evaporated.

"This is Mister Tibbles, Master Peter's solicitor," Mrs Freeman introduced, wiping her face with a lace handkerchief. "I'll get some tea, whilst you two talk," she thoughtfully announced, reminding herself she was not only the housekeeper but also a servant.

Confronted by this imposing figure who blatantly refused to greet or acknowledge Mathew's presence reminded him of the last time he endured such treatment when lined up in formation to be scrutinised by a Sergeant Major. Breaking the silence, Mathew interrupted Tibbles' blatant rudeness by forcing a response.

"Good morning, Mister Tibbles. My name is Mathew Hobbs."

Before continuing, Tibbles cut the conversation short.

"Yes, I thought you might be." His tone was similar to the way he often heard officers talk. "I'm here to make an inventory of all Major Church's possessions. After we received notice of his unfortunate demise, it is my duty to itemise everything beholding to his last will and testament. And if you'll pardon me, Sir, I'm not in the habit of being interrupted. I shall be finished soon."

"Oh, yes, I'm sorry. I apologise" Somewhat taken back by his brusque manner, Mathew purposely diverted Tibbles attention, just to annoy. "It's just I'm surprised at the speed of telegraphs between the War Office and the bereaved families. If they used the same urgency on the front line, this war might have finished a lot earlier. But you don't know anything about fighting, do you Mister Tibbles?" Mathew's sarcasm did not go unnoticed.

"You must understand, Mister Hobbs, when a member of the Church family dies, it is deemed important to relay that information back to England as soon as possible. The family are held in great esteem." Tibbles's feathers had been visibly ruffled.

Abruptly, before the conversation could begin, it was over, leaving the solicitor alone to diligently itemise

Church's belongings. Searching through a labyrinth of corridors and turnings, Mathew found Mrs Freeman in the kitchen, waiting for a kettle to boil on the oversized coal stove.

"He's not a very nice person, is he, Mrs 'F'?" Mathew announced his arrival, endeavouring to lighten her remorseful mood.

"Oh, take no notice of him. He's just doing his job," she defended, a smile spreading across her face for the first time. "I'm just so happy to see you are alive, Master Mathew. Nobody had any idea where you two disappeared, but after we got the telegraph and knowing you are inseparable, we all assumed you both perished. What on earth were you two doing in France?"

Slipping effortlessly into a newly found character, Mathew related a story about being on a special consignment for the government, leaving out the bit about the assassination. It appeared to appease the old lady, seated on the opposite side of a farmhouse kitchen table, pouring tea.

"Tell me, Mrs 'F'. I knew Peter only for a short time, but apart from the little he told me, I knew nothing about his upbringing. Can you fill in some of the missing details? I know he didn't get on with his father. From what Peter told me, he sounds a nasty piece of work, but there must have been a bigger reason why he hated him so much."

Apparently ignoring his questions, Mrs Freeman awkwardly raised her arthritic limbs to carry a third cup of tea out of the kitchen for Tibbles, leaving Mathew pondering her reaction to what he said. Maybe she didn't know, or just didn't want to talk about it. It really wasn't an issue if it brought back remorseful memories.

Scuffing her left shoe slightly on the flagstone hallway alerted Mathew of her return. Purposely ignoring him, she tended to a dirty plate requiring washing, then moved on to place it on a high Welsh dresser shelf, grimacing at the effort to succeed. Dropping her arm weakly back to her side, she brusquely turned on Mathew.

"I swore I would never say a word about what happened, not to anybody, but now with Master Peter gone and because you ask, I feel I owe it to his memory."

She paused, attempting to regain her youthful dignity by straightening an ageing back; a time when instead of getting married to a man of her own class, she chose to stay single and try to attract Church senior's eye. Oblivious to her subtle advances and obvious affection, he married into wealth, an organised marriage producing only one son, but, as Mrs Freeman thought, destined to fail. Staying faithful to her belief that the day would come when she would rightfully inherit the General's love and bear his children, the fateful day finally arrived, signalling those days were past and time really had run out. She'd given her life to the General's family, but after years of servitude, she was considered by her secret lover to be no more than a carer for Peter.

"I've carried this secret around with me since Master Peter was a frail, six year old little boy. You see, it was at that age when he lost his mother. It all happened when his father came back from Africa after fighting the Boers. The General learnt his wife had an affair resulting in Peter's brother being born. As he hadn't seen his wife for over a year, it didn't take much working out that the baby wasn't his. Do you know what the bastard did?"

She paused, taking a deep breath. Her right hand holding a teacup began to shake. Mathew knew a secret, hidden for decades, was about to be released.

"When the General returned home in 1902, the first thing he did was to come back here and shoot both mother and baby with his service revolver. The police found them huddled together in one of the bedrooms upstairs with a bullet hole in each of their heads. As he was Sir General Cuthbert Church, Kitchener's right hand man, the

Government hushed it all up with no charges ever brought against him. Let's face it, how could they hang a national hero, let alone bring it to the public's attention. Before she died, Peter's mother left a letter with her solicitor for it to be opened only on his twenty-first birthday. In it she wrote about her infidelity, how sorry she was and what might befall her when her husband returned. She knew something terrible would befall her, but stayed in the house waiting for him. I don't blame her for finding love elsewhere. I just hope she found some enjoyment in her life during the period he was away, as living with the monster must have been unbearable. Although I was smitten by Master Peter's father, I could see what a nasty person he was. He had something in him that wives hate, a roving eye. I know it's true, because I witnessed it on several occasions and was the only one she trusted to console her when it happened and might I say, it happened on a regular occurrence. He was a very nasty individual"

Poking his head round the door, Mathew cursed Tibbles for interrupting her tirade whilst she was in full flow.

"Excuse me for disrupting your afternoon tea, but, as you two are the only recipients in Master Peter's last will and testament, it appears it might be a convenient time to join me in the drawing room to finalise the settlement."

Mrs Freeman turned, looking at Mathew with a quizzical look on her face.

"Come on Mrs Freeman. Take me by the arm. I think this man wants to tell us something."

Tibbles led the way having previously arranged the seating arrangements for this impromptu gathering. Two chairs facing a desk where he would sit opposite.

"Please make yourself comfortable."

Sounding confidently stern, as though facing a courtroom jury, Tibbles waited till his clients were seated.

"I have before me the last will, and testament of Peter Alfred Magellan Church. Dated the 2nd of November, 1918, and witnessed by my associate, Mister Gordon Forsyth." Peering over half-moon spectacles to confirm their attention, he continued. "To my dearest friend, surrogate mother and housekeeper; Ethel Freeman, I bequeath my home, Green Manor and all the furniture in the inventory."

Mathew heard an audible intake of breath from the lady sitting by his side.

"To this, a pension of £500 per annum to be paid, not only for the upkeep of the house, but also for Mrs Freeman to enjoy being mistress of it."

An intake of her breath was released, only to be replaced with a giggle, something Mathew thought Mrs Freeman was incapable of achieving.

"We now move on to you, Mr Hobbs."

Deserving to benefit for her devotion, Mathew showed his pleasure. Not entirely surprised by this magnanimous gesture, he assumed the major portion of the estate had been bequeathed to another, so a little something would be appreciated in remembrance of a special friend.

"This is the first time it has happened to me, or my company whereby a will of this nature has had to be scrutinized by a high court judge before a finding of this kind can be safely, by law, be passed on to a recipient. Due to Peter's father dying before Peter, theoretically, all his assets are passed onto his only son."

Oh, the irony of Peter's father death, Mathew thought. Peter would have passed away a happy man if only he knew he'd outlived him. He wondered how the old bastard died.

"So, Mister Mathew Hobbs, this brings me to you. Not only do you inherit Peter Church's estate, but you also inherit his father's. To put it bluntly, you inherit the lot. A seven-story house in Holland Park, London, two Rolls Royces, a farm here in Yorkshire and approximately, after the accountants have been finalised, a sum, the amount of two million, seven hundred thousand pounds. There is, I'm afraid, a codicil addendum. A sum of five thousand pound is reserved to pay the servants salaries of the London residence for the following ten years. I hope this doesn't inconvenience you, Mister Hobbs?"

Tibbles words drifted over Mathew's head. The ability to hear deserted him before the mention of the London residence. Regardless of the figures, there was more stashed away in a bank account in London.

"Master Mathew, are you alright?" Mathew heard her voice, but had difficulty placing its origin.

"Mister Hobbs." He recognised Tibbles barking voice.

"Yes, yes, I hear you." Shaking off the desire to faint. Mathew regained a shaking composure. "Sorry, Mister Tibbles. You were saying."

"If both of you agree to the settlement, would you sign these papers so I can safely say my business is done here and that I congratulate you both. All the necessary documents are on the desk concerning change of ownership and for you, Mister Hobbs, your new bank account just requires your signature. Should you, of course, require advice, please contact the office of Tibbles and Forsyth. We would only be too honoured to represent you."

Tibbles' fierce, upper-handed manner became a distant memory. His chameleon-like persona bestowed reeking graciousness in conjunction with false smiles. Oh, how Mathew wished Peter was here to witness such snobbery from this law-man snapping his briefcase together, waiting for an answer.

"Well, Mister Tibbles." Mathew paused, assuming responsibility to talk on Mrs Freeman's behalf. "We thank you for your kind attention to this matter, but the sooner you get out of Mrs Freeman's house, the better both of us will feel."

Mathew heard a splutter, then another giggle. Tibbles couldn't see any humour in what was said, but quickly made his way unescorted to the front door.

"Oh, Master Mathew. You shouldn't have said those things, but it did make me laugh."

Uncharacteristically, Mrs Freeman poked him in his ribs.

"I think this calls for a celebration. I'll get the bottle and glasses, while you remember where you left off telling me about Peter." Reminded Mathew, shying playfully away from an exuberance he thought she never possessed.

"Mrs Freeman, or can we put all that formality behind us and allow me to call you Ethel? Why did Peter always call you Mrs Freeman, when you informed me, you never got married?"

"Oh, it was something Peter wanted to do after his mother died. He said..." She replicated a giggle when recalling. "And remember he was only about seven when he said it. 'If you become my new mummy, I can't call you Miss Freeman, so I'll have to pretend you're married and call you Mrs Freeman from now on'. He was such a lovely boy."

Mathew saw her delve into past memories. Bringing her out of her trance before sinking too deep necessitated verbal distractions.

"Now where were we? You were saying, Ethel."

It was imperative he learnt the true story about the man responsible for his new found fortune.

Sitting, overlooking the expanse of garden on one of her newly acquired antique settees, something she would never dream of doing before her inheritance, a contented smile creased her face

"Here's to you Master Peter. I thank you." She turned to Mathew, raising her glass. "There isn't a lot more to say, really. Except, on Master Peter's twenty-first birthday, Tibbles released his mother's letter and from that day onwards he utterly despised his father once he knew the circumstances leading to her death. We all thought, that is those of us in the village who knew the family, how ironic it was for Master Peter's father to be assassinated in France at the armistice signing on the same day as his son's death."

A sudden chill swept through Mathew's body. Oblivious to his glass tumbling towards the carpeted floor, he scrambled to his feet, startling Mrs Freeman by his unexpected action. Making a dash to the door, jolting Mrs Freeman further into a look of wide-eyed amazement, he appeared to be disappearing out of her life as quickly as he entered. Before reaching the front door, Mathew turned to call down the corridor where Mrs Freeman sat surrounded by all her new belongings, totally bewildered by his sudden rush of manic activity.

"Ethel, I'm terribly sorry to leave you in the lurch like this, but I've just remembered something really important. I have a boat to catch in Southampton, but before I leave, promise to get George Pinkerton over here for a drink. I think you two could become really good friends. And when he's here, supping some of Peter's favourite malts, drop into the conversation he no longer needs to pay rent, because he now owns the farm. Tell him it's a gift from Salvation. He'll understand."

THE END
(or is it?)